THE SALAMANCA DRUM

Joshua was ensconced heavily on his side of the bed. He sighed and muttered into his pillow. He was suddenly tired, and perhaps the evening had gone off well enough. Matilda was too clever for him, that was the trouble.

She was climbing into bed beside him. Her green eyes had a soft swooning look. "Don't let's talk any more," she murmured. "I have other things in mind."

She curled up against him, her slender body adjusting to his more solid curves. Her voice was heavy with sensuousness. "Turn round and look at me, Joshua." She had never before taken the initiative and, although he was reluctant to give up his displeasure, he was finding her surprising behavior enormously exciting.

"You waste time talking when all we both want is a son," she grumbled sweetly. "Isn't that true?"

"Perfectly true, my darling."

"Let's get ourselves a son, Joshua. . . . One this year, one next, one the following year." She was laughing breathlessly. "I'm so greedy, you don't mind, do you?"

"Not if this is the way you show it."

THE
SALAMANCA
DRUM

Dorothy Eden

A FAWCETT CREST BOOK • NEW YORK

To Bruce Hunter

THE SALAMANCA DRUM

THIS BOOK CONTAINS THE COMPLETE TEXT OF
THE ORIGINAL HARDCOVER EDITION.

Published by Fawcett Crest Books, a unit of CBS Publica-
tions, the Consumer Publishing Division of CBS Inc., by
arrangement with Coward, McCann & Geoghegan, Inc.

ISBN: 0-449-23548-3

Alternate Selection of the Literary Guild, June 1977

Printed in the United States of America

10 9 8 7 6 5 4 3 2 1

First Interval

The bedroom door was slowly opening. Matilda turned her head on the pillow and watched. Her visitor must be someone prowling, for after the first tentative push, the door was closed again.

Someone spying on her? Lally? That bossy nurse whom she detested? Not Mab. Mab never wanted to come into this room. She sensed decay and death and very sensibly ran away. She was quicksilver, hypersensitive, unpredictable, but not mentally deficient, thank God. She was just another Duncastle, high-spirited, uncontrollable, overbred. At least, that was how Joshua would have described her. He hadn't had much time for the Duncastle pattern, as he called it. Bred to shoot guns and become cannon fodder. Unemployable in these modern times now that wars were over.

But the wars were not over. It was in the nature of man to fight, to destroy, to conquer. Matilda knew this, none better, for that old ineradicable scene was forming again in her mind. Although it had been so long ago, and she had been only fifteen, the trauma of it had affected her for years afterwards.

Now that she was old the memory had become more alive than ever. As if it had happened not an hour since, that scene in the dining room at Sanctuary became vivid again.

Grieves the butler had come in and whispered to Papa, and Papa had sprung up and left the table without an apology. Mamma had guessed a disaster at once, for she had become very pale, and had pressed her table napkin to her lips. Then she had said to Matilda and Julia, "Finish your meal, girls. I must just go to Papa. I have a feeling—I hope I am wrong—"

But she had not been wrong. Matilda thought she must have anticipated this happening from the day they had all said goodbye to Hillary, her only brother, when he was about to embark on the voyage to the vast and largely unknown continent of Africa lying awaiting dissection by the western nations. Great Britain was the forerunner in this race, as she had been the forerunner in colonization for the whole of the nineteenth century. She stood astride the world, a glorious and powerful nation created by the efforts of families like the Duncastles with their proud record of service to their country.

Hillary was twenty years of age. He had all the best qualities of his family, the erect stance, the controlled eagerness for action, the proudly held head, the alert bright eyes, the belief in himself and the sure knowledge of his duty to his Queen and country. He would make a fine soldier in the family tradition, and add to the already famous collection of medals and trophies.

Would. . . . a word already out of date, for the news Grieves carried in the War Office telegram was that First Lieutenant Hillary Richard Gordon Duncastle had been ambushed and killed by a Zulu spear. He had only landed on that treacherous black continent a month ago. There was not even a battle being fought when he had met his wasteful and tragic death.

Matilda had not allowed herself to be drawn into her weeping mother's arms, as had Julia. She had run blindly and instinctively to the room where all the military trophies were stored, the faded, torn and scorched battle colours, the rifles and swords, the rows of medals in glass cases, the captured helmets of the enemy, and the drum. The famous Salamanca Drum.

She had picked up the drumsticks and beaten the drum softly, then louder, building up to an angry crescendo. She shut out the pictures of Hillary doing this, with fierce expertise, when they had played war games as children, and made herself see that other and first Hillary Duncastle who had begun the family tradition. Hillary Richard Duncastle, aged fifteen, drummer boy to a regiment of the line in the Duke of Wellington's army, marching against the French on the plains of Salámanca. Young Duncastle, his eyes red-rimmed with the dust and drifting smoke, his boy's face scarlet with courage and determination, drumming the rushing stumbling cursing troops towards the increasingly terrifying sounds of battle. And suddenly falling, wilting like a scarlet poppy over his drum, as all the blood ran out of his young body and the drumsticks slid from dying hands.

Hillary Richard Duncastle, slain on the field of battle. Never to have a bride or children, never to grow up, but to become the family's hero forever. Surely an enviable destiny, the fifteen-year-old Matilda had thought on that long-ago day.

And the eighty-year-old Matilda's head slid sideways on the pillow as she was awakened by the sound of the door giving another cautious click.

"Who's there?" she asked, sleep-dazed.

No one answered. In the distance there was a hubbub of voices and shuffling feet. She remembered now. It was the yearly bazaar for war widows and orphans. Her own pet charity. People had come in the past because she was a famous hostess. They liked to see her house in the historic old square. It had a nice collection of pictures, Dutch shipping scenes and flower pictures chosen by Joshua who had conservative taste and a good sense of value. It also had, in the room that the children had satirically nicknamed the Death Room, the carefully preserved military records of the Duncastle family, the medals on their faded ribbons, the sheathed swords, the Salamanca Drum.

Nowadays people came in smaller numbers—surely the

Government took care of orphans—but it was still a habit of the older generation to turn their footsteps to the tall house in Kensington Square on the day of the bazaar. Even if the rather alarming Mrs. Joshua Webb were confined to her bedroom and refusing to see anybody except her daughters, Imogen and poor slow Lally.

There were no boys left in the family. The brave fighting blood of the Duncastles had been drained away. Like England, the England of which those young men and thousands like them had been so proud in her great days of empire. Going, going, gone . . . Memorials in country churches, graves in foreign cemeteries, Death Rooms in private houses . . .

And what are we left with? Matilda wondered confusedly. It's all very well for Joshua to argue that he wants his sons safely behind desks in the city. But what for? To live in this modern-day atmosphere of money-seeking, corruption, lack of ideals?

I'd choose to follow the great Duke down the long hot dusty roads to Salamanca, marching with glory in my eyes, to the beat of the drum. Rat-a-tat, rat-a-tat . . . Because she had always known she should have been a boy. Hillary, Gordon, Frederick, Richard, Robert . . . The roll call of young Duncastles who had served their country. Majors, Colonels, Generals. In the Crimea, the Indian Mutiny and the horror of Cawnpore, Zululand, Afghanistan, Khartoum, South Africa and the Boers. The Marne, the Somme, Passchendaele with that dreadful drowning mud, Dublin in Ireland a long time ago, Tobruk and Tripoli, even the sparkling English channel which had reached up to devour the brave airmen. But by that time England too was bleeding to death.

The drum beat more loudly in her head, merry, demanding, deadly . . .

Where was she? How had she come to this house? And whose was that cheeky freckled face seen briefly round the door? It did not belong to Hillary. He had had the lean aristocratic Duncastle good looks. Richard had taken after Joshua, to her disappointment. She had prayed that her children would favor her and her parents and all their ancestors. She had been saying that prayer on the evening so long ago when she had been presented with an unwanted suitor, and had cut off her hair.

She had been only twenty years old, a mere child to have so much responsibility forced on her. It had made her hard, people said. Hard on her sister Julia, and her children, and that Irish waif Deirdre, and pale little Mab. And Joshua. But he could always look after himself.

The rooks were fighting in the mulberry tree again. It was strange how they came to her London garden, as if to remind her of Sanctuary in Somerset, and Mamma and Julia taking their lonely walks down to the lake or through the woodland.

It was getting dark, too. Where was Fish to light the lamps?

"Fish?" she called querulously, and someone began telling her that Fish had died thirty years ago, and there was a cheeky common little boy sneaking about the corridor.

Then lights flashed on, and another picture came piercingly into her confused mind. She was looking at her pale narrow twenty-year-old face in her dressing table mirror in her bedroom at Sanctuary. She was briskly dismissing her eternal regret that she had not been a boy, another Duncastle to take her brother Hillary's and dear dead Papa's place, and deciding to do something about the woman that she was. Something as devastating as the events about to happen to her.

Thoughtfully she had pulled the pins out of her hair and, as it tumbled warmly on her shoulders, she had picked up her embroidery scissors.

Chapter 1

Nobody regarded Matilda as a beauty. Julia was the beauty of the family. Yet Matilda was fully aware that she, too, was admired. To be more accurate, she was admired rather too obsessively by one man. Which features did he like particularly? she wondered with detached curiosity. Her thin curved eyebrows, her emphatic Duncastle nose, her coils of reddish hair, her green eyes, her lips rather too narrow and very determined, her neck as long as a crane's. She thought she looked like a high-stepping bird.

Yet she had points. Her narrow hands, her erect carriage, her slim ankles which she sometimes deliberately shifted her skirts to display. Though not to Joshua Webb. Nevertheless, even without a glimpse of her ankles, he had noticed her attractions. Or the advantages of her class.

She had met him only twice. Once, when Papa, ill and old and tired, was putting his estate in order, and "that man from the bank" had come down. He had had luncheon with them, and while making abrupt and awkward conversation with Mamma and Papa, had never stopped staring at Matilda. He had scarcely looked at lovely Julia who had been on her best behaviour that day, but only at her, the elder daughter, who had extended him the barest courtesy possible. From the look of harassment on her father's face, she had known the bank clerk had done something to worry Papa deeply. She had been angry with him for that.

The second occasion on which she had seen Mr. Webb had been at Papa's funeral three months later. He had stood discreetly in the background, a stocky anonymous figure in his dark city clothes. He was there only because his bank was Papa's executor. He actually owned a bank, it seemed, albeit a small one. He had come back again the day after the funeral, accompanied by Mr. Deane, Papa's solicitor, and there had been discussions in the library for hours, ending only when Mamma had emerged in tears.

Matilda was lurking in the hall, filled with unexplained apprehension. "Why are you crying, Mamma? Did that Mr. Webb make you cry?"

"No, darling. We can't blame Mr. Webb. It seems he actually helped Papa when no one else would. That's the shame of it. Papa had been gambling, you see, for a long time." Mamma's head was high, her tear-streaked face fiercely loyal. "You know he never recovered from Hillary's death. He couldn't face the thought that he had no son and the family was finished." Mamma was not quite coherent. "Men do things to forget. Some drink. Your Papa gambled. And lost a great deal of money. A very great deal."

"Haven't we anything left? Are we poor? Then I'll go to work and keep you and Julia."

"Nonsense. How absurd. What could you do?"

The impossible suggestion seemed to restore Lady Duncastle's self-possession. The whole situation was really too incredible to be believed. Sanctuary, the home of the Duncastles for generations, was now owned by the bank, owned, it seemed, by that forceful young man Joshua Webb, who had been responsible for lending Papa so much money. Such a catastrophe simply couldn't be true.

Surely she and Matilda and Julia could go on living here very quietly, with two maids and a gardener. They could give up entertaining, give up the carriage, never go to London, do without new clothes, so long as Sanctuary remained their home. They must simply refuse to leave it.

Although she had encouraged her mother in this determination, Matilda soon enough realized the total impracticability of it. There were endless discussions with relatives, legal advisers and friends in the cold library (cold because Lady Duncastle had begun ferocious economies and refused to have fires lit although it was chilly October), but no solution was offered. Until the ultimate hopelessly awful one came from Joshua Webb, the bank clerk as Matilda persisted in calling him, the man who seemed to hold their futures in his hands.

When it came it seemed as if everybody, including Mamma, had been expecting it. There could be no question of its refusal, they all said. There was simply no alternative. Under the circumstances, it was a Godsend, for Mamma, for poor Julia, even for herself. But no one had seriously asked Matilda her opinion. It was accepted that she would be a dutiful daughter. From the moment the offer was made, it was regarded as a *fait accompli*.

They sat around the table in the library and arranged her life. And she, trained always to obey, imbued with conscience and a strong sense of duty, was temporarily speechless. She sat aghast while the busy words of the assembled company flew round her head.

"He isn't too bad-looking, and he's educated."

"At least there'll be enough money."

"It's vitally important to have Julia's future taken care of."

"Matilda will soon teach him social graces."

"Kensington Square is a very good address."

"Lady Duncastle can stay at Sanctuary until her death."

"Extraordinarily ambitious young man, I must say."

"When will the wedding be?"

And belatedly, "How does Matilda feel about it?"

How did she feel? Dazed, numb, astonished, outraged, above all cheated. She was twenty years old and she had expected to have some choice in life, although she had known, ever since Hillary's death, that she would have to bear more responsibilities.

But not such a shattering responsibility as this.

She looked round the familiar room, loving it as she had always done, the faded leather spines of the books, the heavy military histories and stories of colonization in which her family had taken such a prominent part, the panoramic paintings of famous battles, and the smaller sketches of favourite chargers, fellow officers, tented encampments, the last tragic photograph of all, of Hillary in full-dress uniform, taken just after his passing out at Sandhurst.

The Duncastles had fought for their country since the time of the great Duke of Marlborough and Malplaquet and Blenheim. There had been Duncastles in British regiments under the command of the Duke of Wellington in the Peninsular wars, and later at Waterloo. The late general's father, Sir Gordon Duncastle, had fallen at Balaclava in the Crimea, and his brother, grievously wounded in the Ashanti wars, had returned to England to die. There had been a Duncastle in the long-drawn-out Opium wars in China. India, that great hungry arid subcontinent, had demanded its sacrifices during the bloody Mutiny. India and the Royals were family history. Hillary and Matilda had both been born in Delhi, but Julia's birth had taken place at Sanctuary surrounded by civilised comforts, and with the best medical skill.

Papa had been given a baronetcy and made a Commander of the Indian Empire when he had been home on leave at the time of Julia's birth. The tap of his sovereign's sword on his shoulder and the new baby, as delicate and pale as thistledown, had been satisfying rewards for his arduous and dangerous life. At first he would have preferred that the baby had been another boy. Later, because of her mental condition, he was to be thankful that she was a girl and that she could be left in England with Matilda and Hillary, and suitable nurses and governesses, while he, with his wife, returned for another tour of duty in India.

He had been retired for only one year when Hillary had been killed, leaving him without a son and heir. It was a tragedy too painful to be faced. General Sir Richard Duncastle, C.I.E., escaped into the frenetic activity of gambling clubs and racecourses. When he came home he aired grandiose dreams of the kind of man Matilda, his elder daughter, must marry, to produce more brave fighting sons for England. Perhaps this hypothetical suitor could be persuaded to take Matilda's name so that there would still be Duncastles in famous regiments.

But Joshua Webb was not going to take anyone else's name, that was certain. He would have a great deal of stiff pride about his own which, from a humble beginning, he was making into something he thought important.

The only way to avoid having to marry him, Matilda decided, was to make him dislike her. The first step was to ruin what looks she had, for it was her looks that had at first interested him. That was why she sat at her dressing table cutting fiercely at her loosened hair. She must be a bit mad, she thought, for the shorn locks left a peaked white orphaned kind of face which she regarded with approval. Now for her eyebrows. The scissors snipped at the thin golden hairs. She daren't touch her lashes, lest the sharp points of the scissors slip and damage her eyes. She would need all of her eyesight if she were to earn her own living and support Mamma and Julia.

All the same, when she laid the scissors down, she was a little cross with herself for her impulsiveness. When would she be able to go out in society again? But she had finished with society, hadn't she? So what she had done must be carried through with panache. She would scrape her ragged hair back and secure it with pins, and hold her chin in the air. She would look hard and angular and ugly, and Mr. Webb would surely turn away in dismay. Or if he had any sense he would.

And serve him right for his impertinence in thinking that he, an insignificant bank clerk, could so easily marry into one of England's finest military families.

Someone moved behind her. Julia, coming in in her silent way, like a white mouse.

With deliberate suddenness Matilda turned to face her, to test the effect of her transformation. The result was more than she had bargained for. Julia gave a single long screech and hid her face in her hands.

Matilda silently scolded herself for her stupidity. She should have thought of Julia's extreme nervousness. She had only meant to make herself plain, not terrifying. But Julia was notoriously afraid of everything, shadows, a dog whining, a piece of torn wallpaper that might flap in the dark, curtains billowing, loud voices, even of a door banging.

Now she thought Matilda had dressed up to frighten her. Indeed, did she realize it was Matilda and not some ghost? One never knew the tormented fancies in her mind.

"Julia dearest! Don't be silly. It's only me."

The familiar voice made the girl draw her trembling fingers from her face. Her wide lovely startled eyes stared timidly, and then, at last recognizing her sister, she began to laugh. She had a high-pitched laugh that could be a little eerie unless one knew why she laughed. Her amusement often came from things visible only to herself.

"Oh, Mattie, what fun. You've dressed up for a game."

"Not for a game."

"Then why have you cut your hair? It's all over the floor."

"I'll tell you a secret, Julia. I've cut it to scare that awful Mr. Webb away."

Julia laughed again, clapping her hands.

"How clever you are. Do you think it will frighten him?"

"You were frightened."

"Yes, I was, but I'm—" Julia paused, then said carefully, as if repeating a lesson, "I'm a terrible coward."

Matilda said warmly, "No, you're not. I know Papa used to say that but he didn't understand that you see things other people don't see."

"Papa was so brave. He didn't like having a daughter

who was a coward." That was another lesson painfully learned.

"Papa thought you were beautiful," Matilda said firmly. "I got the brains and you got the looks. Everyone knows that. But," she returned to her own appearance, "it's Mr. Webb I'm planning to frighten, not you."

"I hate him," Julia said with intensity.

"So do I. That's why I've made myself look like this, so he'll stop wanting to marry me."

Julia's face cleared of its tortured doubts. "You're so clever, Mattie. I knew you would find a way not to marry him. We will be able to stay here, won't we?"

Matilda loved Sanctuary. It was ancient, romantic, and had always belonged to her family. When Julia had gone to dress with the help of Fish, the elderly maid she and Matilda and their mother economically shared (without supervision Julia would just as likely have come down to dinner in the dark stuff dress she had put on when she had got out of bed that morning) Matilda drew back the curtains and stood in the embrasured window, looking out.

The moon was bright tonight and the lawn sheened with frost. It was very quiet. If there were any live creatures in the shrubbery, foxes, badgers, rabbits, hares, surely such a peaceful night would bring them out. But nothing stirred. The trees, each one known to Matilda like a person, were ink black. The Lebanon cedar had a convenient branch stretched out like a couch on which generations of Duncastle children had sat. Rooks always built their nests in the same elm. The willows by the lake hung over the chilly water. The old pear tree that now bore only small and scrubby fruit had been Hillary's favourite for playing sentinel duty. The espaliered peaches and apricots spread over the old brick wall.

It was not only a garden but a secure secluded world. How could she leave it? How could she be instrumental in allowing strangers to live here?

Yet here she was, in her plainest dress, her cut hair tied back severely with a black velvet ribbon, looking forbidding enough to drive away Sanctuary's prospective saviour.

Mamma tapped at the door and came in.

"Matilda—" She gave a gasp. "What have you done to yourself? You look a perfect fright. Where's your new dress?"

"In its box."

"But, my dear, we bought it for tonight."

All that pink silk with black lace flounces. It was a beautiful dress that she would gladly have worn for a welcome suitor.

"I know."

"Then why—oh, my goodness, Matilda, now I see what you've done. You've cut off your hair!"

"Yes." Matilda's voice was belligerent, but she was a little less certain now. She hadn't wanted to bring additional anxiety to Mamma's worn face. It had become too fragile since Papa's death.

"But why? Mr. Webb will think you ma—" Not that word, it was too traumatic for a Duncastle. "—out of your senses."

"I hope he does."

"But darling girl, he is to save us. You, and Julia, and me." Mamma's voice had trembled. She fumbled for her handkerchief and began to weep.

"Mamma! Please! I didn't mean to upset you."

"You can't go down looking like that. So horrible. Even the servants—"

"He is coming to ask me to marry him," Matilda said flatly. "If he doesn't like the way I look perhaps he will spare himself the indignity of being refused."

"So complicated a way of saying no. Why didn't you tell us you hated the idea so much?"

"I suppose I'm a coward," Matilda said. "If Mr. Webb doesn't propose I won't have it on my conscience that I denied you and Julia security for the rest of your lives."

"Don't think of me. I don't matter at all. But we have to think of Julia. Not every man would be so kind and self-sacrificing about accepting a problem like that."

Matilda refused to believe that Mr. Webb had any but the most personal motives. Self-sacrifice didn't come into it. He wasn't that sort of man.

"I can look after Julia, and you, too, without the help of someone like Mr. Webb. If we must sell Sanctuary we can live in rooms."

"Sell Sanctuary! But it has been in the family for two centuries."

Would you sell your daughter instead? Matilda wondered. This whole sorry business was Papa's fault. It was only beginning to come out now how much he had lost at gambling, roulette, chemin de fer, baccarat. Hundreds, sometimes thousands, in a night. Some he occasionally won back, but the immutable pattern of gambling remained. In the end he lost disastrously. How dare he have exposed his wife and daughters to such a poverty-stricken and humiliating future?

Yet Matilda remembered him in his proud days, a splendid figure on horseback, inspecting a parade on the barracks ground at Delhi or, in full-dress uniform, attending a dinner at the Viceroy's Palace, or leading Mamma out on to the ballroom floor. He had been an overpowering personality to his children, a stern and respected officer to his men. She remembered the light in his eyes at Hillary's passing-out parade, and so soon afterwards his crushed despair at Hillary's death. She realised now that he must have partially lost his sanity at that time. How else could he have forgotten discipline and self-respect so much that he had gambled away his entire fortune, and then had had to seek help from a man like Joshua Webb? Normally he would have gone to a long-established bank for his loans. Or had he done so, and been refused?

Webb's merchant bank, in Cheapside in the City of London, was small but beginning to prosper. It had been begun by Joshua's father (who had been the eldest son of a market gardener) in two rooms. It now occupied a respectable but still modest two-storey building, with gold lettering across the windows. It was beginning to make substantial profits from shrewd money-lending to tragic and foolish gentlemen like General Sir Richard

Duncastle. Joshua Webb, the new young ambitious chairman, didn't deny that these customers were meat and drink to him, but he also maintained that he prevented suicides, that last resort of the desperate gambler, by lending aid. And he had many other irons in the fire besides impoverished gentlemen with family assets. He was intensely proud of his growing business, intensely ambitious. He saw himself spreading into Europe, an English Rothschild.

But he needed solid connections. Matilda knew that she was meant to be one of them, a connection in every sense. His wife.

"Matilda dear!" Mamma was saying placatingly, her tears dried, her worn face anxious. "It may not be so bad. Mr. Webb has many things in his favour. He may be a little uncultured, but you are clever enough to improve him. Could you look on it as a challenge?"

Mamma had been married to such a dominating man that she had long ago taken the line of docility and obedience. It was, in her opinion, the correct role for women. She could not struggle with the troubles that assailed her, bereavement and financial ruin and the permanent burden of Julia. Therefore she expected Matilda to accept with gratitude a comfortable home in Kensington in London, a strong clever ambitious husband, and security for them all. After all, she wasn't in love with anyone else, was she?

No, she wasn't. What was love? A dream, a tremulous fantasy seldom realised. So many marriages of convenience turned out happily. Or so she was told.

"I just dislike people telling me what I must do," Matilda said, her voice hard and fierce. "It's all very well for onlookers. But I'm expected to go to bed with that man!"

"My dear child, don't be coarse."

"I'm just facing facts, Mamma. And supposing," she went on, "I give birth to another Julia. What will Mr. Webb think of that?"

Mamma pressed her handkerchief to her eyes.

"You're too cruel. You suddenly look—"

"How? Ugly?"

"Not a girl any more. Much older. Hard."

Matilda nodded. "That's how I want to look. It's time someone in this family stopped being sentimental. When is Mr. Webb due to arrive?"

"About seven. But please, Matilda, don't go down looking like that."

"I can't pin my hair back on. If Mr. Webb wants me like this he can have me. It's my private test of him. At least he'll know what my feelings are. So he'll need to be a brave man." She added, thoughtfully, "I suppose I would have to respect him for that."

Joshua Webb might have come from a humble background, but he had learned. He knew how to dress for dinner with the gentry, and how to behave with a certain instinctive gallantry. He was not adept at small talk. His conversation was spasmodic and uninspired. He would much have preferred dinner with business colleagues to these three starchy gentlewomen in the house that was now rightfully his. He wished there had been some way to dine alone with Matilda, in order to get the future settled quickly. But if he were to move in upper-class circles, as was his intention, he would have to dance the social minuet. He anticipated that at a certain stage after dinner the mother and the younger sister would withdraw, leaving the two of them alone.

The thing he was most determined on was that Matilda, his future bride, should be made to stop looking at him with contempt. She was a brat, really. She represented a challenge, like a tricky business deal. He enjoyed challenges, otherwise he would not have been a successful businessman. Now he was impatient to see this proud green-eyed young woman presiding over his table in the house he had recently bought in Kensington Square. She was a business deal, too, but hopefully much more than that.

The house in Kensington was a handsome, narrow-fronted four-storey building. It had been owned by three elderly ladies, daughters of a long-deceased duke. Joshua had succeeded in buying a good deal of the furniture and hangings with the house, having the sense to know they fitted better than anything new on the market. So that the long dining table was Jacobean, as also were the high-backed chairs, dark oak with tapestry-covered seats (no doubt stitched by the Ladies Ursula, Elizabeth and Jane). The drawing room had heavy silk brocade curtains, one set of windows facing the square, the other the long, walled garden at the back of the house. There were some dark pictures in old gilt frames on the staircase, and a four-poster bed in the main bedroom. Also a Wellington chest (Matilda, descendant of generations of soldiers, would appreciate that), massive wardrobes, faded carpets in the five second-floor bedrooms, and patchwork rugs in the attics. The basement kitchen was stocked with shining copper pans, there were area steps for tradesmen. The house was an old one in an historic square within easy walking distance of Kensington Palace. The traffic down the High Street, cabhorses, tradesmen's drays, shouting barrow boys, was comfortably audible. Joshua didn't care for the lonely silence of the country, it was too unfamiliar to a boy born in the noisy virile City of London.

Although his Kensington house bore no comparison to the ancient dignity of Sanctuary he could not imagine a woman, even Matilda Duncastle, not being impressed by it. Why should she not enjoy living in town rather than mouldering away in this desperately quiet old mansion which had lost its last thread of vigorous life when the general had died? She would make a splendid hostess. He knew that. She would do things with style, which was what he wanted. Moreover, he wanted children from her, girls to inherit her long elegant figure, boys who would combine her breeding with his business genius. He was not modest about himself. He knew he would go a long way in the City, especially with the right connections.

All these thoughts went through Joshua Webb's head as he waited in front of the fire in the shabby yellow drawing room at Sanctuary. His strong pugnacious face, however, showed nothing but a carefully bland politeness. He knew Matilda called him the bank clerk. It amused him. He would enjoy teaching her his world. It was such a lively place compared to this backwater with its laid-down arms, its ghosts of dead soldiers.

The Duncastles had served England and the Empire with great distinction. Their name would always be an honoured one in military annals. But with the death of the last son the family was exhausted. He would inject new healthy blood. He wanted his sons to come into his bank and build up a commercial fortune. That, too, was serving England. Matilda would learn.

Chapter 2

Matilda found it too infuriating that her carefully de-nuded looks seemed to pass completely unnoticed by Mr. Webb. He greeted her in his usual manner, with a stiff little bow, and made some banal remark about the weather. That it was a frosty night, or some such thing. Perhaps this was an oblique reference to the meagre log fire, since Mamma was persisting with her economies.

Julia, exasperatingly, got a fit of the giggles. She was inclined to do that when she was nervous, not because she found a situation amusing. One had never seen the light of pure fun in her beautiful blank eyes. Malice, fear, rage, but never humour or, sadly, happiness. She was a creature of terrors and apprehensions and there was no doubt this stranger from London, associated as he was with Papa's death, was one of her terrors.

It was unfortunate, but of course Mamma and Julia would stay in the country when Matilda married—rather *if* she married Joshua Webb. Matilda couldn't bring that speculation to a conclusion. She could only realise that it was her social position rather than her looks that had made her attractive to Mr. Webb. What an arid thought.

Yet he was endeavouring to be pleasant, as indeed he ought to be. Sitting down to dinner at a table laid with crested family silver and fine crystal and porcelain, waited on by a butler and two maids, having three gentlewomen with whom to converse, was surely an event that had never before happened to him. Out of his element as he obviously was, it was galling to admit that he was behaving with a certain rugged dignity. One suspected that if he didn't know the right cutlery to use he would regard the matter as being of small importance.

Perhaps a bride with chopped-off hair was of small importance, too. After all, the essential woman remained.

Matilda, instead of enjoying his discomfiture, was discomfited herself. Why wasn't he repelled by her? Why did he forgive her for this very dubious joke, and sit there eating his grouse with relish, and making quite intelligent remarks about hunting and shooting. He had not had the opportunity to take part in these sports himself, but he was sure that all the Duncastles had been fine shots.

"At the enemy," Matilda said crisply. "We don't particularly like murdering feathered or four-legged creatures."

"In war, of course," Mamma murmured.

"My brother Hillary could hit a target in the dusk right between the eyes."

"Splendid," said Mr. Webb. "My sons, I hope, will devote their time to ledgers."

"Are you a pacifist, Mr. Webb?" Matilda asked, with deliberate contempt.

"War isn't my profession. I would be very bad at it. That fellow lurking in the dusk would have shot me long before I saw him."

"Yet you get rich on people like my father who defended this country for you, and your sort."

"I wasn't aware that this country had been under attack, Miss Duncastle."

Matilda was put out and snappish. He was too unexpectedly bland and self-possessed.

"Not this country, of course, but parts of the Empire. The Crimea, Egypt, Zululand. And there's always Ireland."

"Ah, yes, a terrible menace."

"Mr. Webb, are you making fun of me?"

"Pay no attention, Mr. Webb," Mamma said. "Matilda is being provocative, and rather bad-mannered, I'm afraid."

"I'm just intensely proud of my family," Matilda said. "Is that a fault?"

"Far from it," said Mr. Webb. "I'm proud of mine, too. That's an admirable sentiment."

What a lot of big words he knew, for a bank clerk, Matilda thought sulkily. And how dull, dull, dull he was. His sons bending over ledgers, indeed. They might as well be tax collectors.

Julia began to giggle again.

"Mattie, he never noticed your hair," she whispered audibly.

Mr. Webb had attacked his grouse again, eating with concentration and pleasure. He enjoyed the claret, too, and nodded as Sands refilled his glass. He might declare that he disliked war, but this meal, and the present company, were obviously being appreciated as the spoils of war. What a beastly ink-stained man he was, issuing his bonds and his letters of credit and his loans. Imagine not being able to handle a gun or a sword, or ride a horse. What did he do for recreation? How did he perform on a ballroom floor, for instance? She swore she would not marry a man who constantly trod on her toes.

She knew nothing about him except that he apparently had defective eyesight, since, as Julia correctly observed, he had not noticed her spoiled looks. She must have been mistaken in thinking that he had admired her appearance. How galling!

Mamma had signalled to Sands to clear away the main course and bring the sweet, one of cook's special confections, usually prepared only for honoured guests. The last time Mrs. Patch had made this elaborate pyramid of jelly, creamy mousse, and glistening cherries and almonds had been when Papa's old regimental officers had come to dinner. Mr. Webb would probably have preferred plum pudding or spotted dick.

Matilda frowned, a moment of honesty touching her. Wasn't she too niggling in her criticisms? A person's character couldn't be established by his preferences in his food. Only his background. She might even have consented to like him mildly, if only he would stay in his place and not make demands on her.

However, time was inexorably passing. Mrs. Patch's famous sweet was demolished, the port arrived, with cigars for Mr. Webb. Coffee, Mamma said, would be served in the drawing room after Matilda and Mr. Webb had had time to talk as she knew they wanted to. Convention could be ignored this evening. She and Julia would withdraw, and Matilda could stay and perhaps sip a little more wine while Mr. Webb enjoyed his port.

They faced each other across the candlelit dining table. Mr. Webb poured himself a glass of port. His thick black brows twitched once or twice over his intent luminous eyes almost as if he were nervous. He had hypnotic eyes, Matilda thought. They could almost make one not notice his plain pugnacious face. That must be how he succeeded in his business, fixing that domineering stare on suppliant customers, demanding his extra half per cent interest, or the deeds to a family home. What a bizarre proposal this was to be.

Indeed, she wasn't going to let it be a formal proposal. She would spare herself that hypocrisy by talking in the business terms he understood.

"Do you still want to marry me?" she asked.

His eyebrows twitched again, either with nervousness or amusement. How could she guess what it was since she didn't know the man?

"That was the object of my visit tonight. A splendid dinner thrown in is a bonus."

A bonus. That was the language he understood. Yet he was honest. She touched her hair, ragged and uncompromisingly tied back.

"In spite of the fact that I can quite often look a fright. Or hadn't you noticed?"

"I'd noticed. I thought you had had some accident, but that it would be impolite to comment on it."

"What sort of accident? Catching my hair in a candle? No, I cut it deliberately."

"To scare me off?" Suddenly he gave a great laugh, hearty and genuinely amused. "To tell the truth I rather like a woman not tricked up with curling tongs and ribbons. You have a relentless face. Strong. Interesting."

The last thing she had expected was that he would admire her naked face. Or was he just being very clever and adroit?

"Do you really want a bride who makes herself ugly for her husband?"

"Don't be melodramatic. I might have expected your sister to behave like this, but not you." He stretched across the table and had laid his hand over hers before she could withdraw it to the safety of her lap. The candlelight shone in his eyes giving them a yellow flare. His palm was surprisingly soft. Why shouldn't it be? Had she expected callouses on the flesh of a pen-pusher? She had a breathless feeling, almost as if he were lying on her, suffocating her.

"Did you think you would disgust me and drive me away? My dear Miss Duncastle, we must get acquainted. You'll learn that when I want something I must have it."

"If I am the something you have your desires fixed on—" Her careful self-control broke. *"Why?"*

He sat back, picked up his glass of port, and took a long swallow.

"First of all, let's get matters straight. I'm not responsible for your father's death. He was dying before he got into financial trouble. Neither can I be blamed that he came to me for help, and that I demanded, as a responsible banker must, adequate security. I didn't know of your existence until I came here. I had intended only to protect my banking interests. If a man must mortgage his whole estate to satisfy his passion for the gaming tables, then his family must blame him for their subsequent poverty. Not the man who paid his bills and saved him from the disgrace of the bankruptcy court. So, Miss Duncastle, I came here purely to salvage a rather ill-judged investment, in whatever way I could. Then I had the privilege of meeting you."

Matilda's eyes narrowed.

"In other words, I'm the sort of wife you'd never dreamed of getting."

"Oh, perhaps I would have. But when I was older and richer. I'm only thirty now although I suspect you think me middle-aged. I could have waited to marry. I have always been determined to have the best. But when you came into the room on my first visit here, I thought you looked like a queen."

Matilda gave a snuffle of laughter, her long fingers pressed against her lips.

"Which queen? Marie Antoinette? The Empress Eugénie? Surely not Queen Victoria?"

"No, a Tudor, I think," he answered, with gravity. "Your hair will grow. And if you cut it again I'll beat you."

She was beginning to lost control of the conversation. She was being bested by a bank clerk whose honesty had a certain dignity. She hated having to admit that. She felt angry and vindictive.

"Supposing we have children and one of them is like Julia?"

"Impossible!"

"It's not impossible at all. It happens in this family. I remember when I was small, we had a Great-aunt Tatiana kept in one of the back bedrooms upstairs. My brother and I were never allowed to visit her, but sometimes we saw her at the window."

A wraith with her silver hair and pale, pale face. A ghost that had sent a frisson of fear over a small girl. When Matilda had looked at Julia's snowdrop face in her baby carriage the same queer apprehension had touched her. Years later she had been amazed at her early perception.

"Mopping and mowing, I suppose," Mr. Webb said, but his eyebrows were twitching again, as if he had been disturbed.

"No. Just looking sad and lost. As Julia will one day if she isn't loved and cared for."

"How many of these"—Mr. Webb hesitated for want of a tactful word—"have there been in your family?"

"I don't know. It began when one of my ancestors fought in some old war in Scandinavia, and came back with a Swedish bride. She was fair, like Julia. Pale blue eyes. There's a portrait of her somewhere. I think Mamma hid it, after Julia was born. She didn't like looking at it. The girl's name was Cristina. She was unhappy here and very lonely. She found she had married a soldier who neglected her. So finally she lost her wits, as they said in those days. Or perhaps she had never had many in the first place. Anyway, she had a tame arctic hare that she had brought from Sweden, and it used to hop about the garden, especially when there was snow on the ground. The servants were supposed to have been scared of it. It had huge ears and dark eyes that glowed against the snow. They said it was uncanny. And then the story got about that it was the girl in a bewitched state."

"The Swedish bride?"

"Yes. It's only a myth, of course. Those were superstitious times. It was just such a strange pet to have, not like a cosy King Charles spaniel or a cage of canaries. Are you superstitious, Mr. Webb?"

"Not in the least."

"Then you'll laugh about the sequel to all this. There's a story that whenever the white hare is seen—"

"Seen?"

"Yes, people do still see it. Or think they do. Mamma swears she saw it, leaping about on a snowy night before Julia was born." Matilda had the satisfaction of seeing a startled look cross Mr. Webb's face. "You see, when a pregnant Duncastle wife sees this beast she is probably going to give birth to someone like Julia, and Great-aunt Tatiana."

"What absolute balderdash!"

Matilda felt tired suddenly, and disinclined to scare off Mr. Webb any more. The dark strain in her family was another nightmare altogether.

"Julia exists, doesn't she?" she said flatly. "My brother

and I were both born in India. Papa said Julia should have been born there, too, and then it would have been all right. But she was conceived and born at Sanctuary."

"I don't believe a word of this superstitious nonsense," Mr. Webb said vigorously. "Even if your sister is a——"

"Lunatic?"

"I didn't use that word."

"It's the word. Or more politely, in our family, they are called touched. But Julia is fine when she's happy. That's why it's important to keep her happy."

"Aren't I making that possible?"

Matilda saw the repressed distaste in his face. He was never going to grow accustomed to Julia. If one of his own children—no, one mustn't even think of it.

"Our children will be born in London," he went on, "if that's what's worrying you. Good God, some animal from a Scandinavian fairy tale. I've never heard such far-fetched nonsense. We'll consult the best doctors when you're expecting a child, I promise you that. I expect, to tell the truth, your family has been too inbred. That would explain the old aunt and Julia more than a nonexistent white hare."

"Yes, that is true," Matilda conceded. "Sometimes cousins married, in the past. The army tradition and the looks had to be preserved. The Duncastles are very vain."

"I've observed that."

Matilda flushed. "Not me, tonight."

"Very much you tonight. Why did you think I'd be so put off if you made yourself look plain? That was vanity, pure and simple. Ego. But then I like a woman with ego."

She was thoroughly discomposed. Was he going to see through her all his life? She must grow more subtle.

"But now," he went on confidently, "vanity must be sacrificed to breeding from healthy stock. Will you marry me, Matilda?"

She had seen his shock about Julia, and now she saw his resolve. Papa would have liked that. He would have said that here was a man who would behave well in the thick of battle. That was his supreme criterion.

"If I must," she said reluctantly, then made an effort. "Thank you for the compliment."

When they went into the drawing room Mamma and Julia were huddled over the small fire. Julia's face was pinched with cold, or anxiety, or both. She had always clung to Matilda. She knew Mr. Webb was a threat to her security. She would have to be handled very gently. Mr. Webb must learn.

Matilda sat beside her and took her hand.

"Goodness, it's chilly in here. I'm going to ring for more logs, since now we can afford them."

Mamma's worn face got its tremulous look, half regret, half relief.

"Oh, my darling—you've decided?"

"Yes. Mr. Webb and I are going to be married." She was pleased with the steadiness of her voice. "Why don't you sit down, Mr. Webb?"

"Couldn't it be Joshua, now? Won't you call me Joshua, Lady Duncastle, since I'm to be your son-in-law?"

"Certainly. A good Biblical name."

"It goes back in my family to a great-grandfather who came up from the country to London with no possessions but a knapsack on his back. Like Dick Whittington." Mr. Webb laughed heartily. "He didn't become Lord Mayor, but who knows what's in the future for another Joshua Webb, eh?"

Lord Mayor of London. Were *those* his dreams? Matilda thought that if she had loved him, or even had a fondness for him, she would have been tender and indulgent about his ambitions. Now, they only seemed ridiculous. And certainly she would not allow any son of hers to bear such an ugly name. A son of theirs? She and this stranger with his strong, thick-set body. They might produce a lance corporal, she could hear Papa saying. Even a sergeant-major. But not one of those slender elegant whipcord young Duncastle officers, all fire and courage.

"What did he become, this great-grandfather?" Mamma asked stiffly.

"Oh, he leased some land on the outskirts of London, between Chelsea and Kensington. He began a market garden. He came of farming stock and knew the land. He prospered reasonably well. But when his eldest son, my grandfather, took over the land he had the idea of starting a shop to sell the produce. He was a good businessman. Then his eldest son, my father, who was clever with figures, decided to move on further and start in banking. It meant moving to the city. I was born within the sound of Bow Bells, so I suppose I can claim to be a cockney. I have one sister, but soon after her birth my mother died. Father and I were left to look after the baby. We managed well enough, I think. When I was old enough, I went into the bank with Father, and my sister kept house for us. She still lives with my father who is an invalid in the old house in Cheapside."

"Not married?"

"She has a squint."

Matilda was shocked at his insensitivity, then realised he was simply stating a fact, an unchangeable condition. She touched her ragged hair.

"Does that put marriage out of the question?" she asked pointedly.

"It lessens the probability, don't you agree?"

"Oh, yes, I agree. But she must have other qualities."

"Clara has my dogged nature," Joshua said. "I hope you will like her, Matilda. She'll make a splendid aunt to our children."

Witless Julia and squint-eyed Clara. Suddenly they seemed to be the visible symbols of this utterly wrong marriage. Matilda wanted to pick up her skirts and run out of the room, out of the house, into the cold clean night, away from this overconfident man, so sure of his superiority over three helpless women, no, four, counting the unfortunate sister. She simply couldn't go on with it.

Then she caught her mother mopping at a furtive tear with her permanently damp handkerchief and knew that dear gentle Mamma understood, and suffered with her, but still depended on her. Running away was no use because she would have to come back.

The hardest thing to accept was that Joshua Webb had no idea of the undercurrents in the room. He stood in front of the fire, shutting off its feeble heat from the three women, and went on with his confident plans.

"Clara will stay in the Cheapside house, of course. That was arranged when I bought my place in Kensington Square. Matilda and I will be confortable there, and you and Julia, Lady Duncastle, will be able to remain here until the end of your lives. I doubt if I'll sell the place then, since Matilda values it, but I'll be frank and say I don't much care for living here myself."

"Naturally not," Mamma said, with her gentle politeness. "It's much too quiet for someone accustomed to the city. But Julia and I are grateful for your generosity. We'll be quite happy here. We hope you'll visit us at Christmas and on other occasions. It's very pretty when there's snow on the ground."

"And the white hare leaps about?" Joshua said jovially.

Seeing the startled look on her mother's face, Matilda said, "I made Mr.—Joshua laugh about our family—" She hesitated, aware of Julia's tense attention, "—our four-footed ghost. He doesn't realise all old houses have queer tales to tell."

"I'll believe this ghost when I see it, my dear."

"Oh, men never see it," Mamma said quickly, then, regretting the implication of her words, added, "I thought I did once, but it was only that one of the grooms was keeping a white cat in the stables. You know how cats play in snow. My husband never stopped laughing at me."

But Julia had been born six months later, not in the heat and discomfort of army headquarters in Pondicherry, but in a cool beautiful English summer, in a haunted house.

"Mamma, I never heard that explanation about the cat," Matilda said, too gaily. "You disappoint me. You are supposed to be the only one with the distinction of having seen our ghost."

"You must have listened to servants gossiping, dear. You must think us absurd, Mr. Webb. It comes from living in an old house in the country. You'll be very wise to avoid it. Kensington won't have ghosts."

"Well, I don't know. My house is old enough and I believe some of the houses in the square have secret passages. We might even produce a headless ghost, though I doubt if the three elderly ladies who lived there previously would have put up with that sort of thing."

"Don't, Joshua," Matilda reproved. "You're frightening Julia."

Indeed, Julia's eyes had got the shine of suppressed frenzy. She clutched Matilda's hand and whispered that she would never have to live in that house, would she?

"You're staying here with Mamma. Joshua, could you remember that my sister is very sensitive?"

"Sorry," said Mr. Webb perfunctorily. "Clumsy of me." Again, an expression of distaste had crossed his face. He didn't like Julia. He felt repelled by her. It was going to be difficult to make them friends, for Julia would always be bothered by his loud voice, and he would have little patience. Patience, one realised already, was not one of his virtues.

But he must have others, please God. And if he, on his part, thought he was acquiring an obedient wife he was mistaken. She would fight him on every issue on which they disagreed. She suspected there would be many battles ahead. A marriage of this kind either succeeded, or became a small private war. And she was a Duncastle with fiery blood, and, on occasion, a witheringly sharp tongue. What would they both become?

On the first day of the new year 1890, Joshua put the deeds of Sanctuary into Matilda's hands. They were his wedding gift to her. He wanted to assure her that he was a man of his word. The property had been transferred into her name, so that after her mother died it would be hers to do with as she wished.

Matilda looked at the fine spiky writing on the parchment. It testified that the new owner of the property known as Sanctuary was Matilda Mary Webb of Kensington, London, Married Woman. The date was that very day, an hour after Mrs. Matilda Mary Webb had come into being. And only half an hour later she and her husband were quarrelling.

It wasn't her fault. Because of his generosity over

Sanctuary, Matilda had had a sincere impulse to draw Joshua into the family and to have him share her pride in it.

The obvious way to her was to show him the Salamanca Drum and to relate its history. And what better time than on her wedding day. So she drew him away from the small knot of guests in the drawing room (because of Papa's recent death it was a very quiet wedding) and took him to the room where the military relics were displayed. She said she did not intend to remove all of the collection to London as Sanctuary was their natural setting, but the little drum must come. Because, she said, it was so much a part of her life and the life of every Duncastle.

She was already seeing two, three, four boys with the whippy strength and slenderness of the Duncastles, marching off to some future campaign. Where would it be? She hadn't a notion, only that it would further the glory of the Empire.

She saw the blank look on Joshua's face and was deeply affronted. How could it be possible that he didn't share her pride? When he said with a tact she failed to recognize, "Wouldn't it be better to leave it here where it belongs?" she felt a quick flash of indignation. Where would Joshua Webb be if that drum hadn't beaten bravely at Salamanca, if many other proudly preserved weapons hadn't hacked and spat their way through enemy lines? Safely dealing in bills and debentures in the City of London in a sound economy? Never.

"But you must know it's an utterly vital part of my family," she said. "One of my ancestors, Hillary Duncastle, aged just fifteen, and small for his age, they said, was a drummer boy at the battle of Salamanca. He fell on the battlefield. Someone retrieved his body, and the drum. Both were covered in blood. But the battle was won."

"Of course," said Joshua.

"Why do you say 'of course' in that way?"

"Well, for one thing I would say the incident was a little overcharged with emotion. And for another you can't expect me to believe that a drummer boy wins battles."

"I didn't say Hillary won the battle, but he gave the troops tremendous inspiration. The Duke of Wellington referred to him particularly afterwards. Isn't that something to be proud of?"

Joshua remained stubborn.

"I refuse to treat this object like a holy relic. You'll oblige me by leaving it at Sanctuary. It isn't a vital part of my family. Nor will it be of yours and mine. Don't get ideas of that sort in your head, Mattie." (He had taken to calling her Mattie, which he thought more friendly.) "I'm not having my sons spilling blood in deserts and jungles where they have no right to be, anyway."

"Joshua, how can you be so unpatriotic?"

"I'm a realistic fellow. Haven't you found that out yet?"

Could she ever be happy with a man like this? He did have good points, she had fairly acknowledged them. But their ideas and ideals were so disparate as to make an harmonious marriage impossible, without one of them giving way. And it wouldn't be her. The drum was coming to London, to their house in Kensington. She would deal with the execution of that plan later.

Now, a photographer was waiting in the library to make a painstaking record of their marriage.

Matilda knew she would come out in the photograph like a stiff poker. She could almost hear her children saying, years later, "Mamma, you don't look a very happy bride," and herself answering, "Photographs don't show feelings." Though if they knew her well enough they would recognize the light of battle in her eyes.

Chapter 3

Joshua's father had been too much of an invalid to come to the wedding, and his sister Clara would not leave the old man. Therefore, strange as it seemed, Matilda did not meet Joshua's family until she came to London as Joshua's wife. Then Joshua wasted no time in hurrying her across London to visit his father and sister in Cheapside.

Still in mourning for her own father, she was dressed quietly in grey, a bunch of violets tucked in her waistband. Joshua had stopped the cab and bought the violets from a street flowerseller. That was not, as Matilda had at first thought, a romantic gesture, but an attempt to satisfy his own vanity. He wanted his bride to look cherished and festive.

The house in Cheapside was narrow-fronted and un-pretentious, squeezed as it was between two other such dwellings in a rather mean street.

"When my parents moved here they thought they had come up in the world," Joshua said. "They never wanted to move again."

"Why should they?"

"Because prosperity ought to be visible. It then leads to more, it becomes a snowball." Joshua sounded slightly impatient with her naïveté. He expected his wife to be intelligent enough to realise this first law of success. "Why do you think I bought those rugs and pictures from Kensington House before it was pulled down?" He was referring to an enormous monstrosity of a house that had been pulled down within a few years of its erection. The auction sale of its contents had had a certain cachet. Anyone who bought them now owned a rich man's possessions.

He rapped the door-knocker vigorously and presently the door was opened by a small skinny maid in cap and apron.

"We're expected, Janey. How is my father?"

"Poorly, sir." The girl darted a quick inquisitive look at Matilda. "But he be sitting up waiting for you."

"Joshua," came a welcoming voice from the little hall. "Have you brought her?"

"Of course I've brought her, Clara." Joshua took Matilda's arm. "Here she is."

The woman who came towards Matilda with arms outstretched was indeed squint-eyed, as Joshua had said. But apart from this very noticeable flaw her looks were pleasant. She had a feminine softness and a warm smile. Her defect obviously had not soured her.

"I'm so happy to meet you," she said. "I've always wanted a sister. My, Joshua, she's so fashionable. But I always knew my brother would want a smart wife. I hope he'll look after you properly, my dear."

So she didn't know about the arrangement, Matilda thought. No doubt Joshua wouldn't boast about his piece of blackmail. Naturally he would prefer people to think she had married him willingly, for love.

She made herself smile, and allowed Clara to kiss her. The house smelt of beeswax, with another underlying sickly smell. Matilda noticed Joshua's eyebrows twitch, the sign she had come to recognize of distress and nervousness. He didn't care for death. He had never been on a battlefield when the smoke of battle was drifting away.

He was perhaps a coward in this respect. He had felt distaste for Julia's queerness, too. That was what he politely called it. He liked people to be healthy, mentally and physically.

"Will you come upstairs and see Father now? He's awake and waiting." Clara took Matilda's arm. "He begins to wander in his mind later in the day. He had a stroke six months ago and it's left him with one side paralysed. He had never meant Joshua to be head of the bank so young, and he worries about it."

"I'm managing," Joshua said shortly.

"I'm sure you are. Although you're in too much of a hurry, Father thinks. But go in and talk to him."

The grey head on the pillow, the gaunt grey face, the piercing eyes which had been inherited by his son, looking at Matilda assessingly, just as Joshua's had done, as if she were again being valued as a gilt-edged security. Presently the colourless lips opened and a grating voice came out.

"See now why you chanced your luck over that bankrupt old General, son. Might have known you had a trick up your sleeve."

"This is my wife Matilda, Father," Joshua said. "And you're mixing your metaphors. I neither chanced my luck nor had a trick up my sleeve. I deal only in certainties. How are you?"

"There's something wrong with my eyes," the old man said petulantly. "Can't seem to read balance sheets any more."

"Never mind, Father. Read something relaxing. What about Dickens or Trollope? You think of something, Clara. Make him forget the bank."

A flame flickered in the deep-set eyes of the old man.

"Forget the bank, he tells me. You wait until you're dying, son. See who wins, Master David Copperfield or the financial report on those Balkan railways. How are they, by the way?"

"Flourishing, Father."

"Well, as long as Germany drops her warlike attitudes. Never trust wars, my dear, what's your name—Matilda? They create havoc with finance."

"My wife's family has always thought of the glory of military victory rather than the state of the economy, Father."

"Oh dear me, yes, the General. A famous military family, I believe? Well, that's no way to breed strong generations. It's too wasteful, too dangerous. You can be thankful you've married a stay-at-home banker."

"I'm very proud of my family," Matilda said, getting a chance to speak at last. The dubious look on the shrewd old face on the pillow made her go on determinedly: "We have so many wonderful relics. They make me cry with pride. The Salamanca Drum, the colours captured from the French at Waterloo, medals and swords and guns. The history of England is written in the archives of families like mine. And on their tombs."

"Joshua, how did you come to marry this warlike young woman?"

Joshua gave a sudden confident grin. "I'll tame her, I promise you."

He held Matilda's arm possessively. He looked pleased, because she had gone through her paces, shown her breeding. She might almost have been a prize of battle.

"Well, teach her that money can talk just as effectively as bullets. And less fatally." The old man had slipped down on his pillows. He was looking drowsy and exhausted. "Don't want a clutch of sabre-rattling grandsons."

"He's tired. You'd better go now," said Clara, coming into the room. She motioned to Matilda to precede her out. "He likes you. He hasn't talked so much for a long time."

Matilda was still feeling heated from the indignation that had filled her. The way they thought money so important, and courage merely foolhardy. What terrible standards to have.

However, her good manners prevailed and she said, "I'm afraid I behaved badly. I showed off."

"So did Father. He's as proud of his past as your family is of theirs."

"They're such different pasts." Matilda believed she would be able to talk to Clara, who seemed to have the sensitivity her brother lacked. "Joshua and I are so different. I really don't know—"

"Know what, dear?"

"How successful our marriage can be," Matilda confessed. "It took place for—various reasons."

"We've always known Joshua has a way of getting what he wants," Clara said equably. "Perhaps you'll complement each other." Her smile was friendly, her crooked eyes oddly attractive. "I hope so, because I like you. And I was born to be a good aunt."

Joshua had no intention of sitting in Clara's neat sitting room drinking tea and wasting time listening to women's gossip. While she was about it, he said bluntly, Matilda had better see the rest of his empire. As it was Sunday, they would have the place to themselves.

So, with the chiming of church bells in her ears, Matilda stood on the muddy pavement watching Joshua unlocking the stout oak door of his bank. He tried to be casual, but his face was stiff with pride. Guiding Matilda across the foyer, he said he didn't imagine she would be interested in all the paraphernalia of money, the ledgers and scales and cash drawers and telling counters, or indeed in the vaults which were dark and chilly, and he didn't want to disturb the caretaker who had rooms in the basement. Actually, this diverse explanation was meant to hasten her across the tiled floor to the mahogany door which bore the inscription MR. JOSHUA WEBB SENIOR and MR. JOSHUA WEBB JUNIOR.

The door opened into what Joshua was proudly calling the partners' room. He crossed to the windows to pull back heavy velour curtains, and as the wintry light shone in he stood in the centre of the Turkey carpet silently inviting her to enjoy the simple solid expensiveness of the room.

Matilda had to admit that it had exactly the right air of modest success and stability. The partners' room. It sounded important.

"What if there aren't partners?" she asked.

"There almost always are."

"Your father's going to die, Joshua. You'll be Mr. Webb senior then and there won't be a Mr. Webb junior."

"Not as yet, Mattie. But one day—"

Matilda avoided his hand, which had made a move to land heavily on her shoulder, by walking round the room examining the pictures on the panelled walls, two banal but good-quality shipping scenes and a mail coach marooned in snow. The space over the mantelpiece was empty. What was it being kept for? A portrait of the bank's owner in a stuffy dark suit with a heavy gold watch chain across an expensive waist? How different from the romantic portraits of army officers to which she was accustomed, and which gave her those dark, rich dreams of courage and deeds of valour. This place smelt of money. She could almost hear the coins chinking, as Joshua must have when he sat on his side of the wide desk in that nice Georgian mahogany chair, and listened to the tellers counting the sovereigns, the silver and the copper, on the other side of the door.

"Will you take another partner when your father dies?" she asked airily.

"Perhaps. But not to share this room with me. I'm keeping that privilege for my own son."

"You told your father you dealt only in certainties."

"That's a fair certainty, I think."

"Is it?"

"Why, of course it is. Your son and mine. The Duncastle looks and the Webb financial genius, eh?" He was roaring with laughter, and she had one of her moments of detesting him for his complacency, his sureness that he would always get his own way.

"We'll see," she said tightly.

"I thought I might bring down some of that Waterford glass we had as a wedding present. Liquor looks good in it. A customer enjoys a nice tot of whisky or brandy when a deal's completed. Yes, to tell the truth, I have been thinking of a partner, but not for London." He was confiding in her, all at once, and this was one of his private cherished dreams, judging by the sudden intensity in his eyes. "I think the time's right for expansion, a European venture."

Was that safe? Matilda was uneasy. She had made too big a sacrifice to risk having him lose his money.

"You're not a Rothschild, Joshua."

"No, not yet. But who knows? I want to explore the possibilities in Austria. We're investing in the Balkan countries fairly heavily. But I'm in no particular hurry. By the end of the year, perhaps. Would you enjoy that, Mattie? We could go to the opera in Vienna. Banking isn't as dull as you imagine it to be, you know."

The church bells were muffled by the closed windows. There was a plane tree in a small courtyard outside, a patch of pale sunlight on its trunk. She could imagine a working day in here, when the fire burned brightly in the polished grate, the electric light shone on the carefully chosen pictures, the Waterford glass and the silver-mounted inkwells, and Joshua sat at the opposite side of the impressive desk, opening his calfbound ledgers and waiting to interview a succession of customers, foreign gentlemen in black fur-trimmed overcoats, business men in pin-striped trousers and bowler hats, retired army officers in mufti, defiant and furtive and desperate . . .

She shivered slightly. It was cold in here, she said, in answer to Joshua's look of enquiry. She knew that money had saved Sanctuary and taken care of Mamma's and Julia's future, but she still thought it a cold-blooded profession. It bred power and desperation. She didn't think she would ever change her mind about it, even though she personally enjoyed its benefits. She must sound a hypocrite, but there it was. That was how she felt.

"I like honesty," he said, unperturbed. He looked at her standing in front of the fireplace, and his eyes suddenly gleamed. As if he saw her as a pile of newly minted sovereigns. "By jove, I like you, Mattie."

Chapter 4

~~~~~~

Mamma's weekly letter arrived regularly on Monday mornings at the house in Kensington Square. It seemed to smell of the country. Matilda would hold the pages to her nose, imagining woodsmoke from the fire in Mamma's bedroom, and the delicate scent of winter jasmine, before reading the spiky handwriting.

My dear Matilda,

I have so little news, life is very quiet here. It has been raining too heavily for Julia and I to go for our daily walk, consequently Julia is restless and fretful. She misses you so much. I have started her on a new piece of embroidery, but already it is speckled with blood, she pricks her finger constantly. On the other hand, in spite of yours and Joshua's kind invitation, I do not think it wise to bring her to London just yet. She is still very jealous of Joshua taking you away, and needs more time to grow accustomed to this situation. I am sure she eventually will, especially when your baby has arrived. You know how she adores babies.

Babies. Dolls. One doubted if Julia knew which was which. She had a favourite doll that slept in a cradle by her bed—it closed its wax eyelids in the most realistic way—and this seemed to entirely fulfil her maternal longings. She might well find the new baby in Kensington Square fascinating and lovable, but she must be watched carefully with it. She was unpredictable. Her loving fingers could turn into talons.

Mamma went on to say that she herself had been a little unwell, but would recover as soon as the warmer weather arrived.

Matilda sitting in her favourite place in the window seat of her panelled drawing room resolved to have them both to stay, in the spring, before the baby was born. They would find the garden cramping, after the spaciousness of Sanctuary, but not unattractive when one had grown used to it.

At the bottom of the long narrow garden, there was a mulberry tree planted, it was said, in the reign of William and Mary (who had built Kensington Palace and brought fashionable society to the formerly modest suburb of Kensington). The mulberry tree was no match for the cedar at Sanctuary, but it was crooked and pleasing against the brick wall. Already there were crocuses spearing up through the black earth. The thorny skeleton branches of climbing roses spread over a pergola. Elderly Tomkins, the gardener, who had also gardened for the previous owners, the duke's three daughters, assured Matilda that there would soon be a mass of daffodils, and then wallflowers which thrived in the sunny shelter of the walls. The bird bath attracted a great variety of birds, plump thrushes and blackbirds, robins, blue tits and finches. And sometimes crows that came from neighboring elms. Their cawing would make my lady feel at home and think she was in the country again.

Tomkins always called Matilda my lady, no doubt because he was accustomed to this manner of addressing the late residents, the duke's daughters. He had a rosy weathered face surrounded by a scruff of white whiskers. His bright blue eyes had assessed Matilda on their first meeting, as if she were some kind of delicate plant to be watched carefully while she took root. When he called her my lady she knew she had passed whatever test he had applied to her. She had her private doubts that Joshua had similarly passed. Tomkins's face became inscrutable when the master was mentioned.

"Can't expect a city man to know about flowers, my lady. Pigeons and sparrows and soot, and a bit of loosestrife and ivy or a geranium in a pot would be what he knows." His voice was scornful. "But then he'd be too busy to notice, most likely. No, you and me'll attend to the garden. I'll give you a lavender border and some peonies and sweet peas and delphiniums at the back and some climbing roses."

"I like delphiniums, Tomkins."

"And a bit of old-fashioned snapdragon, and some sweet william."

"Thank you, Tomkins." Matilda spoke with deep sincerity, knowing the old man had recognized her homesickness. Perhaps her unhappiness, too, although she hoped she kept that hidden. It was one thing to pine for a beloved country home, another to admit that she had not yet succeeded in loving her husband although she was already carrying his child.

The trouble was that she didn't understand businessmen. She had never had to live to such an implacable routine. Breakfast punctually at eight each morning. If it were a minute late the roof might have fallen, such was Joshua's noisy irritation. She was going to have to teach him that shouting at the servants did more harm than good. She herself had always inspired loyalty in servants, because she was honest and fair and recognized their problems. Papa had taught her that, his knowledge gained from long years of commanding men. You would never get a good day's work out of anyone with a grievance, he had said. You must hear the man out, and apply a remedy. Never mind if the remedy didn't work, the man felt he had been cared for by his commanding officer. A house was a little like an army encampment, from the master and mistress at the top to the humblest kitchen maid at the bottom. Let your subordinates know you had their well-being at heart and you'd get loyalty. Perhaps love, too. Armies were not solely concerned with killing. They supplied order and discipline and a desire to serve, all emotions that enhanced a human being. Matilda would have made a great soldier, he had often said.

As it was, she was now applying her natural ability to being a good wife. Though often this strained her patience.

For when breakfast arrived, eggs and bacon, toast, hot muffins, plenty of strong tea, Joshua immediately disappeared behind the *Times,* which he read with silent absorption. Her presence was superfluous. She could have had a tray in her room and rested longer, especially now that she was feeling unpleasantly queasy in the mornings. But he was the kind of man who expected his wife at the breakfast table, presiding over the teapot, ringing the bell for more hot toast, chiding Polly if the eggs were underdone or overdone, or anything else was not to his liking.

Joshua considered that this was a wife's duty. Was marriage all duty? What a dreadful prospect. And how unfair of Mamma to thoughtlessly remind her of Julia's unhappiness when this whole situation had been planned to protect Julia's future.

She had been trying to regard the affair as an uncomfortable campaign in some wild unknown country to which she had been sent, and where she must acquit herself with distinction. But the future was a prospect on which she avoided reflecting. She must think entirely of the baby that was coming. If it were a boy he would be a soldier, of course. On that matter she was determined. Perhaps, if she were by then in a mood to please her husband, there would be a second son to share that impressive partner's room at the bank. Perhaps. But even if she had six sons she would like them all to serve their country. In this respect, as in the matter of the Salamanca Drum, she had no intention of being an obedient wife. And she knew that she would be like a tigress with her children, because she had deep stores of emotion and possessiveness which were not able to be expended on her husband.

But she would be fair to him until the time came for the revolution. If such a time came. In the meantime she had regained her pride and took care of her appearance. Her hair had grown back to its full length and thickness.

Pregnancy had not yet caused her to lose her slim waist. She wore the clever expensive clothes Joshua admired exceptionally well. He regarded her narrow white face as an asset because it made her different from the ordinarily pretty women. People looked at Joshua Webb's strange-looking wife. He was a bit of an upstart, in spite of his brilliant financial brain, but his wife was something else, poised, well-bred, with an intriguing hint of ruthlessness. So out of curiosity Kensington society came to the Webbs' house in Kensington Square. People had left cards, and presently, at her first tentative parties, Matilda received the smart social dilettantes, the young men who played at the gaming tables and who might need financing in the same way as General Duncastle had, the owners of the big department stores on Kensington High Street, a judge, a well-known writer, some of the famous painters from the Melbury Road enclave, even a bishop.

When Matilda's soirées became modest successes, Joshua expressed his appreciation. In this respect his wife had done very well. The more intimate aspects of marriage, the living together, the punctual attendance at breakfast, the well-planned dinners when they dined at home alone, the housewifely interest Matilda showed in the house and garden were also entirely to his satisfaction. Even the most private part of all, the nights in the big four-poster in a room that overlooked the tall owl-haunted trees of the square, could not give him legitimate cause for complaint.

Matilda turned to him when he demanded her to do so. She was sweet-smelling in her lawn nightgown, and amenable. Even on their wedding night she had not shed tears, as he believed most women did. Her face, when he had been impelled to light the candle, had been calm and inscrutable. He had admired that, knowing a sheltered delicately-bred woman might find the first experience of physical love a shock. If it had been so for Matilda she hadn't allowed him to see it. This augured well for the future. He would soon have her loving him and showing some passion. He believed she could be a deeply aroused woman. It would be a bonus to have a loving wife as well as such a useful and decorative one. He might, though regretfully, say goodbye to the friends of his bachelor days, Rosie and Hilda and the rest. With Matilda at his side, he was going to be an important and highly respectable man. She had once seriously displeased him when he discovered that, along with various medals in glass cases, and a fine set of lead soldiers, she had disobeyed him by bringing that shabby old drum to London. When he saw it in one of the empty attic rooms he had meant to have a row about it. Then he had suddenly been amused at how his wife had got her own way. This had been only an act of defiance and he liked her spirit. The drum looked pretty sad and ineffectual away from the rest of the Duncastle armoury of weapons. It was foolish of him to have imagined it could be a threat to their happiness in any possible way.

Joshua Webb had fairly sound intuition, but this time it had failed him. He had misinterpreted how important a symbol the drum was to his wife, and he had incorrectly read the thoughts behind her passive face after their lovemaking. He didn't guess her despair and disappointment, because she would not permit him to. Up until the last moment she had nourished the forlorn hope that she might find him an appealing lover, that some miracle would happen when, as the parson primly said, they were joined together.

There had not been a miracle. It had all been exceedingly distasteful and she would happily never pursue such antics again. Unfortunately, in her role of an obedient wife, these antics happened all too frequently. Her husband was a virile man. However, when she became pregnant, he unselfishly sacrificed some of his pleasure, and the devouring arms closed round her only once or twice a week.

It was all a great, great pity. She had dearly wanted to love whomever her husband might be. But that felicitous state had become an unattainable dream. This was nothing unusual, she gathered from the low-voiced confidences of some of her newly-made married friends. One was lucky to love one's husband, but if one didn't the children provided compensation. Matilda would discover this for herself shortly. With money, a certain position, and several children, life could be very tolerable. She could be a matriarch, the shaping of her children's lives in her hands. Wouldn't that be more satisfying than being a besotted wife always hastening to do her husband's bidding?

Yes, she and Joshua were settling down together, she wrote to her mother, though it had been difficult, she admitted frankly, to live with someone who was so much a stranger. Now they were beginning to understand each other, and so long as they avoided such topics of conversation as England's military history, or the excessive merits of being a banker, they got on amicably. When the baby was born she would be a completely fulfilled woman, she wrote determinedly. It was no use dwelling on what might have been. She was quite reconciled to her life (this reassurance was for dear Mamma's peace of mind), and when the spring came Mamma and Julia must come on a visit.

Chapter 5

Four months later Matilda's mother was suddenly dead, and Matilda was sitting in the London-bound train with Julia at her side, clutching her hand and scarcely ever removing her wide alarmed gaze from Matilda's face. Joshua was pacing up and down the corridor. Train journeys made him restless. He was not accustomed to sitting idle, he said. But Matilda knew that he was avoiding Julia's company. He disliked being in the same room with her, much less in a small compartment on a train. Her oddness gave him a revulsion he had not been able to overcome.

He would have to overcome it eventually, since the three of them had many years ahead of living in the same house. At least he had kept unhesitatingly to his promise that he would be responsible for Julia's future even if he did not exactly envisage that future being lived in Kensington Square. Matilda suspected that in a discreet time he would be suggesting that Julia would be happier in a suitable home among others of her kind. Such a move Matilda intended fiercely to oppose. Julia was her sister, her only surviving relative, and must be looked after with love and understanding. It was what Mamma had expected when she had encouraged Matilda's marriage to Joshua. Custody of Julia was the unwritten term of the marriage settlement.

Mamma's death had come as a dreadful shock. No one had known she was dying. Her heavy cold had turned to a lingering bronchitis, still not causing alarm until, without any previous warning, her heart had failed.

Sanctuary was closed now. They had spent a hectic and sad week arranging Mamma's funeral, and then packing away possessions, closing and locking cupboards, drawing the shutters, selecting Julia's possessions needed for her new life in London (including her favourite doll which Joshua viewed with astonishment and ordered to be packed out of sight—he was not going to travel on a train with a grown woman clutching a doll), and finally leaving Sanctuary in charge of Tom Rowley and his wife, who would live in the basement. Tom would keep the garden in order and Mrs. Rowley could be depended upon to do a daily tour of the empty rooms. They would all come down to stay after her baby was born, Matilda said. Perhaps they would spend next Christmas there. Julia would like that and Joshua had never known the pleasures of a Christmas in the country.

Joshua, fidgeting to be gone, made no comment, although Matilda guessed his thoughts. He had taken from Sanctuary the only thing he had wanted, its elder daughter, and he had no more interest in the place. He would never be a country man. Besides, being now saddled with the pale and witless Julia, he might have thought of that other figure, poor Great-aunt Tatiana, appearing like a ghost at one of the upper windows. It was an aspect of the Duncastle family he did not want to dwell on, especially since his wife was pregnant. He would forget it if he were not near this grey ghost-like old house. Even if the presence of Julia in the Kensington house constantly reminded him of this hazard.

But she did not intend to have an idiot child, Matilda reflected, hugging Julia to her in the rocking train. She intended to have a fine Duncastle son bearing only an insignificant resemblance to his father. She clung fiercely to this dream. She believed that it was the only hope the future held for her.

Fish was waiting for them when they arrived after the long journey. Matilda was glad to see her, unexpectedly glad too to be in the cosy comfort of the Kensington Square house, after the sadness of Sanctuary. She had been awfully afraid Julia would have hysterics on the journey. Joshua would not have cared for that.

As it was, Fish was ordered to take Julia upstairs at once. "Into the main guest room," Matilda told Fish.

"I think not," said Joshua. "Your sister will be happier on the second floor. She could have a bedroom and a sitting room, couldn't she? After all, if she's to remain here for any length of time, she will need a life apart from ours."

His voice had a false benevolence. For the benefit of the servants, Matilda thought with contempt. His real intention was to keep Julia as far away from their own bedroom as possible, and so ignore her existence. To make her another Great-aunt Tatiana. Someone to be kept out of sight and hearing.

Matilda sighed. It had suited her so far to please her husband. She had seemed to be an obedient and amenable wife such as a man had a right to expect. This was an illusion that had to come to an end. Joshua was about to be shown her mettle.

"No, I don't think the second floor is at all suitable, Joshua," she said. "Julia will be lonely up there. She has always been near to Mamma or me. She's extremely nervous, isn't she, Fish?"

"Yes, ma'am," said Fish in her well-trained expressionless voice. Far be it from her to come between master and mistress. But she had taken Julia's hand and was chafing it anxiously.

"Then let Fish sleep next to her. Or in her room, if necessary," Joshua said shortly.

"Yes, we may consider that in a few weeks, when Julia has settled down. But at present she is to occupy the room next to ours." Matilda tapped Joshua's arm lightly. "You may give orders in your bank, but I give them in my house. Fish, take Miss Julia upstairs. Go with Fish, darling. I will come up in a little while and see you settled. Have the fire lit, Fish. And I think Miss Julia might have her supper in bed tonight. It's been a long strange day for her." Fish tugged Julia's arm. Fortunately the drooping girl followed without remonstrance. She was too tired even for hysterics, Matilda thought with relief. She herself wanted nothing but to follow the same recipe, the fire lit, a tray in bed and the room to herself.

But she had to face Joshua's outraged gaze.

"Did I say something wrong?" she asked innocently. "Is this not my house? Aren't I supposed to tell the servants what to do?"

"Of course it is. Of course you are. But you know how I feel about your sister. A grown woman carrying a doll. If she's to stay here, she's to be kept out of sight."

"Like our Great-aunt Tatiana?"

"No, no. I don't mean locked up. I mean discreetly out of sight. When I'm at the bank you can do what you like, but when I'm home—I mean out of sight."

"She will eat with us, of course," said Matilda smoothly.

"Every night? Oh, my God! Not at dinner parties? That I will not tolerate."

"Not at dinner parties unless she expressly wants to, and I don't think she will, since strangers frighten her. But with us, alone, yes. She is my sister, Joshua."

"Are you trying to make me angry, Mattie?"

"You're angry already. You've been angry all day. You hated that train journey, didn't you? The rising young banker having such an entourage."

"Mattie! Behave yourself!"

Matilda laid her hands on her stomach. "We won't have a child like Julia if that's what you're secretly afraid of."

"By heavens, no!"

"All the same, if we did, I would expect you to acknowledge it and love it. That was what you promised in our marriage contract."

"I didn't bargain for—"

"Not for Julia so soon? Neither did I, to tell the truth. But now we have her we'll make the best of it. And stop glowering at me, Joshua Webb. I'll make you a good wife and give you a healthy baby, but I won't be a meek 'Yes, sir,' 'No, sir,' creature. You must have guessed that from the beginning, so don't look as if I've cheated you. Now I'm going upstairs to talk to Fish about Mamma, whom you seem to have forgotten in your own selfish discomfort."

"I haven't forgotten her," Joshua said stiffly. "I hope I expressed my sympathy."

Matilda wavered. Fairness struggled to prevail. But she was too travel-weary and emotionally exhausted for common sense.

"Then go on expressing it by being kind to my sister. She isn't a leper. She's much prettier than I, as you'll see when we get her calm and nicely dressed. She's really a beauty. She'll be the rage of Kensington."

"Matilda, I've had enough of this. Will you go quietly upstairs and calm yourself."

It was a pity she couldn't love him. She rather admired his flaming eyes and tightly controlled mouth. He was a real man in his own fashion. He deserved a cosy obedient wife, not her, Matilda Duncastle, daughter of heroes. It was sad that he was going to have to suffer a long slow punishment for making the wrong choice, and taking it for granted that he could make her love him.

She hadn't known how deep her resentment about this was until she had seen his callous behaviour towards Julia today. She realised, with a touch of ashamed horror, as she wearily climbed the stairs that she now had the weapon with which to fight him whenever the need arose. Poor Julia.

She had been right to put Julia in the guest room, otherwise she would never have heard the sobbing in the night. Getting out of bed cautiously so as not to wake the sleeping Joshua (though he lay so quietly that he could have been listening, too) she hurried next door.

Julia was invisible in the big bed. She was completely covered by the blankets and curled up tight like a hedgehog. Matilda dragged her up on to the pillows, gently pushing the tangled damp hair away from her face.

"Dearest child! My baby!" she cooed, as Mamma had so

often done, recognizing that Julia could never explain her fears, and must only be soothed out of them. "Julia, my sweet, you're safe. There's nothing to be afraid of."

When the thin body shuddered and tears welled again, she impulsively climbed into the bed and gathered her sister into her arms. "There, sweetheart, there. I know Mamma's gone, and Papa, and Hillary. But you still have me. I'll always take care of you. I'm very strong. And soon there'll be the baby. It's going to be a boy and you're going to love it."

The tense body relaxed. Julia sniffled and sighed and murmured that she was so tired. And then said tentatively, "That horrid man!"

"You mean Joshua? But you understand about him. He's my husband. He's no one at all to be frightened of. Truly, my sweet."

When Joshua came in unceremoniously in the morning and found them asleep, wrapped in each other's arms, it seemed as if Matilda's optimistic promise may have been untrue. Struggling awake she saw that he was scowling, his face set in deep lines of disapproval.

"Are you getting up, Mattie? Or am I to breakfast alone?"

"Oh, Joshua, I'm sorry. Have I overslept? We were so tired last night. Look, Julia's still asleep."

Joshua's eyes rested for a moment on the tangle of fair hair, then slid away.

"If you treat her like a baby, she'll go on being a baby. I forbid you to do this sort of thing again."

"But last night she was frightened. It was all so strange to her."

"I concede last night," said Joshua coldly. "I'm speaking of the future. And now, if you'd be good enough to ring and say that we'll be down for breakfast in ten minutes."

"In ten minutes!" Matilda protested.

"My dear, need I remind you that I'm a business man and at ten o'clock I have an appointment with a banker from Vienna. It's important, much more important, if I may dare say so, than your sleepyhead sister."

Matilda looked at him wearily. But, shaved and dressed

in his city clothes, he had an advantage over her. He was fighting back, she perceived, and a feeling of elation filled her. Life may not be perfect but at least it wasn't going to be dull.

"Who is this Austrian banker?" she asked in a bored voice.

"He is Count Paul von Klein, and later on after the baby is born, I want you to give a dinner party for him. He may be of importance to me."

"Doesn't he know what a pregnant woman looks like?"

"He isn't yet married. I am thinking only of your convenience, my dear. I don't want you to overexert yourself"—his glance flickered over Julia—"in any way."

"Julia won't overexert me, Joshua. I've known her all my life."

Unexpectedly the person who calmed Julia's terrors the most was Joshua's sister Clara. She naturally had been informed of Lady Duncastle's death and of the new developments. She could not leave her father often, for he was expected to die shortly, but she took a cab to Kensington twice a week, and visited with Matilda and Julia. Perhaps because of her strange crooked eyes, neither of which seemed to be looking directly at anything, Julia showed no nervousness of Clara and was actually coaxed to laugh a little. Under his sister's influence, Joshua, too, showed less obvious distaste for his fey sister-in-law.

"I've told him to make friends with her and not to alarm her," Clara said to Matilda. "And why must she be shut out when people come? No one would expect such a pretty girl to be full of intellect. She can sit quietly in a corner."

"Joshua would never allow it. He's too concerned with appearances."

"He's too concerned with his own affairs," Clara said bluntly. "His bank won't collapse because he has a skeleton in the cupboard. One would hardly call pretty Julia a skeleton, of course. But you can manage him, Matilda. You're clever."

"Looking after Julia was part of our marriage arrangement. Joshua must carry it out faithfully."

"He will. But with a great deal of grumbling. Men are wrapped in their own affairs. I've lived with an ambitious father and brother all my life. I never intend to get involved with another man. I'll very contentedly be an aunt, if I may."

"We'll need you," Matilda said impulsively. She liked the little woman in her simple brown dress and bonnet. A sensible plain-spoken creature, with great kindness. She would make an ally, Matilda thought, when it came to the bringing up of hers and Joshua's children. Because even if they had reached an uneasy truce over Julia, there would be more battles ahead.

When Matilda's baby was born Julia threw away her doll. At least she pushed it into the back of her wardrobe and announced she would have no more time to play with it. She had a live doll now and she was absorbed by it.

Matilda was absorbed, too, though less whole-heartedly than Julia. For the baby was a girl. Both hers and Joshua's ambitions had to be postponed. There was no great future to be planned for a girl, except a good marriage. They named her Eulalie, which soon became Lally. She was not even a particularly pretty baby, though she was plump and engaging. Matilda, who felt that she was the kind of woman who would respond fiercely and possessively only to sons, was content for the baby to have a nurse, and to be petted and dandled a great deal by Julia. She herself, now she had recovered her figure, was occupying herself with social affairs. What else was there to do while she waited to become pregnant again?

Joshua suggested that now was the time to entertain his friend Count Paul von Klein, who was shortly arriving in London on business concerned with his Viennese bank. He thought that his and Matilda's difference over Julia was healed, since now that Lally was three months old, Matilda was turning to him willingly in bed. He knew she was longing for a son—so was he—but he dared to hope that her response was not solely due to a desire to be pregnant. She was a strange difficult creature, but now that she had recovered from Lally's birth she was at the height of her looks, with her long-necked elegance, her charming remote smile, her good taste. True, she hadn't Julia's ravishing prettiness, but she was always the centre of attention. The hint of waspishness in her green eyes and the arrogant tilt of her long nose gave her a piquancy that some men preferred to mere beauty. Did he? Sometimes he wasn't entirely sure. She wasn't a comfortable woman. He didn't always hold the upper hand, as had been proved over Julia, damn that half-witted child. Her premature presence in his house and his life was a factor he had not bargained for.

But things had been better lately, and Matilda was a gifted hostess. People never refused her invitations. This was enormously useful to Joshua, as he had known it would be. Apart from certain new accounts being made available to him (some of these Kensington gentlemen were well-heeled), or the odd loan at profitable terms to himself coming his way, there were much bigger matters such as the Austrian nobleman, Count von Klein, with whom he was beginning discussions regarding a possible merger of their two banks. An intimate dinner party in his own home might just swing these discussions to his advantage.

He had a fancy Matilda might be the sort of woman the Count admired. There was little doubt that he, with his soft only slightly accented voice and grave manner, would appeal to her. He was well-bred and titled, advantages that left Joshua a mile behind. The Count's sophistication would show up certain roughnesses in Joshua's manner. But Joshua had the ultimate advantage. Matilda was his wife. He was quite prepared to use her as a pawn since no lasting harm could come of it. He would enjoy surprising the foreigner with his good taste.

Matilda gave her usual meticulous care to planning this dinner party, not because there was to be a titled foreigner present but because she took pride in the excellence of her hospitality. She vaguely wondered about

Count von Klein. What was he like—a thick-necked Austrian with a loud voice and a curling moustache?

To her surprise he was entirely different from her preconceived notions. The slight gentleman who bowed to her had glossy brown hair, a gentle charming smile and a lively interested gaze. Moreover, as dinner progressed, it emerged that he came from a military family and had, naturally, heard of the English Duncastles.

"I think our ancestors probably attempted to slay each other on the field of battle. In the Napoleonic wars, perhaps?"

"We fought at Waterloo," Matilda said proudly. "And before that in the Peninsular wars."

"And also the Battle of Hastings, I'll be bound." That was Joshua's voice booming from the other end of the table. He should have been paying attention to little Mrs. Lewardine on his right, and not eavesdropping on Matilda's conversation. "My wife's family were famous for having their fingers—or should I say their swords—in any pie that was going."

Matilda gave her charming thin-lipped smile. "I ask my husband where he would be now if there hadn't been a family like mine to preserve our country from the enemy. Do you believe in pride of country, Count?"

"Most whole-heartedly. It comes second to one's family. Or even before family."

Matilda saw that Joshua was about to say "Poppycock" and intervened swiftly, "You have a wife and family then?"

"Not as yet."

"Oh, you must remedy that," Matilda said, and the awkward moment was past. She had been afraid Joshua would say loudly that he hoped Matilda wasn't going to indulge herself by showing off the Salamanca Drum— which was exactly what she intended to do when the opportunity offered itself.

It was a successful dinner party. Although, as was to be expected, Joshua strongly disapproved, Julia had been allowed to come down, and she sat like a pretty doll in her pale blue dress. Not venturing to talk except in almost inaudible monosyllables, but smiling radiantly at everybody. Matilda still had hopes that with gentle and understanding treatment Julia's paralysing terrors and shyness would lessen. Perhaps they had been wrong in shutting her away in Sanctuary for all of her childhood. Some day it was even possible that Joshua would agree, though this seemed unlikely. He could scarcely bear to look at the girl and regarded her presence in his house as the most damned misfortune.

Count von Klein would have understood, Matilda surmised. She caught him making sympathetic glances towards Julia, and once he leaned across the table and endeavoured to engage her in conversation. But Julia blushed furiously and let her hair fall over her face, a sure sign of retreat from communication.

"My sister is extremely timid," Matilda murmured. "She's ridiculously nervous of strangers."

"Then I must endeavour not to be a stranger. May that be allowed, Mrs. Webb?"

"But of course," Matilda agreed, pleasure stirring.

"You have a charming house. Is it very old?"

"Not as old as my family home in the country. That's called Sanctuary and is near Bath in Somerset. We seldom go down because my husband doesn't care for the country. But I intend making a visit before the end of the month to see that all is well for the winter."

"Is that where the military relics are kept?"

Matilda leaned towards him eagerly.

"You've heard about them? Yes, most of them are there, in the armoury, but I brought my more prized possessions to town."

"And what are they?"

"Campaign medals, some rather valuable duelling pistols, the drum." Impulsively she added, "Would you like to see them?"

"Very much indeed. Can we desert the company?"

"Why not? After coffee. Perhaps you would like to see the house anyway. It really is very old. There are supposed to be secret passages to the houses next door, but I've never been able to find them."

"What for? Lovers' assignations?"

"I like to think so."

"How charming."

The thought ran through her head that if only Joshua had this lightness of manner, this gentleness, how different —no, one must not make such conjectures. She must just enjoy smuggling the Count upstairs to the sloping-roofed attic room where her dear treasures were kept.

It was cold up there, and a little dusty, which was her fault for she didn't allow the housemaids in this room. The faded colours were draped on the walls, the medals were displayed in a glass-topped table. The drum stood apart on the Wellington chest. To her ears, there was also the faint echo of martial music.

Count von Klein touched the taut, discoloured skin of the drum with knowledgeable fingers.

"Interesting," he said. "Waterloo?"

"No. Earlier than that. The battle of Salamanca."

"Ah. Your great Duke inflicted a crushing defeat on the French in Spain. And one of your ancestors—may I guess?"

"Yes, yes, of course."

"Drummed his regiment into battle and gave his life in doing so."

"How did you know?"

"Because you have a look of reverence on your face. This is a hallowed object to you?"

"It always has been to my family. You understand?"

"Indeed I do. We have similar things in Vienna."

"Are they meant to be an inspiration to your family?"

"Of course."

"That's why we've always treasured our little Salamanca Drum. And now I mean it to be an inspiration to my children." She paused. "But not everyone understands."

He looked at her with his perceptive gaze.

"I think one must have military traditions in one's blood. I imagine your husband doesn't."

"He has other ambitions."

"So you have your private dream and he has his. Interesting. May I tell you whom you make me think of?" His eyes were twinkling with gentle amusement. "That old English queen Boadicea who fought so bravely for her country. Are you going to be another Boadicea, Mrs. Webb?"

Joshua had thought she resembled a queen too, but he hadn't thought of the most warlike English queen of them all.

Matilda laughed. "I certainly will be if my country needs one. Through my children." She was conscious of his admiring gaze. She felt suddenly acutely alive. There was nothing she could not do in the future, after all. "And no matter what my husband says," she said, answering his unspoken question.

It was evident, when they returned to the drawing room, that Joshua was displeased. He could not be impolite to the Count, and said genially enough. "Has my wife been showing you her treasures? It's a habit she has," and only Matilda recognized that the sarcasm in his voice was anger.

"Where's Julia?" she asked, looking round the room.

"I sent her upstairs. She had an attack of the vapours. A delicate young woman, my wife's sister," he said, addressing Count von Klein. "Will you have a glass of brandy, Count?"

There were things to be settled when the guests had departed and Matilda and Joshua had retired to their room. Matilda knew she was going to be taken to task, and quickly adopted attacking tactics. "I think the evening went very well, don't you, Joshua?"

"Did you need to disappear for quite so long with the Count?"

"I was entertaining him, as I thought you expected me to do."

"He's a banker, not a soldier."

"You shouldn't assume that his tastes are as limited as yours," Matilda said tartly. "His family has a military history. And he was most interested in the drum."

"That damned drum! I won't have it mentioned in this house any more than I will again have your sister at my dinner table."

"Oh, poor Julia, was she a trouble?"

"She's always a trouble. I saw a case of hysterics

developing as soon as you abandoned her, so I sent for Fish."

"Oh dear, I am sorry. I had thought she was getting more confidence. The Count admired her."

"The Count has good manners. I can't see any man in his right mind admiring a semi-idiot."

By this time Joshua was ensconced heavily on his side of the bed. He sighed and muttered into his pillow. He was suddenly tired, and perhaps the evening had gone off well enough. Matilda was too clever for him, that was the trouble.

She was climbing into bed beside him. Her green eyes had a soft swooning look. "Don't let's talk any more about Julia," she murmured. "I have other things in mind."

She curled up against him, her slender body adjusting to his more solid curves. Her voice was heavy with sensuousness. "Turn round and look at me, Joshua." She had never before taken the initiative and, although he was reluctant to give up his displeasure about Julia, he was finding her surprising behaviour enormously exciting.

"You waste time talking of Julia when all we both want is a son," she grumbled sweetly. "Isn't that true?"

"Perfectly true, my darling."

Her fingers slid over his chest, then her arms folded round him and she held him tightly.

"Let's get ourselves a son, Joshua . . . One this year, one next, one the following year." She was laughing breathlessly. "I'm so greedy, you don't mind, do you?"

"Not if this is the way you show it."

Chapter 6

A week later Matilda was in the garden at Sanctuary cutting some branches of winter jasmine when she saw the overcoated figure coming down the curving drive. Actually the rooks had given notice of his approach, flying in circles and discussing the stranger in their hoarse voices.

Bother, she was in no mood for callers. She had come down to attend to matters concerning the house, and to be alone, though this state had occurred to her as being eminently desirable only when she found her privacy about to be intruded upon. However, it was true that she had been feeling lonely, sitting in the drawing room at nights thinking of the dead, of which this house was over-full. Even Julia's meaningless prattle would have been better than the silence. Still, she had wanted to be by herself to sort things out in her mind.

It had not been only the well-being of the house which concerned her. She needed a breathing space from Joshua. She wanted to sleep alone at night for a little while, and discover if after their lovemaking (determined on her part, ardent on his) she were pregnant. With a son. She was only twenty-two, and if she were not to have sons it was difficult to face the future with equanimity.

She had resolutely not allowed herself to think of Count Paul von Klein since the dinner party two weeks ago. That represented danger. It was glimpsing a soft loving world that was never to be for her. Yet, before he was within a hundred yards of her, she knew who her visitor was. And she remembered her unguarded statement that she was coming down to Sanctuary that weekend. Near Bath, she had said. Deliberately.

"Count?" she said on a note of enquiry, walking slowly towards him.

"Paul," he said. "Can't we be more friendly? Am I intruding?"

"You have surprised me. Oh, how cold it is. Do come indoors. Surely you haven't walked here?"

"From Bath where I'm staying in a small uncomfortable hotel. You told me Bath was a beautiful city, but I find the pleasures of architecture don't compensate for the lack of hot water."

"Oh, dear. How unfortunate. Winter isn't the time to visit."

"But winter is when I find Sanctuary with its mistress in residence."

"You came to see Sanctuary?"

He nodded, giving his tentative half smile.

"Please tell me if I am not welcome."

On the contrary, Matilda thought that her welcome must be showing in her face. Luckily he could not see the way her heart was beating.

"Of course you're welcome."

"I know it's bad manners to arrive without warning. I acted on impulse. I wanted to see the home of the famous Duncastles. English country houses are more attractive than our ugly Austrian ones."

"You have a country house?"

"A small ancient castle. Let me carry the flowers."

"Thank you. Come inside. There are fires in the hall and the drawing room. The house was so cold when I arrived. And it's time to light the lamps. We're too far from anywhere to have electricity. How do you light and warm your castle?"

"Just with lamps and candles, and those large porcelain stoves that amuse the English."

"What a pity I can't walk across the fields to visit you."

"What a pity. But not fields. Up half a mountain. I live most of the time in Vienna which is less interesting but more comfortable."

"I've never been abroad," Matilda said, pushing open the stout oak door that led into the hall. The firelight and lamplight were yellow and warm.

"Then you must certainly come to Vienna. With your husband."

"Is he going?"

"If our business progresses satisfactorily."

For a confused moment Matilda had seen herself arriving in the gay Austrian capital alone, dismounting from the train after the long journey across Europe, going forward eagerly to be greeted by the Count who would have a bouquet of violets as big as a dinner plate for her. It was funny how clear that picture of an event never to happen was. She quickly dismissed it. If ever she alighted from the famous Blue Train it would be with Joshua, burly and possessive, at her side.

"I couldn't leave my baby at present," she said.

"You've left her now."

"That's different. There isn't a sea between us. I can return home at a moment's notice. Not that I wouldn't love to come to Vienna some day."

"Don't make your visit too far in the future. Well, are you going to show me your house?"

"Yes, now, before it's too dark, otherwise we'll have to carry candles. Indeed, if we're to look at the portraits on the stairs—they're the interesting ones—we'll need candles. Or a lamp would be better."

"Don't you ever feel you're living with ghosts?" Paul asked presently, as he focused the light on Colonel Gordon Duncastle, hero of the siege of Cawnpore. The glittering resolute eyes, the eagle face, the swirling cape, had given Matilda shivers of awe and pleasure when she was a child. She had felt more of an affinity with Major Richard

Duncastle, slender and very young, astride his coal black charger. She guessed that he had been trying to look intrepid. Shortly after the portrait had been painted he had embarked for the Crimea and had died in the terrible valley of death, he and his glorious charger. He had been posthumously decorated. The portraits of the older and higher-ranking ancestors such as Major-General Henry Duncastle V.C. were more comfortable because they had lived to receive their decorations, to marry and have children. Without exception, they had the family features, handsome hawk-like faces, the resolute eyes. It was the younger ones, the drummer boy with his merry schoolboy face; the youthful cavalryman keeping his rendezvous with the Russian guns; her brother, Captain Hillary Duncastle grinning with the impudent bravado she remembered so well, and doomed to be struck by that fatal native spear, who brought a lump to Matilda's throat, and a sensation of unbearable poignancy and loss.

Once Mamma had said, "Always remember their blood runs in your veins, even if you are a girl," and she had impulsively pricked herself with a pin and watched the red welling. But she was a girl and her blood was of no use to her country.

"I've never thought of them as ghosts. They're real to me," she said at last, in answer to Paul's question.

"Do you think you take it all rather too seriously? And were there no beautiful women in your family to be painted?"

"The Swedish woman from a long way back, and Great-aunt Tatiana, the crazy one," Matilda said lightly. "And Julia. They're the beauties. We weren't so good on women. They were sometimes a little mad." She shivered and laughed. "Oh, a goose walked over my grave."

"A what?"

"Just a saying we have. Yes, you are right, my family are all rather ghostly on a winter afternoon. That's what Joshua doesn't like about Sanctuary. He says it's like living in history, and history might be splendid, but it's not like a warm fire and muffins for tea. So shall we go down and have tea before you face that long walk in the dark. Perhaps you'll come again in daylight and see the armoury."

"Perhaps," he agreed. But later, after Mrs. Rowley had brought the tea and Matilda had presided over the paraphernalia of the brass kettle on its spirit lamp, the silver teapot and the delicate china, he said, "No, I don't think I will come again, Matilda."

She looked up and saw him giving her a long gaze which she couldn't interpret. She only knew that it was sad. Those portraits of all her splendid dead had depressed him. He was like Joshua after all, he didn't care for Sanctuary. Bitterly disappointed, she stared back at him, and he said in a low voice, "I am going home to be married, Matilda. Her name is Amalie. She's pretty and jolly and very good for me since I have a melancholy streak. Because I am Austrian I am not always dancing to Strauss waltzes as people think." He smiled. His gaze, lingering on hers, suggested plainly that he admired her more than jolly Amalie. He would have preferred her. Yet would he? She disturbed him too much. She was Queen Boadicea, a ruthless bloodthirsty woman who stopped at nothing to gain victories for the glory of her country. Was she going to frighten all men, except Joshua, and even him a little?

"I hope you will be very happy," she said formally. She held herself very straight. "And when you come to London next I will have a little boy in the cradle."

"You are a strange woman, Matilda."

"I told you that all the Duncastle women are strange."

"I don't think I will tell Amalie about you, however."

"What is there to hide?" She wanted the unspoken in words. "If you and my husband are business partners we will all eventually meet."

"That will be different. We will be so respectable. Our families will visit, I hope. I will show you my small ugly castle."

He seemed to have left her already. The intimacy was over. He bent to kiss her hand. "A woman like you shouldn't have married a man like Joshua."

"Nobody cared that I had to," she burst out passionately, then, instantly regretting what she had given away, she said stiffly, "I can manage my life very well."

"Who would doubt it?" He had turned to go. His last word she might have imagined. *"Liebling,"* he said.

My love . . . Meaning nothing but a graceful gesture to a courteous charming man like this. A fragmentary episode that she would sometimes remember as life went on. Not important because the questions it had posed would never be resolved. Anyway, she was deeply British and she loved her country to the point of fanaticism, as generations of ancestors had trained her to do. How could she have sons who might march beneath the Austrian eagles?

RETURN HOME URGENTLY JOSHUA

Sanctuary seemed to be a place for alarming telegrams. Matilda clutched the yellow piece of paper and watched the boy cycling away. She must pack her bag, and Tom Rowley must harness the horse into the dogcart. She had to hurry, or she would miss the train. Dread weighed her down. What had happened in the house in Kensington? She had been away only a week. Why did Joshua have to be so mysterious? She was going to be in suspense for hours.

Who was in trouble? Her baby, Julia, Joshua himself? Or Joshua's father, who after clinging to life all summer may at last have given it up?

But she would not have felt this foreboding about a sick old man's death. She had a sense of apprehension and danger that was deeply disturbing.

Had the house burned down? Had Julia, who had seemed happy with Fish, and with Lally to cosset, become uncontrollable?

Would the train never reach London? Matilda looked out the window at the foggy countryside. She rubbed the grimy glass clean and then thought she saw Count Paul von Klein's face looking in at her. The image was purely imaginary and already lost in the gloom, as if he had withdrawn down a long tunnel. She felt tired and a little ill, and more than ever sure that the ordeal ahead was going to be too much for her. If Joshua could not cope with it, how could she?

There was no one to meet her at Euston station. This was not to be wondered at, since she had not telegraphed the time of her arrival. Yet she felt neglected and more uneasy than ever.

She found a cab and asked the driver to make haste.

"In this fog? It's going to be a real pea-souper, Mum. If I whip up my horse we're going to have a nasty accident."

"Can't you take a short cut?"

"It's not a night to risk getting lost, Mum. You can't even read the street names. I'll stick to my usual route down Bayswater Road and across to Kensington. It's just lucky you didn't want Hampstead. I'd never have taken on Hampstead in this fog. So count your blessings, Mum."

Her blessings. Had she any? Of course she had. A good solid house and a good solid husband, her darling bright Lally already able to sit up and clap her hands, perhaps a little son growing inside her.

But come home urgently, Joshua had telegraphed.

The house in Kensington Square had lights in every window. Reassured that it had not been burnt to the ground, and indeed looked festive, Matilda climbed out of the cab and asked the driver to carry her bags up the steps to the front door. She rang the bell, choking a little as the fog wreathed round her and she inhaled the soot and dirt of a London evening. If Joshua had sent for her on some slight pretext she would be very angry.

Expecting Polly to answer the door, she was surprised that it was Joshua who did so. He looked reassuringly normal, and in good health, until he took her arm and pulled her indoors, and under the light she saw his haggard face.

"Joshua, whatever is the matter? Pay the cab driver and bring in my bags. It's a dreadful night. We could hardly see a yard ahead of us in the Bayswater Road. But I did come home at once, as you asked me to."

She was prattling nervously because his drawn face had shocked her. If her baby were dead, she thought wildly, he wouldn't tell her so in front of the cabbie. She watched him push some coins into the man's hand, too many obviously, because of the man's heartfelt "Thanks, guvnor. God bless yer." And that was strange, too, for Joshua was inclined to be close rather than generous with the lower classes.

However, they were indoors and the fog was shut out, and Joshua was saying the police were in the library, an officer and a sergeant, and they would be wanting to see her. When she had freshened up from her journey, of course. Matters were no longer urgent. The doctor had left an hour ago, and it was several hours since Julia had been missing.

"The doctor?" said Matilda, looking into Joshua's bloodshot eyes. "Joshua, what has happened? You're standing there saying these dreadful things and yet telling me nothing."

"First of all," said Joshua, "the baby's all right. She has a nasty bruise on her forehead and slight concussion, but she'll be fine in a day or two."

The dread Matilda had been conscious of all afternoon now bloomed inside her, as cold and suffocating as the fog.

"Julia?" she asked in terror.

"Yes. As you have guessed. She dropped the child on the hearth in the nursery."

"Not intentionally!" Matilda cried.

"How does anyone know that? She was alone with the baby, which should never have been allowed. Both Fish and Polly were out of the room, and when Fish came back Lally was lying unconscious on the floor, and there was no sign of your precious sister. Fortunately Fish had the sense to send for me, and the doctor, and I telegraphed for you. This all happened just after I left for the bank this morning."

"Hours ago! Then I can guess the state poor Julia is in. If she's hiding I'll soon find her."

Joshua grasped her wrist hurtingly, the enmity and dislike in his eyes no longer concealed. They were for Julia, of course. Or were they for her, too?

"You will go up to our child. She is your first concern."

"Both of them are my concern."

"Only Lally. You won't find Julia."

"She can't be hidden that completely. Joshua! Why are the police here? You haven't had Julia arrested?"

"I would like to," said Joshua grimly, "if she could be found. That young woman will have to be locked up. She's no longer harmless. She's dangerous."

"We must find her first," Matilda said feverishly. "She'll be terrified out of her wits. But she'll come out of her hiding place when I coax her. Dangerous? Julia? How absurd!"

"Now listen, Matilda, I appreciate your soothing influence on your sister, but if the police can't find her in this house, neither can you."

Matilda's eyes widened.

"You think she's run away?"

"We've torn the place apart, practically, wardrobes, cupboards, cellars. So she's either in the streets or she's vanished into thin air."

"Julia in the streets! Has she taken outdoor things?"

"No, she hasn't."

"Then she'll be freezing to death. Is that why you sent for the police—to search for her?"

"Given all the circumstances, yes."

"How terrible! Oh, Joshua!" For a moment she was fleetingly sympathetic with him. He hadn't counted on this kind of situation when he had been so eager to marry her. "Do the police want to talk to me? You must wait until I run upstairs to see my poor baby. And then if I'm to be reprimanded I deserve it. You're quite right, I should never have left home."

The baby was asleep, her face still plump and serene, but the bruise on her forehead made a nasty blemish. She didn't stir when Matilda bent over her. Fish, with red eyes and quivering hands, said, "Miss Lally's all right, she's come to no real harm. It's Miss Julia I'm worrying about. I blame myself. You said never to leave the two of them alone, and I didn't. At least, not for more than five minutes. Miss Julia was always so careful with the baby. It couldn't have been deliberate, in one of her fits of temper, because she loved Miss Lally so much. She must have stumbled on the hearth rug."

"Yes, Fish, I'm sure that's what happened. The doctor said Lally was all right, didn't he?"

"Yes, ma'am, he did. As far as he could tell in these early stages."

Matilda refused to hear those ominous words, and said quickly, "Then we only have to find Julia and reassure her. Did anyone see her run out of the house?"

"No, ma'am, but after the master—" Fish stopped, pressing her trembling hands to her mouth.

"After the master did what?"

"After he shouted at her. You know the state she got in whenever he did that."

"I do. And I asked him to never again speak sharply to her."

"Well, he did have to be excused this time, ma'am, he was that upset about Miss Lally looking so poorly, and we couldn't rouse her."

"Were you there when my husband shouted at Julia?"

"No, I was here with the baby, ma'am. I just heard him in Miss Julia's room, or the nursery, or wherever he was. After a while he came in here and it was only later we looked for Miss Julia and couldn't find her. But no one saw her leave the house, ma'am."

"Then she's still in it. I'll find her. She'll come out when she hears my voice. And I'll get rid of those policemen. What are they doing here, anyway?"

"They're circulating a description of Miss Julia, I believe. What she looks like, and being—"

"—of unsound mind," Matilda finished bleakly.

If Joshua, by shouting at Julia, had driven her out to lose herself in the cold foggy dark, then he had virtually committed murder. But he wouldn't see it that way any more than he would believe the accident in the nursery had not been deliberate. After all, wasn't this a wonderful opportunity to get the poor girl locked away, as he had always secretly wanted to do?

Although the police officer assured Matilda that after the search he and his sergeant had made, no one could be concealed in the house, Matilda insisted on making her own search. She described Julia's character and habits to the police, emphasising that, because of her excessive timidity, she was most unlikely to have ventured out in the streets alone. She *must* be hidden in the house or the garden. There was the mulberry tree beneath which she had liked to sit in the early autumn, sometimes talking to Tomkins as he worked in the garden, sometimes with Lally beside her in her perambulator. Could she have thought of the treee as a haven and crept up into its branches? Could she have curled up beneath the shelves in the potting shed?

But these places had already been searched. The police officer looked at Matilda tolerantly, and told her to go ahead. Look where she fancied. But he warranted that even a mouse could not have escaped detection in his own search. No, the young lady must be in the streets, run off in blind panic when she thought she had killed the baby, and Mr. Webb had shouted angrily at her. They would all have been too busy caring for the child to notice particularly the movements of Miss Julia, the culprit.

Morning would find her, the police officer said confidently. If she didn't die of exposure in a doorway on this cold night, of course. She had been wearing only a blue woollen dress, the maid had said. Neither her coat nor her outdoor shoes nor her bonnet had gone.

Chapter 7

No one slept much that night. Matilda made a token effort of undressing and putting on a warm dressing gown. But she couldn't lie down. She kept stealing into the nursery where Lally lay, watched over by Fish who refused to leave the child. Fish felt too guilty about her lapse that morning when she had carelessly left Julia alone with the baby.

That had been only for a few minutes. Matilda felt far more guilty at having trustingly left the entire household for several days. Her guilt went deep, for it was centred round the gentle enigmatic figure of Count von Klein. She hadn't known for certain he was going to visit Sanctuary yet she had deliberately hinted at the rendezvous and guessed that it would be kept. Therefore, indirectly, she was more to blame for Julia's disappearance than was Joshua with his uncontrolled anger. This knowledge unreasonably served to heighten her suspicion of Joshua. How could he have been so much more frightening to Julia than the dark streets? What had he done to her? Had he laid his hands on her, shaken her or beaten her? He swore he hadn't put a finger on her, he had merely lost his temper and spoken severely. But Matilda remembered the dislike in his eyes whenever Julia was present and wondered secretly and fearfully if it could have flared into something more.

Lally fortunately slept soundly though Fish said that she refused to take food. However, the little fair face, apart from the ugly bruise on the forehead, looked reassuringly peaceful.

"She can have her bottle in the morning," Matilda said. "Didn't the doctor say she should sleep as long as possible? She's such a plump little creature, it won't hurt her to starve for a day or two." Tears were running down Matilda's cheeks. "Oh, Fish, *where* can Julia be? I keep thinking of her shivering in some dreadful dark alley, and scared to death. Yet I'm still sure she wouldn't go out alone. She'd hide anywhere rather than the streets."

"Then where, ma'am? Haven't we turned the house inside out?"

"Yes, I know. It's quite inexplicable. What's the time? Only two o'clock. What a long night it is. Joshua's gone out to help in the search." (Privately hoping not to find Julia?) "I'll stay with Lally, Fish, if you'll go down to the kitchen and see that the kettle's kept on the boil. We must have hot tea ready for the police if they come back."

"And for Miss Julia and the master."

"Of course. That's what I meant."

Joshua, however, did not come home until five o'clock, and then he was alone. The police had also gone home to sleep, except, of course, for those on night beat. They would have an eye open for any young person who did not look like the ordinary waif and stray.

"We must wait for daylight, Mattie," Joshua said, his voice thick with weariness. "She'll come sneaking home then, mark my words. After I've left for the bank, I shouldn't be surprised, so that the ogre is out of the way."

"You're not going to the bank!"

"I certainly am. I have important appointments, and I've already lost a whole day over your daft sister, and been up most of the night into the bargain. I've done all that I can. It won't help if I'm here tomorrow."

"What about supporting your wife?"

His tired eyes surveyed her. "When has a Duncastle—male or female—needed support? Is the thin red line wavering?"

"You're being cruel."

"Yes. I'm sorry." His voice was gruff. "I didn't mean to say that. We've both got our nerves stretched too far. Get Clara over tomorrow to support you. She's kinder than I am. How's my daughter?"

"Sleeping quietly."

"Thank God for that. Well, I'm off to snatch a couple of hours' sleep myself." He tumbled Matilda's hair roughly. "You'd better do the same. You look like a ghost."

"Joshua!"

"What now?"

"It's your own fault if Julia thinks you an ogre."

"Agreed. But I can't help it." He was too tired to deny the accusation. "I just can't stand her silly face. It gives me the shivers."

In the morning when Joshua, promising to send Clara over, had left for the bank the two policemen came back. Very politely they said they would like to examine the garden. Oh, nothing for Mrs. Webb to worry about. When a person was reported missing it was the rule to make a complete investigation of the home premises.

Lally had awakened and had taken a little milk, but then had begun whimpering and refused to respond to blandishments. Her wandering gaze settled on nothing.

"Her head's hurting, I expect," said Fish. "Poor mite."

"I think we ought to let the doctor have another look at her," said Matilda. A shaft of pure fear had struck into her heart. She had never before noticed how like Julia's Lally's blue eyes were.

"He said he'd be back this morning, ma'am. And don't worry too much. You can't expect Baby to recover all at once from such a nasty fall."

Matilda did worry, however, and Doctor Grimes did little to ease her anxiety. He said the little lass was doing nicely, but if by any chance she didn't respond in a day or two it might be as well to consult a brain specialist. Just as a precaution. Head injuries were tricky things, especially when the skull was the soft one of an infant. He was sure there was nothing to worry about. The child was crying because she had a headache. And what were the police doing in the garden?

The two policemen were prodding at the soil beneath the small ornamental trees and bushes, and paying particular attention to the compost heap of rotting leaves.

Matilda's mouth was dry.

"Whatever do they think—that Julia could have buried herself?"

Doctor Grimes was obviously sorry that he had drawn Matilda's attention to the garden. He twitched the curtain across, and said, "The law gets some far-fetched ideas in the course of its duty."

Surely they didn't think Julia had been done away with?

Joshua shouting at her in uncontrollable anger, Joshua hating her, saying she gave him the shivers, Joshua strong enough to carry and conceal such a slender body. At the time that everyone else was fussing over Lally? In broad daylight? There had been no broad daylight yesterday, only a foggy half light.

What macabre, unforgivable thoughts, Matilda told herself. The police would find nothing in that innocent garden. Poor Julia was lost in the streets. They must check hospitals, places where they took waifs and strays. And the river, too, the muddy Thames flowing by the Chelsea embankment a long way off, but still within walking distance for a young woman crazed with fear.

Clara arrived, brisk and sensible, before the awful morning was over. She persuaded Matilda to rest.

"I have enough on my hands with Father, without having you ill, too. I'll keep an eye on Baby. She's going to be all right. Tough little creatures, babies. And Julia will turn up, wet and draggled, no doubt, she'll turn up. She'll have to, won't she, because she has nowhere else to go."

Clara's optimism was welcome and soothing, but it

didn't prove to be justified. By nightfall there was no change in the position. Lally was still crying far too much, and Julia had not been found. Joshua came home earlier than usual, and wanted the fretful baby brought to him.

"What does Grimes say about her? Is she all right?"

"She probably has a bad headache," Clara said. "But a few days' rest and quiet is all she needs. Don't joggle her, Joshua. That's the worst thing."

Dandling a baby on his lap, joggling her up and down, was the only thing Joshua knew as far as infants were concerned. The tenderness in his face changed to irritability.

"You're as bad as Mattie, Clara. I can't do anything right in my own house."

"You mustn't blame Mattie. She's sick with worry. Julia seems to have vanished into thin air although we all know such a thing isn't possible. It's bad enough having the police digging up the garden."

"Good God, have they been doing that?"

"More or less. They say it's routine. I wouldn't take it too lightly since you're the prime suspect."

"Me!" Joshua's eyes bulged. Then he began to laugh uproariously. "Now, that's the only amusing thing to come out of the whole affair. So I'm the wicked villain, am I? Then let them prove it."

"I don't want to disappoint you, Joshua, but they gave up several hours ago. Julia is now listed as a missing person. Since she's an adult they rely on her coming home of her own free will."

"What does Mattie say to this ridiculous theory that I'm a suspect?" asked Joshua, a shade warily.

"She knows it's just police procedure," said Clara. "All the same, you might convince her otherwise."

"The best way to convince her is to have her wretched sister turn up."

"Do you think she will?"

"I'm damned if I know. But if she doesn't, where is she?"

Two weeks later the police came back. A young woman's body had been found washed up by the tide on the Chelsea embankment. Joshua was required for the grisly purpose of going to the morgue to attempt to identify the poor creature.

He came back looking haggard, and shaking his head. The dead woman hadn't remotely resembled Julia.

"You're sorry, aren't you!" Matilda said, all the repressed tension of the awful two hours bursting out.

"Mattie, do you think I'm a Bluebeard, or something? But in one way you're right that I'm sorry. It would have solved the mystery. Now I suspect that you're going to spend the rest of your life looking for your ill-fated sister."

He knew her by now. Poor Joshua, fated to have a wife with an obsessive nature. He was perfectly aware that everywhere she went she was going to be searching the faces of passers-by, looking for that lovely forlorn lost face. For the rest of her life, as he had said.

But she didn't resist being taken into his arms. She needed comfort so badly, even the comfort of his strong insensitive body. Not entirely insensitive. She must be fair. She was managing very well to shut out her worst suspicions. Joshua had disliked Julia, but he would never have harmed her physically. Never.

A few days later Lally smiled tentatively, as if she recognized her mother. Matilda held her closely, weeping with relief.

Not very long after that she knew without doubt that she was pregnant. And this time, considering all she had suffered, God could not deny her a son . . .

Second Interval

The old lady in the bed had scarcely dropped asleep
again, the bewildering uneasy sleep of the old, half dream,
half nightmare, before she was awakened by a baby
crying. Footsteps scampered down the passage past her
bedroom door. Someone called, "Come here, you little
brat." Whose voice was that? Not Fish's or Polly's or
Minnie's. It had an accent she didn't recognize, a country
accent from Devon perhaps, or Somerset. Who were
these strange people wandering about her house?

The baby was still crying angrily. It must be Lally.
She had cried a lot since she had had that unfortunate
fall. She had changed from a placid baby to a highly-
strung fretful infant who was driving poor old Fish into
nervous ill-health. Fish, after all, was seventy and would
soon have to be given a pension and retired. She had
never recovered from the tragedy of Julia's disappearance.
Had anybody, even Joshua, who couldn't bear Julia's
name to be mentioned? As if he had some guilt about it.
Nor could he bear Lally's crying. He was afraid there
was something permanently damaged in the child's brain.

Or had she been born that way, and they hadn't noticed it before?

None of the doctors seemed to know. They asked questions about Lally's previous responsiveness, which Joshua swore had been normal, and murmured that some infants were much more slow than others in learning to sit up, and to crawl. Lally, they said, was rather over-weight, and therefore lethargic. Her irritability was a result of her concussion, and would lessen as time went by. None of these vague statements lessened Joshua's anxiety about the new baby, now beginning to show in Matilda's rounding stomach. He was as jumpy and short-tempered as his daughter.

The whole of that pregnancy had been an uneasy time, Matilda remembered, because the house was haunted by Julia. And still was. Now, in the darkening afternoon, she tried to raise herself on her elbow. She wanted to look down the length of the garden to see if Julia were sitting beneath the mulberry tree. Looking a picture in her wide-brimmed leghorn hat and her muslin dress. Looking happy, too, as she tried to lure a robin to her feet. Her pockets were always full of crumbs, Polly complained, either from fragments of cake to feed the robin or biscuits for Lally. The day she had gone missing she had been wearing a blue woollen dress without pockets, so she would not have had a crust between herself and starvation.

Was it Julia whom Matilda could hear crying? In the long dark nights, for weeks after her disappearance, Matilda had imagined she could hear a desolate wailing. But she had said nothing because Joshua would not have the fatal name mentioned.

Thankfully, when Hillary had been born she had stopped having fancies. Hillary was her dream come true in the most sublime way. He hadn't a trace of his father in him. He was a handsome imperious little boy with the long Duncastle nose, the far-seeing blue eyes. Born to command, Matilda had thought with intense pleasure.

When Richard followed a year later she had two of them, spirited lively little boys who obviously would never consent to sit behind a desk in a bank. They could scarcely be made to sit behind their desks in the schoolroom, and, at Matilda's insistence, were packed off to boarding school when they were seven years old and had learned their alphabet.

Imogen, her last baby, had been so quiet one had scarcely known she was in the house. Not that her quietness presaged any of Lally's trouble. She was a sweet-natured little girl who fetched and carried for her brothers and picked up the things Lally clumsily dropped. She was pretty, too, and the apple of her father's eye.

She had had a blue fur-trimmed coat and bonnet that she had worn when they had all made that long-promised visit to Vienna. To stay in a real castle, and to meet the family of Papa's partner Count von Klein and his wife Amalie.

The old lady in the bed frowned bewilderedly. Why was Imogen staying in her mind as that dark-haired gentle little girl? She had grown up, one knew, because there had been trouble. What had it been? Joshua kept saying, "You're too possessive, Mattie. Clara says so, too. You act as if the children are clay and you can mould them."

"But you try to mould them, too," she retorted. "You see Richard as president of your bank."

"I do, too. Therefore I won't have his ears filled with stories of battles and dead heroes. It's dangerous. What do you think you are making our boys into?"

"Heroes. Anyway, what stories can you tell them about a bank? There's nothing romantic about that."

"At least bank presidents don't fall on the battlefield. They live to be fathers and grandfathers . . ."

Oh, dear God, yes, you were right, Joshua. But who is crying? "Fish, where are you? I need you. Make that baby stop crying. It's Lally, isn't it? I expect her head is hurting again."

"But I'm here, Mother," came Lally's docile grown-up voice. "I told those people they weren't to c-come up here, it was private. But I c-couldn't stop them."

No, Lally never could do anything successfully. She had begun to talk so late, and then she had stuttered.

That time in Vienna, when the boys and Imogen were so admired, and Paul—but one had never been able to get used to seeing him with Amalie at his side. One had got touchy and impatient, and had taken out one's ill temper on poor Lally, who never did anything right. Dropping her food at the table, crying in the night from a nightmare and finally falling on the skating rink and twisting her ankle so that Joshua, who never liked fondling or touching her (she always reminded him of Julia) had had to carry her back to the sleigh and wrap her in rugs and have her sent home.

Lally's ankle still swelled from that long-ago accident. She blamed it for her clumsiness when everyone knew she had been born clumsy, poor girl. Now, as she bent over Matilda, Matilda had to repress her irritation. Lally was so large, shutting out what remained of the light.

"Who are those people outside my door?" she managed to ask.

"I don't know. I've never seen them b-before. Really, M-mother, you don't know who c-comes to your bazaars nowadays."

"That's my business," said Matilda, with an echo of her old tartness. But what business was she talking about? Hillary's and Richard's future? The old argument about Sandhurst, the army, one of the elite regiments. But there was no argument. Hillary could not wait to begin his military education, though Richard had his father's pugnacious chin. One was not sure how much influence one would eventually have over him.

"I should have been warned that night when you cut your hair off," Joshua's voice was saying in her head. "That was a sign of ruthlessness, if ever there was one. You'd better be careful, Mattie, or your children will grow up to hate you."

Never! Hillary and Richard, her adored and handsome little boys. Never! Yet the pain struck deep within her, making her groan, and bringing the bulky figure of Lally back to her side.

"Shall I ring for the n-nurse, M-mother?"

"No."

"But you're in p-pain."

"No, I'm not. I'm only remembering."

Paul and Amalie, such a handsome couple, Paul neat and slender as always, Amalie blonde, laughing, already growing too plump from all those Viennese pastries. Imogen and Rudi, as young as the earliest spring, Richard teasing Charlotte and looking unforgivably like his father. Hillary, always standing alone, superior, untouchable. And the drums beating in her head again, relentlessly, full of their irresistible lure, the deadly Pied Piper carrying a drum instead of pipes and dancing down the cobbled streets of Europe . . .

Chapter 8

They were such a large party setting out for their continental journey. Imogen, just six years old, had never travelled anywhere but down to Sanctuary, and was afraid she might be sick with excitement. Mamma would not care for that, since they were going to stay in a castle with a Count and Countess. She had been lecturing them for days on good behaviour. "You have to be an example to those foreign children, Charlotte and Rudolph. You're English, and proud of it. Lally, hold your head up and look at people. I really believe you see nothing in the world but your boots, and they're not buttoned properly either. Oh dear, what a careless child you are."

Mamma, dressed in her long fur cape and the little toque trimmed with green feathers that made her eyes green, went down on her knees to attend to Lally's boots. When she straightened herself again there was a spot of colour in each cheek, and she looked very handsome.

Papa said why wasn't she wearing a practical tweed coat for the chilly channel crossing and the dirty train journey. But Imogen suspected he was pleased Mamma looked so smart, a rich lady travelling abroad with her children and their nurse.

Imogen and Lally wore their blue velvet coats and bonnets, and made a pretty pair. Or so Imogen had overheard Aunt Clara telling Minnie, their nurse. Hillary and Richard, in their Norfolk jackets and tweed caps, also made a handsome pair though Hillary was awfully skinny and had reddish hair, a sharp alert face and a wicked tongue, as Imogen had cause to know. He was a replica of his mother, people said, and also the apple of her eye, her nasty little spoiled pet. Richard had Papa's yellowish hazel eyes, and rumbustious ways. Imogen, who loved her father, was much more fond of Richard than of Hillary. But both boys had a similar craze for war games, and when they were home from school the nursery echoed to the banging of drums and the shouting of "Charge!" and "I've shot you, you filthy Boer."

Now that Britain was fighting the Boers in South Africa Hillary demanded replicas of the latest guns, the German Mausers, and field guns. But Richard was a cavalry man, and desired only a sword and a good horse. The girls had to keep out of the way. Or let them nurse the wounded if they wanted to, the British, of course, not the bloody Boers, who could be left to die on the veldt.

It was a good thing, Papa said, to have this jaunt to Vienna to get away from the war atmosphere that was saturating the country, especially since the relief of Ladysmith. Mamma had constantly put off the trip for one reason or another. The children were too small or they couldn't inflict such a large family on the Count and Countess, or she had too many obligations to her committees for war relief, what with trouble in the Sudan, and then with the Boers stirring dangerously in South Africa, and finally erupting into war.

At last Papa had said, in the slow, contemptuous voice he used only when he had completely lost patience, "Do you really think, Mattie, that England will be defeated in any war, real or imaginary, if you are out of the country? Mind you, I wouldn't say that that was impossible. But I don't think Kruger will completely annihilate the British army in the next few weeks, and there are surely some other capable women to knit socks and roll bandages for a couple of weeks. Anyway, when did you learn to knit?"

"Joshua, you know very well I don't knit, I organise."

"And splendidly, too, I agree. Which means all your committees can survive your absence for a short time. Paul and Amalie are hurt that you've never accepted their invitations in the past, and I want you to see our Vienna branch. I particularly want Richard to see it, as a matter of fact."

"Richard's only a little boy."

"Childish impressions are important. Who knows," Papa's eyes flared wickedly, "even the Major-General may be interested."

That was Papa's joke, calling Hillary the Major-General. Hillary enjoyed it, secretly pleased, but Mamma always winced. Not because she thought Papa was poking fun at Hillary but because it seemed to make her strangely apprehensive. As if she saw some far-off frightening vision.

Count and Countess Paul had military portraits on their staircase, too. One in particular, of a stout whiskery gentleman covered in medals, made the boys giggle.

This levity offended Rudi von Klein, who said, "He's a Field Marshal. You don't need to laugh. He was decorated by the Emperor Franz Josef himself. Papa doesn't talk much about him because Papa isn't a warlike man. Perhaps I will be, however."

"Does your mother want you to be?" Hillary asked.

"I don't think she minds. She says I must do what I like best."

"She's different from our mother, then. Our family all go into the army. It's tradition. It's what made England great."

"She isn't as great as Austria-Hungary."

"She is so. She's much greater. She has an Empire with millions of people. Millions and millions."

"What a bother," said Rudi in his precise English.

"Why?" Hillary's long Duncastle nose was in the air.

"Because people don't always behave. You must need an awful lot of armies to keep the natives down."

"We have."

"I think that's rather bullying."

"You're soft like your father," said Hillary contemptuously. "It isn't bullying. It's keeping law and order."

"Children! Children!" exclaimed Mamma, her delicate eyebrows raised. "Amalie, I'm sorry, Hillary and Rudi are fighting again. I'm quite sure that my naughty son began it." There was an undercurrent of pleasure in her voice, however. It delighted her that Hillary almost always won these miniature battles. The curly-headed Rudi was less ruthless, and ruthlessness and a determination to win were what mattered. Hillary had both of these qualities in excess.

"Paul says the answer is to shut them in separate rooms," Amalie said mildly.

"Confine them to barracks?" Mamma was laughing. "What a pity we can't sit them down to some sewing, like the girls."

What a pity, thought Imogen, frowning over her stitching. She and Lally, and Charlotte, too, rather unfairly since her country was not at war, had been ordered to spend an hour working on the white linen squares which were to be handkerchiefs for the brave soldiers fighting in South Africa. Imogen was sure they would lose them, or get them very dirty. But Mamma said the British soldiers must be properly equipped. It was so good for their morale. It was certain that the Boers would not have white linen handkerchiefs, or any sort of handkerchiefs at all.

But this dull task would be much lightened if Rudi could sit at her side and talk to her. She loved his quaintly guttural voice, his tight brown curls, his teasing eyes. Not teasing cruelly like Hillary, but gently so that she laughed. Actually she loved Rudi. She was trying to summon up courage to ask him to write her letters when she had gone home. Or to persuade him to accept hers. Vienna was a kaleidoscope of joy to her because Rudi lived there. She was never never going to forget him. Indeed, she wouldn't have to, because it was being arranged that when the boys were old enough Rudi should come to the London branch of the bank and Richard should go to the Vienna one. It was to be an important part of both boys' education, a prospect which Count Paul and Amalie and Papa welcomed gladly. Mamma said nothing, but her eyebrows curved a little higher and she looked at Amalie as if she disliked her for agreeing so easily to this arrangement.

Imogen had a moment of disloyalty towards her mother, for who could dislike pretty plump Amalie, so good-natured and comfortably lazy. She would never make little girls spend hours stitching white linen handkerchiefs for soldiers. She would tell them to look at picture books or play with their dolls or skip. Rudi was like his mother. He was indolent, too. And kind. That was why Hillary always won their fights. "If ever we fight the Austrians we'll mow them down," Hillary boasted in his horrid superior way. As if he could imagine facing Rudi with a real gun! He couldn't wait for his portrait to be hung at Sanctuary, dressed in uniform as a neatly be-medalled Major-General.

On their last night in Vienna the grown-ups went to the opera. The children were left at home to have a festive supper, but it was spoiled by the boys beginning to fight again. This time, to Hillary's intense fury, Richard took Rudi's side, and together they pummelled Hillary until his nose bled. Then there was trouble, with Gretchen and Minnie both scolding, blood down Hillary's jacket, and chocolate gateau squashed into the beautiful carpet.

Lally began to cry. Noise always upset her. Charlotte shouted, "Horrid Englanders!" and Hillary, his face very white where it wasn't blood-stained, said ferociously to Rudi, "I'll kill you one day, I promise you."

The result of this fracas was that they were all sent off to bed early and as a consequence Imogen couldn't fall asleep. Apart from anything else she was too unhappy. Tomorrow they were going home. She wouldn't see Rudi again for perhaps ten years, and when she tried to visualise that far-distant day it seemed to be hung over with a cloud of sorrow. She couldn't imagine why this was so. She knew that she was just having one of her unhappy spells, and lay awake listening for the sound of the carriage returning from the opera house. She had an overpowering desire to be held in her father's arms. He would grasp her close, laughter rumbling in his chest, and assure her that people didn't kill each other. Well, enemies did, perhaps, but not friends. And not foolish hot-tempered small boys.

When the carriage came at last, she got out of bed and slipped down the winding staircase, creeping by the portrait of the fiercely-whiskered Field Marshal, then pausing to listen. Where were the grown-ups? In the big salon having a glass of champagne before they went to bed, she guessed. Dare she interrupt them? Countess Amalie and Mamma had looked so beautiful dressed for the opera, Amalie in blue silk with a lacy shawl over her plump shoulders, Mamma rather severe in her favourite green velvet, but with her hair twinkling with diamonds. The diamonds, or Mamma's erect bearing and long neck, had made her seem more like a countess, to Imogen's mind, than Countess Amalie. She sometimes fancied Count Paul thought this, too, because he behaved so politely to Mamma, always taking her arm or kissing her hand.

The hand kissing was a thing foreigners did, Hillary had said scornfully, in private. It didn't mean that the Count loved Mamma or thought two penny farthings about her.

And Hillary, as usual, proved to be right, for lurking at the half-open salon door, Imogen saw that Mamma and Count Paul were alone. Not kissing hands, but staring at one another across the width of the hearth rug as if they were wary of each other. "Everyone looked at you tonight, Matilda."

"Did they?"

"You must have noticed. Joshua was as proud as a peacock."

"Joshua?"

"But of course. You're a wonderful asset to him."

"Asset?" Mamma said drily. "Yes, that would be his word, too. Still, I don't quarrel with an arrangement which I agreed to. I just try to keep my part of it. Am I telling you too much?"

"Nothing I didn't guess. But you're happy?"

Mamma was suddenly bitter. "How can we be when

we both always want to go in different directions? This thing now about Richard and Rudi changing places. I was not consulted."

"Neither was Amalie," Count Paul said mildly, "but she thinks it a splendid idea. Anyway, it isn't for several years yet."

"My children are Duncastles, all of them."

"Isn't that unfair to Joshua? Besides, you are being deliberately blind, Matilda. I see distinct resemblances to Joshua in Richard, and in the little one, too."

"Imogen is a good, obedient child."

"She has Joshua's chin. And very charming in its feminine rendering. But she may oppose you one day."

"I hardly think so. My children are brought up to know their duty."

The Count laughed softly. He provoked one of Mamma's most arrogant moods—that was what Papa called them—but he seemed to be amused by it. "Have a glass of champagne and take off your Britannia helmet. You really are such an obsessive creature. What a lucky thing you and I couldn't marry."

"Marry? Us?" Mamma's voice had faltered strangely.

"Don't tell me that thought never occurred to you. That afternoon at Sanctuary, for instance. You must have known that if you hadn't already been married—but as I say it was lucky for us both."

Mamma stared, not speaking. Now she seemed to have no words to say.

"I admire you very much, Matilda, but I could never have changed my nationality for you. And you most certainly would never have changed yours for me. You're such a patriot. Or do you do this sort of thing because your life isn't happy enough?"

"Do what?" Mamma asked haughtily.

"Think of countries instead of people, patches of imperial red on the map of the world instead of ordinary warm-blooded human beings."

"Why are you talking to me like this, Paul? Have I offended you?"

"Naturally not. But you are the most fervently nationalistic lady I have ever met, and too much nationalism is dangerous. Your husband knows. He believes in peaceful trade between countries. Why don't you listen more to him? Do you realise you have spent most of your time here either talking of the glories of a war against a handful of Boer farmers or inciting our sons to fight each other?"

"Paul, that's not fair. I haven't incited the boys. Why, I'm always being called to drag them apart and make peace. And as for our South African Empire, really it isn't for you to pass judgement."

"Because I'm a foreigner? And Austria has her unruly Empire, too? Very well, I concede you that argument. Do you ever, by the way, concede an argument?"

"Not if I can help it."

Count Paul gave his quiet amused laugh. "Matilda, you are a magnificent woman, and I'm glad we at last persuaded you to visit Vienna. I had a ghost to lay, and this could be done only here, not in London or at Sanctuary." When Mamma didn't speak, he went on, "I'm not sure that I have quite succeeded, but at least I no longer expect it to walk at nights and haunt me. I am being practical, a good Austrian banker watching his best interests."

Mamma picked up her gloves and evening bag.

"Matilda!"

About to leave the room, she paused.

"Don't you think it was a good idea that we had this talk?"

"I can't imagine"—Mamma's voice was distinctly cool—"why you thought it necessary. I have no ghosts to lay. What a presumptuous idea."

Again he laughed.

"You really are magnificent. But only a brave man could live with you."

Then Imogen had to dart behind the big chest in the hall and crouch down out of sight, as Mamma came hurrying out. Instinct told her that this was no time to make her presence known. But although that conversation had been so strange she didn't know why it was making Mamma cry. Crying was something Mamma had always said was a waste of time.

The next day there were noisy and friendly farewells at the railway station. Countess Amalie, looking plump and cosy and rosy-cheeked in her thick woollen cape and little fur hat, had an arm round each of her children. Charlotte waved a mittened hand, and Rudi shouted cheekily to Hillary and Richard, *"Auf wiedersehen, verdammte Englanders,"* and got a good-natured box on the ears from his father.

"Please excuse him," Count Paul shouted over the hissing of steam, as the engine was stoked up for its long journey. "We will teach him better manners before sending him to London."

The whistle screeched and the train began to move, belching clouds of smoke that obscured the figures on the platform. Papa drew the boys back from the open windows, and sat down beside Mamma.

"Well, we're on our way home," he said. "That went very well, I think, except for our lively sons."

Imogen hardly dared look at Mamma. She was afraid there might be tears on her cheeks again, but to her surprise there was a challenging look in Mamma's eyes, and she was giving a determined smile.

"Our daughters survived, at least."

"Not truly, ma'am," said Minnie, who was hot and flushed from stowing away garments and packages. "Miss Lally never ought to have been taken skating. I still can't button her boot over her ankle. And if you could see Miss Imogen's tongue after all those pastries."

"I'm not sick," said Imogen indignantly. "I like being here. And Rudi is going to write me letters."

"Ah ha!" said Papa.

"Joshua, don't encourage her in such an unsuitable idea," Mamma said crossly. "She's only six years old."

"She's female, isn't she?"

"And I will supervise her correspondence until she's grown-up."

Mamma had a red spot on each cheek. Her eyes glittered angrily.

"What's wrong, Mattie? I thought you liked Paul and Amalie."

"Yes, I did. At least, well enough, but one never understands the mind of a foreigner. It's all very well for you and Paul to talk money. That's the same in any language."

"And what dialogue did you have that you didn't understand?"

"Oh—many little things that I'm sure you would think unimportant. But I do say this. I expect our children to marry in their own country." Her bright intimidating gaze swept over the four children. "Do you hear, my darlings?"

Almost a year later, when Imogen was seven and would dearly have liked a baby to care for, Matilda's fifth child was born. Sadly it did not survive birth, and Matilda was not permitted to see it. It had been a girl, a tiny pale barely-formed creature, Clara said. It was best that it hadn't been spared for this world where one needed strength and health and a sharp mind.

A sharp mind? Those were the words that aroused Matilda's suspicions. Had the baby been born alive, but Joshua, on seeing its frailty, its colourlessness, decided it was another Julia, and asked Doctor Grimes to put it away? Or even quietly smothered it with a pillow himself? She would never know, because no one would tell her the truth. She thought Joshua sometimes looked at her oddly and guiltily during her convalescence. "You had a hard time, Mattie. I think this had better be the last."

"Is that what Doctor Grimes says?"

"Yes, it is. He's going to have a talk with you. Don't look downcast. We have four healthy children."

She had wanted six sons, she remembered. An impossible dream now. But at least she wouldn't have to sleep with Joshua any more. That was another duty done. "Always do your duty," she constantly admonished the children. She had nothing with which to reproach herself. Even after Vienna, and Paul's face, gentle, amused, mocking, lodged permanently in her skull, she had made herself to be a good and willing wife to Joshua. It would have been nice to have another child to love. Even a girl. For she found herself mourning her tiny lost daughter.

It wasn't true what Paul had said, that she cared more for her country than for people. Her heart ached for that scarcely-born child, and for some reason Julia was constantly in her mind. Since her disappearance so long ago she had always haunted the house for Matilda. It seemed incredible that no trace of her had ever been discovered. Once, someone had brought in a white handkerchief with the letter "J" embroidered in the corner. It had been picked up near the Serpentine in Hyde Park. There had been talk of dragging the Serpentine, but finally nothing had been done because the handkerchief had not belonged to Julia. Matilda would have recognized the embroidery.

Julia had gone into limbo as completely as had the newborn baby. In Matilda's sad heart they seemed to merge into the same person, both uncomfortable fey creatures, but too harmless for Joshua to have such a pathological dislike of them.

Once again her emotions, apart from those which she could express lavishly on her children, had to be repressed. She knew that people accused her of becoming dry, vinegary and sharp, especially now that the Boer war was over and there was no vital cause to consume her energies. She wasn't interested in the poor. They depressed and disgusted her. Nor, now that Joshua was growing more and more solidly successful, did she much enjoy climbing the social ladder and taking her place as one of Kensington's leading hostesses. Her usefulness to Joshua in this way had been all that he had expected of her. They had even entertained the Governor of the Bank of England, a triumph that had seemed to Joshua more important than persuading royalty to enter their doors. And even that would come, he imagined. His wife was an elegant tigress, whose claws, fortunately, did not become unsheathed too often. But a tigress was not necessarily the best of wives, nor of mothers, he sometimes thought uneasily, then dismissed the thought since after all he was the master of his own house.

But was he?

Queen Victoria had been buried with a suitable display of pomp and mourning, and England had gently slid into a golden afternoon of wealth and power. And pleasure.

But Matilda was not one for all the balls and race meetings and garden parties and country house weekends that King Edward VII loved. She considered herself a serious intelligent woman with a hard-working husband (who rather surprisingly didn't seem to mind that he could no longer come to her bed) and an idle life was going to be unendurable.

The boys were at boarding school, Webb Major and Webb Minor. In the mornings the girls went to a day school, slow-footed Lally led by Imogen, and in the afternoon sat in the garden with Minnie, doing their sewing or their painting, or were taken to visit Aunt Clara whom they loved, in the small steep-staired house they thought cosy and perfect now that the elderly invalid upstairs had died and been taken away. The house in Kensington Square, well-staffed because of Joshua's growing affluence, ran smoothly. Joshua left for work at precisely the same time every morning, checking his gold Hunter watch with the grandfather clock in the hall. Sometimes now he worked late at night, saying that although his business was growing rapidly he could not afford to delegate too much authority. He must keep his shrewd fingers on every sovereign. It would be different when he had taken a partner, but there was only one partner in his mind.

The other side of the impressive partners' desk was being kept for Richard. Or so Joshua said, with his dogged determination. Very well, he agreed, trying to make it seem his decision when he knew very well that it was impossible to override Matilda. Hillary could go to Sandhurst. But Richard, his second and favourite son, came into the bank. Instead of being Webb and von Klein it would be Webb, von Klein and Sons, because young Rudolph von Klein also was destined for the financial world.

Matilda bided her time on Richard's future. She was growing less impetuous, more secretive. Events could change plans. What events? Another war? But what country would have the temerity to provoke England, the most powerful nation in the world? Germany? Austria-Hungary? Russia? People speculated idly, but did not believe such a thing could happen. England was surely to enjoy long years of peace.

Matilda had other views. History could be studied at Sanctuary. The motto of her family was always to be prepared. It should have been the motto of England, but the country was lulled into a false security by past successes. The Government haggled about trivial matters; the rich, led by the stout bronchitic King, went on their pleasure-seeking way. Matilda listened to Joshua's complacent opinions (on his partner Paul von Klein's advice the bank was about to finance a railroad scheme in Serbia), but remained silent. The time would come when the drums would beat again. She might be married to a banker, but she did not intend to be the mother of one.

Chapter 9

Imogen wrote to Rudolph von Klein on the tenth anniversary of that well-remembered visit to Vienna. She began tentatively, but was soon launched into a compulsive personal history.

I wonder if it bores you that an English schoolgirl wants to write to you again although you never answered my first letter years ago. You may think me very forward, or very stubborn, but I have a feeling that you did write to me, and that my mother, who is very strict, did not allow me to have your letters, the reason being that she does not trust foreigners. I expect it is right that mothers should be in charge of their children's lives, but only while they are small. When they are grown-up, as I am now (I will be seventeen this year), I have a right to form my own opinions. That is what my father and Aunt Clara say, but being a mother, as Mamma explains, is different and much more emotional and possessive.

However, I must tell you now that I am writing

to you because Papa says you are at last coming to London to have a year in our London branch, and to learn the English side of the business. I thought it a good idea, since we will be meeting so soon, to send you a letter of welcome and tell you what has happened to our family since we last met.

I will begin with my elder brother Hillary who has always been the most important member, in my mother's eyes, anyway, and what she says tends to be believed by everyone else. This does not mean that things are always amicable because Hillary is very strong-willed and quick-tempered, just like Mamma, so two such similar natures must fight. But underneath quarrelling, which happens only when Mamma forgets he is grown-up, they are as close as if they were one person. No one else exists for her when Hillary is in the room. She is quite silly with pride in him, when he was awarded the Sword of Honour at Sandhurst you would have thought he had been crowned king.

Richard is quite different. He simply doesn't care for the army, and guns, and weapons. He is like you, he wants to become a banker, and dear Papa is immensely pleased. But Mamma hasn't given up the struggle. She talks contemptuously about young men with ink-stained fingers, which is her description of anyone in an office. She thinks clerks sissy, although Richard was in the First Eleven (cricket) at Harrow, and can ride as well as any cavalry man—which, says Mamma, is such a waste if he is not to go into a cavalry regiment.

Hillary has gone into my grandfather's old regiment, the Royals. There has been a Duncastle in it for the last century or more. There is no doubt that my handsome elder brother will eventually be its Colonel-in-Chief. He won't be satisfied with less. Papa still calls him the Major-General, and I am awfully afraid this will be a fact one day. I hope I am married and away from the family before it happens as I am sure Hillary would expect to be saluted all the time, even by his sisters.

But Richard is a darling, he is gentle and funny and kind. His eyes are hazel like Papa's, and go yellow when he is excited or angry. And he has Papa's stubborn chin, which people say I have, too. So we are not Mamma's favourites, like Hillary, although she still wants to *entirely* control our lives.

Since I have told you about the boys in my family, perhaps you will want to hear a little about the girls.

Lally, the eldest, is a rather unhappy person because she knows she is a disappointment to her parents. It is very sad. It isn't her fault that she is slow and clumsy. She really isn't good at anything, Mamma says despairingly, and we all constantly wonder how she would be if she hadn't been dropped on the hearth as a baby. This catastrophe was when the Great Mystery in my family happened. My Aunt Julia, who was the culprit and dropped Lally when Mamma was away, disappeared immediately afterwards, and was never found. Mamma thinks she was terrified of Papa, who can be alarming when he loses his temper, and ran out of the house and lost her way in the fog. Though it is extraordinary that she was never found, even as a corpse. Horrid thought! She was a little simple-minded, and Papa hadn't any understanding of this, just as he doesn't understand poor Lally. He gets particularly impatient with her when he is tired, or something is worrying him, so she has learned to keep out of his way. Which is sad, because Papa is a wonderful man and I adore him.

Now I wonder if it is vain of me to think you might like to hear about me. For one thing, I am no longer a little girl as you remember me—if you remember me at all. I am about to leave school and will come out next year. Lally didn't have a coming-out although Mamma wanted her to, but Papa said the whole thing was impossible. How could Lally be trusted to make her curtsey to the Queen, for instance, she would probably fall over her own feet. And as for finding partners at a ball one did not inflict that sort of thing on the young gentlemen of

England. You can't make a silk purse out of a sow's ear, etcetera. Dear Papa is terribly predictable.

Mamma, of course, knew that he was right, but couldn't forbear taunting him that he was ashamed for society to see Lally. He said quite right, he was, and whose fault was that? That wretched Julia's. Really, parents can be so childish. Are yours?

Although I must say my mother looks truly wonderful when she is dressed for a party or a ball. She says that Papa likes to make an entrance, holding her arm as tightly as if she were one of the bank's gold bars and someone would attempt to steal her!

Anyway, after this long story, it was decided that Lally should be excused social life and stay quietly at home with her knitting and sketching and her pet birds, robins and blue tits and wrens, that she has taught to eat out of her hand. She sits under the mulberry tree in the garden, where my vanished Aunt Julia used to sit, and Mamma sometimes cries a little when she sees her. And it is left to me to fly the family flag and be the debutante daughter. I dread it, but not too much, because I like balls and fun.

Do you wonder what I look like, Rudi? I am not anything special at all. I have always wished I had blonde hair instead of dark, but perhaps it is a good thing I haven't, as that would remind Papa of his *bête noir,* Aunt Julia. I have dark blue eyes, and some freckles on my nose, which is not patrician, like Mamma's, but simply a little turned-up and ordinary. I am five feet three inches tall and have stopped growing, so I will never be a stately lady and the cynosure of all eyes when I come into a room, as Mamma is. Mamma says I must make up for my lack of being conspicuous by vivacity and animation. I think she emphasises this because she is driven wild by poor Lally being so inanimate.

I do like to laugh—Richard makes me laugh, he is such a clown—but I also like serious things like music and poetry. When we spend the summer holidays at Sanctuary I wander about the house and dream of its centuries of memories. I even get romantic about all the military portraits, though I don't study them as Hillary does. He knows every *single minute* of the Duncastle family history, and when we were younger he always made us play war games. We have fought every historic battle since the Battle of Hastings. He is handsome but also *vulnerable* in his lieutenant's uniform. He seems too young, and too thin, but Mamma says that is the way the Duncastles are. He is like our famous ancestor of the Salamanca Drum which I will tell you about one day. I am so afraid Hillary may have a similar fate. The church at Sanctuary is full of memorials to Duncastles who died young. Of course one is proud, but terribly sad, and one can only pray there is not another war. Though secretly I suspect Hillary, and Mamma, too, are lusting for the excitement and high unbearable courage of it.

Is your country likely to go to war again? If it is, do be like Richard and stay safely in the bank, and forget about courage and loyalty and all those things that only, as Papa says, leave you dying on some lonely plain for the vultures to pick at.

As you can see, I am not very good at talking about myself. I can only say that I am not likely to make a really successful debutante. All the same, I am cherishing the hope that since you will be in London next year you will come to my ball and dance with me.

I remember everything about you, which Minnie says is impossible since I was only six years old.

But it isn't impossible.

Have you changed a lot? Don't change, Rudi. And if you tell me you have a girl in Vienna I will *kill* you.

The letter could not be sent, of course. It had run away with her, telling far too many family secrets, far too many of her own secrets, too. A woman should be a little mysterious to a man. Looking at her round young face in the mirror, Imogen thought hopelessly that she could never even pretend to be mysterious.

Yet she felt happier with all those neatly written pages hidden in the back of an old composition book. Essays about "My Garden," "A Trip to the Seaside," "Kensington in Olden Times," "The British Empire," and now this outpouring to someone whom she remembered vividly as a little boy, but who was now twenty years old, a man, a stranger.

Chapter 10

The dining room at Kensington Square was a pleasant room with its polished furniture, its panelled walls, its cushioned window seats and its long low windows looking over the square. When the candles were lit and the table laid with the good silver, porcelain and crystal that Mamma had brought up from Sanctuary the room looked rich and inviting. Papa's family had no heirlooms. What could you expect of market gardeners but an antique turnip or two? he was apt to say jokingly. However, he took great pleasure in nice things and often, halfway through a meal, would stop eating to study the hallmark of a silver fork or spoon, as if he were assessing its value. Mamma found this a disconcerting and vulgar habit. He behaved like a dealer pondering on what offer to make for the silverware, she said, but he said no, he was simply taking visual pleasure in it. Like looking at a good painting. Or you, Mattie, my wife. Was that vulgar?

It seemed that at the beginning of their marriage Papa had been extremely ambitious and had been prepared to kowtow to the gentry, or to the merely rich, in the hope of persuading them to use his bank either for investment or loans. Now his business had expanded so much that there was no need for any more boot-licking. He had reverted to being himself, blunt and honest, and he believed people liked him better for it. At least they liked his aura of success.

Although that was not to denigrate the value of Mamma's contribution to his success. It had been immensely important in those early years. It was still important, but less so, and Papa's gratitude was tempered by Mamma's attitude of implacable opposition to Richard's career in banking. She had been in a terrible mood ever since Richard's departure for Vienna a week ago. Lally, always timid and apprehensive, had kept out of her way, and so had the servants as much as possible. Imogen had been able to ignore the storms and frowns, because she was in a state of trembling rapture about Rudi's imminent arrival. Papa had pretended not to notice the glacial chill in the air, but he had come home later at nights, sending apologies not less than four evenings in succession that he would not be in to dinner.

Tonight, however, he arrived home sharp on time and accompanied by young Rudolph von Klein.

There were not to be any other guests. Papa had said the occasion was purely family. And how, asked Mamma, did Rudolph von Klein so suddenly become one of the family? If Papa was going to treat every bank employee as belonging to the family circle they would shortly be entertaining cashiers, bookkeepers and messengers.

He would like it that way, Papa said amicably. No doubt one day a social levelling-out would happen, but in the meantime he expected just such a display of the best silver and porcelain as Paul and Amalie would provide for Richard in Vienna.

So Mamma rather maliciously went to the other extreme and ordered the kind of menu she usually reserved for her most important guests, including minor members of the royal family and Hillary's aristocratic friends from Sandhurst and Aldershot, young sprigs of the nobility who were going to command England's future armies. This was not done with any genuine feeling of hospitality, however. Not only was Rudolph von Klein a bank clerk, but his father had once humiliated her by mocking her and making her weep. She was always extremely cool to Count Paul on his visits to London. She was not a forgiving person.

Imogen, with the intuitive wisdom of her eighteen years, imagined that in other circumstances Mamma and Count Paul might have fallen in love. They were certainly far better matched than Mamma and Papa were. But this had not been able to happen and therefore, beneath a veneer of smiling politeness, they found subtle ways of wounding each other. At least, it was Mamma who excelled at this game. Life was untidy and haphazard, Imogen thought, and unhappy people became cruel. It was very important to be happy.

Inevitably, there was an argument over the dress Imogen had put on for dinner. It was the one that had been specially made for her for the occasion of the visit of one of Hillary's friends, the King's second cousin (who proved to be a fleshy young man with a pink face, not half as good-looking as Hillary). The dress was rather a dream, white lace with a blue sash, and far too dressed up, Mamma said, for a simple family dinner. Take it off at once, she said, and put on your muslin. Do you want to embarrass this young man? He only works in a bank, you know.

That dreary little-girl muslin! But another thing Mamma insisted on was that Imogen mustn't always outshine Lally. Lally was sensibly dressed in her mauve silk and wouldn't open her mouth all evening because she was so afraid of stuttering. It was significantly the first time she had ever been suggested as a rival of Imogen's. Mamma really was being unfairly hostile to Rudi. She developed these unreasonable prejudices and one had to be very clever to outwit her. Imogen decided to give up the battle over the dress, but to put up her hair instead. This would be much more effective, and she would do it at the last minute so that it would be a *fait accompli* when she walked into the drawing room. After all, wasn't there the famous story about Mamma cutting off her hair the night Papa was to propose to her. This game could be played in different ways.

Why did you never answer my letter, Rudi? she would say boldly, in the hearing of both Mamma and Papa. Not reproachfully but teasingly, and the ice would be broken at once.

But again she misjudged the situation. This was the wrong time for any such intimate remarks, for Mamma, Hillary, and the tall brown-haired young man with the serious brown eyes were engaged in a conversation about the Emperor of Germany, Kaiser Wilhelm, and the war-like sounds that were coming from Germany. Would Austria-Hungary join the German forces in the event of war?

"We saw your Archduke Franz Ferdinand at the King's funeral," Hillary was saying. "I must say he didn't look in the best shape. Does he over-indulge himself?"

"He isn't the old Emperor," Rudi admitted stiffly. "But I think your late king was also rather fat and self-indulgent."

"Indeed he was," Hillary agreed good-naturedly. "He wasn't a bit like the Kaiser who seems to have an obses-sion about physical fitness."

"A little self-indulgence makes a man more human," said Papa, patting his round stomach. "I beware of these exercise fiends. They're tied-up in their minds."

"I wouldn't think Kaiser Wilhelm was concerned with humanity at all," Mamma said. "I've never trusted that young man since the time when he used to come over to make a fuss of his grandmother. Our old Queen Victoria, you know. She may have been taken in by him, but the Prince of Wales certainly wasn't."

"However, now we have a dead king and Germany has a very much alive Emperor," Hillary commented. "I be-lieve the Uhlans are crack troops."

"They ride like grey shadows down the Unter den Linden," Rudi said. "One has to admire them."

"They can't be superior to our Brigade of Guards," Mamma said sharply.

"I would not like to guess, Mrs. Webb. Let us hope

such a thing won't be put to the test. Hillary, do you remember how we used to fight!"

"You were rude to my brother and me. You called us *verdompte Englanders*." Hillary was smiling. He looked marvellous when he smiled, tender and joyous. In repose his face was stern with an underlying sadness perplexing in one so young. He had to practise looking stern, he had once told Imogen. You didn't grin when you gave orders to your company. But why sad? She hadn't actually asked him that question, but she pondered over it. Had he had an unhappy love affair? He was secretive about his private life, perhaps because it was one thing he wanted to preserve from Mamma's possessiveness.

"After dinner I'll take you upstairs and show you the Death Room," he said to Rudi.

"The Death Room!" Papa looked disgusted. "When was it called that?"

"Oh, long ago, sir. Because it's full of deadly weapons and old bloodstains."

"And the Salamanca Drum," Mamma said inevitably, with her familiar look of pride. "That's a precious family relic, Herr von Klein. Hillary will tell you about it. But we're quite ignoring the girls. You remember our elder daughter, Lally?"

"Indeed, yes. Didn't she damage her knee skating?"

Lally blushed, her head bent.

"Her ankle," said Mamma. "And this is Imogen, who was hardly more than a baby when you knew her." A sudden flash in Mamma's eyes indicated that she noticed Imogen's put-up hair. "She isn't yet as grown-up as she apparently would like you to think."

Rudi bowed formally to Lally and Imogen. Imogen didn't expect him to look particularly at shrinking Lally, but he didn't notice her either, not her put-up hair, not anything. He was still thinking of the Salamanca Drum and that macabre Death Room which obviously excited him as it did Mamma and Hillary. Oh dear, was he going to be another one who couldn't resist the sound of martial music, and thoughts of death and glory? Perhaps he would rather be one of the splendid Uhlans riding down the

Unter den Linden than a banker tied to his desk and concerned only with money.

"If Germany does go to war," he said, reverting to the subject that seemed to absorb him as much as it did Mamma and Hillary, "I expect my country would march beside her. We are close neighbours, we speak the same language. And as you say, one can't think of that superb army of the Kaiser's being left idle. But the war will undoubtedly be against Russia, so don't be alarmed, Mrs. Webb."

"You don't alarm my wife by talking of war," Papa said drily. "She's bred to it. She would only be annoyed to be left out of the fun. Germany against Russia, eh? Haven't the Kaiser and his warlords read history? Do you suppose we should stop investing in Siberian railways?"

"My father thinks the Balkans are becoming unsettled. He is writing to you about this. He thinks we should favour munitions in our present investments."

"And I think we will postpone business talks until after dinner," Mamma said firmly. "Let us go in. Herr von Klein, perhaps you would sit beside Imogen. I'm sure she wants to hear about Vienna."

"We had a fine time on that visit, didn't we?" said Papa.

"The opera was very beautiful," said Mamma politely.

"Why did you never answer my letter?" Imogen asked in a low voice, her head bent over her soup. "I waited for weeks and months. I was really a very silly little girl."

"But I did answer it. At least, I think—"

"You don't remember?"

"It's a long time ago. But I'm sure I did. Much as I hated writing letters."

"Are you telling the truth?"

"Of course."

"Then Mamma must have suppressed your letter."

"Really?" Rudi's brown eyes shone softly with amusement. "She would take that trouble over children's letters? Why?"

"Because you're a foreigner, I expect."

"My father always said she was an implacable woman. No, a dangerous woman, I think he called her."

"Mamma dangerous!"

"In her attitudes. Inflexibility is dangerous, he said. But he admires her. Very much. So do I. She's so handsome, so in command of herself."

"The Germans are inflexible, too. And I expect you Austrians are."

"You two, what are you talking about?" Mamma's voice came down the table. "Imogen, it's bad manners to whisper at dinner."

"Rudi, will you have some of this Riesling?" asked Papa. "We thought you would like it. Are you comfortable in your hotel? My secretary will find you permanent lodgings when you decide what part of London you prefer."

"A modest part, sir. My father is very strict about my allowance and I want to do so many things. Theatres, operas. And parties, of course. If I am invited to any."

"I am to have my coming-out ball in the summer," Imogen said in a rush. "Down at Sanctuary, in the country. You will be invited to that. Papa will spare you from the bank, won't you, Papa?"

"In that case I will be pleased to accept," said Rudi.

"Debutantes can be a bit stuffy," Hillary said. "Sorry, Imogen, but it's the truth. I should know. I've been at their mercy. Or their mothers'. But we'll find some pretty girls for you. I know one or two."

"Are we to be told who they are?" Mamma asked.

"No, Mamma. You are not. I take the view that if we are soon to be engulfed in war we must eat, drink, and be merry."

"At least, I'm glad you two young men aren't rolling on the floor locked in deadly combat," Papa said. "As you usually were when you last met."

"Our minds, my dear father, are now on higher things. Pretty girls, champagne, late nights. Late late late nights. Not that I wouldn't hesitate to kill Rudi if we were at war."

"Hillary, are you drunk?" Mamma asked suspiciously.

Hillary didn't seem to be drunk, but he had a glittering

look in his eyes. He looked happy, for once. He must be in love, for he was thinking of girls. Or of a girl. He suddenly stared at Imogen and exclaimed, "Good gracious, I hadn't noticed. My baby sister seems to have grown up. What a naked little neck."

Imogen went scarlet. Mamma said, "She is still a schoolgirl, Herr von Klein."

Rudi said in his slow perfect English, "I wish, Mrs. Webb, you would not make me sound such an old man. I am a year younger than your son, and my name is Rudi. And if I may be permitted to express an opinion, Hillary, I think your baby sister has a charming neck."

But he was only being polite. Beautifully polite. He still wasn't seeing her, and he still thought she was a little girl. His mind was on those sophisticated young women Hillary talked about, perhaps, too, on some Soho tarts. Or were they one and the same thing?

Chapter 11

Sanctuary in mid-summer, the afternoon sun flooding into the yellow drawing room, the front door standing wide open to let the warmth come into the cool flagged hall, the scent of roses and honeysuckle hanging in the balmy air, swallows fluttering in the eaves, doves cooing, the table set for tea on the terrace and the chairs festooned with the shabby striped cushions that were brought out each summer.

Hanging out of her bedroom window, Imogen could see Lally practically hidden beneath her large straw hat sitting in her favourite corner of the garden sketching. She always got out her sketching things when she was nervous, and she was very nervous at present. She had begged not to come to Sanctuary for Imogen's ball. She had wanted to stay safely in London with Aunt Clara. But Mamma had insisted. People would say, where is the elder daughter, as if she were being hidden away. So instead she was hiding herself beneath her big garden hat, pretending to be invisible, while her pencil moved over the thick drawing paper, making her strange exaggerated likenesses of people that Aunt Clara said were very clever.

One felt that Lally's figure blurred by sun and shadow could have been a succession of figures, the blonde and forlorn Swedish bride from long ago, the young strange Tatiana who was supposed to have spent her later years as prisoner in one of the second-floor bedrooms, and Aunt Julia, who had been such a picture, like a white rose, Mamma said. Now there was Lally with her thick fair hair always falling out of its pins to hide her face.

Thank goodness you aren't one of the blonde Duncastles, Papa often told Imogen. You're all Webb, but prettier than me, eh?

No, she wasn't one of the slightly fey women that were part of her heredity, who seemed to shrink from life, or to literally disappear, as Aunt Julia had done. She was healthy, lively and happy. Or she would be happy if Rudi would only look at her as if he saw her, and would dance with her often enough to show admiration rather than merely good manners.

Rudi and Papa would be arriving from London in time for dinner. Hillary was driving over from Salisbury Plain where his regiment was on manoeuvres. Richard was not coming, unfortunately. It was too far to travel from Vienna. But he would soon be back in England permanently. There was so much martial music coming from Berlin, and everyone seemed so restless, the young eager, the old anxious. Some hothead, Richard said, was going to let off fireworks that would make an excuse for war.

"And I would hate that," he wrote to Imogen. "I'm not a soldier, whatever blood runs in my veins. I detest uniforms and guns. So I want to get home and let this explosion happen in Europe, the farther away the better. But I'll be thinking of your ball, Mog, and Sanctuary on a summer night. And *don't* fall for Rudi von Klein. Nice as he is, nice as his parents are. Though the Countess has got rather fat, and Charlotte takes after her. Charlotte is good-natured and jolly, but too much of an armful so I am in no danger!

"It's funny, isn't it, that our father who hates all mention of war—understandably, having had to live with Mamma's histrionics for years—has gone into partnership with a bank that well may be in the centre of the next war. In that case we will have to write off our losses, and also the von Kleins as friends. So remember that when Rudi uses all his charms on a susceptible little female creature like you."

It was June 1914. Imogen was eighteen years old. And she didn't intend to pay any attention to Richard's warnings. It was too late to do that anyway, for she had been in love with Rudi ever since she had been six years old.

Sanctuary, her best-loved place in the world, and a ball on a summer night. Her ball gown spread out on the bed, together with her satin dancing slippers, her long gloves, her programme with its tasselled gold pencil, the posy of white violets that Papa had sent, the necklet of seed pearls from Mamma.

It all spelled happiness, but happiness could be so fragile. Mamma knew. Her dearly loved brother Hillary had died a year before her coming-out. Money troubles were beginning. Her sister Julia was a constant burden. And the bulky unloved figure of Papa was on the horizon.

Imogen, Mamma said, would be luckier. Not that Papa had not been a good husband, but a young girl should not have to marry against her wishes. You will be allowed to make your own choice, my darling, Mamma said, but then came the sting—as long as you choose an Englishman, of course.

It had always been formidable opposing Mamma. Now that she was middle-aged, she had become commandingly handsome, her glorious dark amber hair only slightly streaked with grey, her brilliant green eyes very direct and domineering, her nose seeming to have grown longer and bonier. She expected Imogen to marry one of Hillary's friends, one of those stiff-backed young men who all looked alike, and didn't know how to talk to a girl.

"Why didn't you ever marry, Minnie?" Imogen asked Minnie, who was putting up her hair.

"Well, I had you lot, didn't I?" said Minnie cheerfully.

"Yes, but I expect secretly you wanted to be married. Don't all women? Would you have married a foreigner if a terribly nice one had asked you?"

"Not me, Miss Imogen. I'm like your mother, I don't trust them. Well, they're different from us, aren't they? You stay in your own country, there now."

"Mamma wants me to be an army wife."

"It's the least she'll expect of you, Miss Imogen, seeing you aren't a man and can't go to war."

"So you've noticed that, too. I mean how bloodthirsty she is."

"That's putting it a bit strong. I'd call her patriotic."

"It's more than that. Fighting for your country, acquitting yourself well on the battlefield is the only thing that is important to her. She scares me. But I'll marry who I please, or not at all."

Minnie gave her deep good-natured chuckle.

"Can't see you a spinster, Miss Imogen. Poor Miss Lally, perhaps, but not you. You see what happens tonight."

Yes, everything depended on tonight. And she had her plan, which was to lure Rudi out into the garden. Just about midnight, she thought, when they had both drunk enough champagne to be reckless. Surely the combination of distant dance music, moonlight over the fragrant gardens, the sleeping swans glimmering on the lake, and herself, a little dim and mysterious in her soft white gown, would provide the necessary alchemy.

He would discover that she was a woman. He had looked on her for too long as Hillary's and Richard's young sister, and the baby of the family. He would discover that she had dignity, poise, a touch of imperiousness, and that to be allowed to kiss her would be a great privilege.

"If you go on looking as fierce as that," said Minnie, "I doubt if anyone's going to dance with you, even if it is your own ball."

"I was trying to look mysterious."

"Ha! That's funny. You look just like a cross little

Pekinese. Now you laugh and be happy, Miss Imogen. That's what's natural to you."

One doubted if Sanctuary had ever been so gay as it was on this night. The motors, interspersed with some now decidedly old-fashioned carriages, began drawing up to the door at nine o'clock. Hillary, accompanied by three noisy fellow officers, drove a bright red Bentley. He swept round the curved drive like a miniature fire engine, his finger on the hooter, and finally stopped in the middle of the lawn. Then the four officers charged up to the front door as if they were storming an enemy redoubt, Papa said disapprovingly. He took Hillary aside and advised him to persuade his friends to go easy on the champagne. This was his sister's ball, not a drunken mess room party.

Hillary stood very erect and saluted.

"Troops will be informed, sir."

Papa didn't look amused, but Mamma, with the radiant soft look she reserved for Hillary, pulled his head down to kiss him, and told him to behave. "The band's beginning in a few minutes. You and your friends will see that all the girls get partners, won't you? We don't want any wallflowers."

Hillary murmured something about a certain Daisy Martin, was she there, a redhead, he had specially asked that she be invited. Imogen knew whom he meant, and also knew that Miss Martin had not been invited. Mamma considered her too fast. There had been some scandal, apparently. Hillary was not going to be pleased when he discovered her absence. He liked racy types. Innocence, the outstanding element of a debutante dance, bored him, and when he was bored he was apt to drink too much. Though he was never disgracefully drunk, only high-spirited and uncontrollable and with that hint of desperation in his eyes. As if he had some secret unhappiness.

Actually it was Rudi, the outsider, perhaps to Mamma's chagrin, who behaved impeccably that evening. He danced with all the girls, including Lally, who stumbled reluctantly round the floor with him, then fled to her refuge at

Minnie's side on the stairs. Imogen, Rudi decided, rated two dances. Only two. Hadn't she already too many partners lining up to claim her? This was true, but she counted every dance she had with handsome slightly inebriated army officers as a waste of time. The night was slipping away, and her state of angry frustration was increasing. Honestly, even when Rudi told her that she was astonishingly pretty, he was behaving to her like a brother. She wanted to aim a sharp kick at his ankles.

"Are you always going to treat me like a little girl with a skipping rope? Don't you ever *look* at me?"

"All the time," said Rudi amiably.

"Then can't you see that I'm Hillary's sister and I can be just as difficult as he can."

"What's the matter? Have I done something wrong?"

"Only taken me for granted."

"Oh, is that it? So what should I do to make amends?"

"First, get me another glass of champagne. Then I would like to be kissed. And really, you must see that it's very humiliating to have to ask."

Rudi gave her a slightly surprised look. Then he made a small bow.

"I will endeavour to fulfil both requests to your satisfaction. The champagne at the bar, the kiss—"

"On the terrace. Or shall we be daring and go down to the lake? It's more private there." She looked at him hard. "Or don't you have any desire to kiss me? It has to be equal on both sides."

It was a little while before he said thoughtfully, "Oh, yes. I think I can promise you equality. Shall we discuss this point afterwards?"

Imogen began to giggle.

"You're so pompous. I do love you."

"Love?"

"Love. How do you say it in your language?"

"*Lieb.*"

"Then that's what I'm talking about. Isn't it nice that we understand each other at last?"

"Imogen, do you think you should have any more champagne?"

"Oh, I'm not drunk. I'm just being honest. Or perhaps

I'm drunk enough to have the courage to be honest. Now could someone who is drunk think so profoundly?"

He slid his arm round her waist.

"And since when did you grow up?" he asked interestedly.

"Imogen! Where are you going?"

That was Mamma, barring the way on to the terrace. She looked splendid in her black and gold dress, slender and immensely straight, smiling in that quiet way that only Imogen recognized as intimidating. They could have excused themselves and pushed past her, but Imogen knew Rudi would not do this. He was too courteous.

"You were not planning to go into the garden, Imogen darling? You can't disappear at your own ball. That would be terribly bad manners. Let me see your programme."

"I've lost it," Imogen mumbled.

"Now that's a naughty little lie. I can see it in your reticule. May I just look? Ah, I see you are about to have this dance with Peregrine Webster. Isn't he one of Hillary's friends? A charming young man. Rudi, the next dance is a waltz, I believe. I love to waltz, and whatever talents my husband has, dancing isn't one of them."

Rudi gave Imogen a quick rueful glance, then made his correct little bow to Mamma.

"May I have the pleasure, Mrs. Webb?"

As always, Mamma had reduced her to childhood. Imogen blinked back angry tears. That lost kiss in the moonlight by the lake, she thought tragically. None that might take place in the future would ever make up for it. The fragile beautiful moment had escaped her forever. It was going to be hard to forgive Mamma for that.

"Our dance, I believe?" came the stiffly polite voice of Second Lieutenant Peregrine Webster. His pink face loomed over her. "I do hope I can keep off your feet. Over-indulged myself with the champagne, I'm afraid. It's an absolutely top-hole party."

"Is it?"

"Absolutely top-hole."

"Is that all you can say?"

"I'm sorry, am I boring you?"

"Yes." (I sound like Mamma, Imogen thought, in a kind of muted horror.) "You'd better come along or our dance will be over."

Once, across the room, she caught sight of Mamma's erect head, and Rudi's glossy brown one. She steered her decidedly unsteady partner in the opposite direction. When the music stopped and the couples wandered off the floor there was Mamma talking to a group of chaperones. There was no sign of Rudi.

Later, Papa danced with Imogen, holding her lovingly, his feet trampling over hers.

"This is my first dance, baby. I haven't dared tread anyone else to death."

"You're doing jolly well, Papa."

"I hate this damn house, but I'm here for you, so my heart's in it, you might say. All the same, I think it's been a good party. Hillary had better not drive himself back to barracks, but at least he holds his liquor like a gentleman. I suppose that's one thing the army has taught him."

Imogen pressed her head against the familiar solid chest.

"I adore you, Papa."

"And I you, little one. You and Richard. You make my life bright."

He didn't mention Mamma, or poor Lally from whom he winced, or Hillary who could have been a replica of several of the portraits on the stairs of the house that he hated. He had learned to compromise, dear Papa with his belligerent chin and his tired eyes. Did life always force one to compromise? Or was it the wise who submitted to those relentless rules?

The music was stopping and allowing other sounds to be heard. Some sort of disturbance outside the ballroom. A shouting, and footsteps running down the stairs.

"What's this?" Papa muttered. "Have I been too optimistic about the Major-General holding his liquor?" He gripped Imogen's arm and hurried her to the door.

The noisy altercation had stopped now. There was a circle of embarrassed young men in the hall, and

Mamma, like a statue in her glimmering dress, was half-way up the stairs, staring at Sanctuary's most famous work of art, the portrait of Major-General Sir Henry Richard Hillary Duncastle, V.C. It was horrifyingly splattered with ink, very black ink that was trickling slowly down the bright painted uniform. A silver-lidded inkwell (Imogen recognized it as coming from the library) lay broken on the stairs.

Papa was up the stairs in three bounds. He took Mamma's arm and said loudly, "A prank, my dear. That'll clean off. I rather think the old boy might have enjoyed this sort of thing in his heyday."

"It's not a prank, Joshua. It's desecration. Deliberate desecration." Mamma spoke as if the agony of being struck by the heavy inkwell had been hers.

"Well, we can't have a post mortem at present." Papa's voice was lower. "Ah, Minnie, that's a sensible woman."

Minnie was on the stairs gathering up the broken glass and mopping up the ink.

"Boys will be boys, sir," she said in one of her uncomfortable platitudes. "Even if they think they're grown-up men."

The group of young men in the hall stirred and muttered. They were all flushed and a bit dishevelled. Hillary, Imogen noticed, was not there, but Rudi was. He was neither flushed nor dishevelled. On the contrary he was pale and tight-lipped.

"The canvas is torn," Mamma cried. "Who could have done this vile thing?"

"Leave it now, Mattie. We'll go into it later," Papa said.

"No, it must be now, while we have witnesses." Mamma's outraged white face looked down at the group in the hall. "Which of you saw who threw the ink?"

No one had, it seemed. No one spoke. They were officers and gentlemen. They were not going to betray anybody. Then suddenly Rudi, his head held very high, made a step forward.

"It was I who did it, Mrs. Webb. Hillary and I were having one of our old arguments. You remember as boys we used always to fight. Hillary made me angry. He said his family militarily was much superior to mine, as evidenced by this illustrious soldier on the wall. It is regrettable, but I lost my temper and threw the inkwell. I apologize deeply. I think you would prefer me to leave the house at once."

Imogen thought she would never forget the glittering antagonism in Mamma's eyes. She looked at Rudi as if he were an enemy to be run through with a sword. Really, she was treating the unfortunate prank as if Rudi, the foreigner, had desecrated not only Great-grandfather Duncastle, but England itself. Her rage was quite out of proportion to the accident. A cold fearful suspicion settled in Imogen's heart. Great-aunt Tatiana, poor Julia, poor Lally, the long-ago pale unhappy wife from Sweden. Was Mamma a little touched by the Duncastle women's instability?

"I'm grateful for your confession, Herr von Klein," she said icily. "At least you have had the decency to clear these other young men. But yes, I would like you to leave my house."

"Now come, Mattie, the lad can't catch a train at this hour," Papa protested.

"Then he can wait at the railway station until one comes."

"Nonsense! I'll have none of it. If you insist on his leaving I'll motor him back to London myself. Be glad to shake the dust of this unlucky place off my feet, to tell the truth."

Perhaps Papa had meant his last words to be inaudible, but he, too, was outraged, not by Rudi, but by Mamma's inhospitability in front of so many people. He was deeply shocked. Yet he should have known after so many years how implacable she could be. Now there was going to be a scandal. The initial fracas between two young men a little inflamed by drink had been blown up into a major event.

The music had stopped, the ball was over prematurely, people were getting their wraps in an embarrassed silence. The ink had dried on the ruined portrait. And there was still no sign of Hillary. But Lally, who could always be trusted to do so, had burst into noisy sobs, and Papa, coming downstairs in his city clothes, exclaimed, "Make that crazy girl shut up," which remark was not going to lessen the scandal.

Imogen grasped at Papa's arm.

"Couldn't I come back with you?"

"I don't think so, little one."

"But Papa, I know Rudi isn't drunk. No one could have done that unless they were drunk."

"Perhaps he will be by the time we get to London." Papa's eyes were flaring yellow, a sure sign of his anger. "Perhaps I will be, too. So you'd better stay here, and help to clear up the mess." He chucked her under the chin. "It was a shame to spoil your ball, but everything in this life has to be paid for in one way or another. It forms character, they say. Now where is my young George Washington?"

Rudi appeared in the doorway, also with his overcoat on. He didn't look at Imogen, or at Mamma locked in her icy rage. He walked out, erect, stiff-shouldered, as if on parade. Papa followed him, and they were lost in the darkness.

Before Lally had stopped sobbing Hillary appeared. His face was ashen, his eyes red-rimmed. He looked as if he had been crying, though that was a preposterous idea. His eyelids were simply inflamed from too much alcohol. He went straight to Mamma and took her in his arms.

"Don't grieve, you silly old thing. Great-grandfather has been dead a long time. He isn't going to care if his good looks are spoiled."

"It's the insult, Hillary. It's quite unforgivable."

"Don't be such a tragedy queen, Mater. I believe you're enjoying this. Poor Rudi. Have we started a new war?"

"Don't be so foolish, dear boy. One act of vandalism doesn't start a war. But that young man ought to be punished."

"Everyone gets punished in the end," Hillary said, with a strange weariness. He really was the worse for all the champagne. "Now I've got to get back to barracks. Where's my little sister? Sorry about the abrupt end to your ball, Imogen. We'll make it up to you. Won't we, chaps? Now who's going to volunteer to drive because I can promise you I would end up in a ditch."

His white face had the bony austere handsomeness of his ancestors. He should have been a little blood-stained, Imogen thought, broken lance trailing in his hand. He was as accomplished at histrionics as Mamma was. But he had the authentic air of leadership that was a necessary part of being a Duncastle. His fellow officers were already automatically following him out into the night, as they would follow him, their ravaged young hero, in a charge against a real enemy.

"Oh, damn and hell!" said Imogen under her breath in a most undebutantelike way. But she was no longer a debutante. She had grown up too suddenly and with too much pain.

Chapter 12

The long night was not over although everyone had gone to bed. At first light Imogen was at last drifting into an exhausted sleep when her door was pushed open and the dim figure of Lally in her nightdress appeared. She looked ghostlike with her long hair unplaited and hanging loose round her wan face.

"Are you asleep, Imogen?"

"No."

"C-can I c-come in with you? I keep having n-nightmares." Lally was stuttering badly. She was always much worse under stress.

Imogen was too tired to be welcoming. But something had to be done when Lally was in this state, otherwise she graduated to hysterics. She pushed back the blankets resignedly. "What are you having nightmares about? It isn't you who has lost a lover."

"A l-lover? Rudi?"

"He would have been," Imogen said forlornly. "Except for Mamma. Dear interfering hateful Mamma. You'll have to watch her, Lally. I can take care of myself, but she'll gobble you up."

Lally crept into bed, shivering beside Imogen although it was a warm morning.

Imogen sighed despairingly. She had wanted Rudi, and what she got was silly scared Lally.

"She shouldn't have s-sent Rudi away," Lally said into the pillow. "It wasn't Rudi who threw the ink. I s-saw."

Imogen sat upright.

"I knew he didn't. Not that I cared if he did. Why should he admire our ancestors? But who was it, Lally? One of those dumb friends of Hillary's? I thought it was a typical mess room prank, but why did Rudi have to be such a gentleman?"

"He was l-looking after Hillary."

"Hillary!" Imogen was incredulous. "Hillary couldn't have done that. Not to his revered great-grandfather."

"He d-did. I saw him."

"Lally! Are you sure?"

"I was behind the f-ferns in the hall. Hoping no one would ask me to d-dance. I hate d-dancing." Lally clung to Imogen. "M-mamma m-mustn't know. P-please don't t-tell her. She would d-die."

"Yes. I believe she would if her darling Hillary were disgraced," Imogen said soberly. "But whatever could have made him behave like that? Was he showing off? Had Rudi provoked him?"

Lally shook her head back and forth. She was momentarily not there, her eyes vacant, the tip of her thumb in her mouth. Then she gave a small shudder and said, "It wasn't a p-prank. Hillary was c-crying." Abruptly Imogen remembered Hillary's drawn white face, his red-rimmed eyes. She couldn't take in the significance of Lally's information. Because if it were true it meant that Hillary, unlike Rudi, was far from being a gentleman. He had done the unacceptable. He had permitted someone else to take the blame for his misdeed.

"He—r-ran upstairs afterwards—when p-people came," Lally said. "I couldn't tell, c-could I?"

"But that means Rudi has been blamed for something he didn't do."

"Hillary's our b-brother. You d-don't t-tell on f-family." Lally's words were almost unintelligible.

Imogen made an abrupt decision. She leapt out of bed and began pulling clothes out of her wardrobe. Her lined coat and skirt, her straw boater, her strapped calf shoes.

"But neither do you let other people suffer," she said.

"What are you d-doing?" Lally cried in alarm. "You're not going to M-Mamma?"

"No, I'm going to London by the first train. I'll have to wake Rowley to drive me to the station. You can tell Mamma—" Imogen cast a glance at Lally's desperate face. "No, I'll write her a note and leave it on my pillow. Then you can say you knew nothing about it. I'll tell her I'm going to stay with Aunt Clara for a few days because, like Papa, I hate Sanctuary."

"But I thought you l-loved it."

"Not any longer. It's got too many interfering ancestors."

Lally's eyebrows rose in perplexity. Imogen leaned over and gave her a gentle push out of bed.

"You'd better go back to your own room. And don't make a noise."

"B-but—"

"This is my life, Lally, and I intend to manage it myself."

Aunt Clara, who had quietly but firmly refused to come to Imogen's ball because she said she did not belong in such a setting, had always been welcoming to all the children when they visited her in her small neat house in Cheapside. Today in spite of her surprise at the sight of Imogen clutching her small wicker travelling bag, standing on the doorstep in the hot mid-day sun, was no exception.

"Why, my dear child, have you run away?"

"You must know what happened last night," Imogen said breathlessly. "Hasn't Papa been here?"

"He has. But he only said that he and Rudi were in disgrace. What a shame on the night of your ball. But I believe Sanctuary does something to Joshua. It brings out the worst in him."

"Papa was wonderful," Imogen insisted. "So was Rudi. That's why I'm here." Aunt Clara's eyebrows raised a fraction.

"Does your mother know?"

"She will, by now."

"And am I to expect any more refugees from Sanctuary?"

"Not for a few hours, I expect. May I stay with you, Aunt Clara? I don't want to go home for a—well, for quite a long time."

"You know you're always welcome. But your mother isn't going to be very pleased with me for harbouring you. And your father must be told."

"I'm going to see him now."

"At this minute? No, you're not, my darling. You're going to freshen up and have some food and tell me what this is all about."

It had always been easy to talk to Aunt Clara, perhaps because she could never look intimidating. Her crooked eyes should make her a perpetual clown, but they didn't. They were oddly attractive. So was her plain gentle face. She wore a veil when she went out, yet Imogen thought her wrong to hide what she called her undistinguished face. Imogen thought it highly distinguished, much more so than Mamma's with its patrician elegance.

"Besides," Aunt Clara went on, "your father isn't in a very good temper. He was banging on my door at seven o'clock this morning, looking absolutely fagged out. He had just dropped Rudi at his lodgings, he said, and he wanted a couple of hours' sleep before going to the bank. I asked him what had happened, had a war between Austria-Hungary and England broken out, but all he said was that it was imminent. Did he think to enlighten me further before going to the bank? No. So the whole story is yours to tell me when you have refreshed yourself."

Another merit of Aunt Clara's was that she was a good listener. She had always given undivided attention to the most trivial of the children's stories. This story was not trivial. But she listened without interruption until Imogen had finished.

Her first question was, "Does your mother know about Hillary?"

"Not yet. How are we to tell her?"

"You don't tell her."

"But why should Rudi be the scapegoat?" Imogen demanded indignantly.

"Why did he choose to be, I wonder?"

"Because he wanted to save my mother distress. Because he's a true gentleman. Unlike my cowardly brother."

"Cowardly? Hillary?"

"I know it's hard to believe. He's always been Sir Lancelot and Sir Galahad and St. George rolled into one. But what else would you call him after running away like that? What will he do in the face of the real enemy?"

"Perhaps he regards your mamma as the real enemy," Aunt Clara said reflectively.

"Mamma! But they adore each other passionately. Oh, no, Aunt Clara, he was just drunk and didn't know what he was doing. Perhaps it was a dare."

"Perhaps it was. Does Rudi know?"

"I intend to find out. That's why I've come to London. I'm going over to Papa's bank now."

The tiled banking hall, the polished mahogany counters and the mesh grilles, the chinking of money like a small, twittering conversation, and the pervasive smell of cigar smoke, the grave gentlemen sweating on this hot day in their dark city clothes, conducting their business in low voices across the counters, were all familiar to Imogen. She was only infrequently allowed to come here, it was a male world and unsuitable for a young girl, Mamma had decreed. But she loved the solid rich atmosphere and the friendly smiles of the clerks. Once she had begun irrepressibly to skip on the black and white tiles, and the head cashier, bearded and solemn like Moses, had surprisingly become human, and winked at her.

Unlike Lally, the partners' room had never intimidated her. She simply knocked on the gold-plated door, saying, "I want to see my Papa," and marched in, whether Papa was in conference with a customer or not.

If the conference were important she was peremptorily ordered out, but if it were not, Papa sprang up and presented her to his customer.

"My younger daughter, Imogen. I believe she's come to take me out to luncheon. You must excuse us, sir."

And they really would go out to luncheon at Kentners in Soho or Simpson in the Strand, and all the waiters would make a great fuss of her, which she adored.

Papa would not be in conference today because he had not been expected at the bank. Nevertheless, seeing him was only a gesture. It was Rudi she wanted. He worked in one of the offices upstairs, and would have to be sent for.

"I want to see Rudi," she said imperiously, although noticing with a pang the wearily slumped figure of her father. He looked exhausted.

"Rudi isn't here. I took him to his lodgings and told him to get some sleep. I could do with a bit of that myself." Papa yawned noisily. "What a carry-on. And what are you doing in London, may I ask? Why aren't you helping your mother to sort out last night's mess! Why aren't you cleaning the ink off Great-grandfather God, eh?"

"Because Rudi didn't put it there. I know."

"You do, do you?" Papa's eyes, sunk in folds of weary flesh, had a faint but unmistakable cynicism.

"You know, too," Imogen exclaimed.

"Not because our gallant knight Rudi told me. I merely used my fairly reliable intuition."

"You *know* who it was, Papa?"

"I can make an inspired guess."

Imogen sighed with weary relief.

"Then you understand the awfulness of it. I mean, Hillary letting Rudi take the blame."

"I don't remember seeing the Major-General around at the time. Perhaps he didn't know about Rudi's gallant act until we'd gone, and then he felt the moment—or the need—for confession was past. I don't understand my elder son, Imogen. All I do understand is that he isn't part of me. He's all Duncastle."

"Mamma has made him that."

"True. But there are his looks as well. If she had sculpted him with her own hands she couldn't have made him more like all those bloody—sorry, my love—all those Duncastle ancestors. It's a bit uncanny, really. But what do you think? Should we keep this nasty bit of truth from her?"

Imogen shook her head slowly. She was terribly tired. Too tired to imagine Mamma's stricken look, as if something within her had been brutally killed.

"That's what Aunt Clara said, as well. I'd like to, but not at Rudi's expense."

"I fancy Rudi wouldn't mind."

"But he'll never be allowed in our house again if Mamma doesn't know the truth. Won't he mind that?" Imogen's eyes implored her father to make the right answer.

"A week ago he might have, but not now. I have to tell you, little one. Rudi's waiting to hear from his father. He's expecting to be summoned back to Vienna. We got the news when we arrived back this morning. The Archduke Franz Ferdinand has been assassinated."

"The heir to the Austrian throne? The fat prince who came to King Edward's funeral?"

"The fat prince who is never going to enjoy overeating again. Some Serbian madman was the assassin. Although he would call himself a patriot, no doubt. But it's madmen who change the world."

Apprehension, and then the chilly finger of fear, touched Imogen.

"Will Austria-Hungary go to war?"

"Very likely. If they were a naval power like the British they'd send a gunboat. As it is they'll deliver an ultimatum and then march, I've no doubt. Then the Russians will mobilize on one side of the border and the Kaiser's armies on the other. Do you know one thing, Imogen? I'm afraid the courage of our own Major-General is going to be tested properly before very long."

"You don't suspect Hillary's courage, Papa!"

"Now you sound just as outraged as your mother would be. No, I don't doubt it, but neither do I believe it. I simply don't know my son. To my knowledge he's a good-looking body in a uniform, but what motivates him I don't know."

"Is there really to be a war?" Imogen asked fearfully.

"What was it Shakespeare said? Something about greyhounds straining at the leash. Those grey Uhlans Rudi talked about, all the guns and the shells and the bayonets and the battleships. They're not intended for the scrapheap. So things get into their true perspective. The inked face of the hero of the Crimea becomes just a schoolboy prank, doesn't it? Rudi will be going, little one, and I'll be sending for Richard."

"Oh, Papa!"

"So in view of everything don't tell your mother, eh? Kinder to keep her in ignorance. And if you want to wake Rudi to say goodbye here's the address of his lodgings. In Bury Street, St. James. You can get a cab. It's a respectable area for a young lady. He's a fine fellow, Rudi. I wish he were my son."

"But then he'd be my brother, which I wouldn't like a bit!"

Papa's hand descended on Imogen's shoulder.

"Nothing can come of this now, you understand. You might think you're in love, but you're so young. I don't know how Rudi feels, of course, but I rather suspect you bowled him over last night."

"We might have kissed," Imogen said furiously. "If Mamma—"

"There you are, you see. Obstacles. Insurmountable. You'd have to wait until after the war—if there is one. And then—who knows?"

Imogen flung herself into her father's arms.

"Papa, don't look so like doom. I can't bear it."

"Sorry, little one. I'm thinking of our Balkan railway debentures. We're going to lose catastrophically on them. Worry about that for me, and stop interrupting serious business with flippant things like young love. Now run off and give Rudi that belated kiss."

"I can go alone? Mamma would say my reputation would be ruined forever."

"To hell with reputations. Live, girl, live." Papa pinched her cheek, but his eyes were bleak. "Anyway, wait until you see Rudi's landlady."

As Papa had warned her, Rudi's landlady was a person to be reckoned with. A small voluble lady with a tight knob of grey hair and inquisitive black eyes, she stared at Imogen with suspicion and disapproval.

"Mr. von Klein didn't come in until breakfast time this morning. I think he's sleeping. What his boss is saying about his not being at his desk I don't know. But he's a German, what can you expect of them? And the house rules are no young ladies in young gentlemen's sitting rooms."

"He isn't a German, he's an Austrian," Imogen said. "It happens to be my father he works for, and it was my father who sent me here."

"To wake him up?" said the woman, with a sharp look. "I could do that for you."

"Then will you? I have to see him urgently. If you won't let me go up to him, have you a room downstairs where we could talk?"

"Well—I suppose you look a respectable young person. You'd better wait in the front parlour. What's the trouble? Lovers' quarrel?"

"I just need to talk to him. Please!"

The front parlour was a most unlikely place for an assignation. It was neat and drab, antimacassars on the chair backs, dark brown walls, lace curtains drawn across the narrow windows, a collection of coy china kittens and puppies on the mantelpiece. No one could possibly converse in here. The sterile atmosphere would dry up words, just as it was drying Imogen's tongue and making her tense with uncertainty.

She could hear the landlady's voice at the top of the stairs.

"A young lady to see you, Mr. von Klein. Who? I didn't ask her. She looks respectable, otherwise I should have sent her packing. Says you work for her father.

What? Yes, I thought that would wake you. I'll tell her you'll be right down."

Rudi could not have been asleep because he came running down the stairs in the immediate wake of his landlady. He was fully dressed, the only sign of discomposure his ruffled hair and a slightly crooked cravat.

"Imogen!" he exclaimed. "What are you doing here? But I am glad you have come because it gives me an opportunity to say goodbye to you. I'm on my way home. In the last hour I've had a telegram from my father. Have you heard the disastrous news?"

"About the Crown Prince?"

"Yes, he's been assassinated, and the army is mobilising. This is an historic hour for my country. One can hardly call last night's events fortuitous, but they have turned out to be so, because I would in any case have had to return to London immediately to arrange my affairs."

He was so full of anticipatory excitement that Imogen had to repress angry tears. Did he need to make it obvious how glad he was to be going home to an imminent war? He was as bad as Mamma. The two of them were war horses tossing their heads at the distant sound of guns.

"This room smells of mice," she said distastefully, and for no particular reason. When Rudi looked at her in surprise that she could make such an irrelevant remark she began to giggle. "It really does. Couldn't we go outdoors? Or do you have to catch a train this very instant?"

"Not this very instant. But I have things to complete at the bank. I must say goodbye to everyone, and do my packing."

"You have to say goodbye to me, too. You can spare me at least half an hour. Less than that I would consider bad manners."

His brows were raised quizzically.

"You sound just like your mother."

"I'm not in the least like my mother. Are you blind?"

"Not any longer."

Imogen blushed beneath his very intent gaze, and was annoyed with herself. At last she had what she had longed for, his complete attention, and she was colouring like an unsophisticated schoolgirl.

She took refuge in asperity.

"Why did you tell that lie last night?"

"What lie?" he asked airily.

"You know very well. It was Hillary who threw the ink, wasn't it? I know because Lally told me. She saw."

"Oh, dear. How inconvenient."

"*Why?* Because you want to be a hero or a martyr or something? Rudi, that's *childish*. If Hillary did it he must take the blame. Or are you such a gallant gentleman that you think you must protect my mother from painful things?"

"I wasn't protecting your mother. I was protecting Hillary. I know we argue and fight but I am fond of him, you see, and I think he is fond of me. If you forgive me for saying so, I don't think anyone in your family understands Hillary."

"We all know that he likes himself immensely."

"Does he?"

"Of course he does. He has from the moment he was born. First he was Mamma's pet—he still is—then he was the good little schoolboy passing all his exams, and later the outstanding cadet at Sandhurst, as everybody expected him to be. He's a born leader, he has the good looks that all Mamma's family have, he's pursued by all the prettiest girls. How couldn't he like himself, with so many advantages?"

"Then why does he drink too much?" Rudi asked.

Imogen hesitated, suddenly uneasy as she remembered Hillary's white face and reddened eyes.

"They all do in the officers' mess. Or at a party. Papa complains endlessly about Hillary's mess bills. He says they must bathe in champagne, and that being a soldier is a daft profession because you could never produce a balance sheet showing profit. Why do you think he drinks, Rudi?"

"Because he's afraid."

"Hillary! I can't believe that."

"It's true, nevertheless. Under all that born leadership, as you call it. He can't stand the thought of blood and the noise of battle, and dead men. He has a nightmare that he will run away when he has to face the enemy."

Imogen was appalled.

"But that's being a coward!"

"Which is inconceivable for your brother?"

"For anyone in my family. I mean courage is our tradition. We hear it enough from Mamma. All our lives we've had to look at those portraits and listen to stories of valour. Oh, Rudi! Is that why Hillary threw the ink at Great-grandfather? Because he hated him?"

"It was a nice idea," Rudi said, grinning. "It did Hillary a lot of good. He had been telling me that he felt as if all his brave ancestors were on his back. He hated them all. He finally even included *my* great-grandfather, the Field Marshal, in his dislikes."

"He must have been very drunk."

"He was. So naturally I protected him."

"How terrible!" Imogen whispered.

"No, no, it was nothing much to me."

"I meant how terrible that Hillary should have these secret fears. How awful for him keeping up a pretence all the time. And Mamma thinks he's the one who values our war trophies. He was certainly the one who named the Death Room."

"Doesn't that speak for itself? But he really is impressed with the Duncastle history and the trophies. He admires the dream but fears the reality. He has too much imagination. But don't look so worried. Soldiers who overcome their fears are the bravest."

"Supposing he doesn't overcome them. Oh, no, one can't contemplate that. It would kill Mamma if anything shameful happened."

"Nothing will kill your mother," Rudi said emphatically. "Oh, she might be embittered but alive she will be. Now have I offended you?"

Imogen's lips quivered, half between tears and laughter.

"Rudi, you're so nice. I adore you. Is it immodest to tell you?"

She thought his tender smile was beautiful.

"Do you know, I quite adore you, too. But could we do this mutual adoration out of this mice-smelling room in the park? For an hour. Sixty whole minutes." He took her arm. "I would have made this declaration last night, but for your mother."

"I hate her."

"Ah. That's a pity. Because people you hate always live forever."

They sat on a bench by the lake in St. James Park. The swans moved lazily on the green water. The sun was very hot. Most people had sought the shade, but they sat in the full blaze of the heat, Imogen's little straw boater only half shading her face, Rudi's unprotected skin looking damp and tanned and healthy. His brown curls were rumpled, unbrushed after his daytime sleep, his full lips pouted a little as if with an unwilling recognition of sadness.

"Are you afraid too, Rudi? I mean, if war actually comes." Imogen knew the question was unnecessary. This calm young man had none of the taut restlessness of her brother.

"No, not a bit. But I'm a dull fellow. I can't conjure up scenes of nightmare."

"You want to go!" Imogen accused.

He nodded. "But I want to stay here, too. Which gives me a dilemma. May I hold your hand?"

"Please."

"May I kiss you?"

"Please, yes."

Afterwards he said, "You're very sweet. Very very sweet." His voice lingered over the words as if he tasted them, as if they were part of the sensation his lips had just experienced.

This had not happened, as Imogen had planned, beside the lake at Sanctuary in the moonlight, but in glaring daylight in full view of passers-by. It wouldn't have mattered, Imogen concluded, if it had been in the middle of Piccadilly Circus or even in Mrs. Consett's dreadfully proper parlour. His lips would have tasted the same, the brushing of his cheeks against hers have given her that astonishingly delicious feeling.

"Am I the first English girl you have kissed?"

"No. But the nicest."

She sighed. "Why did we leave it so late?"

"I know. I've been a fool. I suppose I thought of you as part of our two families."

"No, it's not that, it's simply that you haven't looked at me."

"That's what I'm telling you." He traced her eyebrows, her nose, her lips, with his forefinger. "I did see you last night."

"But it's all too late! You're going away and there'll be a war, and when will we ever see each other again?"

"We can write."

"We can't. The letters will never come. It won't be Mamma stopping them this time, it will be some horrid military censorship."

"No, no, Austria isn't at war with England, only with Serbia."

"Then what is everyone talking about? War, war, war, they're all screaming. By just talking about it they'll make it happen."

The sun glittered on the ornamental lake, the water-birds dived and emerged, shaking crystal drops from their feathers, a Canada goose followed by a skittering tail of goslings foraged in the trim green grass.

"Is ours going to be the lost generation?" Imogen asked, with uneasy premonition.

"Now your imagination is worse than your brother's. Stop looking so sad. Have dinner with me tonight. I know a quiet little place in Jermyn Street."

"But you're leaving tonight."

"I've suddenly decided to make it tomorrow."

"Not so that you can have dinner with me?"

"Yes, exactly."

"Oh, Rudi, truly?"

"Can you escape the various dragons in your family?"

"Aunt Clara isn't a dragon. Neither is Papa. And Mamma's at Sanctuary, getting Great-grandfather repaired, no doubt."

"Splendid. I will call for you at seven o'clock."

The perfection of the moment brought tears to Imogen's eyes.

"I really have always loved you. Since I was six years old. Is that boring for you?"

"Very. But today I will endeavour to endure it."

She pinched his arm sharply, then ran away across the grass, her hat flying off and disturbing the goslings. They fell back into the water with liquid plops. Rudi caught her at the water's edge and she could see themselves reflected in the glassy surface. A merging and separating shimmer of whiteness and darkness.

We will always be here, she thought. This is our place.

Mamma was sitting in Aunt Clara's parlour.

Imogen rushed in, hot, excited, dangling her hat by its ribbon, ready to exclaim to Aunt Clara that she had had such a heavenly time.

And there was Mamma, like an empress on a throne, ready to raise a sword and personally slash off an erring subject's head. She was dressed in her neat black and white travelling clothes, and hadn't even removed her hat, though she had pushed her veil above her glittering green eyes.

I hate her, she had said to Rudi. Now, in a moment of terrifying honesty, she knew that those harsh words were true. Not all the time, perhaps, but certainly now when her freedom and happiness were threatened.

"So you've come to London, too, Mamma," she said with deliberate flippancy. "Poor Aunt Clara must wonder what this invasion is all about."

"She must, indeed," said Mamma in her iciest voice.

"Where's Lally? Has she come, too?" (How does my face look? Is it giving away all my secrets? I have to meet Rudi tonight. I have to.)

"Lally is at Sanctuary with Minnie. She is waiting for us to return."

"Tomorrow?" said Imogen airily. "Of course, Mamma."

"I had meant this evening. There's a train at seven fifteen."

"But, Mamma, you can't do that long journey twice in one day. It's too exhausting."

"Do I look decrepit?"

"Of course not, but in this heat—"

"You're the one who looks exhausted. You're very flushed. Are you feverish?"

Imogen's hands went to her hot cheeks.

"I'm a little sunburnt, that's all."

"And how did you contrive to get sunburnt in the city?"

"It's this ridiculous hat." Imogen threw the hard little boater on to a chair pettishly. "Such a stupid fashion. I was only having a walk in the park. Papa—said I could."

"Alone?" No one had such an uncompromising voice as Mamma. It was a waste of time and energy to pretend to her. Oppose her, yes, but lying to her never succeeded.

Imogen sank tiredly into a chair. "I was with Rudi. As you very well know. And honestly, Mamma, you can't blame me because I had no opportunity last night to say goodbye to him. You ordered him out of the house, don't you remember."

"Don't speak to me in that impertinent way. I'm very angry with you. Surprised, too. It would have been most undignified of you to run after any young man, but that you could do so with a bad-mannered undisciplined one like Rudi von Klein is beyond my belief. I forbid you to see him again."

Suddenly, in Imogen's mind, there was a small hazy picture—the diamonds twinkling in Mamma's beautiful hair, her high held head, her rigidly controlled anger as Count Paul von Klein gently punctured her regality, making it theatrical and just a little absurd. Understanding, but not pity, came to her.

"Don't you ever forgive anyone, Mamma?"

Mamma, who couldn't possibly have known of that picture in Imogen's mind, said emphatically, "Not rude young men who abuse hospitality. But then Rudi is a foreigner."

Imogen's moment of weariness passed. She sat up vigorously.

"But he has two arms and two legs, and two eyes and a nose and a mouth and a stomach and lungs and heart just the same as us. Foreigners are human beings, Mamma."

"Now, don't get hysterical, child. You're being absurd.

I'm merely telling you that as my daughter I forbid you to have any more associations with Rudi."

"I'm Papa's daughter, too. He doesn't forbid me."

Mamma's face tightened.

"It's my place to guide you, not your father's. Men are too soft and sentimental about their daughters. So we will go back to Sanctuary tonight, and you can have a few quiet days to recover from this foolish escapade."

"But haven't you heard about the Austrian Archduke, Mamma? Don't you know we're on the edge of a terrible catastrophe?"

"Such pompous statements for a little girl. Why should we in England be concerned with Austria's domestic affairs? Of course, if Germany interferes and England has to declare war, that will be an entirely different matter."

"But Rudi's father has sent for him to come home at once. We have to say goodbye. It might be forever."

Mamma's voice remained brisk and sensible, although it seemed that her eyes had softened.

"Then isn't it better to forget the whole thing? Now, before you're both too involved. You're much too young, my darling. Besides, if there is a war your duty is whole-heartedly in England, not sympathising with the enemy. Haven't you thought about patriotism?"

Imogen's lips were quivering with desolation.

"I believe, I really believe, you love sacrifices, Mamma. If Hillary has to go to war you'll hold up your head and smile with joy."

"With pride. Which is entirely different. Yes, I do believe in being able to willingly make sacrifices for a just cause, a cause involving one's own country. That is the strength of the British. My family has proved it over and over. If there is war, Hillary's regiment will be one of the first to leave these shores, and I will watch it go without tears. Tears, my dear Imogen, are an impermissible weakness. You will learn. So—come here—let me dry your eyes. Silly baby."

She hadn't entirely grown up after all. Mamma's hypnotic power was having its effect once more. Kind, sensible, practical, even loving—once she had got her own way. Imogen made to get up and run out of the room, devastated by her corruptibility—it was like being unfaithful to Rudi already—but a strange dizzy darkness struck her. She swayed and stumbled, and Mamma had to catch her to prevent her from falling.

"Imogen! Are you ill? Clara! Come quickly."

They laid her on the couch, and the two kind faces looked down at her, Mamma's concerned and maternal, Aunt Clara's nodding knowledgeably.

"Not surprising, Mattie. Up all night, rushing about in this heat, not eating. Eighteen-year-old girls are vulnerable creatures. I'll take her upstairs to bed. She can sleep until dinner, and you'd better put any ideas of going back to Sanctuary today out of your head."

"How tiresome!" Mamma said. "Yes, I expect you're right, Clara. But can you give me a bed, too? I've shut up the Kensington house. And I'll have to send a telegram to Sanctuary; otherwise I'll have another daughter in hysterics. You're very wise, Clara, not to have had daughters."

"Or sons?" Aunt Clara asked quizzically.

"Oh, sons are a different matter entirely. They don't let their emotions run away with them."

Chapter 13

"Aunt Clara," Imogen said urgently. The dizziness had passed, but she felt desperately tired and was very glad to lie down in the small spotless bedroom that Aunt Clara kept for her and Lally's use.

"What is it, my dear?"

"Rudi's coming here tonight. What am I to do?" Aunt Clara's face showed no surprise or perturbation.

"Send him away, I expect."

"I can't do that! He was going to take me to dinner, just by ourselves. It's to be a farewell dinner, so I must go. It's the last chance I have in my life to be happy."

"H'mm. At eighteen. And you fainting across the table in the restaurant, no doubt."

"I won't faint, don't be silly."

"One never knows what emotional girls will do. However, I can see that isn't the problem. It's the difficulty of your mother being here, isn't it?"

"Why did she have to come? I'll have to sneak out while you keep her occupied and then you'll have to say I'm fast asleep and can't come down to dinner."

"What makes you think I'm on your side?"

"Oh, darling Aunt Clara, you always have been."

"Don't try blackmailing me. What can I do about this?"

"You'll think of something. Talk to Papa. Make him persuade Mamma to be more understanding. Can't he remind her of when she was young?"

"I doubt if that would be the right thing to do," Aunt Clara said drily. "Your mother was brought up to have a great sense of duty. Victorian girls were."

"But I don't expect she had any temptations. Not real ones. She would have been far too well-behaved."

"Now, Imogen, my dear, being young and headstrong doesn't excuse you being stupid. Tomorrow Rudi will be gone and whether you think so or not you'll need your mother as a friend. So don't misjudge her. Don't think she's heartless."

"No, I don't think that," Imogen said reluctantly, again remembering that long-ago scene in Vienna when Mamma had obviously repressed and conquered violent feelings.

But couldn't she have given way to those feelings, wouldn't that have made her more human, more understanding, less set on those tiresome paths of discipline, unselfishness, orderliness and duty?

If she had given way, however, Papa would have been stabbed in the heart. So would Rudi's mother, the comfortable jolly unsuspecting Countess Amalie.

One had to think of both sides of a situation, one had to be fair.

"Aunt Clara, I intend to marry Rudi."

"Of course. When the war is over."

"It isn't our war. He isn't an enemy."

"We'll have to wait and see, won't we? But certainly, when the war is over, he'll no longer be an enemy. Myself, I'd like to blow up that gaggle of Field Marshals and Generals and Kaisers and von Hindenburgs, sit them on a powder keg, the whole dangerous lot of them."

"Aunt Clara, if you talk like that you and Mamma are going to get on like a house on fire."

Aunt Clara's face was aggressive and angry in a way Imogen had never seen it.

"I was a Victorian young lady, too, you must remember. We were not taught to think of ourselves. I love you dearly, little one, you know that. But I won't have you wallowing in self-pity. You'll hold up your head, and if we've got to fight you'll be proud of being an English-woman. And be damned to the enemy."

"Goodness, Aunt Clara!" Imogen gave a faint giggle.

"But I suppose I must see what can be done about your Rudi. Now for the moment stop being grown-up. Be a child again and go to sleep."

When Imogen woke up Rudi was sitting by her bed.

She couldn't believe it. She put out her hand to touch him, to see if he were real, and he grasped it between his and held it tightly.

"I fell asleep. Is it late?"

"Pretty late. Too late for dinner."

"Oh!" Imogen peered at the bedside clock drowsily. "No, it isn't. It's only eight o'clock. Couldn't we—"

"No. I am sorry."

Wide awake and furious, Imogen sat up.

"They've got at you downstairs."

Rudi nodded. "What else could be expected with your mother here? But she has permitted me to come up to say goodbye. Briefly."

"Very briefly, you can be sure. She's against lovers."

"Only the wrong lovers, perhaps."

"But we're not wrong, we're right!"

"Except that an eagle presided over my birth and a lion and a unicorn over yours."

"We're star-crossed," Imogen said with a forlorn feeling of pride. "Romeo and Juliet. Family feuds."

"Your mother was fair enough to let me come up and see you. Your Aunt Clara is a wonderful lady, and of course I have the greatest respect for your father. By the way, Richard is to come home, too. So you will have him to comfort you."

"I won't. He'll be pushed right into the army, if I know Mamma. It's the opportunity she's been waiting for."

"Nevertheless, he will be in England. I have to go now, *liebling*."

"Oh, I love it when you call me *liebling*. Don't go. Stay here. Please!"

Rudi shook his head. The light was too dim to see what was in his eyes.

"This was a special concession. After all, I am the man who blackened your great-grandfather's face."

"Rudi, you're standing there as if you're visiting a sick aunt. Come and kiss me."

He backed towards the door. "No, I think not. It will make it harder. You're so soft from sleep. So pretty and pink, like a crumpled rose." Now, in the dark, she could see his eyes gleaming. "I promise I'll be back as soon as I can come."

Imogen's voice quivered.

"I'll wait. If you want me to."

"Don't grow too old in three months, eh?"

"Only three months?" she said hopefully. But she knew it would be more. Much more.

"That's what I believe," he said and turned and was gone, clattering down the stairs. Fearful of the temptations of that warm dusk-filled bedroom, sad at leaving, but eager to be gone to the deadly excitement of his soldier's world.

A little later Mamma came up, carrying a tray. She had changed from her travelling clothes and was wearing her olive-coloured tea gown. She must have sent to the Kensington Square house for night things. She would never have slept in her petticoats, or indeed in a borrowed nightgown of Aunt Clara's. Not Mamma. Correct in all things. Except that she had let Rudi come upstairs to see Imogen alone in her bedroom, an unbelievable concession. But in spite of the softness that the ruffled tea gown gave her, she could not hide the glitter in her eyes. It was the same look that Rudi had had, of anticipation, of sheer excitement at the knowledge of the struggle ahead. Of determination and courage and patriotism and intense pride.

People like this were dangerous, Imogen thought confusedly. They provided ammunition for the war makers. Whatever lay ahead, even something so dreadful as Hillary being disgraced, Mamma was never going to let that proud mask slip and show her agony. One had to admire her. But to be wary of her, too. She could be insidiously persuasive, hence the tray with its steaming bowl of soup and fingers of buttered toast, which she had carried up with her own hands. Yet she was made of iron.

Rudi was not made of iron. He was still pliable. But now the war had taken him and if he ever came back he would be different. It was inevitable.

Abruptly Imogen began to cry. She supposed she must have wanted Mamma's arms, clad in their soft, scented silk, round her. This was reverting to childhood. It was something she couldn't control. But even while she pressed her face against Mamma's breast she knew that although through fate and other things she had lost this first adult skirmish, she would not allow herself to lose the next. She could be made of iron, too.

"Dry your eyes, Imogen. Here's my handkerchief. And eat your supper. You'd be surprised how often it's only an empty stomach that makes one think the world has come to an end. And Richard is coming home. You'll like that, won't you?"

"Only to g-go into the army." She was stuttering like Lally.

"Naturally. If war is declared. But it hasn't been yet, and we'll have time to all be together at Sanctuary. You know how Richard loves being there. And Hillary will get some leave before the summer's over. Just think, it's nearly July already. The peaches will soon be getting ripe."

The soothing words meant nothing at all. The glitter in Mamma's eyes, sunlight on steel, cancelled them out.

Third Interval

Now the old lady, waking again, realised why it was so dark. The curtains had been drawn because of air raids. One never knew when that monstrous German invention, the Zeppelin airship, would loom out of the clouds and sail on its destructive way across London. She thought she could hear the cracking of anti-aircraft guns, frustratingly out of range of that great airborne whale.

She must go to Lally who became petrified with fear at anything beyond her understanding. Or was it Julia of whom she was thinking? It was perhaps as well that Julia had not lived to endure this war. If she were actually dead, of course. After more than twenty years one had to assume she was. No, it was Lally who shut herself in her room when the Zeppelins sailed overhead, Lally who could never be taken to the seaside at Sandwich or Deal because when she heard the distant boom of guns in France she began to weep, and wept for hours. She was thinking of Hillary and Richard, she said, lifting her permanently tear-splotched face.

"And Rudi," Imogen reminded her.

Imogen had been forbidden to mention Rudi's name

since he was now fighting on the Western front, killing British soldiers. At least, so Papa had heard through some underground network from the bank in Vienna. Imogen's face had lost the round soft contours of girlhood and become sharp and starved looking. Starved! Matilda thought indignantly. Her children! There was still plenty of food. The threatened submarine blockade had not begun.

But how did she know about the German submarines prowling the Atlantic, menacing shipping, trying to cut off England's lifelines, if the blockade had not begun?

She stirred fretfully on her pillow. She was afraid she was dreaming again, muddling the past with the future, remembering shadows. Shadows they all were now— Hillary taking her to tea at the Ritz on his last leave, crumbling his cake, talking in half-finished sentences, beside himself with eagerness to get into the fight. At least, that was how she interpreted his feverish restlessness.

"I've made my will, Mamma."

"Your will, dear boy?"

"It's just routine. We all have to make wills. Some of the men have practically nothing to leave, their stamp collection or their best Sunday suit. One left his dog to his girlfriend."

No, it wasn't at the Ritz that she remembered Hillary most vividly, it was entraining at Victoria station, marching at the head of his company, rigidly erect, pencil slim, proudly wearing his newly acquired badge of rank. Captain Hillary Duncastle setting out to war. No, of course he was Captain Hillary Webb. But as a soldier in uniform he was forever a Duncastle in her eyes.

Imogen, my dear little sister, I can't describe the utter foulness of this war . . . Don't tell Mamma . . .

That was a letter she had not been meant to see and had forgotten so completely that only now the searing words sprang again before her eyes.

My dear Mother, It is almost quiet again after the last battle, at least quiet enough to hear a few birds singing. We found some windfall pears in an old orchard, but the early frosts had got at them. It's getting cold at nights . . .

Cold at nights . . .

The old lady in bed shivered violently as if the same

chilly early Flemish frosts, or another more sinister cold, were raking her emaciated body.

With an enormous effort she dragged herself out of the shadows. But the rat-tat of a drum, ragged and unsteady, had begun again in her head. Of course it was young Johnnie. She had showed him how to beat the Salamanca Drum with his baby fingers, and Imogen had been furious.

"I won't have my son corrupted."

Corrupted? Whatever did she mean? The little boy adored the drum. He always demanded it, in his imperious Duncastle way.

"I'm going to play my drum now, Granny."

My drum. A Duncastle through and through, even if Imogen angrily rejected the fact. So life went on. Nothing was ever ended.

Or was it ended? For who now was there to beat the drum? Except the ghosts in her head.

"Mrs. Webb, you've been ever so far away. Are you dreaming again?"

That damned nurse intruding once more.

"I've been marching down a long road lined with dark trees. Those dark, pointed trees like black candles. What are they? You must know. They're in France."

"It's mostly poplars along the roads in France, Mrs. Webb. You must be thinking of the trees leading to the cemetery where your husband's buried. Cypresses."

Not cypresses! she wanted to shout. Young trees, newly-leaved willows, hawthorn frothing with white blossom, poplars if you like, lindens. No, lindens were in Vienna.

She hadn't been crying at Joshua's funeral. That was a sober fact. But for some reason she wanted to cry now. Because of the children's voices, the fat eager fingers banging away at the shabby drum.

"Johnnie will wear it out, Mamma." Imogen was always so disapproving, so hostile. "And a good thing, too."

"I've brought you a nice cup of tea, Mrs. Webb. All that mob downstairs will soon be gone, and you can have some peace."

Peace? For her?

Chapter 14

For once, later that summer, they were all at Sanctuary, even Joshua. Richard was back from Vienna. Since the Germans had invaded Belgium, and Great Britain and France had declared war, calling the Kaiser's bluff, Richard had enlisted as a private, although he would have to resist pressure to be sent on an officers' training course. What Duncastle had ever been a private?

"But I'm a Webb," he said, with a stubborn pride that made Matilda tighten her lips and Joshua's eyes go moist.

So Joshua had two sons in the army after all, but one only on loan, so to speak. Please God, Richard would survive to resume his banking career, and not attempt the sort of crazy and unnecessary acts of heroism that it was almost certain Hillary would perform.

Matilda, from the moment war had been declared, had gone into action. She was organising committees, urging on the lethargic or the stupid or the hysterical or the plain scared. It was her belief that every woman was much happier and more sane if she were busy, not to mention the matter of the contribution she could make to her country. There was so much to be done, especially if the war should last a year or more. And what well-informed person, knowing the strength of the Germans, could expect a victory in less time than that?

She had never longed so much to be a man. When Hillary finally embarked for France she would want to march with him every step of the way down the long dusty roads towards the sound of the guns.

Since this could not be, she plunged fiercely into work, and even had an audience with the Queen, discussing all the useful and necessary roles women could play. Apart from emergency hospitals and convalescent homes (the enormous country houses of the rich could be put to this use), and volunteer nursing services and comforts for the troops, there were the bereaved, the mothers, the widows, the war orphans. That last service she would like to make her special province. After all, as a member of a military family she had an inherited knowledge of loss. It helped a mother's grief a great deal to be told that her son had died in that most privileged of ways, for his country. She would make England a nation of heroic women.

But during that late autumn week down at Sanctuary she relaxed and wore pale-coloured floating gowns and looked, said Imogen, like a rose going brown at the edges. With a worm consuming it, she added cruelly. She was a menace with her over-developed sense of patriotism, a vampire waiting for young fresh blood to flow.

"She can't be an overblown rose and a worm and a vampire," Richard said lazily. "And when did you become so vindictive, Mog?"

"She's the kind of person who doesn't flinch from war," said Hillary tightly. "You should be proud of her."

"She glamorises armies and martial strength," said Richard. "That's unhealthy."

"Rudi's a soldier and she doesn't glamorise him. That's where she's not fair." Imogen, desperately anxious about Rudi, was going through one of her hating-her-mother phases, convinced that people like her were responsible for wars, just as much as the German Kaiser was.

"It's the Kaiser and his minions we're supposed to be reviling," said Richard. "Not our brilliant clever handsome efficient flag-waving mother. Actually, she'd make a splendid wife for the Kaiser."

That took the bitterness out of the conversation. They all laughed, Hillary the loudest. He would make nothing but nervous trivial conversation, giving a convincing imitation of a smart young officer without any intellectual interests. The three of them lay at ease on the summer-browned grass, and a little distance away Lally sat in a deck chair and sketched them.

"While we're all t-together," she said, making her curious spiky portraits that bore an uncanny likeness to her sitters, despite their haphazard quality.

Imogen thought that this kind of thing must often have happened at Sanctuary, the family gathered for the last farewell before another Duncastle son left for India or the Crimea or to follow the Duke of Wellington across the heat-dazzled Spanish plains.

The Germans were over-running Belgium, the immaculate Uhlans armed with lances, sabres and pistols trotting down village streets, victorious and lethal, hauling down the Belgian flag and raising the black eagle of the German Empire. No one knew how heavy the losses the British Expeditionary Force had suffered because censorship stifled the news. There were stories about raped women and children, about babies impaled on bayonets.

Where was Rudi? Imogen had had only one message from him, a comical sentence scribbled on the train and dispatched from Dover. *"My dear little goose girl, When you visit our feathered friends in the park, you will remember me perhaps? Your Rudi."*

As if she needed to feed the ducks and the geese in St. James Park to remember him. He was everywhere, all the time. She had intended to take Hillary to task for never confessing his part in the ink-throwing episode. But the empty space on the wall, now that the Major-General was away being cleaned and restored, was a little uncanny. It made Imogen feel superstitious. Supposing Hillary, who was secretly afraid of battle (if Lally and Rudi were to be believed), also left an empty space, this gay young officer clowning, drinking champagne, pretending to be brave enough to slay dragons. No, the accusations would have to wait until after the war. At present one must help Hillary to maintain his façade. Mamma's calm and determined demeanour was natural. Hillary's was a gaiety covering desperation. One saw his slack pale face when he thought himself unobserved.

It was easy now to see why Papa found banking comforting. He had only to worry about the freezing of the bank's assets in enemy countries, the depreciation of foreign bonds and debentures. Not flesh and blood.

And shortly he would find ways of financing industries profitable to his bank. Why not? Someone ought to get something out of this crazy war.

"I heard that Rudi blotted his copybook," Richard said to Imogen. "Or Great-grandfather's face, to be more explicit. Doesn't sound like old Rudi to me. I thought he was a model of good behaviour."

"Don't ask questions about that," Imogen answered. "It's all—well, something we don't talk about to Mamma. But don't blame Rudi."

"Ah—do I get the gist?"

"It doesn't matter any more." Imogen was bitter and angry. "Rudi's supposed to be our enemy now—as if he could be, no matter what Mamma says about foreigners— and what happened that night is just trivial compared to what he's facing now." She added with certainty, "I know that's what he'd be thinking because I know how he thinks."

"You and Rudi had begun something, hadn't you?" Richard's voice was gentle in the way that Papa's could be. Both being aggressive outspoken men, their lapse into gentleness was a potent weapon. Some day a woman would find this out about Richard even if Mamma had never allowed herself to recognise it in Papa. But Richard would not marry a woman like Mamma.

"I love him," Imogen said, tears starting to her eyes. "Yes, you're right, it was just beginning for him, but for me it had been always."

"It's not particularly practical to be faithful to one love, Mog. It's a long life."

"You wait and see for yourself."

"Oh, I'll never be like that. I knew a nice little girl from Grinzing. Flaxen hair, pink cheeks, soft as a cushion. Lottie. She cried when I left. But now I can hardly remember what she looked like. Except for a rather devastating dimple in one cheek. Men are pretty base creatures, on the whole. And talking of that, do we have to cover up for our not-so-brave brother?"

"Richard, you know about that!"

"I'm reasonably intelligent. After all I'm only a year younger than Hillary. I've lived with him all my life. Even at school he put on an act. Very successfully, too. He should have been on the stage."

"Oh, poor Hillary!"

"He won't let the side down. He never did. Just had his private nightmares, and played with his toy soldiers. That was all right when he could pretend war was a game. He could reconstruct almost any famous battle, especially the ones our side won. Everyone said he was destined for a famous military career. Poor devil!"

"Are you frightened, too?"

"Of course. No one except fools and liars would say they weren't. But I'm not paralysed, as Hillary can be. I've seen him staring into his glass of port when he's had a bit too much. But I'll make you a bet he'll come home with a decoration, the Victoria Cross most likely. Then, of course, it will be even more impossible to live with our fire-eating mother. Well, Mog, what are you going to do with your life when the war's over? Or while it's on, since you can't sit at home brooding about Rudi."

"I have a plan."

"Tell me. Is it a secret?"

"From Mamma, yes. She's going to wash her hands of me when she hears it. She thinks I should be a nursing aide, at least, or handing out comforts to Tommies. But Papa is beginning to lose all his young clerks because they're enlisting. I want to go into the bank."

"Goodness me! Can you count?"

"Of course I can count. I can write neatly, too, and I could soon learn how to keep ledgers. Why shouldn't a girl be able to do that as well as a man?"

Richard grinned. "Don't scare me. You sound like one

of those peculiar women who chain themselves to railings campaigning for women's rights."

"A suffragette? Do you know, I believe Mamma might have some sympathy for that if I did it in the grand manner. But you know what she has always thought about bank clerks."

"She was forced to marry one. You have to remember that."

"And I've been forced to part from one," Imogen said bitterly. "So don't expect me to be too sympathetic to Mamma. I'm thinking of Papa, and I know he'll be delighted. I'll tell him I'm keeping yours and Rudi's places."

"A female tycoon?"

"Dear Richard. Were you planning to be a tycoon too?"

"I was planning to make a success of the job. I enjoy juggling with money. I've inherited Papa's genes, but here I am, forced to take on Duncastle traditions and shoulder a rifle. I could almost believe Mamma had invented this war to get me into the army."

Imogen frowned with anxiety.

"It won't be for long. Everyone says so. And the moment the war's over I'm off to Vienna. I'm going to save every penny of my wages."

"There's a wonderful restaurant in the Vienna Woods. Very romantic. Get Rudi to take you there."

"Oh yes, and we'll drink the young vintage wines you've told me about."

"Go easy on them. They can be pretty potent. If you want to get drunk do it Hillary's way, on champagne."

"I haven't Hillary's style."

"No, but you're going to be a survivor."

"How do you know that?"

"I can tell."

"You be one too, please!"

"You think a Boche bullet could go through my thick skull? It's as solid as a bank vault."

Imogen took his hand lovingly. Dear Richard, he could always make her laugh, even in her present constant desolation. She prayed the war wouldn't take away his natural merriment. Nor hers, either. Laughter was in short supply in this family at present.

Dinner, on the last night of Hillary's leave, took Joshua back to the night he had first dined at Sanctuary, and he had been mad for Matilda. He hadn't been young even then, so he couldn't attribute his marriage to a mistake of youth. Anyway, by and large, it hadn't been a mistake. But it hadn't been a real marriage either, hampered as it was by that idiot sister, and the tragedy of Lally, entirely attributable, in his view, to her unfortunate fall. He knew that doctors had divided opinions, and that they talked about genes, but he had always remained convinced that Julia should have been put into a suitable home for cases of her kind. Then his elder daughter might have been as vital and alive as Imogen.

Imogen and Richard represented the credit side of his marriage; poor, nervous flawed Lally and his strange, handsome, withdrawn elder son the debit. On the debit, too, was his wife's failure in bed. Because no matter how much he had pretended to himself in those early years she had not deceived him. She had used him for begetting children, preferably sons, then, with relief on both sides, conjugal relations had ceased.

What a term—conjugal relations. It could kill any romance. Rosie, and lately Prudence, his favourite (and what a misnomer that was for that generous, warm, good-humoured woman, always welcoming, always laughing) had dismissed such inhibiting language and said they preferred the simple words of fun and loving.

Nevertheless, he knew that if he had not been able to marry Matilda he would have been haunted by her all his life. Those overbred good looks had had a mesmeric effect on him. He had thought that possession of such a woman would make him grow inches in stature. He was still immensely proud of her, although in too many aspects his marriage had been a disappointment. They had never succeeded in communicating, either verbally or physically. Prudence had made him see that, but she had taken the bitterness out of his failure by commenting that that young Joshua Webb must have been an awful ambitious young rooster.

Now secretly comforted and cherished by a warm-hearted woman, he was able to endure Matilda's crankiness more patiently, even feeling a little sorry for her. Though God knew she was not sorry for herself. She was the most self-assured woman he had ever known. Although she was far too intelligent not to realise that they had never succeeded as a husband and wife, she defended herself by saying that she had been blackmailed into marriage, therefore she was entitled to nourish resentment. She kept her emotions entirely for her children. Even when they didn't please her, Richard expressing his determination to represent the son in Joshua Webb and Son, and Imogen, poor little lass, embarking on her ill-starred romance with Rudi von Klein. But for Hillary, who had inherited Matilda's curious long-nosed elegance, and become a perfect puppet soldier (he would remain a puppet in Joshua's eyes until he had proved himself in action), she showed a shameless preference.

Hillary was her darling, her pride, her joy, her reward for the sacrifice she had made in marrying Joshua. He represented all her ambition. It was a wonder he had become a man at all. He had, for Joshua knew of his affair with a certain young woman in Pimlico, and thank God for that. Matilda would have preferred him to have married one of those doll-faced debutantes and produced an heir, another blood-thirsty Duncastle, before he went to war. But even she could not stop the onward rush of militarism to give Hillary time to marry. Nor, he believed, would she have wanted to.

Her blood was up. She was enjoying this supreme test of patriotism and sacrifice. She intended to be a model to British women. They were all in for hell, didn't they realise it, he wondered, looking round the candlelit table at the fresh young faces of his children. Were they as naïve as he had been twenty-five years ago, sitting at this same table and lusting for the cool strange beauty of the red-headed Duncastle girl? It infuriated him that his pugnacious masculinity had had such little impact. He had thought then that Mattie had been excitingly like a newly-minted sovereign, but he had overlooked the hardness of that particular metal.

"Papa, you're looking awfully serious," said Imogen.

"That trans-Siberian railroad stock?" Richard hazarded.

"Joshua, you're not thinking of investments tonight," Matilda said severely.

"I'm about to pour everyone some more wine," said Joshua, "since Simmons seems to be unaccountably absent."

"He enlisted this afternoon," said Matilda.

"Oh, good God! He's middle-aged."

"He'll get a job behind the lines, in stores probably. Won't he, Hillary?"

"I expect so. But he won't be decanting Château Lafitte, poor devil. This is a jolly good vintage, I must say. Thanks, Pater."

"Laid down by your grandfather, I believe," Joshua said drily. "So don't thank me."

"Make the most of it while it lasts," said Matilda. "We'll be able to see out the war, thanks to your grandfather's foresight, but after that you must start laying down some new stocks, Hillary."

"After the war. It's like a litany." Hillary raised his glass and drank deeply. "I wonder if Grandfather said that before he went off to India to quell a mutiny, or Great-grandfather departing for the Crimea said, 'Remind me to restock the cellars when I return.' As if they were going to live forever."

"So will you," said Matilda.

"But they didn't face German guns. When did the British last face German guns? Not even at Waterloo. I know we're not an inferior race, but we're not that superior. So I'm not at present going to tempt fate and start brushing up my knowledge of French wines suitable for consumption in the nineteen thirties."

"Darling, you're so amusing," said Matilda. She moved her head and the diamonds in her hair twinkled in the candlelight. She had wanted this to be a real party tonight, and was dressed accordingly.

"Do you really find that amusing?" asked Richard, leaning forward. "Do you, Mamma? *Pour out the red sweet wine of youth.* Haven't you read your Rupert Brooke?"

"Can't stand sweet wine," Hillary said flippantly.

Matilda's chin lifted.

"What witty clever sons we have, Joshua."

"You have a clever daughter, too." Imogen had drunk much more wine than she was usually permitted. Papa had kept deliberately filling her glass, and giving her small winks. He thought he could cheer her up, bless him. "Do you know what my war work is going to be, Mamma?"

"No, darling, but strong young girls will be needed in hospitals. I intend speaking to Princess Louise."

"You'd be wasting your time," Imogen said. She laid her hand over Joshua's and winked back at him. "Papa's going to teach me how to keep ledgers. He's losing all his clerks because they're joining up. It's that poster of Kitchener's that's responsible: *Your country needs you.* Well, Webb's bank needs me, doesn't it, Papa? So I'm going to be a bank clerk."

"Imogen! You're making fun of me."

"No, I'm not, Mamma. I'm deadly serious. Aren't I, Papa?"

"I believe so, little one."

"Joshua!"

"You can't put everyone in uniform, Mattie," Joshua said mildly. "Someone has to stay at home and mind the shop."

"Don't use that word 'deadly,' Imogen," Hillary drawled. "Damned morbid." He drank some more wine. "But postpone your fight until tomorrow. Tonight we're supposed to be enjoying ourselves."

I've always hated this house, Joshua thought suddenly. Damned mausoleum.

However, dinner finally ended in uproarious laughter as Richard and Hillary capped impossible stories. Even Lally laughed, although it was obvious she didn't see the jokes. Afterwards everyone except Hillary went somewhat somnolently to the drawing room. They had dispatched half a dozen bottles of the 1887 Lafitte. Even Mamma was unusually flushed and in no mind to take up Imogen's challenge.

Imogen, after a little while, went to look for Hillary. She found him in the library bent over the collection of medals he had known by heart since childhood. They seemed to endlessly fascinate him.

"Hullo," he said. A lock of hair hung loosely over his forehead. Otherwise he gave no sign of having drunk a bottle and a half of wine. The army had certainly taught him how to hold his liquor. Or perhaps this, too, was a Duncastle characteristic.

"Look." He held up a medal. "That's my favourite. It's so bizarre. 'Kirkee and Poona.' Whoever heard of that little skirmish? Look, here's the 'Relief of Lucknow.' 'The Relief of the Legations in Pekin.' 'Corunna.' 'Waterloo.' 'Talavera.' 'Northern Kurdistan.' My, our ancestors got about the world. And all I'm going to manage is crossing the English channel."

"You and Richard will be adding to this collection," Imogen said.

"God, now you sound just like Mamma."

"Oh, I didn't mean to. But it is a fact, isn't it?"

Hillary stared at her from sunken eyes. Red-rimmed, as Lally had described them. Fearful.

"Hillary—"

"Yes, I am scared," he said loudly. "But don't you say it. Just don't you dare put it in words."

"I'm not saying it. I only think you have too much to live up to. Not only going to war, but all these medals, for instance, not to mention the Salamanca Drum."

"I wish I had that drum here, now. I'd beat it until it fell apart."

"That wouldn't help. Mamma would mistake your motive. She'd think it was bravado."

"So it would be."

"You're not the only one who's scared."

"Rudi isn't."

"I don't know. Perhaps he has a different way of seeing things."

Hillary was looking at her sharply.

"You know about Rudi and me, don't you? That pot of ink, and—oh, my God, it was glorious while I was doing it."

Impulsively Imogen wrapped her arms round his slen-

(162)

der tense figure, as hard as steel, as vulnerable as mortal flesh and blood.

"Rudi understood. So do I now."

"Do you, Mog?"

"Write and tell me anything you want to. Don't pretend, as you'll have to for Mamma. Promise, Hillary."

"All those brave ancestors of ours," Hillary muttered resentfully. "They gave me their looks, but they forgot the guts."

"Perhaps they were frightened, too. That little drummer boy with everything rushing at him, soldiers in front of him, soldiers behind him. You can't tell me he wasn't shaking like a jelly."

"Drummer Boy Hillary Richard Gordon Duncastle, aged fifteen years. I blame the precocious little sod for this whole bloody myth of our brave family."

Imogen stared at him in surprise. Then suddenly, because it seemed so irreverent, the family being looked at honestly at last, she began to laugh, and after a moment Hillary joined her, his eyes lighting up with a half-crazed merriment.

"I never saw the funny side before. Does the poor wretched Hun know he's going to be fighting the terror of rebel tribes, the terror of Chinese peasants, the terror of Zulus without guns, the terror of the starving Irish, the terror of the Emir, the Mahdi, the Maharajah, not to mention Napoleon Buonaparte?" Hillary stopped to draw breath. "We'll have it all over by Christmas, Mog," he said quietly. "And Rudi will be home."

Chapter 15

Propped up against the gnarled pear tree which had shed
the rotten pears he had gathered up from the long grass,
Hillary continued the long letter he had begun to Imogen.
It was becoming a saga. He had been writing it off and on
for days. He must end it soon and send it off.

Funny how he felt he could talk to Imogen more than
anybody else. That had happened only recently, perhaps
after Rudi had left and he had realized she had had her
first experience of the pain of maturity. She would understand the turmoil of feelings he poured out on these scraps
of paper, although he was beginning to doubt whether he
would ever post this letter. It was becoming too revealing.

It was very cold today. There is a lot of mist about,
and the frost hasn't thawed. After all the rain last
week the roads are in a frightful mess from the
endless traffic, gun carriages and mules and cavalry
and the poor plodding infantry up to their ankles in
mud. This morning there was a very thin coating of
ice on the puddles, a sheen of it like moonstones.

Now the leaves are falling the landscape has a kind of grand desolation, grey, black and faded brown, lit up now and then by distant flashes from gunfire and exploding shells. Like a distant and rather harmless fireworks display, though no doubt I will change my mind about their harmlessness when we move up tomorrow. I promise to finish this letter today, since it may be the last I will write for a while.

I'm writing to Ma, too, and reassuring her about my safety, though I wonder if she really wants me to be safe. A serious but not fatal wound, perhaps, as I really can't imagine an unscarred Duncastle after he has been to war. There would be something out of character about that.

I am sitting on the damp ground huddled in my greatcoat, and thinking that surely all our ancestors fought battles in blazing heat, in Spain, India, the Crimea. And here I am, frozen to the bone, queasy in the stomach from those wormy pears, and shivering like a nervous terrier. This is a relatively safe billet, in fact as safe as houses, my batman assures me, which is ironic considering that the houses are destroyed, their timber sticking up like broken bones. The village got in the way of the retreat from Mons and God knows what happened to the villagers, although on the way here I saw some evidence. An unburied body, several weeks old, is a very nasty bit of debris. Why can't we rot cleanly like old turnips or mangel wurzels? I wake up from nightmares that I am crawling with worms. I had the most overpowering impulse to run for my life after I stumbled over that first corpse. It was dressed in a peasant smock. It hadn't even been a combatant. But where could I run to? There is all this mad shattered landscape and nowhere to hide.

Yesterday a deserter was executed by firing squad. I heard the shots. They came from behind the ruins of the village church, so perhaps God heard them, too. And said, "My son, I should have given you more courage when I made you. It was an unfortunate oversight for which I apologise."

I can't let my men down. It would be the most horrible unthinkable thing. But will I be able to avoid it? I don't get any thoughts of glory, only of the utter foulness of rotting bodies. The chaps coming back from the front lines say the noise is the worst thing. Cadet Hillary Duncastle's drum wouldn't have been heard in these battles. But even so, in that chessboard battle, he died, didn't he?

I expect I'll come back in some shape or other, but if I don't, Mog, would you do something private for me? There's a girl, Gwen Spark, living at 11 Haven Road, Pimilico. I'd like her to have the gold watch I had for my twenty-first birthday. It's in the top drawer of the Wellington chest. She'll probably sell it, but on the other hand she might not. It doesn't matter. Just so long as she knows she meant something to me. I don't suppose I would have ever married her, she's what Ma would call common, but she knows how to be comforting and loving. Will you do this errand yourself? I couldn't trust anyone else.

I only write like this because this is such a stricken place, meant for death. Or do only I feel its doom, the dying leaves, the frosty grass, the low grey sky, as if some withering hand had been placed on everything. It has a horribly morbid effect on me, and I believe I am rapidly advancing towards melancholia! I need some of that Bollinger 1910 we had at your party.

However, even without it, I can still manage the expected cheery words to my men. All the time despising them for their stupid grinning gullibility. Heroism, patriotism, duty, are three words I would like struck from the English language. They have so little meaning for me. Or I won't allow them to have, because I know what they entail. My chief fear is of being blinded. I saw some poor chaps yesterday who were. They stumbled along in a wobbly line, like lame ducklings, holding each other's shoulders. I wondered who they would have to look after them at home, how they would spend the rest of their lives. I can't imagine any woman wanting to devote the rest of her life to me, not even Gwen. I'm too full of self-pity, too self-absorbed, too introspective. Horrible, really. I even let your nice Rudi down. I'm haunted with the fear that my next letting down will be on a much bigger scale. If it happens I pray God Ma never knows. I believe I'd rather face a firing squad than her—I mean, than disappoint her so cruelly. Because I love her terribly, and I never know how to say so . . .

It was shaming to have to put down his pen to wipe the tears off his cheeks. He was thankful he was alone in this damp chilly place. But he felt eased and emptied by that outpouring, and folding the thin sheets of paper he tucked them inside a slender volume of Palgrave's *Golden Treasury* that he carried in his breast pocket. He had decided that such a letter could never be sent. Imogen was too young to be burdened with such a confession. It was more for a priest, he supposed. Anyway, it was done, and he felt calm, almost brave. In this mood he could march unflinchingly down the muddy road towards the sound of the guns. The very vital thing was not that he killed the enemy and received decorations, but that he retained the image he hoped his men had of him, brave, debonair, dashing, an amusing chap at a party, something of a performer on the banged-about old pianos they had in French estaminets, a good officer, a deadly marksman. They'd follow him all right. So long as he led . . .

Now, while he was in this more relaxed mood, he must write to his mother, and get that duty done. This was a letter that would be sent.

My dearest Mother,
      This may be the last opportunity I have to write for a little while, so I can tell you I am in the best of health, apart from a slight stomach ache from eating some windfall pears I found in an old orchard. They were a bit wormy. My splendid batman is a great forager and yesterday we had rabbit stew. Make the most of it, he said, because there'll be no cuddly little rabbits left if this war goes on. They'll

all turn into rats! He has a longer face than Tomkins, but he's a sound chap, and my billet here has been dry and almost comfortable.

I don't know how the war is going. When you're in it you can't see the wood for the trees, but the men are in high spirits. If you'd heard them singing "Pack up your troubles" last night, in pouring rain, you'd understand what I mean.

I hope all is well in Kensington Square (I imagine you have shut up Sanctuary for the winter), and I'm sure you are working twenty-five hours a day. Don't overdo it, Ma. I want you fit and well when I come home. I'd like to say sorry now for all the times I've fought with you—only, really, to assert my masculine superiority, and you have to admit you're a very strong-minded lady. And can I be sentimental and tell you a picture I have, fixed somewhere in the back of my heart, of you in that almond green dress you used to wear to the Opera, dragging Richard and me unwillingly with you, giving us a cultural education, you used to say. I can't remember anything about the opera, but that image of you sticks with me. It's cool and green and springlike in this grubby muddy place. The winter isn't going to be a joke. It's getting cold at nights . . .

There was another picture in his mind that he didn't mention, that of his family pressed against the barrier at Victoria station the day his regiment had entrained for Dover and France. Lally was sobbing in her all too familiar unrestrained fashion, Imogen's usually cheerful face was pale and streaked with tears, Papa in his city clothes, with his stranger's face (one had never got to know Papa, Mamma hadn't allowed it), had been stern and unsmiling, Minnie who had begged to come to get a last glimpse of Master Hillary had been jumping up and down to see over the heads of the crowd.

But Mamma, dressed in her sable-trimmed dark brown cloak, with a little feathered hat perched at a particularly jaunty angle on her glorious hair, had been erect, tearless and proud. Exactly as one had known she would be. Oh, my God, that pride. It had shivered through him, making him burst into tears of apprehension and gratitude, love and hate. How dare she put such a burden on him? How could he ever be the hero she expected?

He had been forced to straighten his contorted face, and to dash a hand over his humiliatingly wet eyes, and pray his men hadn't noticed. If they had, they would probably attribute his loss of control to the fact that he had been waving goodbye to a cherished lady friend.

Not just his mother. No one would understand that. No one else had such a mother.

"The nights are getting cold," he ended his letter lamely, forgetting he had already said that. He could have said the days were cold, too, for at only four o'clock in the afternoon he was shivering violently.

Chapter 16

Christmas, 1914, and London a dark subdued city, lights dimmed and blinds drawn for fear of Zeppelin raids, a muffled quiet in the streets. The sound of groping footsteps round the tree-dimmed gloom of Kensington Square made going outdoors after nightfall a little eerie. London was so full of all kinds of people, refugees pouring across the Channel from war-torn Belgium, or enemy aliens trying to escape internment, bewildered young soldiers having their last night's leave before embarking for France, revellers seeking to blot out thoughts of the ordeals ahead.

Matilda forbade Imogen and Lally to go out after dark unless properly accompanied. Lally would not have dreamed of doing such a thing, but Imogen rebelled and planned defiance. She was in more danger, she pointed out to her watchdog Minnie (who was developing a pathological fear of Zeppelins), from being knocked down by a careless cabbie than blown up by a bomb.

She was still determined to persuade her father to take her into the bank, but he was hesitating about the wisdom of this. Not for Mamma's reasons, but because he thought she might grow stooped and frowning, sitting over a desk. It wasn't woman's work. He wanted her to be soft and feminine when Rudi came back. If Rudi came back. He made a compromise that she should wait until February next year when she was nineteen. In the meantime she could please her mother by knitting mufflers and mittens, meeting hospital trains to comfort blood-stained gaunt shocked young men with cups of tea and encouraging words, escorting the frighteningly silent refugee children from Belgium to orphanages. That, according to Matilda, was what a patriotic young woman did in time of war.

Lally, whose fingers were so skilful with pen and pencil, was extremely clumsy with knitting needles. Nevertheless, she persevered and until the mornings became too cold, sat under the mulberry tree in the garden, surrounded by her sketch books and balls of khaki-coloured wool.

She had made a clever sketch of the crowded troop train leaving Victoria station, Hillary leaning out to wave, his nose and forehead two decisive strokes of her pencil that didn't look like anything and yet captured the essence of Hillary in a very clever way. Matilda had looked at it for a long time, and then said she would like to keep it, together with the sketch of Imogen, Richard and Hillary sprawled at ease on the lawn at Sanctuary. Imogen had thought her mother was merely humouring Lally, who worried so much about her general ineptitude, but there really was something remarkably lifelike about these sketches. They seemed to tell more than a formal photograph. Anyway, it was nice that Mamma could be sentimental about mementos.

Joshua, in his usual shrewd fashion, was taking practical steps in this time of emergency. At the outbreak of war there had been a shortage of uniforms, and new recruits had drilled in all sorts of incongruous clothing, blue trousers, red jackets, anything that bore a resemblance to army issue. But factories had quickly adapted to production of standard wear for the modern British soldier, and Joshua Webb was financing firms with sound management. The turnover in army boots and uniforms was colossal, not because the garments wore out but because their wastage was a figure one could bear only to relate to account books, not to human life. One didn't think of all the khaki jackets and trousers, blood-stained and torn by shrapnel, rotting on the battlefields or in shallow graves, or burned in hospital furnaces. One thought of keeping the living British Tommy warm and well-equipped.

Someone made money out of a war, and Joshua was doing so because he was a businessman. He knew that he was doing a necessary job more capably than most of his kind. The profits were a bonus he didn't seek. He guessed that Paul von Klein in Vienna was doing exactly the same thing. And that the wives of each of them would be lavishly handing out donations to war widows and convalescent homes and the permanently disabled, so that, in a way, things came full circle.

They also had both given sons to fight for their country. There was no real reward in war. One fitted into one's place like a piece of a jigsaw. And carried on. It was a damned wasteful tragic business.

Joshua's eyes had unexpectedly stung with pride and repressed tears when he had watched Hillary, his elder son, leave. But when it had come to Richard, not the polished soldier that Hillary was, a bit abashed in his private's uniform (that was because he was too aware of his mother's embarrassment at having a son serving in such a lowly rank), Joshua had had to turn away and blow his nose violently, and vow he would never go to a public leave-taking again.

From then on he spent sixteen hours a day in the bank, and every other evening with Prudence in her small flat near St. Paul's cathedral. Home was a place to be avoided. Either it was crowded with the members of Mattie's committees or it was enlivened only by the deadly depressing click of knitting needles. Imogen, poor lonely girl, had to be supported, but otherwise his presence was almost unnoticed, certainly not desired.

However, Christmas was to be different because Matilda had said it was their duty to invite a Belgian refugee family to dinner. There was not yet any shortage of food in England, and these wretched people were entirely dependent on the charity of the British.

The parents were peasant farmers, sturdy, dark-faced, shocked and surly. The two children, Pierre and Angelique, were aged six years and seven years. They were exactly the right age to enjoy a Christmas tree.

Imogen was told to get out all the baubles, candles, silver stars, ribbons and toys treasured from other happier Christmases, and the fir tree, purchased from old Elijah Hook who made the rounds of the square each Christmas with his handcart piled with spicy spruce branches, was dragged into the hall.

At least this was a livelier occupation than the endless knitting, and as the servants came up to help, Minnie and cook and even old Tomkins who had to put up the step ladder and hold it securely, everyone became merry in a muted way.

Toys for the children, a doll for Angelique, a little wooden horse and cart for Pierre. One wondered if they spoke any English and what it had been like having the German soldiers trampling over their farm, ruining their wheatfield and probably slaughtering their animals. Supposing the little boy had had a pet rabbit. Hillary, in his last letter to Mamma, had talked of a rabbit stew. Soldiers foraged to relieve the monotonous diet of bully beef and tinned jam and particularly vile (so Hillary said) tinned mashed potatoes.

Cook had bought a turkey in the market. She had made the plum pudding three weeks ago, also two smaller ones which had been included in parcels for Hillary and Richard, though whether they would get them in time for Christmas was a matter for conjecture.

Imogen wondered if Rudi's parents had sent him a plum pudding, or perhaps one of those celebrated Viennese chocolate cakes. She was always wondering things like that. She wondered when Rudi slept, when he woke, when he was cold, hungry or in pain. She wondered the same things about her brothers, but to a much lesser degree. She could still see Hillary's and Richard's faces quite clearly in her mind, but Rudi's features, his ruddy cheeks and merry brown eyes, were dissolving away into mist.

As if she were willing this so as to ease the pain of recollection.

But things were definitely more light-hearted in Kensington Square. Until Christmas Eve. Until the telegram from the War Office came.

Minnie had opened the door because Polly was in the basement helping cook stuff the turkey. She looked at the yellow envelope in a dazed way, apprehension shuddering through her. The master was not yet home. It would have to be the poor mistress who took the shock of this news.

Which one was it, Master Hillary or Master Richard?

Minnie knocked at the door of the drawing room where the mistress was having a brief rest before dinner. She had been at one of her fund-raising Christmas fairs all day.

"Oh, ma'am," Minnie said, and burst into tears. Only because it had seemed that two little boys, one on each side of her, had tugged at her hands as she went in. She could have sworn she had felt their warm impatient sticky fingers.

"Now, Minnie, what's the matter?" Matilda asked in a slightly hoarse voice. She had been talking all day. The last thing she wanted just now was servant troubles.

Then she caught sight of the yellow envelope in Minnie's hand. She snatched it before the fear could possess and paralyse her.

Hillary or Richard?

Her fingers trembled.

Oh, dear God, Hillary. Killed in action . . . Deeply regret to inform you your son Captain Hillary Webb . . . Killed in action . . . *Killed* . . . The harsh word stabbed her as if it were the bayonet penetrating Hillary's slender body. Or had it been a bullet, hopefully instantly fatal? Or had a shell—fragments of flesh blown everywhere, a foot with a boot still on it, a little finger, that young haughty face so beloved . . .

"Ma'am, are you all right? Can I get you some brandy? Oh, ma'am, it is about the boys, isn't it? Which one?"

With a supreme effort Matilda lifted her head.

"My elder son," she said in a formal voice, as if Minnie were some visitor to the house. "Hillary. He—I had a letter from him—"

"Just last week," said Minnie. "Oh, ma'am."

The room began to focus again.

"Minnie, you know I can't stand crying. Pour me a little brandy and stop making those disgusting noises. Then I'd like to be alone for a little while. I'll ring shortly for the girls, and my husband."

"The master isn't home yet, ma'am."

"Then when he comes in—let me know." She straightened herself with a visible effort. "Christmas must go on, of course. We can't disappoint those children. The war's no fault of theirs."

"Like ice she was," Minnie reported downstairs. "Not a tear. Scolding me for blubbing like a baby. She held her head ever so high and said we couldn't disappoint those foreign kids. She's a great lady and we've got to do our bit and see that turkey is cooked and eaten. I know every bit will choke me. Oh, my poor dear Master Hillary, my brave little soldier."

"I can't help saying," cook confided, "that if it had to be one of them I'm glad it's not Master Richard."

"You shouldn't have favourites," Minnie said bleakly. "And it'll be him, too, like as not."

Imogen knew that she would never forget that Christmas day. It was only by Mamma's example that everyone remained calm, even smiling. Though the smiles were for the shy children who could not be persuaded to say a word. They could eat, however. The table after dinner, said Papa, looked as if locusts had marched over it. And when the balloons and toys were taken off the Christmas tree, they even began to make timid sounds of pleasure.

It had been arranged that the little family should live on a farm in Norfolk for the duration of the war. Mamma managed to convey this information to the parents. Mamma was terrifyingly erect, terrifyingly composed. She wore an elegant grey silk dress with a diamond brooch pinned at the throat. She had pushed her food from one side of her plate to the other, however, her only sign of distress. As far as Imogen knew she hadn't eaten all day, nor last night. She certainly had not slept for her skin was waxen, her eyes glittering. Neither had she talked, beyond making the stark announcement of Hillary's death, adding that she did not want a display of grief. Nevertheless, Imogen had cried half the night, not so much for Hillary as for Rudi. She had had a curious foreknowledge of Hillary's death, and now only prayed that he had died facing the enemy. But the tragic briefness of his time in action had made her desperately afraid that Rudi's life would be similarly brief. Richard's, too. How awful and hopeless it all was. Yet Mamma said one must show only pride. Hillary had died in the most privileged of ways, for his country.

Even Papa had unashamedly wept. For the loss of a son, for the crazy waste of youth. War shouldn't be glorified.

"But your mother is a strange proud woman," he told Imogen. "She'll keep her eyes dry and she won't crack, but she'll pay in other ways. She'll die a bit inside, and no one will guess. So be kind to her, little one. She'll need you more than anybody. I think that idea of yours of coming into the bank had better be postponed for a while. Eh? Help your mother. Don't let her be alone."

"She's never alone!" Imogen burst out. "She always has her committees and her meetings."

"That's not real company, is it?"

"I know they bore me dreadfully. I can't spend all day working with all those women."

"What about looking after the boys back from the front?"

"That's different. Yes, that's different, Papa. They do need me. Or anyone cheerful."

"Anyone cheerful. That's the ticket. You keep them happy and your mother happy."

"And you, Papa?"

"I'll manage."

"All those late nights that you work."

"They're good for me," Papa said, rather abruptly.

"They take my mind off Richard. And Rudi, too. My God, Imogen, war is a terrible thing."

"I know," Imogen said, sobbing in his arms.

But neither of them broke down at the Christmas dinner party. When all the candles had been lighted, and a large fire glowed, the room became quite gay. Unexpectedly, too, Lally had a frail gaiety. She enjoyed watching the children unwrapping their presents, and blew up the balloons, and skipped about with them in a childish way that would normally have irritated both Mamma and Papa. Today, however, they were grateful for their elder daughter's retarded behaviour. The Belgian family didn't seem to find anything amiss, and the nonsense helped to bridge the silence.

Imogen found the whole thing horrible and artificial and pathetic, and was astonished when Mamma became affected by the noise and suddenly came to life in the most unexpected way. She swooped up the two stolid Belgian children, one under each arm, and said that she was taking them up to the Death Room. It was fitting that, with their country ravaged by war, they should see the military mementos of another country, the one that was at present pouring out much blood to save them.

"*Ah, non!*" the mother cried, but the children, thinking there was another adventure ahead in this rich house, had stopped being afraid.

When they had gone the warm festive room became very silent. Lally was disappointed to lose her audience, Imogen knew something awful was going to happen. The Death Room. What a lucky thing those kids didn't understand English.

A few minutes later there were shrieks from upstairs, not of fear but of laughter. And then the drum began to beat. The Salamanca Drum. On this Christmas day, a century after the Battle of Salamanca, the little drum spoke again. *Rat-a-tat, rat-a-tat, rat-a-tat* . . . bold and confident, and the children shrieking with excitement.

"Les Boches!" the Belgian woman exclaimed in alarm.

"No, madam," Joshua assured her. "Only the British, winning the war in their own eccentric way."

"I've never heard Mamma play the drum before," Imogen said. "Should I go up, Papa?"

"No, leave her, leave her. It's her mood. I imagine it's something she wants to do."

Rat-a-tat, rat-a-tat, rat-a-tat . . . The throbbing went on for another five minutes, then came to an end in a crashing crescendo.

A little while later the trio came back into the room, Mamma pushing the children who were now chattering excitely in French. Mamma herself had lost her frozen look. There were spots of colour in her cheeks, her eyes gleamed.

"Did I startle you?" she asked pleasantly. "It was just that I had this sudden urge. I did the same thing when my brother Hillary was killed in Zululand. It's strange, it releases something in me. I think I know why drummer boys are so brave, and indeed why the troops follow them. The sound is hypnotic, isn't it?"

"It's black magic," Papa growled. "Even the African tribes know that."

"I have played Hillary's lament," Mamma said, in a low voice. She sighed deeply. "Now I think I could sleep. Joshua, see these people get a cab when they're ready to go. We managed the party pretty well, didn't we, considering everything."

Considering the elder son of the house had left its roof forever. Yes, they had managed very well. Joshua nodded his head slightly. He would never understand his wife, but she certainly had special qualities. What those ancestors of hers would call the undefeatable spirit of England, he supposed. Did it thrive on grief? One didn't know. Only let Richard come home safely . . .

If it had been possible for Matilda to hold her head any higher she would have done so when the letter arrived from Hillary's commanding officer telling her that Hillary had died when silencing a German sniper of deadly accuracy who had been decimating the British lines. He had succeeded in this attempt by making a wide circle behind the man who was hidden in the ruins of a farmhouse, and creeping up on him. But almost at once he had been caught in a burst of fire from German guns.

His death had been instantaneous. He was being recommended posthumously for the Military Cross.

So there was going to be another medal to add to the Duncastle collection, Joshua thought ironically. Actually he was secretly sceptical of the official story. It sounded too much like the sort of propaganda the country was being fed, heroic young officer showing outstanding initiative and gallantry. He wouldn't have thought Hillary had had it in him.

But Imogen believed it. She thought that in a desperate effort to overcome his fears Hillary had tried to do something mad and dangerous. And solitary. So that if he failed there would be no witnesses.

Needless to say, Matilda never doubted any of it, and was comforted by that lonely fatal act of courage. She was going to cherish the knowledge of it until the end of her life.

There was no reason why she should disbelieve the story since she was not shown the letter that arrived for Imogen some weeks later, brought by a very young second lieutenant to whom it had been entrusted. It had been found on Hillary after his death, tucked in a copy of Palgrave's *Golden Treasury* (yes, Imogen knew that book, she had given it to Hillary herself). The letter had seemed to be pretty private so the commanding officer had suggested that Second Lieutenant Barrett deliver it himself, since he was going on home leave.

That was why, a few days later, Imogen stood on the doorstep of a shabby rooming house in Pimlico. She had found the gold watch where Hillary had said it was, because so far Mamma had not wanted Hillary's things disturbed. It was now in her handbag, to be handed over to Miss Spark, who had answered Imogen's note by saying she would be home at five o'clock that afternoon.

What was she, a clever scheming tart or one with a heart of gold? It didn't matter. She had meant something to Hillary and his wishes must be carried out.

The girl who opened the door on the first landing of this bleak house was slight and young, with a lot of cloudy dark hair round a waif-like face. She was neatly dressed in a blouse and skirt. She didn't look more than eighteen. She had been crying.

"You're Miss Spark?" Imogen asked in surprise.

"Yes."

"I'm Miss Webb. I believe you knew my brother."

"I told you in my letter," the girl said with forlorn dignity.

"Yes, you did. It's just—you look so young."

"I'm twenty-one. And I'm not a tart, if that's what you're thinking. I'm a shopgirl and I met Hill—your brother, when he was buying a blouse. For his mother, I think. He made me hold it up in front of me to see how it looked and then laughed and said I wasn't stately enough. It made him look at me, see? He seemed a bit in awe of his mother so he was glad I wasn't like that. He was waiting outside the shop when I was going home that night, and asked to walk with me. After that, he used to come and see me when he was on leave. We—didn't do anything wrong, Miss Webb."

"What did you do?" Imogen asked in frank curiosity, unable to see the elegant Hillary with this little dark mouse.

"We just walked in the parks or by the river, and talked. He seemed to be able to talk to me. Oh, I do apologise, Miss Webb. Here I'm keeping you standing outside. Won't you come in and have a cup of tea. I mean, if you don't mind."

She was so unsure of herself, so gentle and soft-voiced, with those big listening eyes, that Imogen began to understand the odd friendship. It must have been just what Hillary needed. A person he didn't have to live up to, who listened, and made no demands.

"We could never get married, of course," she said, becoming more relaxed after the cup of tea. "But it's so wonderful to have his watch. To have him specially remember me. I'll wear it on a chain inside my bodice. Could you tell me how he died?"

She cried again as Imogen related the heroic story.

"I knew he would do something like that," she said. "He used to try to tell me he was scared, but he never was, was he? He just liked telling me he was so I'd say I didn't believe a word."

Imogen's throat ached.

"He said you were a great comfort to him."

"Did he say that? Did he really?"

Imogen walked the entire way home, helplessly angry and sad. Miss Gwen Spark, a shopgirl, who was going to treasure a gold watch for the rest of her life. This was war. They were all going to be casualties in one way or another. At least Miss Spark was fortunate in that she knew the truth, bad as it was. Nothing could be worse than living forever in uncertainty as she was doing about Rudi.

A few days later Mamma said, in a sternly composed voice she now used when speaking of Hillary, "I've been going through Hillary's things and I can't find his watch. You know the gold one we gave him on his twenty-first birthday."

"Can't you?" said Imogen.

"I hoped you might know if he had put it somewhere special. Or given it away."

"No, Mamma."

"Then where can it be? I must find it."

"Why?"

"Because naturally I want to keep it. With the Military Cross and other things."

"In that horrible Death Room."

"Wherever I choose to remember my son," Mamma said austerely. "I will have a memorial window put in the church at Sanctuary, of course. But for his personal things—if you know, Imogen, I hope you will tell me."

Imogen instantly flushed deeply. Oh, God, she never could tell lies without giving herself away. Had Mamma noticed? If so she said nothing.

But that night, with her senses heightened too acutely, Imogen knew her drawers had been searched. She had hidden Hillary's letter under her notepaper and muddled correspondence in the top drawer of her writing desk. She quickly established that it was still there. But not tucked inside the book of poems as it had been. Pushed underneath them. By someone distressed, and forgetting to be careful.

She should have hidden it more cleverly. But one would never have thought Mamma would stoop to searching for the missing watch in her writing desk.

So now Mamma knew the truth about Hillary. She knew he had not been lion-hearted after all. Serve her right for snooping!

Poor, poor Mamma.

The American Ambassador, Mr. Walter Page, sprang up from behind his desk as the tall woman dressed in black came into the room. Another bereaved mother, he thought, tearless, composed and proud, as all these Englishwomen seemed to be. He admired them so much and felt such sympathy for them.

"Mrs. Webb?" he said, holding out his hand. "You wanted to see me, I believe. Come and sit down and tell me what I can do for you."

"What I hope you can do for me, Ambassador."

Mr. Page indicated her black garments.

"Your son? Is he missing? We can sometimes trace prisoners of war through the German and Austrian Embassies. As you well know, we're trying to run those as well as our own. It's an onerous and very sad task." He was talking to give his visitor time to relax. She was as stiff as a poker in her determination not to show emotion. "I'm besieged by pleas for help from people who have suddenly become enemy aliens. They want news of their families, of their parents, or sons. A curtain has come down between us and Europe."

"I know," said Mrs. Webb. "That's why I too am begging for a little of your time. It isn't about my son. He has recently been killed in action. It's about a young Austrian friend of ours, a particular friend of my daughter's. We think he may have been in action for some time. His name is Rudolph von Klein. His father is Count von Klein, a banker from Vienna."

"Ah, a notable family. It may not be too difficult to discover something. Do you know his regiment?"

"Naturally not."

"H'm'm, yes, of course. The enemy. You'll have to give me a few days to make some enquiries. I'll do what I can."

"I'm very grateful, Ambassador, when you have so much on your hands."

"Believe me, we would like to do much much more. I'm very sorry about your son."

"He died for his country."

Mr. Page bowed his head slightly. What else could he do in face of that dignity? This woman didn't want sympathy. It would break her up. She had to cling to her terrible pride. He noticed that she had amazing green eyes, pure and dedicated. A difficult woman to live with, he imagined, but these were the people who had made England great. They would win this war as they won all wars. But at what a cost. And did a man want a wife who was so invulnerable? Who was Mr. Webb? Nothing to do with him, Mr. Page thought tiredly. Just get on with the job.

Two weeks later Imogen came home from a particularly harrowing session at Victoria station. The hospital train had been carrying some grievously wounded. She found Mamma sitting alone in the drawing room. And idly at that. It was so surprising that she exclaimed,

"Is there something wrong? Are you ill?"

"No, I'm not ill." Mamma stretched out her arms. "Come here, dear child."

Alarm leaped in Imogen's throat.

"Richard?"

"No, not Richard, darling. Rudi."

"Oh—oh, no!"

"I'm afraid so. Two months ago on the Russian front."

Imogen jerked away, her eyes blazing.

"I don't believe it. You're making this up so I'll forget him."

"I'm not making it up, but it's true that it would break my heart if you spent useless years of your youth waiting for him. No, I'm not making it up, Imogen. Here's the letter from the American Ambassador."

"How could he know?"

"I asked him if he could make enquiries for me. He has ways, since he's officially in charge of the Austrian Embassy. He has been very kind."

Imogen snatched at the letter. Then her face crumpled in desolation.

"All this time I imagined him alive. I *made* him be alive."

"And it would have been tragic to go on doing that," Mamma said, very gently. "It's better to know the truth. If Hillary had been reported missing, I don't think I could have faced the uncertainty. But knowing—" the barest quiver shook the composed voice. "It really is better, my darling. I haven't been cruel. Just wise."

"An eye for an eye!" Imogen cried. "That's what you're thinking, isn't it? Rudi for Hillary."

"Imogen! I shall forgive you for that only because you're in a state of shock."

"But you're glad I'll never see him again."

"I shouldn't have wanted you to marry him, if that's what you mean. But be angry with me. Scold me. It will do you good. Then we can be friends again."

Deep in herself, Imogen knew that Mamma had been acting for the best, and that it was far better to know the truth than to go on dreaming about someone who had long been a corpse. But the shattering news she had just imparted made her seem like a vulture. Her lack of tears, her composure—the composure she also expected Imogen to have—were inhuman. At least that was how they seemed in this black moment. Perhaps time would soften this nightmare. Perhaps one day she would even love Mamma again. It didn't seem possible now. It seemed so certain that she was gloating over the death of one more of the hated enemy.

Chapter 17

April 1916 on the Curragh in Ireland. A hazy spring green over the low hills, a bluebell sky, a mist-laden wind.

Richard had got a ride that morning on Trooper Morgan's bay gelding, a fine big brute of a horse that ate up the ground. His thigh had throbbed a bit, but not too badly. After this temporary posting, he would be pronounced fit for service in France again. It was a bit of a bad joke the way they sent the half-fit or the indifferent soldiers to poor old Ireland. It was also tragic that any army had to be maintained here at all, when England's resources were completely stretched in France and Flanders and on the Dardanelles.

But there were always undercurrents in this troubled country. It was rumoured that the Sinn Feiners were plotting again. Did they ever stop? They were so in love with this perennial game of attempting to oust the British that, if victory ever came, they would hardly know what to do with it. No more secret plans to whisper in public houses where the Guinness flowed as freely as the talk, no more rendezvous in barns or wet ditches in the perpetual misty rain; what would a man do when his adrenalin ceased to flow?

However, gloomy as the climate was, apart from rare spring days like this, and even though one could never trust the natives, Richard was glad of the peace and quiet. He had an acute dread of returning to France. The memory of its particular brand of horror could be suppressed in the daytime, especially among these charming entertaining Irish who thought one thing and spoke another. Didn't he do the same himself about life in the trenches when trying to bolster up the courage of new recruits, poor devils, boys hardly out of the village school, hardly old enough to do the paper rounds or deliver the milk.

He had been unable to avoid becoming an officer, after all. They had promoted him on the field. Promotions came rapidly in this war. He had quickly gone from second lieutenant to first, and then to captain—only, he told his mother, because all of his predecessors had been killed and they were desperate for more silly mugs who were willing to die for their country. He didn't want to die. He badly wanted to stay alive, for the most simple reasons. To lie on the newly-cut grass at Sanctuary and listen to uninterrupted birdsong, to crumble clean earth in his fingers, clean, not that diabolical muck of Flanders, that witches' brew of mud and blood and rat droppings and sewage and stinking portions of human bodies that had missed the burial parties.

"Have you seen my hand? Has anyone seen my hand?" he had heard an anguished voice calling. "It's the right one. It has a gold signet ring on the little finger. And the fingernails are regrettably—rather—neglected . . ." The accent was Christchurch, Oxford, the voice tight with its attempt at facetiousness and its repressed panic. The demand went on, more feebly and waveringly, until the stretcher, bumped along between the narrow walls of the trench, was out of hearing.

"If we find it, sir, we'll give it a proper burial," someone shouted.

Black comedy, the only kind possible. That was in Flanders. It was rumoured that there was going to be a big new offensive, bigger and more costly than Ypres, worse than

Loos, worse than the tragedy of Verdun where France had lost the elite of her nation. It would be on the Somme and it would be the biggest noisiest most unimaginable battle known to mankind.

Compared to that, a little bit of Sinn Fein fireworks in Ireland was light relief. One had to remember that the cunning devils had a habit, through past centuries, of striking the Englishman in the back when he was at his most vulnerable. But the Irish Brigade of Guards was fighting with distinction on the western front, and there were plenty of raw and apparently willing recruits being trained for service with the British army overseas.

It was good to be active again. Richard was glad to have escaped from convalescent hospitals and from home which was now permanently Kensington Square because Sanctuary had been turned into a hospital for the shell-shocked and severely disturbed. Their despairs must be putting poor Aunt Julia's and Great-aunt Tatiana's mopping and mowing ghosts to shame.

But home in Kensington Square in its own way was not much more cheerful. Mamma was waging her own private war with her small army of helpers, who raised funds, did nursing duties, drove ambulances. Imogen, the light gone out of her eyes, had tried for Richard's sake to be smiling and lively but the environment and her own personal grief for Rudi defeated her. Papa disappeared into the citadel of his bank every day of the week, including Sundays, and sometimes he remained there all night. He was reduced to a staff of middle-aged, elderly and physically unfit. Only Lally, who seemed to have retreated more than ever into childhood, and Aunt Clara, who remained quiet, unfussed, loving and undemanding, provided a cheerful atmosphere.

There had been Zeppelin raids, and the black-outs added to the gloom. There was also a growing shortage of fuel and certain foods, bad news about shipping lost to German submarines increased, and there was a dreary preponderance of khaki in Piccadilly Circus and the brighter night spots.

Yes, it had been a relief to come to Ireland to put himself together again after the long nightmare. He would probably always have a slight limp from his thigh wound, but provided he kept out of trouble on the Emerald Isle, the medical board said facetiously, he would be fit for active service in France by the autumn. Sometimes he wondered if Hillary were the lucky one, poor old Major-General who hadn't revelled in war as he should have done. But not often. He was too in love with the small things of life. He thought he would be content with very little when the war was over. He no longer even wanted a place at the partners' desk in the bank. Perhaps one day he would, but he doubted if money would ever have any importance for him again. He just wanted to live, to have women or preferably only one much loved woman, to dig in a garden, to have a pet fox, or a badger, to forget the terrible brutishness latent in human nature. Perhaps Mamma would give him Sanctuary. She must, since Hillary, the true heir, was no longer alive. Oh, that he would like.

But now it was Easter Monday and if he could get leave that evening he had promised himself a meal at Jammet's where the Irish stew was reputed to be the best in the country. Today everyone who could get there, the Irish being a horseloving people, had gone to the Fairyhouse races.

Fairyhouse. Now there was another of those whimsical Irish names. Leprechauns, no doubt, evilly sat on the jockeys' shoulders. Armed with rifles, most likely, elderly weapons that should be in museums, but were nevertheless capable of killing dead anyone wearing a British uniform. If the leprechauns took up the Irish cause then England was going to be in real trouble. He must write that to Imogen. It might make her laugh.

When the news burst on him at noon, after an agitated Colonel Cowan in Dublin Castle had got through to the Curragh (before the telephone lines were cut, he said extraordinarily), Richard really did think the little people must have taken over. No one else could have been so mad. Except the Irish, of course.

It seemed that a small motley force consisting mainly of young men scarcely out of their teens, but armed with Lee Enfields and German Mausers, and dressed in the dark green uniform of the self-styled Citizen Army, had burst into Dublin Castle, then had taken over the Post Office in Sackville Street, and impudently raised the green Irish flag. Now there was vicious sniping going on in the streets, houses and shops were being broken into, wounded, dead or dying lay in gutters or doorways, and there were the inevitable inflammatory harangues being made from vantage points.

It all sounded like a particularly devilish form of Irish hoax. It couldn't be true. Rumour even had it that a woman, a Countess no less, theatrically dressed in a green blouse and knee breeches, had led troops on to St. Stephen's Green, and was commanding them with military efficiency. She was a crack shot herself. All the toddlers, watched over by nannies (English surely), the elderly sunning themselves in the delightful weather, the lovers, had had to flee from the green lawns and park benches of the green.

In a state of disbelief Richard had got his company of the Mobile Column into battle order. He was in the grip of an overwhelming feeling of *déjà vu*. There had been bland sunny days like this in Flanders lulling one into an illusion of peace. Then the great guns had boomed, the shells begun to fall. He kept listening now for the doom-laden roar of the cannon, for enormous black masses of smoke to blossom on the horizon, for the screech of approaching shells, the rattle of machine guns, the whole diabolical orchestra of death.

But the afternoon remained quietly peaceful, there was no sign of trouble except for a distant low smudge against the blue sky. Smoke? Fires? The smell of burning?

So there went his dinner at Jammet's that evening. Unless this rebellion could be nipped in the bud in a couple of hours, dying of lack of volition. The talking, in this country, usually took preference to action. But there certainly were armed men with murderous intentions about. Murder so often came under the heading of patriotism, something that none of these hotheads (and including my own mother, Richard thought) would admit.

It was going to be ironic if he could survive the massive

onslaught of the German attack and then die in a Dublin street.

This, to his dismay three hours later, seemed all too possible. When attempting to take cover in Merrion Row leading to St. Stephen's Green where the most disturbance seemed to be, he found himself involved in a dangerous little guerrilla war, masquerading, as always, under the beguiling rebel songs and perorations. There were snipers in the buildings opposite who had a deadly accuracy. Two of his men had been hit already, one killed outright, the other, hopefully, able to limp to safety. The warm sunny day was drawing to a close, and although British troops, including the splendidly caparisoned Lancers on their polished black horses, had arrived in force, there was no sign of this rebellion being quelled in a few hours.

Richard was getting the impression that it might go on all night, perhaps all the week, judging by the determined fire of the rebels, and the unwieldy barricades, constructed of overturned motor cars, carts and even furniture and mattresses dragged from nearby houses and thrown across the streets.

He was thirsty, dusty, tired and enraged. Ireland was to have been a rest cure, not another war. Crouching in a doorway, waiting for the right moment to signal his men to rush the barricade, the thought of the awful futility of dying in this squalid situation had barely crossed his mind before the stunning blow of the bullet hit him. He remembered only its sledgehammer impact, and nothing more until he opened his eyes in a gloomy quiet room, the setting sun slanting through long windows, dim portraits hanging on the walls, a finely carved ceiling above him. He seemed to be lying on a couch. There was a cushion under his head, a blur of yellow that his straining eyes eventually saw was a bowl of yellow tulips on a table beside him.

Civilisation! Had that senseless fury in the streets been nothing but a nightmare? Had he strayed into Dublin Castle? He couldn't think clearly. His vision kept blurring, and when he tried to sit up an agonising pain shot through his right arm.

Oh, God, not his arm as well as his leg. He surely

wasn't going to be a cripple. Better to go the way Hillary had, cleanly and finally. He saw now that his sleeve was slit to the shoulder, and a tourniquet was tied tightly round his upper arm. He couldn't lift his hand.

Far in the distance, in that nightmare world, he could hear shots and explosions, splintering glass, and wild cries. A little more consciousness drifted into his brain. The mad Irish. The rebellion that had sprung up like an autumn bonfire. The crazy fools ruining this soft spring day.

What, he wondered, in sudden desperate anxiety, had happened to his men? What was he doing here?

"I'd advise you to keep still," came a woman's voice somewhere in the gloom behind him. "You were bleeding rather badly, and I'm not sure if I've tied that thing tight enough."

The voice was soft and musical. It had the barest hint of a brogue. This room, the soft couch, the garden in the green gloom of twilight beyond the windows meant that she must be one of the upper-class Irish. Perhaps even a British sympathiser, although after this afternoon that was hard to believe. The whole of Dublin seemed to be in a state of rebellion.

"Couldn't you come where I can see you?" he managed to say.

"If I were you, I'd be more interested in finding out whether I was going to lose my arm."

The pain had become insistent, his weakness alarming.

"Is it that bad?"

"Bad enough. You British can certainly bleed. Patrick Pearse and his friends will be glad to know you've got some vulnerable points. You might as well know I'm glad myself."

She had moved within his range of vision, but his eyes were maddeningly weak. He could see only a mass of soft dark hair, a slim-waisted figure. Tall. Her hair was tumbling down a bit as if she'd been in the fighting.

"Are you—one of them?"

"In sympathy, yes. Oh, sure, I don't fire a gun. I'm not parading on the Green, like the fire-eating Countess. Now, if you get in the sights of her gun you won't live to tell the tale, and that's for sure. But I don't believe in dressing up to look like a man, and my mother and father would disown me if I did. No matter that I was killing you British pigs."

"So—you're like them all—a bonny talker."

He sensed rather than saw the anger flash in her face.

"Is that only talk that's going on out there now? Don't you taunt me, Captain, or I'll have that tourniquet off your arm and you can bleed to death."

Amazingly, Richard was beginning to feel stronger. His adrenalin was flowing again. The woman's soft voice, filled incongruously with hostility, stimulated him.

"If you feel like that, why did you bring me in here? I presume it was you who did so."

"Not without help. You're a big fellow."

"But why? Didn't you want a corpse on your fine doorstep?"

"To tell the truth, because you had rather a nice look to you. I wanted to see the colour of your eyes."

As she spoke she turned on a light and the room, and the young woman herself, took shape. Richard wasn't interested in the panelled walls, the marble fireplace, the dark portraits, the proportions and furnishings of a fine Georgian house. He looked only at the girl, and saw her pale three-cornered face (one of the cat variety, a lynx perhaps, pure and ruthless), her smoke-grey eyes fringed with extravagantly thick black lashes, and the abundance of her tumbling black hair. A beauty, no less. Unless his judgement was marred by his abominable tiredness.

"Well?" he said.

She was studying his own eyes. "Not grey, not brown. An in-between colour." She sounded disappointed.

"We call it hazel. I take after my father. My mother has green eyes."

"Is she a great beauty?"

"No, she's a—a holy terror." He heard his voice from a long way off. The girl was suddenly kneeling beside him.

"Now, don't go and faint on me. I'll give you a mouthful of brandy. My father will be in any time now."

"Is he"—the words were difficult to enunciate—"to administer the *coup de grâce?*"

The soft gurgle of her laughter delighted him, and made life stir in him again.

"I should hope not. He's Doctor Brendan O'Connor, highly respected in his profession. I'm his only daughter, Deirdre. And don't make any mistake about me, I hate the British. I intend throwing you out of here as soon as that arm is dressed. It's your fighting arm, thanks be to God, so you won't be raising it against us again."

Nor against the Germans, Richard thought confusedly. Had this episode in a Dublin street saved him from the awful holocaust of the trenches? From Ypres and the Somme?

"Now, just a wee sip of brandy."

The arm raising his head was as soft and gentle as a meadow of clover blossom. He fell asleep, thinking he could smell the fresh summer scent. Or perhaps lost consciousness, as he did again when the burly bearded man bent over him and stripped the bandages from his arm, causing intolerable pain. Long afterwards when he woke in the night—he found he was in a comfortable bed—he wondered if he had imagined the words he had heard.

"Bullet's gone right through, but there'll be permanent damage, withering maybe, poor young fellow."

He didn't sleep again that night, partly because of pain, partly because spasmodic firing ruined the quiet. When dawn came there was a fusillade of shots, and the smell and crackle of burning.

This was awful. He had to get out of here to find out what was happening to his men, to report his wound and to swear he had not voluntarily taken refuge with the enemy.

But when he got out of bed the room spun darkly, and he collapsed to the floor.

"Loss of blood," he heard someone saying. "The lad will have to rest for a day or two. Get him some breakfast."

"Are we to harbour him, Father?" The girl's voice was incredulous.

"What did you mean to do when you brought him in?"

"Just not let him bleed to death outside our front door. That seemed too barbarous."

"And so it would have been. I like to save my patients, not murder them. What the lad needs now is a pot of tea and some of Bridget's fresh bread. Get Bridget to bring it up if you think such a task will sully you."

"No, I'll bring it. The fewer people who know he's here, the better. Mother mustn't know."

"Damned lunatic farce, the whole thing," the doctor grumbled. "Do you know those crazy Sinn Feiners are killing more of our own people than British. Innocent Irish people are dying in the streets. Wars should be fought in other countries, not your own."

"We ought to be used to that by now," the girl said bitterly. "Should we try a landing on the English coast, do you think?"

"It might make more sense than burning down Dublin. We'll be paying for this mess for a century to come."

"Shame on you, Father, the British will be paying. Very well, I'll feed the brute, if only to get him strong enough to be thrown out of here." A slight amused lilt came into her voice. "But he is rather a good-looking one, isn't he?"

"He is. Perhaps you can pass the time teaching him to sing the 'Green Flag.'"

Richard, who had lain immobile listening to this highly diverting conversation, opened his eyes in full consciousness when the girl, Deirdre O'Connor, returned, carrying a breakfast tray. She had to help him to sit up. His arm hurt vilely. But he was also starving, and he was sure the hot strong tea and the bread, still warm from the oven, and deliciously crusty, would revive him sufficiently to enable him to get out of this house. Judging by the sloping ceiling, he was in an attic, probably being kept out of sight and sound of the rest of the household.

"This is terribly good of you," he said.

Now his sight was clearer and it was full daylight, he could see what he had suspected last evening, that the girl was a beauty, one of those fine-boned passionate young women the Irish now and again produced. Lovely and wild and contrary and perhaps a little devilish. Ready to die for their beliefs, be it their religion or their country.

If it came to that, his mother was the same, but he doubted that even in youth she had had the fire he could read in this girl's smoky dark eyes. Mamma was contained and ordered and implacable. Deirdre O'Connor, he suspected, would change like the light over the Wicklow hills from hour to hour. She intrigued him greatly. Even though he was starving, he had to contemplate her first. Afterwards, he would eat.

"Don't thank me," she said. "I'm only hoping to get you strong enough to get rid of you. Father says you should stay for a day, but it's too risky. For you and for me. You can leave by the back door across the garden. You'll soon be picked up by your friends. The streets are full of patrols."

"Aren't you taking a risk, supposing some of *your* friends see me go?"

"They'll kill me if they find you here," she said simply.

"The bloodthirsty Countess?"

"Don't be making fun of me, Captain."

"But she *is* bloodthirsty, isn't she?"

"So are others. And we're winning, I might tell you."

"For how long?"

She flung round, her long dark hair swinging. "Oh, be damned to you, you supercilious Englishman. We know very well this rebellion isn't going to make a big enough coffin to bury the British army, but it's going to to put a good big nail in it. Now eat your breakfast and be getting ready to leave. I'll come back in an hour and help you to dress."

Now he was stiff and on his dignity.

"I can manage very well myself."

"We'll see."

He was forced to let her help him. He could manage his trousers, but when it came to his jacket, split and blood-stained, he had to hold his head in his hands until the pain ebbed from his upper arm. Was the arm going to wither, as the doctor had said? Oh, God, preserve him. Preserve everybody, even the madmen who had read their brave proclamation from the steps of the General Post Office, Irishmen and Irishwomen: In the name of

God and of the dead generations from which she receives her old tradition of nationhood, Ireland, through us, summons her children to her flag and strikes for her freedom. . . . The girl had recited it to him as she firmly, but with considerable gentleness, helped him into the damaged jacket. His puttees were beyond them both. They would have to be left.

"I'll burn them," she said. Her eyes became mocking again. "Will you be demoted for not being correctly dressed? Some of our boys are fighting in shirt sleeves, and I wouldn't be surprised if some of them are barefooted. The ignorant peasants, you know."

"Stop that!" he said angrily. "It's cheap."

"Oh, well. We use what weapons we can."

"Mostly words, I've found."

"Then that was a dangerous word that hit your arm. A really nasty one. Can you walk down the stairs if you hold on to the bannisters? Can you be careful not to make a noise?"

"Are Patrick Pearse and others hiding beyond the arras?"

He could have sworn she almost gave a sputter of laughter. But instantly she was an icicle again.

"It's my mother. She isn't strong, and she's been very upset by all the shooting. If she thought a British soldier was in the house she'd probably die."

With her slim figure—she was wearing a white blouse and a plain grey skirt—going ahead of him, he somehow contrived to reach the bottom of three flights of stairs without fainting again. It was a near thing, at the bottom, but the girl had anticipated it, and on a table in a tiled passage there was a bottle of brandy and a glass. She quickly poured a generous portion and made him swallow it. As he made to thank her, she hissed,

"For the love of God, don't think I'm doing this for you. I'm saving my own skin. Now I'll open this door that leads into the side garden. If you go down a path between the syringas you'll find a gate that takes you into the street. I don't think it's under fire, but I can't be sure. You'll have to take the risk."

"I must thank you—"

"I don't want thanks, I tell you. Just get away from here."

"And God go with you," he finished for her. With the kind of devoutness he might have expected her to express. If they had been friends . . .

Chapter 18

Matilda and Joshua were waiting for Richard's return
from his medical board. It was the reason Joshua was
spending a rare Sunday afternoon at home. Usually he
went to the bank, to tidy his desk for Monday morning,
he said. Occasionally he put on casual clothes and disappeared for a long walk, then called on his sister Clara
for tea. Kensington Square, the home of which he had
been so proud when he had brought Matilda to it as a
bride, no longer seemed to interest him. He behaved
as if it were only a place to sleep (for a scant four or
five hours each night) or a place to give his business
friends as good a dinner as possible under war conditions.

These friends were no longer Austrian counts or Swiss
bankers. They tended to be members of the Government
concerned about equipping the fighting forces, and the
country's economy. There were vague hints that when the
war was over Joshua would receive a knighthood. Not
for getting rich, he was doing that, too, but for bringing
his keen financial flair to the aid of his country. That,

combined with his wife's outstanding contribution to the women's war effort, and indeed, the loss of his sons, one dead and the other disabled, were all factors to his credit. He had become a man of stature and influence.

This did not surprise Matilda. She had recognized his potential before she married him. It was a pity the financial world, the wheels turning behind the scenes, bored her, and she had no hankering to be Lady Webb. Now that Hillary was gone and Richard almost certainly due to be turned down by his medical board her spirit had faltered. She spent too much time in the Death Room, fingering medals, including the posthumously awarded Military Cross, looking through old photograph albums, occasionally touching the torn and grimy battle colours, or nursing the little drum on her lap, as if it carried within it a living spirit. Why hadn't she had six sons? Then she wouldn't have had to concentrate all her deep aching grief on Hillary.

She had deliberately read that letter which Imogen had hidden too carelessly. She knew it by heart. She didn't believe a word of Hillary's expressed unhappiness and fear. He was merely being over-dramatic, the young hero waiting nervously for his baptism of fire. Striking an attitude as he had so often done as a child. Nervousness was understandable. Not fear.

She treasured his words at the end of the letter, the poignant sweetness of them after the preceding bitterness. "I love her terribly and never know how to say so." They moved her so agonisingly that she couldn't cry. She had never cried for him.

She knew about the insipid little shopgirl he had befriended—he had been a kind sensitive young man—and had made a point of occasionally anonymously sending her gifts of money. The girl deserved that since she seemed to live in some poverty. But she didn't deserve Hillary's gold watch. That must one day be retrieved. When the war was over.

At first, while Richard was still unharmed, things had been tolerable. She still had a son upholding the family tradition, bearing arms for his country, and destined for honours. Perhaps not the honours Hillary would have achieved since he had not been to a military academy, but certainly promotion to the rank of Colonel, perhaps even Brigadier.

But now all those hopes, too, were destroyed. That sordid treacherous scuffle in Ireland had left him permanently disabled. She was furious and utterly unforgiving. She rejoiced when the Irish traitors were executed. Some people talked about the inhumanity of it, the squalid execution yard, the white-faced boys lined against the wall, still defiant, still begging prayers for Mother Ireland. But Matilda said calmly that these were justified punishments, the price of treachery, the rules of war. Besides, those men, boys, what you will, had not only seriously wounded her one surviving son, they had wickedly and deliberately stabbed England in the back at the time of her greatest crisis, when submarines were decimating her shipping and when Gallipoli was proving a tragic failure and the costly and monstrous battle of the Somme was about to begin. Oh no, she would never forgive the Irish.

"Where are my daughters?" Joshua grumbled. He was already bored at having to sit at home. "This house always seems like a morgue nowadays."

"Imogen is at the hospital," Matilda said. "Lally's somewhere upstairs. She feels safer in one of the attics, since the Zeppelin raids, I don't know why. I think it's the smallness of the room, the low ceiling or something. I suppose a psychoanalyst would say it was a desire to get back into the womb." Matilda was talking to avoid the awkward silences that too frequently occurred between her and Joshua. "Julia was just the same. As a child, she would hide in cupboards."

She stopped, inwardly scolding herself. Even after all these years Joshua still hated any mention of Julia, and the never-solved mystery of her disappearance. As if they were going to discover her poor little crouched body in a cupboard one day. He frowned and said testily,

"I wish Lally'd be less of a coward."

"She can't help it, Joshua. She isn't able to rationalise her fears. She does her best about things."

"I suppose so. Isn't it time Richard was home?"

"I should think he would be here soon. One can't tell how long he'll have to wait to see the doctors."

"Like lame birds, these young men," Joshua muttered. "Winged by some monstrous duck shooter. I tell you, Mattie, I'm not having him going back to France."

"It won't be anything to do with you, my dear."

My dear. How long since she had called him that? Was it because he was looking elderly and defeated, and she understood the raw pain he was suffering over Richard. She knew it was very real, but not what she had suffered over Hillary. No one but a mother could suffer so acutely.

Yet she was afraid that if Richard failed his medical board, and was always with them, limping a little, holding his damaged right arm across his breast, but staying alive, she would begin to resent him keenly. And also Joshua for having the good fortune to keep his favourite son alive. It would be so unfair.

"I'll have him at his desk at the bank," Joshua said. "He may not be able to use a pen very well, but he can use his brains. He has a good financial head on him, that boy. I'll make him a partner at once. Joshua Webb and Son. Eh, Mattie. What I've always talked about."

Matilda stood up with a rustle of her stiff silk skirt.

"You sound as if the war's over, as if everything is back to normal. Why should you be so fortunate, when others—"

Her voice failed and she stared at him with her bleak eyes. She knew he had never suffered deeply over Hillary's death. He had once said that Hillary had made him feel a clodhopper and always on the defensive, as if he was not part of him. Now he never mentioned Hillary's name.

"Everything normal when that boy may carry a useless arm to the end of his life," Joshua exploded, with his old vitality. "Eh, well, Mattie." The anger died out of his voice. "I know you miss Hillary badly. You ought to talk about it a bit. Can't we comfort each other?"

She did lay her hand on his arm. The loneliness, for an unguarded minute, had overcome her. But his expression instantly became shy, almost embarrassed, as if he had never known her in any way, and now she had become the kind of woman who alarmed him.

She remained in that isolated state of loneliness even when Richard came home and kissed her cheek almost apologetically and said, "Well, I'm here for keeps. I hope you're pleased, Mother."

But he wasn't looking at her. His gaunt young face was turned hopefully to his father.

"Who was this girl?" Imogen asked with deep interest. "You say she hated the British and yet she bothered to save your life."

"Well, she said she didn't want me bleeding to death on her doorstep. It was a very handsome doorstep. And she knew how to put on a tourniquet."

"She must be practical."

"As a doctor's daughter, yes. Not in other ways. She wanted to join those rebels. She thought the Countess Markievicz was a heroine."

"Pity she isn't on our side," Imogen said drily. "With her and Mamma we'd have the war won in no time at all."

"Should I write to her?" Richard said tentatively. "It would be only polite, wouldn't it? There wasn't time to thank her that morning when she bundled me out. Besides, she wouldn't have listened then. She was in too much of a hurry to get rid of me."

Imogen looked at him, fondly and sadly, this changed Richard with his thin face and haunted eyes. It was so unlike him to be indecisive and unsure. Would he ever get back to being his old vigorous cheerful self? They said the powers of recuperation of the young were strong, but she had seen too many of them in convalescent hospitals, listless and inert, living in some endless nightmare. Men had never before been called on to stand weeks and months of living in the ground, overcome by claustrophobia, disgust, fear and sheer physical misery. Richard had recovered from his leg wound very well, but now that his arm showed continuing paralysis and withering he faced a lifetime of being maimed. Imogen knew that he was wondering if any girl, apart from this headstrong Irish beauty, would love him with a maimed right arm.

"I believe you fell in love," she said.

"With that spitfire? Hating me like poison?"

"You were dressed as a British soldier. When she got your jacket off didn't she get kinder?"

"She did say something about my having a nice look. I rather think she was making fun of me. Treating me like a little boy."

"Yes, I'd write to her," Imogen said.

"Would you?"

"If I were you. Of *course,* Richard. Even if it ends in nothing—well, Rudi and I had two hours one hot summer day, and that's a lovely shining thing that I remember all the time. If I never fall in love again, it's there, inside me. You're lucky because your Deirdre isn't as much of an enemy as Rudi had to become. That Sinn Fein rebellion is over, and I expect we'll soon be friends again with the Irish. Even the wild lot. They must see there's no sense in going on killing the British."

"Deirdre—she mightn't want to kill me, but I think we'd fight like blazes."

There was dawning animation in Richard's eyes, a bit of the old stubborn lively brother she so much wanted back. Oh, let him begin to live again. Let them both begin to live.

She leaned forward.

"If you promise to write to Deirdre I'll tell you my secret."

"Have you got a secret, Mog? A man?"

"In a way. Yes, I think there is. I'm not in love with him, but he's nice. Shy and clever. He works as an orderly in one of the hospitals I go to. He really wants to write books." She gave Richard a direct defiant look. "He's a conscientious objector."

"Good God! Does Mamma know?"

"Heavens, no."

Richard suddenly gave a great shout of laughter. He sounded just like Papa.

"Me with an Irish rebel, you with a conscientious objector. Oh, dear, what is the family coming to?"

Imogen's lips twitched. "It isn't funny. Well, it is in a way." Giggles overcame her. "I don't know whether I'm serious about Desmond and you may never get anywhere with your Deirdre, but think of Mamma's face. No, it isn't funny. Only I can't be worried about Mamma. She expects such enormous sacrifices and I'm not able to live on that scale. I'm just an ordinary human being."

"I want to live at Sanctuary," Richard said. "Do you think, if I were to marry a Sinn Feiner, Mamma would give it to me?"

"She has to. You're the heir now Hillary's dead. Anyway, you'll love it more than Hillary would ever have done."

"Mamma's so complex. But I think she does love us, Mog, with what feelings she has left from Hillary."

"And according to her rules."

"I suppose so. Where would you and Desmond live?"

"Hampstead. That's where all his friends are. I mean, people who think as he does, that you don't kill. It isn't cowardice, Richard. You simply don't kill."

"I'd like to meet him."

"Would you? He won't look on you as a wounded hero, only as a damn fool for getting into the firing line."

"Perhaps he's right."

"Oh, darling Richard, thank goodness we have each other."

"And Papa."

"And Aunt Clara. She's always on our side."

"But Mamma—"

"We're not Hillary," Imogen said fiercely. "She'll never be as affected by our actions as she would be by his. Actually, in some ways I think she's almost glad he died. She's got her young hero forever. Is that a bad thing to say?"

"I suppose it could be true. I think there are quite a lot of Englishwomen like Mamma about at present. It's a kind of defence, really, otherwise they couldn't bear things. They would let the side down by going to pieces, and then we might lose the war."

"Do German mothers cry?"

"Great fat oceans of tears, I should think. So do some of their sons. I saw blubbing prisoners of war. Not over their wounds, or anything, but when they sat looking at their cherished photographs of sweethearts and kids. They can fight like lions and then be squashy inside. Perhaps their contrary nature is what makes them want to be the victors, all the time."

"And the Irish?"

"They're born victims, poor devils. Although I don't know what they'd be without their grievances. They wear them like their clothes." Suddenly a flash of humour showed in Richard's eyes. "My God, what am I thinking of? If I can ever persuade Miss Deirdre O'Connor to come to Sanctuary what is she going to make of Great-grandfather and all his relations. The hated British red-coats. She'd have them off the wall in a flash."

"I don't think so," Imogen said slowly. "She admires courage, doesn't she? She'll probably find that our great-grandfather fought alongside hers at Balaclava. I'll make a bet she has an ancestor who was one of the Duke of Marlborough's Wild Geese at Fontenoy."

Richard folded his strong left arm round Imogen, hugging her tightly.

"Darling Mog, you're a tonic."

"So are you, brother. Oh, do let's begin to live again."

But no letter arrived for Richard from Dublin. His face grew more and more sombre. He was starting a habit, Imogen noticed, of hugging his partially helpless arm across his breast. He was much too thin. Joshua said it was painfully difficult for a young man to adjust to dis-ablement and also, in a lesser way, to a business life again, but Richard had plenty of good sense. He would be fine when he settled down. Perhaps he needed to do something a bit wild.

Although even Joshua hardly expected the wildness to take the form it did. Richard announced that he intended to spend the weekend in Dublin. To revisit the scene of the crime, he said lightly. He had the greatest desire to see that fateful doorstep in Merrion Row again. And also, of course, to express his gratitude in person to a certain young woman, Miss Deirdre O'Connor, who had saved his life.

"Who is she?" Matilda asked sharply.

"The daughter of a Dublin doctor, Mother. Blood doesn't frighten her, and she knows how to put on a tourniquet."

Matilda thawed slightly.

"How fortunate she wasn't one of the rebels."

"But she was. Or so she said. She regretted she wasn't on St. Stephen's Green blazing away beside the Countess Markievicz."

"That terrible woman!"

"She was only doing what you would do under the same circumstances, Mother."

"Don't be ridiculous, Richard. I've never fired a gun in my life."

"But you've beaten the drum. Admit it. See another point of view for once."

Matilda's face had its pinched look of hauteur.

"There isn't another point of view as far as the Irish are concerned. And when you look at what they've done to your arm, I don't see how you can have the faintest sympathy for them."

"Oh, I don't love them *en masse*."

"Only this young woman, presumably."

"I only mentioned thanking her, Mother, not loving her."

"Richard, you wouldn't seriously think of bringing a member of that illegal organization, the Sinn Fein, into my house?"

"I would think of it, but I doubt if I'll have any success. Miss O'Connor can hate as fiercely as you can, Mother. She wasn't exactly anyone's idea of a ministering angel. That's what I liked about her. I've been at the mercy of too many ministering angels over the past few months. Bless their pure hearts."

"Richard, are you crazy?"

"Mattie!" Joshua interrupted. "Shut up!" When Matilda turned to him in affront he went on, "If this girl can make Richard look as alive as he does at this minute, then for my part I don't care if she belongs to the cohorts of the Devil. Just leave them alone. Let them find their own way."

It was a soft day, as the Irish termed this kind of weather, with the warm mist-laden wind, the smell of washed green leaves and clean grass. Richard knew the way to Merrion Row, although not the exact house on whose doorstep he had lain unconscious. Much of the rubble of the fighting had been cleared away, but there were still burnt-out buildings and shuttered windows. Scars which the rebels would be in no haste to remove, wanting to remind the Irish people of the deep underlying bitterness of the declared peace.

However, it was not a difficult task to find the house, for the Georgian doorway with its elegant half-moon fanlight bore a small brass plate announcing the residence of Doctor Brendan O'Connor, and the surgery hours.

Aware of a foolishly accelerated heartbeat, Richard rang the bell. What did Deirdre O'Connor do when she wasn't fighting the British? Sit in the garden and sew? Not likely.

He had no time to speculate further before the door opened and a rosy-cheeked maid, wearing her cap crookedly, looked at him and smiled in a friendly way.

"Were you wanting the doctor, sorr?"

He could well have been, with his arm gripped tensely across his chest. His civilian clothes disguised his nationality.

"I came to see Miss O'Connor. Is she in?"

"Miss Deirdre? She is not, sorr. Would you be seeing the mistress instead?" The door opened wider. "She's in the back sitting room if you would be caring to come in. Did you get that wound at the front, sorr?"

"You could say that." He remembered Deirdre's urgent words that her mother must not know of his presence in the house. Yes, he did have a great desire to see this lady who was no doubt as fiercely hostile as her daughter. He followed the plump maid into the hall. The smell of beeswax and roses sent his nerves tingling. They belonged to the gloom of the drawing room where he had lain on the couch. "Yes, I'd like to see your mistress, if I may."

"She'll be glad of your company, sorr. She's been terribly lonely since Sean. Who shall I say it is, sorr?"

"Mr. Webb. Mr. Richard Webb."

The back sitting room was bright with flowered wall-paper and many small pictures. A couch was half pulled across the window that looked on to a long narrow garden. On it lay a fragile-looking woman with enormous tragic blue eyes that turned towards Richard with weary interest.

"Forgive my not getting up, Mr. Webb. I've been rather poorly. I don't think I know you." She noticed his arm. "Are you back from the front? Have you come to tell me about Sean?"

"Sean?"

"My son, Major Sean O'Connor. He was killed on the Somme. The Irish Guards were heavily engaged and then outflanked. But they held their ground until the last man. They say the carnage among the horses is frightful. That's why Sean wouldn't join a cavalry regiment. It's no war for horses, is it, Mr. Webb? They can't charge guns without the most fearful massacre. Deirdre agrees with me. She rides with the Galway Blazers when she stays with friends in Connemara. But while the war's on hunting has stopped. Deirdre's heartbroken about her brother, of course."

What about that other war, right on her doorstep? Richard was wondering with intense curiosity. Had this frail voluble lady thrilled to the sound of guns fired by Irish rebels?

As if answering his question, the low dry voice whispering like summer grass went on, "But at least it's taken her mind off that shameful affair here in this city last Easter. I expect you heard about it in France. Sean wrote asking if we'd all gone out of our minds. Was Ireland set on destroying itself? I asked Deirdre what she thought, but she was a little secretive. I don't really know what that girl gets up to. Do you? Are you a friend of hers? I'm a little afraid that she may have some undesirable friends. Oh, I do apologise, I didn't mean you. Please do sit down, Mr. Webb. I see so few people that my tongue runs away with me when I have a visitor. Of course my husband's utterly destroyed about Sean. We all are. Tell me about him. Don't be afraid. I can bear to hear it. They protect me too much in this house. I'm still very much alive, you know."

"You're making a mistake, Mrs. O'Connor. I didn't know your son. But I'm sorry to hear he's been killed. My own brother was killed, too, just after Mons."

"And your arm? Where were you wounded? On that dreadful Somme?"

"Right here in Dublin, ma'am," Richard said boldly. Mrs. O'Connor started up.

"At the Easter rising? You were not one of the rebels?"

"I'm sorry you should take me for one of them. I'm British. I was fighting your rebels."

"Not *my* rebels," Mrs. O'Connor said tetchily. "I'll have nothing to do with that wild mob. And they did that to your arm? The divils!"

> Soldiers are we
> Whose lives are pledged to Ireland . . .

The words, sung in a low mocking voice, made Richard spin round.

"Well, who have we here?" Deirdre O'Connor asked, her face as pale as a candle within the frame of her smooth dark hair. "Is it yourself, Captain? You've changed. You're tidier, for one thing. Cleaner. And out of uniform, thanks be to God. But, oh dear"—a genuine look of distress crossed her face—"your arm. It really was a bad wound, then."

"Our countrymen did that to this nice young man, Deirdre," Mrs. O'Connor exclaimed. "They ought to be ashamed! And you singing that rebel song."

"So you think I should be ashamed, too, Mother? But I'm not. And if I offended Captain Webb I have no intention of apologising because he wasn't invited here in the first place."

"I'm no longer Captain Webb. I'm plain mister," Richard said mildly.

"Are you invalided out of the army, then? Well, that's one less of you to be got rid of."

"Deirdre, why are you being so rude to Mr. Webb? Do you know him?"

"She saved my life, Mrs. O'Connor," Richard said. "I've come back to thank her. Since answering letters doesn't seem to come as easily to her as tying tourniquets."

"You did that, Deirdre? Why wasn't I told?"

"Because we couldn't trust you, Mother."

"We?"

"Daddy and I. If you'd told people we had harboured a British soldier we'd have had our house burnt down, most likely."

"I don't understand you, Deirdre," Mrs. O'Connor complained. "In one breath you're singing rebel songs, and in the next you're harbouring a British soldier. Now there, Mr. Webb, you have the mystery of the Irish temperament."

"Well, isn't Mr. Webb contrary, too, wanting to shoot us one minute and thank us the next?"

Mrs. O'Connor's blue eyes, going from one to the other of them, were suddenly shrewd.

"I suspect this is all a more fundamental thing. Isn't it, Mr. Webb? Though why you should want to see my tomboy daughter again I fail to understand. Deirdre, ring for a tray of tea. Do you know that Mr. Webb knew Sean? No, now I'm getting muddled. I thought, seeing his wounded arm, that he had come from the front to tell us about Sean."

"Yes, my brother died fighting a British war," Deirdre said angrily. "Don't you find that ironic?"

"And heroic," Richard said.

"And unnecessary."

"If he'd stayed here on your side he could have died in the Easter rising."

"But he'll never be a martyr lying there on the Somme among a million others. Here," Deirdre's voice was wistful, "we'd have made him one of our Fenian dead."

"Deirdre!" Her mother spoke sharply. "Stop that dangerous nonsense. Building a nation on martyrs' graves. It's unhealthy, to say the least. And you a doctor's daughter."

There was a sudden gleam in Deirdre's eyes.

"You're one of the crazy Irish, too, Mother. You have a terrible lack of coherence. But anyway, let's give the English usurper some tea."

The hot strong tea revived memories, the fresh brown bread was fortunately sliced and buttered so that he did not need to manipulate his weak right hand. He wondered if Deirdre had thought of that when she had ordered the tea, for she was saying, "Have you had a proper medical opinion on that arm?"

"I had one when it happened. Your father's."

She nodded slowly. "Yes, he's a great diagnostician. But I hoped he was wrong."

"Hoped?"

"No one wants to see a fine young fellow crippled. I'm not a gorgon, Captain."

"Mister."

"Mister Webb. And what are you when you're not a member of His Majesty's Fighting Forces?"

"A banker. My father's just made me a partner in his bank although I've got an enormous lot to learn. He was comforting me, you understand? I'm no longer a whole person and I've done nothing to get a military decoration as my brother did—so I've become 'and Son.' What do you think of that?"

"I'm not thinking particularly about it," said Deirdre.

Mrs. O'Connor rose, fluttering her lacy Shetland shawl like a dusty butterfly.

"Deirdre dear, I think I must go and have my rest."

"In the morning, Mother?"

"Yes, I feel rather tired and self-indulgent. You will excuse me, Mr. Webb? My daughter will look after you. See if he'll stay to lunch, Deirdre. Daddy would like to meet him."

"Daddy's already met him."

"But again, at a more peaceful time. We can all talk about Sean."

"Mr. Webb has nothing to do with my brother," Deirdre said sharply.

"But they were both fighting the same battle in

France, weren't they? Wasn't it Shakespeare who wrote something about a band of brothers? I must look that up."

"Mother!"

"I'm just on my way, dear. A short nap and I'll be much better company at lunch. I don't enjoy good health, Mr. Webb. But now my beloved Sean comes to me when I close my eyes."

As she went out of the room Deirdre burst into tears. Richard started towards her. She motioned him away.

"No, leave me alone. Talking about Sean upsets me. And trust Mother to make an exit line. I'm sorry, I'm inclined to do this. I'm a weeper."

He put his arm tentatively across her shoulders. He could feel the small bones beneath her wool dress. She was shaking a little, but growing calmer. She didn't repel him.

"I'm glad you're a weeper. I get intimidated by all the heroic dry-eyed women in England. My mother's one of them. Her eyes stay dry and glitter like glass. Yours are—let me see?" With his fingers under her chin, he gently tilted her face. "Yes, as I thought. Stormy weather over the Irish sea."

She snatched herself away.

"My goodness, do many Englishmen talk in such purple prose?"

"When inspired. Cry for your brother, Deirdre. It's the best way. Cry for me, too, if you like, because I have this crazy hope that some nice young girl might be persuaded to love me, with my useless arm."

"Would you be wanting a nice young girl, Captain— Mr. Webb?" She was looking at him through her thick damp lashes.

"Richard," he reminded her.

"No, I haven't come to first names yet."

"Can't you stop thinking of me as a British soldier? Can't you think that your brother and I were on the same side?"

"More fool he. And don't try that soft talk on me about a useless arm and no girl loving you. You with your lion's eyes."

A powerful feeling of joy shot through him.

"So you can use purple prose, too."

"Oh, I frequently do. But I'm not English. It comes naturally to me."

"And not to me?"

Her lips quirked. "You're not too bad, at that. But I'd think you'd need to keep it out of banking language."

"I'll do that easily enough since I won't be wanting to make love to my clients."

Her cheeks coloured vividly. He stared at the transformation from pale cream to geranium. It enchanted him.

"That arm doesn't handicap you much. You're getting impertinent."

"Am I invited to lunch?"

"It looks like it, doesn't it? I'd better go and tell Bridget."

Chapter 19

Imogen, who was still not entirely sure of her feelings for the dark quiet young man, Desmond Morrison, found a crisis precipitated by her mother. The nephew of some friends in Kensington, Sir Henry and Lady Falconer, was home on leave from France. He was a little battle-shocked and needed taking out of himself. Therefore his aunt and uncle were giving a dinner party for him. They needed some suitable young people including an unattached young woman. Imogen Webb, of course. Pretty, lively, well brought up, understanding with the silent withdrawn young men newly back from the trenches, but not seriously involved with anybody. There was some story of her having lost someone she had cared for early in the war.

She and Ian Falconer would have many things in common.

Middle-aged and older women were awfully smug about arranging one's life, Imogen told Desmond. It was probably because they had been Victorians and had themselves had to submit to rigid rules. But she was a rebel. She had never told Desmond about Rudi. Now she did so. Watching the understanding in his dark serious eyes, her feelings for him developed from a warm and sympathetic friendship to love. Or so she thought, in the relief of remembering and then burying forever Rudi's healthy vital young body.

"It wasn't just a boy and girl crush, as my mother would like me to think. It would have lasted if Rudi and I had ever had a chance. But now I want something safe."

"Won't you find that a bit dull?"

He was too intelligent, and she had to vigorously deny his suggestion.

Impulsively she leaned across to kiss him. She wanted to feel and taste his lips, to see whether Rudi's ghost intruded. They hadn't kissed before.

Of all unlikely places, they were on the top of an omnibus, travelling through Westminster to St. Thomas's hospital. Although her action in kissing Desmond in such a public place had been on the spur of the moment, she immediately found herself enjoying feeling wicked and fast. People stared and she was excited. She realized that under other circumstances kissing Desmond might not have been exciting, and it was highly important that for this first time it should be.

She was growing up, too, because this wasn't a clumsy boy and girl kiss. She could detect the hunger in his lips, and felt his thin hands clutching at her waist. She liked that. It stirred an immediate response in her. Now she was positive she was in love.

The time had come to tell Mamma and Papa, and the unlucky Lieutenant Ian Falconer would have to go back to the front without having been cheered up by a nice English girl.

She began to giggle, and Desmond, still a little bemused, with his arm round the previously forbidden area of her waist, asked what was funny.

"Cuddling and kissing on an omnibus. Mamma would say it was awfully common. Do you love me, Desmond?"

He pressed his face into the curve of her neck and shoulder. She could feel his intensity.

"Very very much."

"Enough to marry me?"

Above the rattle of the omnibus she heard his whisper, "Please!"

"Are you brave enough to face my mother? She can be pretty annihilating."

Then she had lost him, or their mood of love. He straightened himself away from her, his face thin and ferocious.

"So you think me a coward."

"No, Desmond, I do not. I never did. I think you're extremely brave. You went to prison for your beliefs, and that was terrible, especially for someone like you. I agree with you absolutely about everything. I hate, hate, *hate* killing!"

For a few moments she reflected sombrely, clenching her hands, the unbidden image of Rudi slipping into her vision again. Now it bore the blanched features of death.

"Fares, please," came the voice of the conductress suddenly, and Desmond had to grope in his pocket for the necessary pence. The uncomfortable little spell between them was broken. Imogen slipped her hand back into his.

"Filthy lucre," she said. "But it has a nice normality, hasn't it? Papa says he only feels real when he's counting money. Mind you, I think he's exaggerating. I have an idea, Desmond. Let's start by telling Aunt Clara and Papa and Richard. We'll graduate to Mamma in three short lessons. And Lally, of course."

"Of course. Lally mustn't be forgotten." That was what was so nice about Desmond, his sympathy for the weaker, the underdogs. He was gentle now, that moment of ferocity like a small wild animal inside him, was gone.

"I ought to tell you," Imogen went on, "that we have a Lally recurring in our family. We had an Aunt Julia who disappeared before I was born, and before her a strange great-aunt. You have to know, because I want children."

"We'll have children, never fear."

Imogen hugged his arm. "You see how brave you are, taking on me and an unknown crop of slightly batty daughters."

He didn't laugh, he seldom laughed, but he gave a disbelieving smile.

"You're the last woman I could imagine having a batty daughter."

She nodded. "Thank you for saying so. Anyway, Lally's like she is because she was dropped on her head when she was a baby. She's quite happy in her own quiet way. She'll be awfully impressed by having a brother-in-law who writes books."

"Hold on, I haven't had one published yet."

"But you will, and I'll be so proud. Though can I ever live up to being a writer's wife?"

"I'll have to find out first if I have anything to say." He looked moodily out of the omnibus window. "I doubt if any other writer will have been driven like me."

"Why?" Imogen was a little alarmed by his intensity, her happiness faltering. There was indeed going to be something to being a writer's wife.

"Because I've got to justify staying alive, haven't I? I was probably destined to die in a foul stinking trench."

"Nobody can change their destiny."

"I have, by defying the military. And why should I deserve to be alive when so many are dead?"

That was a question that was always going to torment him, she suspected. But she answered lightly.

"That's exactly what my mother is going to say, I'm afraid. I might as well tell you we'll never convince her otherwise."

"We?" he said tentatively.

"It's you and me together, now. I'll always be at your side, Desmond. Indeed," Imogen gave a fleeting grin, "I'll be the first Duncastle to strike a blow for peace."

"You said Duncastle?"

"That's my mother's family. She's never really regarded herself as anything else, even after getting on for thirty years of marriage to poor Papa. She's a very strong lady, my mother. She'll be looking for an heir to all the family military relics, but that will have to be Richard, not us. I only hope Richard marries the right sort of girl."

Chapter 20

With middle age, Aunt Clara's face had acquired a strange handsomeness, her crooked eye adding to rather than detracting from her look of distinction. She was very thin and upright, plainly dressed as always, her grey hair bound into its usual neat knob on the top of her head. This morning she had an authority that matched Matilda's own.

"Now, Mattie, I've come to discuss the children's future. I will give Imogen and Desmond my house, and you will, naturally, give Richard and Deirdre Sanctuary. Oh, I know you can't turn the convalescent soldiers out, but the war surely can't last too much longer. And as for me being turned out of Cheapside, that's going to happen anyway."

She had successfully distracted Matilda from the main thorny issue. "What do you mean, Clara?"

"I'm sorry if this comes as a shock to you, but I haven't a great deal longer to live. A carcinoma of the left lung. I've known it for some time. There's nothing to be done."

"Clara, my dear—"

"Now I don't want your sympathy. You're a very unsympathetic woman, Mattie, and I wouldn't want your small reserves of that commodity wasted on me. Save it for your children. Don't oppose them so determinedly. You make yourself into an unfeeling monster, and I don't believe you're that."

Matilda's face sharpened and hardened.

"Thank you for that small concession, Clara. But you're like Joshua, you simply won't understand the importance of the traditions of my family, my very *proud* family. Imogen and Richard are making those traditions worth nothing, with their cowardly conscientious objectors, Irish rebels, and all that rag bag collection of friends. What my father would have said I can't imagine."

"Your father isn't here to say anything, Mattie. And I must strongly protest at Desmond being called cowardly. He spent six months in the trenches, didn't you know? Before he had the exceptional courage to stand by his principles and refuse to pick up arms any more. Then he endured a tortured six months in prison, and ever since he has been working as an orderly in a very busy hospital, doing the most menial and distressing tasks. If ever a young man deserved some happiness, he does."

"He's protecting his own skin, isn't he? He's alive while my son is dead."

"And his staying alive won't bring Hillary back. Nor Rudi, whom you seem to have forgotten. Anyway, can't you think of Imogen's happiness?"

"I'll never be able to hold up my head again."

"What's all this to do with *your* head? The miracle would be if you could ever lower it."

Matilda's chin jutted angrily.

"You really don't understand, Clara. I *am* thinking of Imogen and Richard, believe it or not. But I'm also thinking of what my grandchildren will be. We have traditions to be carried on. Hasn't this war shown that? Britain as an island is no longer safe. It has to be defended at all costs. We'll need another generation of brave men. But my grandchildren are to be bred from a young man who refuses to fight for his country, and a squalid little Irish traitor."

Aunt Clara gave an astonished laugh.

"Are you speaking of Deirdre? That beautiful girl? To tell the truth, Mattie, I believe you've met your match in her."

"Never! I only object to her as a daughter-in-law because one will never be able to trust her. Her sympathies will always be with those wicked Sinn Feiners. As for her beauty I fail to see it. She looks a skinny waif to me."

"She's been living on a diet of potatoes, do you suppose?" Aunt Clara asked ironically. "And haven't you by any chance noticed how Richard has come back to life? Or doesn't that matter to you, you stupid woman."

Matilda's eyes gleamed icily.

"Don't call me a stupid woman, Clara. You know I'm not that. And Richard would have come back to life, anyway, given time."

"Mattie, I really believe you're being contrary just for the principle of it. You can't care so little about your children's happiness."

"It's just so unfair," Matilda cried in deep bitterness.

"But war's not fair, is it? I'd have thought you, of all people, with your family history, would know that. Was it fair that the poor little schoolboy should die beating his drum on the plains of Salamanca? Of course it wasn't, no matter what undying myth was established. The Irish have myths about martyrs, too. You must learn to be more tolerant of each other, both you and Deirdre. And Desmond, too. Isn't there enough quarrelling going on in the world?"

"Joshua's put you up to this," Matilda accused.

"No, he has not. But I agree that he'd expect it of me. Now, if I may make a request, in view of my uncertain health, I would like both weddings to take place as soon as possible. Because I want to enjoy them while I can. I don't want to look like a skeleton at the feast."

She gave a small wryly triumphant smile, knowing she had played her trump card. Matilda was nonplussed, her feelings divided between pity for this woman whom she had never disliked, and deep resentment at having her authority over-ruled. Clara was playing a mean trick on her. And was she going to be left in this house with only Lally for company? She was almost back to full circle, Matilda and poor Julia thrust into the cold world alone.

Joshua had not bothered to hide his pleasure about Imogen's and Richard's unfortunate attachments. And now

Clara was issuing this unanswerable challenge. Would she deprive a dying woman of her last request?

Yes, she would, a thousand times—if she could. But this time she knew she couldn't. The Duncastles were temporarily in retreat. She would have to be a graceful loser. The weddings would take place. But they needn't think they had crushed her spirit, because Hillary would be standing on one side of her, holding her hand, and Papa on the other, telling her to stand straight in the face of the enemy.

One thing, she thought, she would never let that treacherously soft-voiced Irish wildcat defeat her.

There was always the possibility—never would she admit this thought to a soul—that Deirdre, absorbed into the English atmosphere at Sanctuary, might breed fighting loyal British sons.

At this moment there was Clara to be cared for. One could not hold the cruel things she had just said against her since her mind must be clouded by her illness. Poor creature. One must be gentle and kind with her.

"I'll think about what you've said, Clara. I'm not as unreasonable as you suppose."

"You just know you're beaten," Clara said.

"I'm far from beaten. I simply must form a new strategy." Matilda gave the charming smile which she had once bestowed on her children when wanting to woo or coerce them.

"Now, shouldn't you be resting, my dear? I'm going to ring for some tea. Or would you prefer a little hot bouillon? Then I will have a cab called for you. When you begin to suffer too much, my poor Clara, will you come here to be nursed? I can arrange for nurses. I know they're scarce nowadays, with so many wounded arriving all the time, but with my connections at the hospitals, something can be done."

"Are you getting round me, Matilda? No, I'll stay in my own home. Joshua is making arrangements. He has friends, too, you must know. But thank you all the same. And I'll tell you the truth, I've always admired you, even if I haven't liked you. That's been a pity, hasn't it?"

Fourth Interval

The shadows are beginning to lengthen across the ground . . .

Where had she heard those words?

She believed it had been at a cricket match at Lord's. The measured voice of the commentator, strictly impartial as always, had come over the radio, and she, sitting at home on a summer afternoon, had imagined the shadows, dark and elongated, staining the sunny pitch, slowly blotting out the exuberant play. England had been winning, she thought. Or losing?

They had begun to lose, lately, and not only cricket matches. Buffeted by blows, near bankruptcy after the crippling cost of two world wars, stupid self-seeking politicians, the Commonwealth countries growing truculent, South Africa, even India, the prize jewel of the Victorians. Would it be the Africans, fired with ambition, hysteria and ignorance, next?

After two such long-drawn-out and terrible wars when the cost of winning seemed more than the cost of losing, was the spirit of the players temporarily diminished? As hers was, although she tried very hard to conceal the fact.

Oh yes, she was tired. Deadly tired. And that woman with something white on her head would keep moving across her vision. Surely it wasn't a bride's veil she was wearing.

"Now, Mrs. Webb, time for your tea. I'm going to prop you up with another pillow."

The woman wasn't a bride after all, but a nurse. The one she had got for Clara in spite of her protests. At least it had enabled Clara to die in her own home as she had wanted to do. Poor creature, turning into a gasping ivory bone. And after her death Imogen and Desmond deciding how they would rearrange the narrow small-roomed house, with a nursery on the top floor, because a baby was coming.

Imogen had been a very pretty bride, though not, one had to admit, a radiant one. There had been a shadow in her eyes that only she, Matilda, her mother, could interpret. A memory of her lost love, poor romantic girl. Well, she had wanted this dark moody young man and now she had got him, so she might have had the grace to sparkle for him.

It was a little galling to remember that the Irish bride had been the admired one. Deirdre with her delicate troubled beauty. Yes, Clara had been right, she was a beauty, and a fiery one at times. Richard was not going to have a calm life with a wife who constantly felt guilty about deserting her country and her revolutionary beliefs for love of an Englishman. But the Irish thrived on conflict, and Richard probably didn't want a calm life. He was besotted with the girl, and she, obviously, with him.

Did those feelings last? Matilda asked this question of the empty air, for she would never know herself. She had never been blindly in love, except with Hillary and to a lesser degree with her other children. But that, one knew, was a different kind of love, though it could be no less painful.

And with the little ones, of course. Johnnie, Patrick, little Mab.

Ah, Johnnie . . .

"Mother, Desmond says Johnnie isn't to stay with you

any more because you will fill his head with dangerous ideas."

"Dangerous ideas! What do you mean, Imogen?"

"Ideas about loyalty, about the glory of fighting and dying for one's country."

"To call that dangerous is a traitorous statement."

"No, it isn't. You must know how gullible children are, how these over-romantic notions take root. Johnnie's our only child and it's worrying Desmond terribly that you're encouraging him to think of nothing but beating a drum. Desmond says, if he has to, he'll destroy the Salamanca Drum, and all the rest of that morbid Death Room."

What an empty threat that was. Desmond was incapable of violent action as he had so shamefully proved during the war. So the drum was still safely in the Death Room, beating merrily, drowning the distant babble of voices and the occasional furtive scrabbling in the corridor, as if someone were spying on her.

Rat-a-tat, rat-a-tat, rat-a-tat . . .

One had known for a long time that it must have been Hillary who had thrown the inkpot at Great-grandfather's portrait. But not in malice, of course, only in youthful high spirits. He would have confessed one day, if he had lived long enough.

That was why she had taken all that trouble to find out for Imogen what had happened to Rudi. But Imogen had misunderstood and had not been in the least grateful. Poor child. She had been too young to suffer such a painful bereavement.

Rudi was dead, and so, later, was his father.

"We won't be resuming connections with the Vienna branch now the war's over," Joshua was saying. "I've just heard that Paul von Klein died of influenza last winter. I don't want to begin again with new people. I was fond of Paul. I think you were, too, in spite of everything."

"In spite of what?"

"He was a foreigner, wasn't he? You always kept saying so. You do have this obsession about foreigners, Mattie. You should have lived in the Middle Ages, in a moated castle, and kept watch over the battlements for the invader.

Anyway, Vienna, the whole of Austria, is going to have a bad financial crisis. Worse than ours, if that's possible."

"We did win the war, Joshua."

"But there are no spoils in modern wars, Mattie. The victor is left with an enormous debt that may very well break his back."

"What about the ideals we fought for?"

"Intangibles, Mattie. They don't seem to mean much nowadays."

So there was no more Paul. Nor the brief secret love that had perished, like a fragile butterfly, overnight.

Why did Deirdre, with her swift radiant glances at Richard, or her violent tempers that ended in soft tear-stained reconciliations, always make her remember Paul von Klein? Count Paul coming to Sanctuary on that grey winter afternoon . . .

"It's no use scolding me, Richard. Deirdre and I are like oil and water. We simply don't mix. Of course I'll go on airing my views on bringing up Patrick, even if his mother never listens to a word. Just don't let him visit his grandparents in Dublin too often. You know the Irish aren't to be trusted. If ever I hear of Sinn Fein meetings at Sanctuary I'll set fire to the place."

"Mother, the Irish have their independence now."

"Which makes them foreigners, you know very well."

"And Patrick is only eight years old."

"And he has a wild look to him, just like his mother. No, I'll be polite to your wife, but I am quite unable to love her."

"Are you able to love anyone, Mother?"

"How dare you say that to me!"

"I know you have a terrible possessiveness, Mother, but that isn't love."

She was picking at the bedclothes, struggling with those old acute emotions. No one, no one, could have loved more than she could have. Given the chance . . .

My emotions were nipped with frost—when I was very young—when I had to marry unwillingly. But they rage inside me, Richard . . .

There was no Richard there to listen to her, she re-

alized fretfully. He was a country squire down at Sanctuary, doing all the rustic tasks of which he was capable with his helpless right arm. No shooting, no gardening, but a little riding, and chiefly breeding horses, jumpers, because that was Deirdre's thing. Bloodstock equal to the big-boned brave horses bred in Ireland.

Richard had decided long ago, when Joshua's bank had been part of a merger, to give up being "and Son," as he put it. Nor was either Patrick or Johnnie to be "and Son." Joshua would have been desperately disappointed.

Matilda moved again, restlessly, pushing away the hot wrinkled sheets. Her memory was suddenly becoming too clear, too uncomfortable. The things she wanted to forget were vivid, the happier things . . . What happier things?

"M-mamma, are you too hot?" Only Lally called her Mamma nowadays. "I've told Nurse to go downstairs for a cup of tea. Is there anything I can get you? All those p-people will be going home soon. We've made quite a lot of m-money, but we're going to be left with the usual horrid old junk. I'll p-put it in the attic for next year."

She clearly recognized Lally's perpetually anxious stammering voice. Couldn't she have stopped being anxious after—after what?

"Lally, why must you make your drawings so cruel? Do I look like that? A hawk about to strike?"

"With your nose, M-mamma—it does stick out. You shouldn't be ashamed, M-mamma. Some faces are just b-blobs."

"I'm never ashamed, you foolish girl."

"Mamma, you always forget, I'm n-nearly sixty."

"Then you're old enough to button your dress properly. Look at that, crooked as usual. You get more like Julia all the time. I wonder——"

"What, M-mamma?"

"Where she is."

"B-but don't you remember——"

What was it she was supposed to remember! She said fretfully, "I wish Richard's girl wasn't so fair."

"Mab? I thought she was a little like me."

"God forbid."

"Only in looks. She hasn't got my stupid brains. She's t-terribly clever, Mamma."

"Naughty and sly. She's trouble. But what can you expect, with the mother she has."

"M-mamma, do drink your tea. I'll hold the cup. The p-people are beginning to go. It's nearly dark. And M-Mab's mother is dead."

The shadows are beginning to lengthen across the ground . . .

Chapter 21

Deirdre flatly refused to come to the will reading. She thought it a barbaric custom. Besides, she was expecting another baby and her pregnancy had been complicated by two near miscarriages. It was because, against the doctor's orders, she would insist on riding. She had ridden until Patrick was seven months on the way and no harm had come to her, or to him.

But after the second episode she reluctantly agreed to stay off horses. She wanted this baby very much. She had always hoped for a large family, six or seven at least, she said, but after Patrick there had been eight years of barrenness. She and Imogen had had to console one another, for Imogen was in the same position, with only Johnnie, a difficult highly strung introverted little boy, clattering about the house and making his father, who worked in the small back study downstairs, shout with impatience. But Imogen had not conceived again, although she was far too young to give up hope.

And Deirdre was now six months pregnant, although her slender body, cleverly dressed in the bright loose gowns she loved, emerald green and crimson, scarcely showed the coming baby.

Nevertheless, although she had been well enough to go to Joshua's funeral, she declared herself too frail to attend the will reading the following day.

Of course she would be strong enough for a funeral, Matilda thought. The Irish took a morbid pleasure in the panoply of grief.

There had been a long line of yews, dark tapers, leading to the graveyard. The small grey-spired church at the end of the avenue had seemed infinitely far away, as if Joshua's last journey were never-ending. Yet in reality his life had ended very suddenly, with his collapse at the bank, sitting at his cherished partners' desk, and then his brief four days in the hospital, fighting, though not very hard, Matilda suspected, to live. He had been worn out from overwork during the war, the doctor said.

Matilda had felt secretly outraged. She had always thought Joshua had had a good war, not bearing arms, doing the work he enjoyed above everything. She was also outraged, or perhaps puzzled would be a more accurate word, by the tight little bunch of violets on his locker in the hospital. Who had brought them? Not Imogen or Deirdre, though both would gladly have smothered him in flowers when he was well enough to enjoy them.

The nurse said a woman, she thought perhaps she was Mr. Webb's secretary, had put them there.

"But how was she allowed in?" Matilda asked angrily. "My husband isn't to see anyone but his own family."

"I don't know, Mrs. Webb, honestly. She must have just slipped in and out."

One would have to check at the bank. Matilda hadn't known Joshua had a devoted secretary. But she hadn't known much about what went on in the bank. She hadn't visited it for a very long time. She had never been interested in it, other than as a source of money. The servants' wages and household expenses had been brought down each week by a clerk and her own cheques were never queried.

Yes, Joshua had kept his promise and given her security. But it worried her that someone else had thought to express gratitude, or some other sentiment, with that bunch of violets. While she could stand at his bedside, disturbed and concerned, but quite tearless.

Wasn't she famous in her family for never crying? So why should she begin now?

Joshua had died a rich man. Three hundred thousand pounds in investments, not including the Kensington Square house. He had come a long way from the bank clerk who had once stared at her stubbornly and insisted that she must marry him. But not further than she had expected. She had known he would succeed as a business man, if not as a husband.

But then had she succeeded as a wife? That thought struck her acutely as she listened to Mr. Briarly, Joshua's solicitor and friend, reading the will in his pedantic voice.

A life interest to her (which will leave you comfortably provided for, Mrs. Webb), legacies of one hundred pounds each to the servants who had been with them for more than ten years, Minnie, cook, Albert the chauffeur, and to three of the older bank employees. Also a hundred pounds each to his grandsons, Patrick Webb and John Morrison, to be spent immediately, and entirely as they decided. Joshua had been aggravatingly sentimental about his grandsons.

After those expected bequests, there had come a surprising one. Five thousand pounds to a certain Prudence Nesbit "whose friendship has meant a great deal to me." Mr. Briarly's voice hesitated only slightly before going on, "On my wife's death, the residue of my estate to be divided equally between my three children, though I direct that the Kensington Square house be transferred to my daughter Eulalie, my other children being already possessed of residences."

It was a very fair will, except for the mysterious legacy of five thousand pounds. This was not a shopgirl getting away with a gold watch, this was a considerable sum of money.

But for once Matilda had no desire to pursue the matter. She preferred not to know who Prudence Nesbit was. If Joshua had meant to humiliate her by giving her this public slap in the face, then she would never let anyone know that he had succeeded. She would push the episode out of her mind. It all went to show that Joshua had never been entirely a gentleman.

They had made a misalliance and obviously Prudence Nesbit was the result. Who was to be blamed?

But it was galling to have failed him so badly. She had never intended to be a failure. If Joshua hadn't had that pathological dislike for Julia, if he hadn't been so opposed to army careers for the boys, if he hadn't secretly disliked Hillary because of his being all Duncastle, even if he had been more congenial, both in conversation and, yes, she must admit, in bed, she wouldn't have failed.

On reflecting further on the matter she decided that Joshua had probably decided that it was more important to make this public acknowledgement of his mistress, for her sake, than it was to humiliate his wife. One must accept those facts and forget the matter.

Imogen, with a curiosity she couldn't hide, said, "Mother, don't you want to know more about this woman? Would you like me to find out?"

"No. I want nothing stirred up. Leave it alone."

"You can't pretend she doesn't exist."

"And why not? What's wrong with that? One couldn't face life without some subterfuges. I don't blame your father. He was lonely, and that was probably my fault. I don't even grudge the money. I grudge Hillary's gold watch far more."

"For that little stick of a girl. Oh, Mother!"

"It was a family thing. Money's anonymous."

"I long to know what she looks like," Imogen sighed.

Matilda drew herself up with her formidable elegance. "Your father didn't find my looks unattractive."

"I know. He admired you enormously. I'll bet Prudence Nesbit can't hold a candle to you."

But she would be warm and cosy and welcoming beneath the bedclothes, and that was undoubtedly the most important thing to a man. One accepted that fact, and put it out of one's mind forever.

There was a slight disturbing repercussion, however.

Just when Matilda had succeeded in believing that Prudence Nesbit did not exist—it was surprising how important it had become to believe that—a small package marked personal was found in a locked drawer of the partners' desk at the bank and sent to Matilda. Mr. Briarly hadn't taken the liberty of opening it, thinking Matilda would prefer to do so.

She found a collection of objects, astonishing for someone as blunt and unsentimental as Joshua. Had she not known him at all?

A plain gold wedding ring (that woman must have given it to him, how dare she!), a briar pipe (he had never smoked a pipe in Matilda's company), two locks of very fine curling brown hair, one tied with a pink ribbon, one with a blue (baby hair, heaven forbid!) and a letter written in childish handwriting.

Dear Mr. Webb,
    When we got to Gran's she took us into the paddock to show us the pony. She said you had given it to us. It is a little beauty. Grandpa is going to teach us to ride it. We are calling it Topsy because it is black and a mare. That was Pansy's choice. Mine was Queenie. Gran said girls should have first choice, but I don't agree. I hope you are on my side. Men should stick together.
                        Your affec. friend Ronald.

In one swift furious movement Matilda flung the entire contents of the package, including the obscene wedding ring, on to the fire.

Now she had forgotten everything. As quickly as that.

"Would you be able to behave as Mother is doing?" Imogen asked Deirdre. "If you discovered after his death that Richard had had a mistress. Mother has successfully convinced herself that Prudence doesn't exist."

"I'd find the woman and tear her limb from limb," Deirdre said. "Make no mistake."

"I'd certainly want to see her," Imogen decided. "If

just to find out what my husband found in her that he didn't find in me."

"And then mend your ways?"

"I suppose if I could."

"That's abasing yourself. If you're the person Desmond wanted to marry, then you mustn't attempt to change. I couldn't. I know I'm me, bitchy and bad-tempered and crazy, and Irish, and Richard loves me in spite of all."

"You sound so sure."

"I am sure. Aren't you sure of Desmond?"

"I think so. But he's such a shut-away person. He gets so deep in the book he's writing."

Deirdre's gaze was far off. She was pursuing her own thoughts.

"But Richard wouldn't."

"Wouldn't what?"

"Have a Prudence. Or a Penelope or a Pamela or any other woman."

"Nor would Desmond."

"So I suppose we can't really know how your mother feels. Does she feel anything? She always looks to me as if she should be on top of a monument with that beautiful frozen nose in the air."

"Oh, yes, she can feel," Imogen said. "When we were children she could be delightful. I remember her coming into my room in the middle of the night when I'd been running a temperature, that gorgeous hair tumbling over a green dressing gown."

"Did your father ever see her like that?"

"Don't be silly, he must have."

"Well, I still think it would be like taking a national monument into bed," Deirdre said, her cat-like face languid and malicious.

"I admit Mother's wildly patriotic, but so are you."

"Granted. Only I'd do the fighting myself, not send my son to die."

"Don't be unfair, Deirdre, you know Mother would have wielded a battle axe if she could have. She did get the O.B.E., you know."

"I know."

"And she said the King's remarks were far more important to her than the medal. He said he knew her family's proud record, and this country was going to need more illustrious defenders, like the Duncastles. So you see what sort of a family you've married into."

"And Joshua took a mistress," murmured Deirdre.

"Deirdre, you're cruel. I wonder Richard doesn't beat you."

Deirdre's eyes gleamed.

"He would if he could. But he has only one effective arm. My beautiful beloved husband."

Deirdre's baby was expected early in the new year. She told Richard that she was feeling magnanimous and would like a family Christmas at Sanctuary. As well as Imogen and Desmond and Johnnie, she would insist on Matilda and Lally coming.

"What shall we drink while your mother's here? I shall need something to nicely blur my senses and make me keep my temper."

"I wish you and Mother would get on better."

"How can we when she only tolerates me because of Patrick? Imogen says she does the same with Desmond, because of Johnnie. Do you think she's safe with our little boys?"

"Don't be absurd, she dotes on them."

"Don't you see, that's the dangerous thing. She tells them long stories of battles, and she shows them those old weapons. Imogen says Johnnie has nightmares afterwards."

"What about Patrick?"

Deirdre pulled Richard closer by grasping a handful of his hair.

"Our son is Irish."

"Half Irish."

"That's enough. Anyway, he says he'd rather have a horse than a gun."

"Naturally, you being his mother."

"I wouldn't mind him having a bit of the financier, like your lovely father, in him. But I won't have the Duncastle side in my children. Those memorials in the church depress me enough, not to mention the family portraits. Tyrants, all of them."

"You secretly admire them. Confess."

"I admit they're splendid-looking men. I do like a good-looking man. And I like to think they had enough time away from battle to scatter their seed a little, so that I got you, my darling. And I do enjoy a bit of a fight myself, I won't pretend not to. But fighting isn't part of being a mother. That's where Matilda and I will always disagree. She wants to drill little soldiers. I want to channel those fighting qualities into other things. I'm like Desmond there, though I'm far from being a conscientious objector. Anyway, your mother's death and glory ideas won't have any effect on our Patrick. He's his own man. I'm not so sure about Johnnie."

"Johnnie always seems a scared little rabbit to me."

"But he's material that can be worked on. If I were Imogen I'd be worried. I expect Johnnie is his father's son and lives an intense secret life. If only Imogen could have kept that beautiful Rudi."

"You're talking an awful lot, aren't you?"

Deirdre snuggled against Richard on the couch. "Don't I always? I think I'd like this baby to be another boy. So long as your mother leaves him alone."

"You have an obsession about my mother, my love. She's just an aging lady living in the past."

"Aging lady, my oath. She's as strong as iron, and she will be until her dying day. If she ever dies." Deirdre sighed. "Don't get me wrong, I admire her enormously. We must persuade her to come for Christmas. She'll make a marvelous decoration in this dark old house."

Chapter 22

The day before Christmas it began to snow. Matilda and Lally, met at the railway station by Eddy, the head groom who was also employed to drive Richard's Bentley, had problems on the icy road. They nearly spun off twice, and Matilda said that she considered the days of the coach and horses much safer. She was wrapped in a long fur-trimmed cape, with a fur toque to match. A vague memory stirred in Lally's brain. Something about a channel crossing and a foreign train, and then a gloomy castle with endless stairs, and her ankle hurting. Or was that a story she had once been told?

Mamma seldom came to Sanctuary now, partly because it was Richard's home and partly because she obstinately refused to like Richard's wife, Deirdre, whom Lally could never stop looking at. She was as graceful and mysterious as a slender young cat. Lally would have liked her to come often to Kensington Square so that she could sketch her. But she seldom came. Just Richard and Patrick, more often Richard by himself.

But now they were to be at Sanctuary for a week she would have plenty of opportunities to sit quietly in a corner and sketch the lovely young mistress of Sanctuary, her body as round as a snowball with the coming baby, her beautiful eyes soft and far-off as if she were dreaming all the time of her new son or daughter.

It was a pity, however, that Mamma had been reluctant to come. It meant she might be in one of her difficult moods all the time. Was Mamma, Lally wondered, ever really happy?

For Lally herself, happiness was sitting under the mulberry tree in the garden at Kensington Square, with her sketching pad and pencils, the friendly robin hopping at her feet. Or going on an ambling undemanding walk with Minnie who was now over seventy and stooped with rheumatism. Or taking a packet of stale bread to the Round Pond so that she could make quick sketches of the ducks as they dived for the lumps of soggy bread crust. Happiness was a state of living that made no demands on her shy and quivering personality. Bliss, to Lally, was being unnoticed, actually invisible. She didn't know why she had been born like that. She didn't understand what old friends of Mamma's meant when they looked at her sideways and whispered, "Julia." She knew there was a ghost called Julia in the old house in Kensington. No one had told her, but she knew. And sometimes people mistook her for that ghost because she slipped about in such a silent way. She had her revenge on people like that by sketching their faces, making them sharp and beaky like ill-tempered birds.

She knew she had been a bitter disappointment to Papa and Mamma, but Imogen and Richard were her friends. Not Desmond. She felt uncomfortable with him, not knowing what went on behind his dark brooding eyes. Deirdre made her shy, she was so quick and witty and unpredictable, but her radiance spilled over and some of it touched Lally, making her want to be in the same room as Deirdre as much as possible. She had never stopped missing dear Aunt Clara.

The two little boys, Patrick and Johnnie, teased her by jumping out at her from behind curtains so that she screamed, or talking to her in deliberately unintelligible language. They giggled a great deal at her bewilderment. But she was secretly looking forward to Deirdre's new baby, even hoping it would be born before Christmas was over. She adored mothering tiny helpless things, fledglings fallen out of nests or stray kittens. She could never understand why she hadn't been allowed to nurse either Patrick or Johnnie unless someone else was present. It hurt her very much not to be trusted. She hoped Deirdre would be more generous with the new baby.

But in the meantime there was the Christmas tree (that reminded her of another occasion when there were those funny foreign children at Kensington Square and Mamma had beaten the Salamanca Drum), there was her old bedroom looking over the Dutch garden (where she had sat sketching Hillary, Richard and Imogen on that long-ago dream-like summer afternoon), and there was her new dress which she had been allowed to choose herself, a dark red velvet like a ripe plum that gave her a warm pleasure. She loved colour. She was beginning to use coloured pencils in her sketches. She wanted to do Deirdre in her long loose violet-coloured dress that made her look like a young Empress. She was really going to be happy at Sanctuary.

There was, unfortunately, a bit of a fuss before dinner the first evening. Since it was Christmas Eve, Patrick and Johnnie had been told they could stay up for dinner, but when the gong rang there was no sign of them. Nor of Matilda.

Deirdre was getting impatient. Desmond went off to see if the boys were in their room. Johnnie always wanted to share Patrick's bedroom when he came to Sanctuary. He adored Patrick, six months older, half a head taller, and apparently scared of nothing. Johnnie, his mother knew, was secretly nervous in this big dark house with its winding passages and unexpected stairways. He missed the familiar street sounds of London, and found the screech of an owl, or some small captured animal in the night, highly alarming. He would never admit this, however. Instead, he became noisy and excitable and sometimes cried out in his sleep, to Patrick's disgust. He was a thin little boy with the long Duncastle nose. He was growing disturbingly like his dead uncle, Hillary. Imogen never commented on this, especially to Desmond who had an academic career planned for his son and did not want any star-struck admiration for military things, or dead heroes.

It was too much to hope that Matilda had not noticed the growing resemblance to Hillary. She made no secret of the fact that Johnnie was her favourite grandson. Patrick was too elusive. "Irish," Matilda said scornfully. "He never listens." But Johnnie listened too intently and never forgot anything.

Desmond came back shortly to report that the boys' room was empty, and so was Matilda's. He had tapped tentatively on that door, and then had looked in to see that the light had been left burning, Matilda's evening wrap was lying on the bed, but she herself was not there. Were there rooms in use on the second floor? He hadn't liked to investigate.

"Nervous, old chap?" Richard asked lightly. "The main room on the second floor is where our great-great-aunt Tatiana was supposed to have been kept in captivity. Isn't that right, Imogen? She was loony. So they said. A lot of families had loony spinster aunts a century ago." Richard decided to enlarge on the subject. Something had to be done to make this party go.

"Then there was our mysterious Aunt Julia who we didn't know, although I believe Lally had the distinction of being nursed by her."

"Me!" Lally exclaimed involuntarily, forgetting that she had meant to stay quiet and invisible so that people wouldn't think they had to engage her in conversation. Besides, she was still thinking of that curiously disturbing thing that had happened while she was alone in her room. She had looked out of her window at the snow deepening over the lawns and weighing down the trees when a shape on the lawn, just near the broken statue of the little boy with vines round his hair, had moved. At first she had thought it was a very large squirrel. With her usual instinctive reaction she had grabbed her sketch book and made one of her lightning drawings. The garden buried beneath the snow, the bending trees, and in the middle of the white expanse the crouching animal. But the long ears weren't a squirrel's. Besides, it was pure white like the snow. Did an animal allow itself to be coated with snow?

"Behave yourself, Richard," Deirdre scolded. "The time for ghost stories is just before midnight. And go and find your mother and the boys, otherwise we'll have cook going on strike."

The three culprits, if one dared to include Matilda in that definition, were at last discovered in the gun room. One might have guessed they would be there, and even what they would be doing. "We're fighting the Battle of Salamanca," Matilda announced. She, dressed in one of her stately dinner gowns, and wearing her diamonds, was holding an unsheathed sword as if it were a baton, and giving instructions to the little boys. "Patrick is on the French side, under Marshal Marmont, and Johnnie is taking orders from the great Duke himself, and bearing the regimental colour."

Johnnie certainly was attempting to carry the dusty and tattered battle colour, but it was too heavy to hold upright, and the dust was making him sneeze. Patrick, however, was showing suitable fighting spirit, if getting a little mixed in history. "Surrender, you dirty British divils! Up with the Irish!"

"No, Patrick, no, you're French," Matilda protested impatiently. "And you're giving ground to the British. You must retreat."

"I'll not give ground to the murdering British. So!" Patrick declared. "Up with the Sinn Fein!"

Matilda sighed exasperatedly, then saw that the door had opened and that she was being watched.

"I'm not mad," she said calmly. "Only a little overheated. I thought I would amuse the boys and give them a lesson in history. Your Johnnie is a real little soldier, Imogen, but Patrick—"

"Patrick isn't required to learn British history," Deirdre said coldly. "His father and I will be the judge of what his education should be."

"And Johnnie no doubt is going on the stage one

day," Imogen said, quickly forestalling Desmond's anger. He was quite likely to pack up and leave the house if he got too upset. The idea of his son being a soldier was ludicrous and insulting. "Mother, you're being very naughty, getting the boys so excited."

"Oh dear," said Matilda, deliberately unrepentant. "Do you all disapprove? But this is such a wonderful house for military games. It has so much more room than Kensington Square. Though we really needed the Salamanca Drum as the British were advancing. Didn't we, Johnnie?"

"I'd beat it until I was shot dead," Johnnie shouted.

"If ever I find you beating that pernicious drum," Desmond said, very quietly, "I'll give you a beating you won't forget."

"Desmond, it's only a game," Imogen protested. "But Mother, promise! Let the boys learn their history out of books. And we're keeping Deirdre waiting for dinner."

"Oh, do forgive me, Deirdre." Matilda was at her most formal. "I momentarily forgot I wasn't in my own house."

"And that Patrick and Johnnie weren't your own sons," Deirdre said.

"Yes. I believe I did forget. Johnnie has an occasional look of Hillary. But Patrick—you must remember, Deirdre, that he's going to be brought up as a British schoolboy. He really mustn't be encouraged to shout rebel slogans. And as for what I do myself, yes, this is your house now, my dear. But its memories are mine. I can't give them away, but I'm always more than delighted to share them with sympathetic people."

"Don't mind her," Richard whispered to Deirdre, as finally everyone went back to the dining room. "I think she's going a bit balmy. If we opened her head I believe we'd find a regiment of the line tumbling out."

There were angry spots of colour in Deirdre's cheeks.

"I believe she's Britain's answer to Ireland's Cathleen n'Houlihan. A blood-sucking female who drives her sons to battle for love of their country."

"Strong drinks all round are indicated," Richard said

soothingly. "We might even spike Patrick's and Johnnie's lemonade."

Deirdre at last began to smile.

"A drop of Guinness would do them both, and me too, a power of good. I've just been wondering what possessed me to marry into this mad English family. I thought we were better at the family skeleton game in Ireland, but I've changed my mind." A sound caught her ear. "Oh, listen! I can hear the carol singers. We'll have to postpone dinner again. They must come in. They'll be snowy and frozen. But how nice!" Deirdre was vivid and glowing again. "It will calm everybody down. You can't fight battles to the tune of 'Silent Night.' "

The little group of carol singers, scarved and overcoated and snow-sprinkled, trooped into the firelit great hall. They were cheerful and noisy. As they began to sing "The Holly and the Ivy" everyone joined in, even Matilda, standing regally in the centre of the group, her diamonds sparkling.

Richard had hastened to pour drinks, whisky or rum for those who wanted to keep out the cold, ginger beer for the children. It became a merry party and suddenly no one was worrying about cook and her spoilt dinner, or any other undercurrents.

When the visitors at last prepared to leave it had stopped snowing. Richard held the door open to a frozen night, not a leaf stirring, not a solitary snowflake drifting down. Someone was clutching him, tugging at his arm, dragging him back indoors. He thought it was Patrick. He snatched his arm away to wave to the departing carol singers. Hell, didn't Patrick know he had only one useful arm.

But it wasn't Patrick. It was Lally and she was pointing at something in the white garden.

"There it is again," she stuttered. "S-see it, Richard. That animal."

"I don't see a thing. You're looking at that old statue of the little boy. It's falling to pieces. Looks a bit like an animal, I suppose. Deirdre, do you see a strange animal on our lawn? Lally thinks she does." Deirdre was at his side.

"Not a thing. What have you been giving her to drink, Richard? Poor child, she's shivering. Come indoors."

Matilda came across the hall.

"What is it, Lally?"

"N-nothing, M-mamma. I just thought I s-saw that animal again."

"Again? What animal?"

"I s-saw it earlier. I m-made a sketch of it. It really was there. It was white, like the snow. I'll s-show you."

They all had to go back to the drawing room where Lally had left her sketch book. She was trembling with some kind of excitement or fear.

"L-look!" she said, thrusting the sketch at her mother, at Deirdre and Imogen. And then at Richard who followed them in a minute or two later, kicking snow off his shoes.

The sketch showed a long-eared animal sitting up alertly. Too big for a rabbit, more like a hare. Though if there were any hares lurking in the garden at Sanctuary they would not be white.

An arctic hare . . .

"She's been having one of her hallucinations," said Matilda sharply. "I was afraid this visit might be too much for her. She lives such a quiet life. On doctor's orders, as you all know. She has such an uncertain emotional balance."

Being the subject of conversation had made Lally retreat into one of her withdrawn states. She crouched by the fire in her gay red dress, her face expressionless, her eyes wide and empty.

"It's a clever sketch," said Desmond. "Imogen, I didn't know your sister drew so well."

"There are no footprints of any animal in the garden," said Richard. "I've just looked. There aren't even bird prints, since the snow's only just stopped. There's a clean slate to be written on out there. Lally must have been having one of her dreams."

"So that—creature was in her head," said Deirdre. Her eyes were dark and enormous. "How odd. Spooky." She shivered slightly.

"Wouldn't someone else have seen it if it were actually there?" Richard demanded. "I suppose there's a chance it could have been a fox."

"Or a hedgehog," suggested Patrick. "There was a hedgehog in the summer."

"Now you're being absurd," said Deirdre. She had recovered her composure. "I could make suggestions myself. Like a small polar bear or a white goose or an albino squirrel."

"Or a goblin," shouted Johnnie in his over-excited voice.

This reduced both boys to a state of giggles that were only suppressed by a prompt removal to the dining room and the delayed dinner.

After dinner Desmond asked Lally to show him more of the drawings in her sketch book. He studied them with growing interest and finally said, "These really are good. They ought to be shown to someone. I believe I'll take them to Bill Cruickshank."

"You mean they might be saleable! Lally's scrawls!" Imogen was surprised.

"Perhaps not saleable individually, but I'd think there's a chance she could make a very clever book illustrator."

"But Desmond, you know how overwrought Lally gets. She wouldn't be up to the responsibility of a real job."

"Try her. Give her a little self-confidence and she could blossom."

"Darling, you're awfully thoughtful and kind, but—"

"Poor Lally is the scapegoat in your family?"

"I didn't mean that. Only how could she have imagined that hare?"

"Because she heard an old story as a child, and it's foxed in her brain," Richard said thoughtfully. "Maybe she saw something, maybe not. I wouldn't put anything past happening in this house. It's just lucky it wasn't Great-grandfather's portrait in the firing line this time. But do you really think Lally has talent, Desmond?"

"I do."

"Mother, do you hear that? Desmond thinks something could be done with Lally's sketches."

"She seems a complete natural," said Desmond. "What's called a naïf in the artistic world."

"Naïf is the word," Matilda said. She had been silent all through dinner, and still seemed to be brooding, her face sharpened and distant. "And I'd rather you didn't draw anyone's attention to Lally's scrawls. I can see what you're thinking, Desmond. That I'm an ignorant philistine who doesn't understand modern art. Or should I say modern fashions, as I refuse to believe Lally's work is art. However, my objections have nothing to do with the quality of the work. They have to do with my daughter's emotional instability. She could never cope with even the mildest publicity. And think what an unkind critic could make of her. Or hadn't you thought of that? Photographs, interviews, making the most of their unique subject. No, I absolutely forbid it. Lally must remain undiscovered and undisturbed. Leave her as she is, as happy as it's possible for her to be."

Later, in bed, snuggling beneath the goose feather quilt, curling against her husband's warm body, Deirdre said, "I wish this baby could be born soon. Tomorrow even."

"Are you getting tired, my darling? You've still four weeks to go."

"I know."

"Everything was too much tonight. I shouldn't have allowed it."

"But it was lovely. In patches."

"Ah well. That's life. Patchy."

Deirdre fondled Richard's withered arm, massaging it gently.

"Perhaps I wouldn't have loved you so much if you'd been whole. Now I have a special tenderness. You know, don't you?"

His strong arm wrapped round her.

"Yes, I know."

"So if our baby—no, it doesn't matter."

"If our baby what?"

"I said it doesn't matter. It's nothing. That goose, or whatever Lally saw, has just tramped over me."

"It was a leprechaun, alannah. And it came to bring us luck."

"Did it?"

"Well, isn't that what they do?"

"I've heard so. I'm not superstitious myself."

"You expect me to believe that! Irish born and bred and not superstitious."

She had stiffened slightly.

"Not English superstitions."

Richard was silent a moment.

"Ah well. I don't blame you. We haven't the Celtic touch." He pulled her head on to his breast. "Go to sleep now, little love." Quite uncharacteristically he heard himself adding, "God keep you safe."

Twenty-four hours later Deirdre went into labour. Richard sat beside her until he was forcibly turned out of the room by the doctor and nurse who had arrived as quickly as the frozen roads would permit. But there had been no need for haste, as it seemed as if the labour would be prolonged. Since the birth was four weeks premature Doctor Woods would have preferred his patient to be in hospital, but moving her, with road conditions as they were, would be foolhardy.

When Richard came out of the bedroom he went down to the library and poured himself a drink with an oddly stiffened hand. My God, if this arm packs up, too, he thought irrelevantly . . . But he had been gripping Deirdre's hand for nearly twelve hours, and now his muscles seemed to be locked in a paralysis.

He had never seen her so distressed. At Patrick's birth she had been excited and jubilant, making little of her pain, only longing for her baby to appear.

But this time she had been half delirious, clinging to him, sobbing, and talking confusedly about witchcraft.

Damn that stupid Lally and her fancies. She seemed to have infected the whole household with some quite unwarranted apprehension.

Richard wanted to be left alone in the library until the doctor summoned him, but inevitably his mother found him there.

"How is she, Richard?"

"Doing nicely, according to the doctor."

"Will the baby be all right?"

"It's premature."

"I know. That was a silly question."

"Deirdre's sorry about spoiling your Christmas. She wanted me to apologise to you."

"It's not her fault. Poor child." Richard realized in mild surprise that his mother was speaking with genuine feeling. She had never before shown anything but veiled animosity towards Deirdre.

"I blame Lally's hysterics," she went on. "Bringing up that foolish ghost story. I hope Deirdre isn't afraid."

"My wife isn't afraid of anything," Richard lied.

"I'm glad to hear that. Our family is one of the finest in England. It isn't tainted, you know."

Except by arrogance and conceit and heroism and dedication to Empire, and a touch of paranoia. But what could one expect, since for generations it had been bled of its best sons?

"What are you thinking, Richard?" his mother asked. "You're scowling dreadfully."

"I'm thinking that Patrick and Johnnie—and this new baby, too—must be allowed to live to old age."

"So they will, my dear. Unless there's another war. We must always be prepared. Anyway, what's so appealing about old age? I can tell you I don't look forward to mine."

The baby was born just before midnight. It was a girl, tiny and wizened. Deirdre lay hugging the tiny bundle against her breast. Richard could see only the crown of the head, naked except for the faintest covering of silky white hair.

Oh, God, it was true, it was one of the blonde ones! An Aunt Julia, a Lally . . .

"Can't I see her face? he asked.

"It's only the size of a button." Deirdre pulled back the coverings, revealing the soft formless face. "She's got to start doing some growing. We must take the greatest care of her."

Was it wise? Hadn't Mother's last child, a girl like this, fortunately died at birth?

"What shall we call her?" he asked, trying to sound completely normal himself.

"She's too small for a long name." Deirdre's face was tired and luminous. She seemed to have been taken by surprise by this minute living morsel in her arms, and was totally enchanted with it. "I'm going to call her Mab."

"Just Mab?"

"I think it suits her. Richard—my darling husband—I think I—Mab and I—are both falling asleep."

He had an odd uneasy feeling, as Deirdre's eyes closed and her thick dark lashes lay immobile on her cheeks, that part of her had left him, and would never come back. It would belong instead to this tiny goblin child.

Chapter 23

Desmond had had his first book, a novel on social attitudes, published two years after he and Imogen were married. It earned him a literary reputation and very little money. Since then he had published three more novels and in addition to his earnings from these, made a small income from reviewing other people's books, and giving lectures. Since Aunt Clara had bequeathed them her house they were able to live modestly on Desmond's earnings. Neither Imogen nor he had any desire for an extravagant way of life. It was only Matilda who was shocked by Imogen's shabbiness and insisted on giving her a new dress from time to time.

Matilda, never very tactful with her gifts, said bluntly that she didn't want to be ashamed of her daughter. Besides, this was only anticipating the legacy she would eventually receive under her father's will, when she would be a comparatively rich woman. How Desmond would accept having a rich wife was not known, but he did deeply resent the interim gifts. He was even less tactful at receiving than Matilda was at giving. He wanted to forbid

Imogen to wear the clothes which he regarded as highly unsuitable for the kind of life they led.

Did being good and having a social conscience and all that have to be so dreary? Imogen wondered privately and with a guilty feeling of disloyalty to her husband. She had been accustomed to quality all her life, and she would swish about in taffeta skirts at literary parties if she pleased, and if she did make most of the other women look shabby and half-starved—as one suspected they were. Artists, she had discovered, were seldom financially successful people, and this made some of them, though not all, a little sour and contemptuous. Desmond was not either of those things. He had too good a mind. He genuinely didn't care about money or possessions, and expected his wife and son to share his views.

The clothes Matilda gave Imogen were a comparatively small matter. The question of Johnnie's education was much more important and contentious. Matilda wanted to send him to Hillary's and Richard's old preparatory school. He was her favourite grandchild, so receptive and responsive, with those wide eyes and pale intense little face. Patrick, freckled, ginger-headed, unruly and inattentive, was, to Matilda's mind, a complete little Irish outlaw. There was, disappointingly, no Duncastle in him. Mab was an odd little creature, not dim as they had all privately feared she would be, but almost precociously intelligent and perpetually restless. She never seemed to stop moving, or to grow, or sleep. She was the size of a dandelion, her silver head a dandelion clock, and she wore everyone out.

But Johnnie, Matilda thought fondly . . . Now there, as nearly as possible, was her lost son Hillary over again. He had the same passionate interest in history and military affairs. He knew the uniforms of every famous regiment, and could recite their feats in battle. He shared Matilda's admiration for the Duke of Wellington, and, to a lesser extent, that earlier military genius, the great Duke of Marlborough. He knew the merits of guns used in warfare, past or present. He enjoyed nothing more than reconstructing battles with the battalions of lead soldiers that Matilda kept in the Death Room. Once they had been Hillary's and Richard's playthings. Now they were Johnnie's and Patrick's, though Patrick was interested only in the cavalry regiments, and then half-heartedly. He much preferred real horses and outdoor games.

When Johnnie was at home he practised drilling in the tiny paved courtyard at the back of Aunt Clara's house, marching up and down with a broomstick over his shoulder (since he was not allowed to own even a toy gun), and shouting commands to an invisible company. He did make sure, however, that his father was out when he played this game. An unspoken agreement existed between him and his mother. She would give him a signal if his father should come in unexpectedly.

However, there was an unfortunate slip-up in this arrangement one afternoon. Desmond did come home earlier than expected, when Imogen was out shopping. He discovered the lonely parade in the courtyard, with Johnnie making efforts to drill his amiable but uncooperative cat, Hector.

"Slo-o-pe arms!" he was shouting. "You! Cadet Morrison! Straighten up. You're slouching like a—like a cat!"

"Johnnie!" called Desmond in the quiet voice that suggested trouble.

Johnnie's skinny figure stiffened. He carefully set down the broomstick, and Hector seized his opportunity to disappear behind Imogen's tubs of petunias and ivy.

"Yes, Father?"

"What's that game you're playing?"

"Just—I was teaching Hector obedience, Father."

"Don't lie to me, Johnnie. You were teaching—attemping to teach a cat to come to attention and slope arms."

Johnnie's chin went up. His nose, that offensively Duncastle nose, seemed to grow longer. He looked elderly and haughty, a small replica of his interfering grandmother.

"There's no one else here to play with. At Granny's—"

"Yes, I'll have something to say about that later. In the meantime you can't have forgotten that I have forbidden you to play military games. Either here or at your grandmother's."

"But—yes, Father."

"You know I'll have to punish you."

"Yes, Father."

"Go up to your room and stay there until supper time. And don't tell yourself you're being confined to barracks. You're simply a disobedient boy receiving some very mild punishment. Though that isn't quite all."

Johnnie shot his father an apprehensive look.

"Yes, I see you've guessed what I'm going to say. You won't go on to your grandmother's on Sunday as usual. Indeed, I'm going to have to discuss with your mother whether you shall ever go there again."

"But, Father! You can't stop me! She's my granny." Johnnie had gone scarlet with emotion. "I mean she has a right to me."

"Has she? I wonder why."

"Because I'm a Dun—because I'm her grandson," Johnnie amended hastily.

"You were going to say you're a Duncastle. You're not. You're a Morrison. You're my son, and you're going to learn to appreciate the worthwhile things in life and achieve something real."

"Isn't being a soldier for your country achieving something, Father?" Johnnie asked with some daring. He had always been afraid of his father. But if he were to be a soldier he had to practice being brave. "I mean, Granny says if we hadn't won the war we'd be the slaves of the Germans now, and we'd have no King and Queen, and there'd be some awful person like the Kaiser or Bismarck being Prime Minister."

"Is that what she's teaching you?" Desmond's face was tight with anger. "Has she told you how many men died in the last war? It was an expensive way of keeping our King and Queen. And I think you're defying me. Go upstairs at once and stay there until I give you permission to come down."

Johnnie's lower lip stuck out rebelliously. He held his head high and whistled with determined defiance as he marched upstairs. He would never let his father see how upset he was.

But the thought of not being allowed to go to Kensington Square so appalled him that on the instant he conceived a daring plan. He would run away to Granny now, this minute, before Father had had time to forbid visits. The urgency of this decision made him tremble with excitement and fear. However, he still tried to plan carefully, as a wise soldier would. He got out his school satchel and packed his pajamas, a clean shirt, and a water bottle (an empty lemonade bottle filled from the tap in the bathroom). He wouldn't need other rations because by bus he could reach Granny's in less than an hour. Even if he walked he could be there in two hours. And Granny would let him sleep in Uncle Hillary's room. If Father arrived he would barricade himself in and begin a siege.

Two hours later Imogen, downstairs, said, "Desmond, he's so quiet. I really had better go up and see if he's all right."

"Of course he's all right. He's just sulking. You do agree with me that he had to be punished?"

"I suppose so, though—"

"Though what?"

"There doesn't seem to be much harm in just marching up and down our backyard."

"Darling, if you don't understand how dangerous implanting militarism in young minds is, then we're never going to get a world at peace."

"We never are, anyway," Imogen said. "Even you can't be as unrealistic as that."

"You mean you can't change human nature, and man's natural aggressions?"

"Exactly."

Desmond moved irritably. "At least we can have less of it. I didn't go through all that degradation and contempt during the war to have my own son a militarist."

"Darling, Johnnie's only a baby. If he weren't playing British wars he'd be playing cowboys and Indians." But

Imogen's voice had softened. "Did you mind so much about the contempt and everything? You didn't tell me. You let me think you didn't mind."

"Then I must have been a better actor than I thought I was."

And she less perceptive? She looked at his dark eyes, seeing their sensitivity, and realising how like Johnnie he was. Only Johnnie's vulnerability carried him into dreams about heroism in combat, where Desmond's battles were fought inside his brain privately. What a pair of introverts they were and how they got at her emotions with their need for protection. All the same, Desmond was right on one point. A great deal of this was Mother's fault for encouraging Johnnie in his fantasy wars, and exacerbating Desmond's wounds.

It was Mother who should be sentenced to solitary confinement. Thinking of the absurdity of this, Imogen smiled and Desmond leaned over to press her hand. They were happy, really, she thought. But no one could tell her a brilliant mind was easy to live with.

She got up and went to the foot of the stairs.

"Johnnie, you can come down now."

Five minutes later she said impatiently, "What is that boy doing? Didn't he hear me?"

"Of course he heard you. If he's sulking then he must do without his supper."

"Johnnie!" Imogen called again. "Desmond, he's awfully quiet. I must see what he's doing."

Desmond, as a man, might seek her comfort in subtle ways. Johnnie, as a child, could be sobbing forlornly into his pillow. Anyway, she did think Desmond was a little severe with him.

The bedroom, with the neat narrow bed, the table littered with books and pencils, the wicker basket of toys, neatly stored and seldom touched, in a corner, had no life in it. Not even Hector, Johnnie's treasured cat, who frequently slipped upstairs to sleep on his bed, was there.

But on the bedside table, propped against the lamp, was a note.

Dear Mother,

Father is forbidding me to do the things I injoy most, so I have to run away. I am sorry if you are upset. Don't forget to feed Hector until I come back. If I ever do.

Your loving son Johnnie.

Between tears and laughter, Imogen rushed downstairs. "Desmond, read this. It's terribly funny, really. But—sort of painful, too. Were you that hard on him?"

Desmond frowned over the note. "Can't he learn to spell? I suppose he doesn't think that's one of the important things in life. Well, we can guess where he is, can't we?"

"At Mother's. Of course. I'd better go there straight away."

"I'll go."

"No, I think this is something I should do."

"You'll cosset him."

Imogen blinked away tears. The pain had superseded the amusement.

"Of course I'll cosset him. He's only eight. Anyway, if I don't his grandmother will."

"Wouldn't it be a good idea to telephone first?"

"Of course. I've stopped thinking logically. When your child feels he has to run away from home—Desmond, who's to blame?"

"All kids want to run away at some time or another." But there was a hint of uneasiness in Desmond's voice. "I did myself, and I didn't have a rich and pampering grandmother."

Imogen knew that Desmond had lived in the East End of London in some poverty. His father had been a labourer on building sites, who had died of a heart attack during the war.

"But you didn't actually go so far as to run away?"

"No."

"That's what I mean. It's a huge step to take, and for a basically timid child like Johnnie—Desmond, we must be going wrong somewhere."

"The boy's being corrupted!" Desmond burst out. "I've kept telling you so."

"No, it's deeper than that. I hate to admit it, but my mother seems to understand some need in little boys."

"She creates a need, a dream world—"

"Desmond love, aren't your own books a dream world?"

"No! I'm setting down realities which I hope my readers take seriously." Now she had hurt him again. She recognized that quick look of pain and knew that once again he saw himself struggling against people's stupidities. He hated war and yet he was inclined to regard most of the world as his enemy. They should have had six children or none at all, Imogen thought wildly. Poor little Johnnie, having to bear alone the weight of his father's social conscience.

"Mother has some realities, too," she protested mildly.

"About proficiency with guns?"

"About character building. Darling, what are we doing quarrelling now? I must ring Mother and get on my way. And promise me you won't scold Johnnie when I bring him home. Not tonight, anyway."

Not ever, she wanted to add. But children, naturally, had to be disciplined.

"While I'm away you might carry out your son's wishes and feed the cat."

"Damn the cat," said Desmond, but thankfully the tight anger had gone out of his voice. When Johnnie was home and safely in bed she knew that Desmond would want her in bed, too. He always did after a quarrel. He never said much in the way of an apology, but his arms tightly round her and his hungry body were eloquent enough. He trusted her to understand him. She, he regarded as a simple uncomplicated person who didn't need understanding. These clever people, idealistic, introverted, egotistical, unconsciously cruel . . . Father, she knew, had never been entirely happy about her marriage. Not for Mother's reasons, that Desmond was a pacifist, but because he was too intellectual, an unknown quantity in her father's world.

Nevertheless, compared to Mother's and Father's her marriage to Desmond was a success. Except for the problem of Johnnie.

Before she had time to telephone Kensington Square, however, her own telephone rang. She snatched at it, expecting her mother's voice.

"Is that you, Imogen?" It was Lally. "M-mamma said I was to ring you and t-tell you——"

"About Johnnie?" said Imogen eagerly.

"Yes. He's here, and q-quite well."

"I guessed it. I was just coming for him. I'll get a taxi and be with you in half an hour."

"N-no."

"No what?"

"M-mamma says n-no, you're not to c-come."

"Lally, don't be absurd. Where is Mamma? Let me speak to her."

"N-no, she won't."

Lally was stuttering worse than usual, a sure sign of tension. She hated the telephone, anyway, and rarely talked on it.

"She won't speak to me!" Imogen exclaimed. "But why?"

"She says—just a m-minute"—there was some distant whispering—"she says Johnnie is t-too upset to go home t-tonight."

"Oh, now, Lally, this is too much. I'm Johnnie's mother. I'll make the decisions. I intend coming over at once."

There was another murmur of voices in the distance, then Lally again, over-excited and voluble.

"If you c-come, M-mog, you won't be able to get in. We're having a s-siege. It was Johnnie's idea. All the doors are l-locked."

"What are you talking about? Has Mother gone mad? A siege! Really, this is carrying play-acting too far. Desmond and I——"

"It's no use, the servants are t-told not to answer the d-door if you ring the b-bell, and the n-neighbours will be—what did you say, Mamma?—scandalised——"

"I don't care what the neighbours will be."

"—and think you and D-desmond ill-treat Johnnie."

Rage beat up in Imogen, making her face hot.

"Oh, stop it, Lally, you're just parroting what Mother's saying. Why won't she talk to me herself?"

"B-because she's in the rocking chair with Johnnie asleep in her l-lap. He was so hot and tired and upset when he arrived, and he's only just g-got c-calmed down."

Imogen stared at the telephone in frustration. She wanted to call Desmond, but knew that would only make matters worse. A siege in Kensington Square. The notion was so absurd that he would explode in angry disbelief. I've married into a madhouse, he would say, as he had done, under provocation, in the past.

But she had a vivid picture of Johnnie asleep on his grandmother's lap and tears of jealousy and failure slid down her nose.

"In the m-morning," she heard Lally saying. "We'll open the d-door then."

Imogen put the telephone down and went slowly back to the living room.

"What was all that about?" Desmond asked.

"Didn't you hear?"

"I was in the kitchen feeding the cat as I was told to do. And have you ever tried to interpret one half of a telephone conversation? I only got the most surprising idea that your mother is being cranky, as usual."

"She's keeping Johnnie for the night. She said he was very tired and upset and needs a rest."

"So she knows better than his parents?"

"Desmond, not that now, please. And perhaps she's right this time."

"You're crying!"

"Yes."

"Because of Johnnie? Or me?"

The dark sensitive eyes were too much for her.

"Both of you. My two difficult men."

"Come here, love. Come here."

Matilda rocked gently back and forth in the dim room. Presently she would put the child to bed. But not for a while yet. The feel of his thin body, curled trustingly in her arms, was too precious a sensation. The drum had rolled away across the floor when it had slid from Johnnie's sleepy arms. But beating it had eased him, as it had eased her in moments of crisis. He had beaten furiously, his face alight with joy.

"I'm brave, aren't I, Granny?"

"Very brave, my little drummer boy." She was so proud of him, having had the courage to rebel and run away.

"Need I ever go home again, Granny?"

No! she had wanted to cry. Never! I'll keep you here and you'll be mine.

She had tumbled the damp dark hair, and said soothingly, "I'm going to have a talk to your mother. But not tonight. You've had a long march and you need sleep."

When he at last fell asleep he looked uncannily like Hillary, the thin nervous face, the long nose.

I'm not wicked, she thought, anticipating Desmond's, that bleak clever man's, accusations. I only believe that little boys must be taught certain essential things like courage and initiative and ideals.

Her mouth twitched as she looked again at the pale blur of her grandson's face.

And I, she admitted painfully, need, so badly, someone to love . . .

The outcome of Johnnie's escapade was that his parents finally consented to his going to boarding school where he would have plenty of companionship and grow out of his unhealthy obsessions.

He went willingly enough, since Granny had promised to visit him frequently, and also to see that a good part of his holidays and long weekends was spent at Kensington Square. One didn't know how she would manage to extract permission from his parents, but if she said she would, she would. Granny didn't make idle promises.

Patrick had already been at school for a year, and had distinguished himself, if that were the word, by the essay he had written on "My Ancestors."

"I am descended from the Kings of Ireland, and my ancestors have fought against Cromwell and the British invader for centuries. My mother took part in the Easter Rising in Dublin. That is where she met my father. My uncle Sean joined the Irish Guards and was killed at

Thiepval on the Somme. This was very stupid of him as if he had refused to fight in the Great War he could have fought the Black and Tans in the Troubles. All my Irish ancestors have liked horses. My English grandmother is very boring about the famous soldiers in her family, but they can't have been very good because they all got killed."

Richard roared with laughter.

"What bog oak have I grafted the Duncastles on to? We'd better not let Mother see this effort. Though I begin to wonder if your influence, my devious wife, isn't as dangerous as my mother's. Leave Mab out of all this rebel talk, will you?"

Deirdre's face went soft, as it always did, when Mab was mentioned.

"That child is never still long enough to listen to anything. She invents her own songs and stories, anyway. What are we going to do with her, Richard?"

"Let her grow up."

"She's going to be trouble for some young man some day."

"Like her mother."

"Oh, I know I have a terrible temper. But it flies over."

"It flies over," said Richard, gently rubbing his thumb under her chin. "How did I ever have the luck to be dragged inside by you that bloody afternoon misnamed the Easter Rising? Like Christ."

"Patrick and Mab came from that."

"And us, alannah. And us."

A week to the day after that conversation Deirdre was thrown from a filly she had wanted to break in herself, because she had a silver sheen to her roan coat, and was small-boned and dainty like Mab. It hadn't seemed a bad fall, but when the groom ran to pick her up her head on its long neck wilted sideways, like a fading flower. She never opened her eyes again.

She wouldn't have wanted to be buried at Sanctuary, Richard said violently, when at last Imogen persuaded him to come out of the library where he had locked himself for two days. The graveyard was full of Duncastle dead. No, he wanted her to lie beside his father in the London cemetery. Joshua and he were the only two Englishmen she had loved.

So again there was a procession down the long avenue lined by the dark tapers of the cypresses. The boys had been brought out of school, and Mab, too, was there. Because her mother would have wanted it, Richard said firmly. Mab, an odd little faery figure with her glimmering white-blonde hair and sharply aware blue eyes, was far from unhappy. She had found a marble angel with outspread wings on a child's grave. She knelt beside it and talked to it softly in her unintelligible language. She was only four years old. They hoped she wouldn't miss her mother too much. They had always been hand in hand, always laughing together. And would anyone know how damagingly Mab missed her mother since she was such a self-contained little creature, even at the age of four keeping her thoughts to herself.

All they did know was that her flashing tempers increased. But, like lightning, they were gone as quickly as they had come, and she was lively and amiable again. As time went by she seemed to transfer her affections to her father, wanting to be near him a great deal.

It was a good thing, because otherwise Richard, who had aged ten years overnight, might never have emerged from his grief. As it was, he remained quiet and diminished, an aging man with a withered arm, and that little white-haired sprite haunting his footsteps.

Sanctuary had never been a place for prolonged happiness.

Chapter 24

There was only one way Matilda would have enjoyed her sixty-eighth birthday, and that was if Johnnie had been able to join the party for dinner. But Johnnie, Captain John Morrison now, was in India with his regiment. Her other grandson was also absent, in Ireland for the Dublin Horse Show. Patrick, however, had never been close to her, so his empty chair would not worry her too much.

Her own children remained loyal to this occasion, which was now no longer one for celebration, Matilda thought, twisting her hair into its usual smooth coil, and noticing how little of the rich bronze remained. She was becoming like an elderly monument, fading beneath the onslaught of wind and weather. A grey-haired lady with a stringy neck (to be concealed by the ruffles of her high-necked chiffon dinner dress), a shrunken bosom, and thin bony hands growing unpleasantly claw-like.

Stepping back from the mirror, she reassured herself that the figure she scrutinised still had its slender elegance and its impressive erectness. Young girls didn't know how to hold themselves nowadays. Look at Lally, round-shouldered from bending over her perpetual sketching pad. And Imogen, slightly thick and dumpy, like her father. And now Mab who, when she was bored, drooped languidly like a parched flower. She would become bow-shaped before she was in her twenties, her grandmother scolded. But sixteen was a difficult age, full of moods and rebellions, and Mab was not easily understandable. She had a wild unpredictable streak. Purely Irish, Matilda had decided long ago, and wished Richard wouldn't always pamper the child. Her short stays at Kensington Square were not sufficient to correct her wilfulness. Indeed, this time she had been too precocious for comfort. She had struck up a friendship with a young man next door.

The Osbornes had recently moved in. Their eldest son Julius appeared to have been sent down from Cambridge, though this was only rumour. As a long-time resident of the square, Matilda did not hasten to make friends of new arrivals. Besides, the right people were no longer living here. The tall narrow pedigreed houses were getting occupants like film stars or successful jockeys. The aristocracy, such as the duke's three daughters who had once lived in this house, the retired admirals and judges, were finding times difficult. England had not fully recovered from the depression. Power was shifting from the upper classes to another kind of person, chiefly, it seemed, to Welsh miners' sons. There must be something about coal that brought out a nuggety grit and determination in a man's character. This was admirable in its way, but it was lamentably narrow-minded and lacking culture and good taste. Matilda found it deeply disturbing. Perhaps it was right that socialists should be coal miners' sons for they possessed a great skill at burrowing beneath the fabric of society.

If there should be another war, what patriotism could one hope for?

But these were not the thoughts for a party. Neither was Mab's flirtation with that fast young man next door. She would have to speak to Richard about that. It might be better if Mab returned to Sanctuary immediately, rather than spend her twice-yearly three weeks in London, to have her wardrobe attended to, and some culture forced into her scatterbrained head.

The subject of war came back when they were seated at the dinner table, Richard at the opposite end to Matilda, Imogen and Desmond on one side, Mab and Lally on the other. There was a rumour that the King was having secret meetings with that dreadful dangerous man Adolf Hitler and his Nazi followers. What was the King of England doing, hob-nobbing with Germans?

"It must be that Mrs. Simpson," Matilda said disapprovingly. "She has a bad influence over him. Why can't he do his duty to his country and make a suitable marriage? He says he'll abdicate if he can't have that silly woman, that he'll find his duties too onerous without her at his side. I never heard anything so ridiculous. Imagine if the Duke of Wellington had decided he didn't want the onerous burden of fighting Waterloo? Where would we be now?"

"Still surviving, Mother." It was only of recent years that Desmond had begun to call her mother. But still reluctantly. "The British are survivors."

"Of course they are," said Matilda. "Even you, in your own way."

"But I don't survive because I have warlike qualities." Although Desmond had never grown to like his mother-in-law he had to admit to a certain respect for her. They had fought every inch of the way over Johnnie's career, but when Desmond knew he was beaten—two against one, for Johnnie would have staged another running away from home if he had not been allowed to go to Sandhurst—he had given in and said simply that his son had unfortunately inherited the incurable Duncastle disease. With his growing success as a writer and lecturer he had mellowed a certain amount.

"I'm so countrified I never hear anything," Richard was saying. "Or suspect people's motives, if it comes to that."

"Every foreigner is suspect," Matilda said, climbing on an old hobby horse. "Look at history—"

"Mother, don't let's beat drums on your birthday,"

Imogen begged. "Mab, what have you been doing in London?"

Mab pushed the silky almost white hair out of her eyes.

"Oh, shopping. Going to boring art galleries."

"Want to come home, mouse?" asked Richard.

"Well—not just yet, Daddy. I do have a project."

"Project?" enquired Matilda.

"Yes, Granny. A secret. Oh, very historical. You'll approve."

Mab's pale blue eyes had a strange luminous quality. She was quite plain, under-sized, under-developed, child-like, chronically untidy, yet suddenly that intelligence, or cognizance or whatever it was, would flash in her face, and she was far from being a child, and far from being plain. An uncomfortable creature. Sometimes Matilda thought a little of Lally's dullness might not have gone amiss in Mab's make-up.

"And when am I to be told what this secret is?"

"When the time comes. Granny, may I be excused now?"

"Before coffee?"

"I'm too young for coffee."

Matilda sighed when she had gone. "Richard, that child is like her mother. She needs a good spanking. And I know you'll never give it to her."

"No, Mother. I have only one good arm." A flicker crossed Richard's face. He remembered saying that once before, a long time ago.

"Then I hope you don't rue the day. She's growing up fast and I want her intact until her coming out."

"Intact? What do you mean, Mother?"

"You know perfectly well what I mean. She's flirting with a rather questionable young man next door. Isn't she, Lally?"

Lally flushed scarlet. "I don't know."

"You do know. You saw them yourself in the square gardens."

"What were they doing in the square gardens, Lally?" Richard asked.

Lally hung her head.

"I didn't m-mean to tell. Lying on the grass, f-fooling."

"Oh, lord," said Richard. "Well, she is growing up, Mother. I'll have a talk with her."

"I'd be glad if you would. I'm getting too old for the responsibility."

"You old, Mother," said Imogen. "I'll never believe that."

"I'll soon be seventy. Very few Duncastles have lived to that age."

"Because they bled to death on foreign battlefields. Don't you remember Papa saying that? Now we have only Patrick and Johnnie left. They'll have to breed."

"If they have time," Desmond said.

"Time?" Matilda said. "What do you mean? They're young men."

"Beloved of the god of battles, don't you remember, Mother? Young men are. And your own Duncastle blood is rising at the thought of another war." Desmond's face was dark and malicious.

"Desmond, you're teasing me!" Matilda said sharply.

But her thoughts had gone inward. It must be age that was making her so fearful, so apprehensive. How could England, still bankrupt from the last war, riddled with strikes, governed (what an inappropriate word) by a succession of weak Prime Ministers who talked pacifism and turned deaf ears to the thunder of the marching feet of that terrible gang of Hitler youth, face another holocaust? Where would the will and the courage and the patriotism come from? Those things were not fashionable nowadays, they were only encouraged by megalomaniacs like Adolf Hitler.

England, still invalidish, slowly recovering from the desperate blood-draining operation of the Great War, was like her own family. The best blood had been spilt. Only Johnnie and Patrick and that little glowworm Mab were left to breed. What was more, they had been infiltrated by people like Desmond Morrison who had a brilliant mind, but a mean and niggling outlook, with no breadth of vision, no grandeur.

And the Irish girl Deirdre, that charming hostile little witch who had infatuated Richard and then by her death reduced him to a shadow as if she had taken him with her into the dark cypress groves . . .

"Mother, where have you gone? You're not listening," said Imogen.

She gave herself a shake, apologising.

"I'm sorry. My mind wandered. What were you saying?"

"Desmond was saying isn't this house too big for you now? Just you and Lally and with servants harder to get."

Her adrenalin was flowing again. She said haughtily, "Do you see me in a small house? Why do socialists always level people down rather than up? I've been accustomed to striving upwards."

"But you were born with privilege. You had an unfair start," said Desmond in the slightly hectoring voice he used when lecturing from platforms. What a chip that young man had on his shoulder.

She lifted her chin in the familiar arrogant gesture.

"I am glad you admit at last, Desmond, that a military family is a privileged one. Shall we have our coffee in the drawing room? And a little cognac, Richard? I have a very good Napoleon brandy. If Desmond doesn't regard that as too privileged."

In her room Mab was making breathless preparations. She brushed her hair, renewed her lipstick, splashed scent on her flat little bosom. Then she took a blanket and pillow off her bed and tiptoed into the adjoining room, an empty bedroom with panelled walls, a fireplace, and an unmade bed. It had been her dotty Great-aunt Julia's room, Lally had told her. "It's where Aunt Julia's ghost is," Lally had said. "If you b-believe in ghosts."

"I do, and I adore them," said Mab carelessly.

One thing was certain, poor disappearing Great-aunt Julia had never done what she was going to do tonight. *That* belonged to the world of the living, and she was very much alive. So alive and pent-up that she nearly jumped out of her skin when the tap sounded on the other side of the panelling. She checked her wristwatch. Exactly on time. Beautiful dependable Julius.

She flew to the wall beside the fireplace and ran her fingers over the panelling, pressing. Yes, there was the sensitive area. The panel was moving, opening inwards. On Julius's instructions she had tested this yesterday and found, with an immense thrill, that it worked. The panel, he said, only operated from one side, as it did in his house. Once inside the secret passage, someone had to heed the signal of the intending visitor, or refugee, or escaping prisoner, or whatever he was, and allow him exit.

The passage must have been built when the houses were built, in troubled times, when persecuted priests or political refugees, or even villains seeking to evade capture and the hangman, had escaped by this route. Perhaps a Regency gentleman avoiding his creditors, or embarassing discovery by his mistress's husband.

Julius had found the entry from his bedroom by accident, and had immediately suggested a use of the passage to Mab. Now they could be private, couldn't they? Not condemned to courting in public parks and gardens.

Mab was not difficult to persuade. She was madly in love with this infinitely sophisticated young man. He was twenty-one, and had been sent down from Cambridge for some as yet undisclosed misdemeanour. She found him devastatingly exciting. This room was never used. They could have an uninterrupted time together. All night, she hoped. There were things she had to learn. She longed to become worldly and experienced. She was old enough.

Granny would have a fit if she knew, and that was part of the excitement.

Julius was stepping into the room. He was a little dusty. He had bumped his head on the ceiling. The passage had been made for small men. Of course they were smaller in those days, Mab said, looking admiringly at Julius's height. Her head came only to his chest. Had he locked the door of his room, and had he propped the panel open so that he could get back?

"Of course, fusspot. Phew, there's a rotten musty smell in that passage. It's quite wide, you know. Someone could hide there for days. And probably did. That's why it still stinks."

"It doesn't stink in here," said Mab, pulling him towards the bed. Her heart was thudding in her frail chest. "Quickly, take your clothes off."

"What's the hurry? Is anyone likely to come upstairs?"

"No. They're too busy discussing the next war. That will take an hour and a half. Anyway, no one will come to my room. They'll think I'm asleep."

"Little Mab, the baby? Some baby."

His fingers were inside her blouse, fumbling knowingly. Her skin was alive and crawling with sensation. She wanted to be naked against him, feeling the delicious contact. If nothing else happened, just their skins together would be enough. For the first time, anyway.

"There's not much of you, is there?" he said, his fingers groping.

"Enough." Her eyes gleamed mischievously. "I'm a slow developer."

"Slow? Is that what you call it?"

Her breath was coming raggedly. His caresses were becoming too imperative. She wanted to slow things down, else she was going to die of heart failure.

"Why were you sent down from Cambridge?"

"The usual reason."

He had dragged his shirt open and her face was against his naked chest, warm, silky with tufted dark hair.

"I don't know what—the usual reason is."

"A girl in my room all night. Silly bitch, I told her to go home at four o'clock, and then again at five o'clock."

"She wouldn't? I don't blame her."

He began to kiss her, on her forehead and cheeks, not touching her lips at first as if he were tantalising her.

"You're cute, little slow-developing Mab. At first I thought you were too young. But you're not, are you? You're a little devil, aren't you?"

"Am I?" How flattering that he thought her a devil. He was so splendid, so powerful, and twenty-one years old. A grown-up man. Now his hand was going down between her legs. She bit her lips to stop from crying out. Oh help,

Granny, I'm being ravished. She began to giggle hysterically.

"Shut up! Hey, you've got your pants on still. Let's have them off."

"Not—too quickly, Julius."

"Scared?"

She caught her breath. "I'm just afraid—I'll die."

"You won't. I promise you."

Neither she would, for just as she was kicking her feet out of her pants, someone called, "Mab! Are you in bed? If not, Granny wants you to come down for five minutes."

Aunt Imogen. They were sitting up tensely, listening. Damn, the door wasn't locked. She hadn't told Julius, but she hadn't been able to find a key. She had been so sure no one would come. Not into this room, anyway.

"Mab, where are you?" Now Aunt Imogen would check the bathroom. In another half minute she would be at this door. There was simply no time to dress. Julius had sprung out of bed, and was standing half naked and shivering. Shivering! Was he cold? Or cowardly?

It was she who had to take action.

"Quick! Grab your clothes. Into the secret passage. Have you got your torch?" She was bundling after him, neglecting to pick up her discarded pants, trying hastily to button her blouse.

In a moment they were inside the passage, the floor cool and dusty beneath their bare feet, the darkness closing on them as Julius pulled the panel shut. She clung to him, laughing shrilly.

"Shut up!" he said nervily. "Don't make so much noise."

"I was only thinking you'll have to let me through into your room, and help me sneak out of your house. I can, when everyone's in bed. Don't be frightened."

"I'm not frightened." But he was. Or upset anyway. And very cross.

"It's an adventure," she whispered.

"I knew you were a child."

"I'm not. I'm calmer than you are. S-s-sh. She's next door."

"Mab, are you hiding? What have you been doing in here? The bed has blankets on it. Good gracious——"

Mab, clinging to Julius, was dissolved with giggles. "She's found my pants. Oh, help! Let's get out of here. Ouch!" Her voice was suddenly raised unthinkingly. "I've tripped on something. Ugh! It felt like a bony rat. Where's your torch? Put it on, for goodness' sake."

The strong circle of light shone on the floor, along the wall.

And then Mab screamed. She couldn't stop herself. She didn't care who heard, who came and exposed them. It was just so ghastly. A small scattering of bones. A skeleton. A human skeleton, one knew without any doubt at all. There was the poor little skull.

Oh, dear God! Let them get out of this terrible sinister place, this death trap. For someone long ago had been imprisoned in here and died. Oh, it was awful, she couldn't breathe, the air was foetid and deadly.

"Help!" she screamed. "Help!"

Julius thrust her through the aperture into his room. Then he shook her mercilessly.

"You silly fool. Why did you have to make such a row? Now we'll both be on the mat."

"But there's someone dead in here," Mab sobbed. "I want to go home. Take me downstairs. I don't care who sees us. Perhaps there was a murder. We have to get the police."

"Now you're losing your head. We don't have to look for trouble. Whoever that is has been there an awfully long time. There's nothing we can do for that thing now. Why not just leave it there."

Layers of illusion peeled from her. If she had wanted to grow up quickly, her wish had been granted, brutally.

"That might be someone you loved, Julius. Or someone some other person loved and is looking for. But you don't care, do you? You only want to run away from trouble." Mab's silvery head was in the air. Had she known it she looked remarkably like her grandmother. "I couldn't love someone who behaves like that. I could only despise them. Don't come down with me. I'd rather go alone."

Her face screwed up maliciously. "I'll leave you to have nightmares tonight about sleeping next door to a dead thing. To having it there forever because you're too cowardly to confess."

When she rang the doorbell she was admitted by a surprised Nellie. "I never saw you go out, Miss Mab. Everyone has rushed upstairs. They heard someone screaming. I never heard a thing, but I always said this house was haunted."

"It is, Nellie. But I've found the poor little ghost. And I think I know who it is." Nellie was half alarmed, half indulgent.

"I don't know what you're talking about, Miss Mab, but who is it?"

"My Great-aunt Julia." Mab's mouth worked. "God rest her soul." She had never uttered those words before. They had come unbidden and quite naturally. It was as if it were her Irish mother speaking.

As the enormity of Mab's discovery was made clear, nothing was said about her dishevelled appearance, or the discarded pants, which no doubt Aunt Imogen would produce at a future date.

There was too much of flurry in sending for the police, in calming Granny who had gone so paper white that it seemed as if she might collapse, and in studying the secret panel which surely somebody might have had the wits to discover long ago so that the secret of Great-aunt Julia's whereabouts need not have remained an unsolved mystery.

For there was no doubt the small bones were those of a woman. The date of death, the police doctor said, would be difficult to establish. He would put it at about half a century ago. And the poor victim, who had obviously sought to hide in the secret passage (which she must have discovered and never mentioned, but then she was half-witted, wasn't she?) appeared to have caught her foot in a bit of rotten flooring and fallen. She must have suffered from concussion. She might even have died at the moment of falling. One thing was certain, she had never cried for help, because had she done so someone would have heard.

"If it is your missing sister, Mrs. Webb," the doctor said

soothingly, "I can reassure you that she didn't suffer. At least not much. If at all."

"She wouldn't have starved to death?" Matilda asked shakily.

"No, as I said, she'd have yelled for help, wouldn't she? If she had been conscious. Anyway," he had no sentiment, this bluff man, "that's your skeleton in the cupboard—sorry, that's your mystery solved at last."

Everything was done tidily. The collection of bones was put in a satin-lined box, and buried quietly at Mortlake cemetery, with an unknown clergyman given a discreet sum to recite the burial service. First Matilda had wanted to take the slender box to Sanctuary, but Richard vehemently persuaded her against doing such a thing.

"Mother, it happened too long ago. And she doesn't know anything about it. Just have a small stone put on her grave. Julia Duncastle, aged—aged what?"

"Nineteen," Matilda said in a muffled voice. "It's just that I feel so sad, having done him that wrong."

"Done who wrong, Mother?" Richard was alarmed, thinking the shock had addled his mother's superb wits.

"Your father. Once—though only very briefly—I thought he might have done away with Julia— It was after she had dropped Lally. He had always disliked her." She held her handkerchief against her face. "He disliked all the Duncastles except me. Poor Joshua."

"Well, never mind, Mother," Richard said uncomfortably. "He loved you."

"A little. A long time ago."

Mab, subdued and quiet and touchingly loving to her father, was taken back to Sanctuary. Nothing was ever said about what Aunt Imogen had discovered. It was assumed that Mab had been playing a rather naughty prank with that young man next door, having led him on, no doubt. She would stay in the country until she was seventeen, and then perhaps have another attempt at London life, if Granny would have her as a guest. But she might prefer to grow up simply at home. Patrick would be there, and his friends. There would be no shortage of company, even if a less sophisticated company than London could offer. Aunt Imogen suggested that that would be much the best idea. Mab would always suffer from having lost her mother, poor child.

Anyway, events took care of the problem. There could be no London season for Mab when she was old enough, for the British Prime Minister, brave and foolish and gullible, had at last done with his ill-judged appeasement of Germany's Hitler, and war had been declared.

Johnnie was on his way home from India. Patrick was learning to fly fighter planes. The children, with child-sized gas masks hanging from their shoulders, were being sent to the country, and all the people who remained in London were hanging dark shades over their windows. As if in mourning. There would be no raiding Zeppelins in this war but there might be bombers.

The drums, imperative and deadly, were beating again.

Chapter 25

Matilda had asked Johnnie and Patrick to give her the
pleasure of their company at the opera. Johnnie, who had
emerged from the disaster and triumph of the retreat of
the British army from France and the beaches of Dunkirk
with a promotion and a decoration—he was now Major
John Morrison D.S.O.—and Patrick, with his newly acquired wings, were tall good-looking young men. She, at
seventy, cut quite a figure herself in her black lace and
her diamonds. Johnnie in particular looked proud to be
escorting her. Patrick said flippantly, "You can still go
through your paces, Granny," as if she were an aged
thoroughbred. From him that was high praise. He admired a good performance even if he had never been able
to love his grandmother. He had used to think she was
rather ridiculous, with her craze for making Johnnie and
him fight old battles. But now, in face of very imminent
danger to England, he had to commend her spirit. She and
Winston Churchill, who was beginning to make stirring
speeches, might well save England between them.

Johnnie, too, had turned out to be all right. As a little

boy he had been excitable and over-imaginative, and too deadly serious about a game. But now the game was real he had become cool and efficient and apparently fearless. Three days and nights on those deadly beaches at Dunkirk, keeping his men together and orderly, was something. His unit had been almost the last to leave. Whoever would have thought that shy skinny little boy would grow up to be so handsome and hawk-nosed and quietly competent. Although he was still very shy with girls, Patrick knew.

Patrick's trouble was a superfluity of girls. He couldn't keep them all happy, and had offered Johnnie a choice of two or three of the most delectable. After all, life could be, most likely would be, short, and therefore morals could be tossed away. But Johnnie, perhaps still suffering from the shock of the painful and bloody retreat from France, or more likely from a deeply injured pride that the British army could be defeated, had spent more time in Kensington Square than anywhere else. He frankly seemed to prefer Granny's company to that of any number of glittering girls.

Matilda herself was superbly happy that night. Her face was stiff with pride, the lines smoothed out, her eyes full of their old green fire. She didn't suppose the boys enjoyed the opera, *La Bohème,* as much as she did, although it had been Hillary's favourite, but this had been what they had to do, sit in the Royal Opera House among the still well-dressed audience, and show the flag. It was an unspoken way of defying Hitler, who would surely hear from one source or another, that the British were going about their usual affairs, and treating with contempt the rumours of invasion.

When the performance was over she gave the boys the choice of dinner at the Savoy, or quietly at home in Kensington Square where she had had champagne put on ice.

Patrick was about to say the Savoy, when he reflected that dinner at Granny's could be over fairly quickly and he still might have time to dash into the Four Hundred. Johnnie didn't hesitate.

"Let's go home, Granny."

Matilda was deeply pleased, not only because that was what Johnnie preferred, but because he called it home.

The lighted candles made hollows and shadows in the faces of the two young men, aging them prematurely. The pain of this last evening together was beginning to exceed the pleasure. Matilda was tired now, and she kept having an illusion that her two guests were Hillary and Richard, young and eager and indestructible. Destined for glory but not for death.

"Where's Aunt Lally?" Patrick asked.

"Oh, she's gone to bed long ago. She's an early bird. Poor dear, she's insisting on knitting mufflers and mittens for the boys in the trenches. She thinks it's the same as the last war, and it isn't, is it?"

"No, Granny. I wouldn't have been flying a Spit in the last war," Patrick said cheerfully. "Marvellous machines. The Germans can't touch them."

"We may need some woollies in the winter," said Johnnie. "We may be dug in on a mountain range somewhere, who knows? Don't discourage Aunt Lally, Granny. Anyway, what are you doing on your committees, because I'm sure you're the Queen Bee as usual."

"Mostly organising convalescent homes. I have plenty of experience to draw on. But we won't be asking for Sanctuary this time, Patrick. It wouldn't be fair to your father who is still one of the last war's casualties. Or to Mab who needs her home."

"If a bomb is dropped on my stables I'll personally take on the whole of the Luftwaffe," Patrick said. "And don't worry about Mab, Granny. She's having a high old time. She may be pint-sized, but she knows how to take care of herself."

"I prefer not to think what Mab might do," Matilda said. "She's—"

"Don't say it, Granny. She's completely Irish."

Matilda sighed. "You know it's extraordinary and rather tragic that the survival of a family like mine should now depend on two young men. Let's face it, my darlings—"

"You want us to make hasty marriages and leave pregnant wives," Patrick said. "It's not on, Granny. It's not fair to the girls. Is it, Johnnie?"

Johnnie shook his head. "No, Granny. I couldn't marry that quickly. Not even for the sacred cause of the survival of the Duncastle line."

His voice was gently humorous. He was being careful not to hurt this old woman whom he loved so deeply. She had been his rock and his refuge always. But he had to move slowly in matters of girls and marriage, otherwise he might make a mistake like his mother had. For surely it must have been a mistake marrying that cold clever man, his father, who so disapproved of wars but neither could he love people. His emotions were all spent grandly and with a lot of public ballyhoo on causes.

"Anyway, there'll be be plenty of time after the war," he added.

"Or are you writing us off, Granny?" Patrick asked.

"No!" Matilda denied vehemently. "Forgive me, I should never have spoken of such things." Her eyes were alive with pain.

"You're just facing facts, Granny," Patrick reassured her. "Very sensible of you. But your cause is hopeless, you know, because the Duncastles are already extinct. Except for you. England has been the death of them, as my mother would have said."

"Patrick, you're teasing me again. Let us talk of something more cheerful."

After dinner Patrick's chances of escaping grew more remote, as Matilda withdrew to allow the gentlemen time to enjoy their port, as she expressed it. She really spoke in a dead language. But the port was exceptionally good. Patrick became resigned to a completely family evening.

"I must say one thing for Granny, she keeps a jolly good cellar. Did she get her knowledge of wines from Grandfather?"

"No, from her father. The cellar at Sanctuary was renowned. You ought to know since you've had the benefit of what's left of it. I hope your father has been laying down new stocks. I know Granny lectures him from time to time."

"He probably has. We seem to be pretty well-stocked. I know when war was imminent Dad shrewdly grabbed some good French and German wines. I must take a closer interest since I expect it will all be mine one day, and I wouldn't want to find the shelves empty. That is—"

"That is if you survive," said Johnnie apologetically.

"No need to pussyfoot about that, old chap. I knew the survival rate when I chose the air force. The trouble was, Dad talked too much about the filthy trenches. So I preferred the clean air. I've got hooked on flying, luckily."

"There won't be trenches in that way in this war. It's a war of mobility. Plenty of armour, that's the thing."

"Where will you be posted next?"

"I'm not sure. I think it may be North Africa. But don't tell Granny or she'll be supplying me with pith helmets or contraptions to keep the sand out of my tea."

"Would you like to marry, Johnnie?"

"Of course. When I have time to do the thing justice. And I want kids for myself, not just to restock the family. Like a damn wine cellar!"

"Me too. But I refuse to be so fatalistic as to conceive a child because I think I'm going to be killed. That's really asking for trouble. Airmen get to be a superstitious lot. Some more port?" Patrick refilled his own glass and held it to the light. "Marvellous colour. Rich, warm, satisfying. The colour of life. Or of blood. What will you miss most, Johnnie?"

"If I don't come back?" Johnnie said calmly. "I don't know. An English summer morning, I think. Early, when you think you're the only one awake in the whole world, and the dawn chorus begins. Cheerful little buggers, birds. Don't seem to know anything about bombs or pollution."

"I'll miss my horses. Oh, girls, too. But a good horse is an absolutely supreme thing. And Sanctuary. That old house makes me more British than Irish, only don't tell Granny. She'll think it a bigger victory for the British than Waterloo."

"I never got attached to a house. Unless it's this one. My home was ruled over by a despot. Anyway, it was never a memorable place. That's why I've always enjoyed camp life. You know, people used to think I was weak and timid, but it really wasn't true. I knew I was born to to be a soldier. In a funny way, as if I were all those Duncastles reincarnated, the Hillarys, the Gordons, the

Richards, not to mention the Major-General and the Colonel of the Regiment."

"You're drunk."

"You don't need to comment."

"Actually I never liked you when we were kids."

"I know."

"But I do now." Patrick sketched a salute. "Major Morrison D.S.O."

"Another memento for the Death Room. You'd better aim at the D.F.C."

"I jolly well will. I won't be one-up-man-shipped by you."

"Or disappoint Granny."

"She's a blood-sucking old leech. Johnnie, were you frightened under fire?"

"Paralysed."

"But you want to go back?"

Johnnie's eyes went dark and inward.

"I think it's like extreme torture. You get sort of addicted to it. You'll find out when you get into a fight."

"I'll be alone up in the sky. No one will see if I turn yellow."

"You won't turn yellow. You'll turn red, or maybe white, with rage. You'll think, how dare those arrogant bastards attack my country."

"My God!" said Patrick. "You bloody well are a Duncastle."

"So are you," said Johnnie. He lifted his glass. "Here's to us."

For Matilda that had been the proudest evening of her life. She would have liked to have died before morning, for she had a premonition of grief to come.

And come it did on a July afternoon when the telephone rang. Richard wanted to speak to her. His voice was almost unintelligible. Patrick had been shot down over the channel. His Spitfire, emitting a fatal tail of black smoke and descending in long lazy whorls, had plunged into the sparkling summer sea. He had been flying in combat for just four weeks. The average life of a Spit pilot, Richard said in his dead voice. Men fighting on the Somme and at

Passchendaele in the last war had often averaged only a few days or a single morning.

"I hope you'll be all right, Mother."

"Why shouldn't I be all right?" Her voice was testy and indignant.

"I know what Deirdre would have said."

She wanted to retort angrily that she hadn't the least interest in what that Irish girl would have said. But she couldn't interrupt his painful meandering voice. "She'd have said, the bloody fool, why did he have to die for England? There's going to be none of us left soon, Mother."

"Richard, you'd better come to London."

"No, I'm all right. I've got plenty of Grandfather's booze. And Mab. I've still got Mab."

For a night or two, Matilda thought. Then she would be off on her glowworm flight. Mab thought the war the most exciting thing. It was so full of lovely men. Was she, that little fly-by-night, to be all the family had left?

For Matilda, standing in her lonely drawing room, knew with certainty what the next news would be. Her two beautiful young men. Her last sacrificial offering to her beloved country.

Pilot Officer Patrick Webb had not lived long enough to earn a decoration. Nor did he have a marked grave. Major John Morrison D.S.O., killed by a bursting shell in the western desert, was buried with full military honours at Tripoli.

After hearing the news Matilda spent all night in the Death Room holding Johnnie's medal, so new and shiny, in her hands. For the first time in her life she was too tired and too sad to beat the Salamanca Drum. Too old, also, for it needed someone with youth and optimism and spirit.

She had none of those things any more. And anyway the last hands to hold the drumsticks had been Johnnie's. Now she would like them and the drum to remain untouched forever.

Imogen tried, without success, to coax her out of her rigid grief.

"What about all your committees, Mother, your bazaars and things? Lally says you won't go to them."

"Not at present."

"Then don't you think you and Lally should go down to Sanctuary? The bombing is going to get worse, Desmond says. He's afraid St. Paul's may be a target, and that could include our house and Papa's bank."

"So Desmond is running away again?"

"No, Mother, he *isn't!* But he thinks you and Lally—"

"Tell him not to organise my life."

"Mother, Johnnie was *my* son," Imogen burst out, weeping.

Only then did Matilda, briefly, touch her hand.

"You must be so proud of him," she said formally, as if she were speaking of someone else. Not of her private and beloved Johnnie whom she shared with no one.

Last Interval

It was Lally shuffling into Matilda's bedroom on those big flip-flop feet. She had never learned to walk gracefully, and now she was bending over Matilda, her flushed excited face hanging only a few inches away.

"Mamma! What do you think, M-mamma?"

Matilda shrank defensively into the pillow.

"Don't come so close. I can't breathe."

"But M-mamma, the gentleman has been l-looking at my drawings. For ages. He says he c-could give me an exhibition. He says I could be a Grandma M-moses." Lally's lips hung loosely, questioningly. Her eyes already had the wateriness of old age. Poor Lally. The flaw in the family. Mab had it too, in another way. She was too frenetic, too restless, and completely unreliable. She had already made two disastrous marriages, neither of which had produced children. "No children, Granny," she had said gaily. "I don't want any white rabbits, do I?"

White rabbits. Whatever did she mean?

"Who is Grandmother M-moses, M-mamma? S-someone f-famous, the man said."

Lally famous? Ridiculous. She had scotched that idea long ago. Her flawed daughter stared at by the world. No.

Was Desmond downstairs making these far-fetched suggestions, exciting Lally unnecessarily? Oh, stop those drums! She couldn't think.

"Who is Grandma Moses, did you say? An old woman who paints childish pictures, I believe." There. She had got out an intelligible sentence. Her memory was suddenly more reliable.

"Not childish, M-mamma. C-clever. Gifted. The m-man said. I could make a lot of m-money, he said. And Desmond says—"

"Don't listen to Desmond. He hates me."

"It's only because you stole Johnnie."

"What nonsense! You can't steal anybody who isn't ready and willing." Her brain really was improving. How splendid. "So now he wants to steal you."

Lally gave her high-pitched burble of laughter.

"Oh, M-mamma, you must be feeling better. You made a joke. Nurse, I think my m-mother might drink her tea now. She seems better."

"Well, we'd better seize the opportunity," the nurse said briskly. "Get some nourishment down her. Oops-a-daisy, Mrs. Webb. She still has a fine face, hasn't she. Look at that nose."

Lally giggled faintly.

"The Duncastle nose."

"What?"

"It's just the f-family nose," said Lally, and her words had set the drums vibrating again in Matilda's head. She shut her eyes in an instinctive desire to disappear, and instantly fell into a light sleep. When she woke there was another face hanging over her, a crumpled pretty middle-aged face. Good heavens, when had Imogen become middle-aged? A lingering malice stirred in her.

"I want Deirdre to have my diamonds," she said clearly. "Your neck's too short."

"Deirdre's dead, Mother. Do you mean Mab?"

"Mab! Would you trust her with diamonds?" What

was it that Mab had done? She couldn't remember, except that it had been disturbing. "Is the war over?" she asked.

"Yes, Mother. Six years ago."

Six years ago! That meant, yes, it really must be true that she was eighty. High time to depart this life.

"Only I keep hearing a drum beating," she said bewilderedly.

"Perhaps it's the bazaar downstairs. We had a band playing for a little while, but it got rather noisy. We're doing very well. Everyone has been asking after you."

"Who could possibly care?"

"Lally and I do. You're unfair to us, Mother. Did Lally tell you an art dealer is interested in her drawings? You know how she always puts some out for sale, but usually they don't create any interest, poor darling."

"How much did he pay?"

"He wasn't interested in them to buy, but to exhibit. He thinks Lally has real talent. Don't you remember that Desmond spotted it a long time ago?"

Matilda opened her eyes wide and spoke clearly. "Your husband's a know-all. And how does he dare to remain alive when everyone else is dead?"

Imogen bent closer. She was about to make one of her confidences that she didn't want the nurse to hear.

"Mother, you must know you haven't too much longer to live. Why do you go on being spiteful?"

"Spiteful! Me! Why, I speak only the truth. I love you dearly, Imogen. I saved you from that German—"

"Austrian, Mother. His name was Rudi."

"Never mind what his name was. I wanted you to marry a gallant Englishman."

"I did, Mother."

With a great effort Matilda produced one of her deliberately scornful remarks.

"You wouldn't be referring to that pacifist, that platform orator who hasn't the courage to hold a gun?"

"Johnnie's father," said Imogen.

Abruptly the tears came, like warm balm, filling her tired eyes.

"Ah, Johnnie. The best of them all."

"I know, Mother."

Matilda sighed. "But everyone's gone now. We're left alone."

"Actually we're not." Imogen was bending closer again, as if she were deaf. And that she was not, for the thudding of the drums rocked in her head. "Mother, are you up to seeing a visitor? Two visitors, to be exact. Nurse! Is it all right to have someone in to see my mother? It's rather important."

The nurse came over to survey her patient with experienced eyes.

"If it's important you'd better get them in. This might be her last lucid interval."

It wouldn't be her last. That nurse knew nothing. When the drums stopped she would be able to think clearly. Just now she was confused by Imogen's action in bringing to her bedside a completely strange woman and a boy of about seven or eight years.

Then she started up. It was the same boy again! The one who had kept peeping cheekily round the door. She recognised his freckled face, his sturdy body, his yellowish hazel eyes, very bright, very direct. He reminded her of someone, she couldn't think who.

"Mother, this is Mrs. Pansy Hall."

She attempted to incline her head. Feeble rage stirred in her. How did Imogen expect her to do her grande dame act on her death bed?

"Have you come to our bazaar, Mrs. Hall?" She managed that politeness successfully.

"Well, not exactly, Mrs. Webb." The woman was middle-aged with a clean rosy country look about her. Nice but totally uninteresting. "I came to see the house, really. I hope you'll forgive me, but I wanted Josh to see it. You know—they say he's like—I didn't want to upset you, Mrs. Webb, but your daughter thought it might cheer you up to see Josh."

"Josh?" Matilda enquired.

"Joshua. My son."

The shock was like cold water, stimulating her muddled brain. Now she was remembering. Pansy and Ronald. A pony. Dear Mr. Webb . . . She really *thought she had forgotten that. She had commanded herself to ignore the knowledge.*

"Where's Ronald?" she heard herself asking.

"He was killed at El Alamein."

"Ah! That must have been about the same time as my grandson. In North Africa, too. How strange. How very strange."

"I was left on my own because Mum had died, too."

"Your mother was Prudence, of course."

"Yes, I thought you would know, Mrs. Webb."

"I can't imagine why you thought that. But what then?"

"I got married and Bill and I had a son and I wanted him called Joshua. Ronald and me"—she was blushing a rather becoming peony pink—"loved our father very much."

"And this is his grandson?"

"Yes. Joshua."

"I can see. He has the same stubborn jaw. He'll beat his own way. My husband would have, too"—she gave a faint chuckle—"with any woman but me. Come here, boy."

The child went forward willingly enough. He didn't seem afraid to stand at the bedside of a very old dying woman. The distinctive yellow eyes stared at her with a magnetism she was suddenly remembering too well.

"And what are you going to do with your life, Joshua? Be a soldier and fight for your country?"

"No, ma'am, I'm going to be a farmer like my Dad."

"A farmer?"

"Yes, ma'am. Dad says that's the best thing to be. England's yeoman farmers have always been her backbone, since the days of good Queen Bess, and if more people grew things than destroyed them—"

"Josh, you're showing off," his mother scolded.

"No. Leave him," Matilda said. "Perhaps I need a sermon on my death bed. Joshua, what are you going to grow on your farm?"

"Wheat and oats and barley mostly, ma'am."

Wheat and oats and barley. The simple names sounded like a poem. So they were back at the begin-

ning, were they, with the loyal yeoman making England strong? How miraculous, and yet how unsurprising. For no one could ever convince Matilda Duncastle, even on her death bed, that an Englishman could be wholly defeated. It didn't matter if the road back was a long one, provided it began in the right direction. Her family had been decimated, and ironically it had been Joshua's tough stock which had survived.

Joshua would have enjoyed that joke. He would also have enjoyed this sturdy little offspring, so sure of himself, so much a youthful replica of the over-confident bank clerk who had had such a profound effect on the life and fortunes of her proud family.

A strange dry sound emerged from her lips.

"It's all right, Josh. The lady's only laughing."

"Mother?" came Imogen's anxious voice.

Matilda wanted to say, without malice, indeed with perfect contentment, that Joshua had won. Though only temporarily. The English temperament being what it was, another Duncastle family would evolve. The heavy weight of history made that inevitable.

But she believed she had spoken her last words. For she was realising in wonder that the drums in her head had stopped beating. And she must not move a muscle or blink an eyelid or even breathe lest the fragile peace be destroyed.